D1008051

THE ICE PRINCESS

A Novel

CAMILLA LÄCKBERG

Translated by Steven T. Murray

POCKET BOOKS

New York London Toronto Sydney

Pocket Books
A Division of Simon & Schuster, Inc.
1230 Avenue of the Americas
New York, NY 10020

First Pocket Books paperback edition April 2011

POCKET and colophon are registered
trademarks of Simon & Schuster, Inc.

For information about special discounts for bulk purchases,
please contact Simon & Schuster Special Sales at 1-866-
506-1949 or business@simonandschuster.com

The Simon & Schuster Speakers Bureau can bring authors
to your live event. For more information or to book an event
contact the Simon & Schuster Speakers Bureau at 1-866-248-
3049 or visit our website at www.simonspeakers.com

Cover design by Lisa Litwack.
Cover credits: ice © Sarah Wilmer/Gallery Stock;
woman © Ilona Wellmann/Arcangel Images.

Manufactured in the United States of America

10 9 8 7 6 5 4 3 2 1

ISBN 978-1-4516-2176-1
ISBN 978-1-4516-2175-4 (ebook)

For Wille

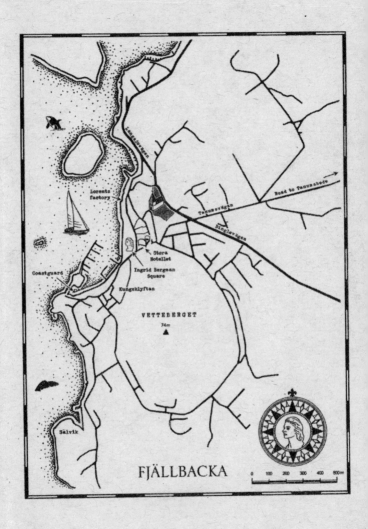

FJÄLLBACKA

1

The house was desolate and empty. The cold penetrated into every corner. A thin sheet of ice had formed in the bathtub. She had begun to take on a slightly bluish tinge.

He thought she looked like a princess lying there. An ice princess.

The floor he was sitting on was ice cold, but the chill didn't bother him. He reached out his hand and touched her.

The blood on her wrists had congealed long ago.

His love for her had never been stronger. He caressed her arm, as if he were caressing the soul that had now left her body.

He didn't look back when he left. It was not "goodbye," it was "until we meet again."

Eilert Berg was not a happy man. His breathing was strained and his breath came out of his mouth in little white puffs, but his health was not what he considered his biggest problem.

Svea had been so gorgeous in her youth, and he had hardly been able to stand the wait before he could get her into the bridal bed. She had seemed tender, affectionate, and a bit shy. Her true nature had come out after a period of youthful lust that was far too brief. She had put her foot down and kept him on a tight leash for close to fifty years. But Eilert had a secret. For the first time, he saw an opportunity for a little freedom in the autumn of his years and he did not intend to squander it.

He had toiled hard as a fisherman all his life, and the income had been just enough to provide for Svea and the children. After he retired they had only their meager pensions to live on. With no money in his pocket there was no chance of starting his life over somewhere else, alone. Now this opportunity had appeared like a gift from above, and it was laughably easy besides. But if someone wanted to pay him a shameless amount of money for a few hours' work each week, that wasn't his problem. He wasn't about to complain. The banknotes in the wooden box behind the compost heap had piled up impressively in only a year, and soon he would have enough to be able to move to warmer climes.

He stopped to catch his breath on the last steep approach to the house and massaged his arthritic hands. Spain, or maybe Greece, would thaw the chill that seemed to come from deep inside him. Eilert reckoned that he had at least ten years left before it would be time to turn up his toes, and he intended to make the most of them, so he'd be damned if he'd spend them at home with that old bitch.

His daily walk in the early morning hours had been his only time spent in peace and quiet; it also meant that he got some much-needed exercise. He always took the same route, and people who knew his habits would often come out and have a chat. He particularly enjoyed talking with the pretty girl in the house farthest up the hill by the Håkebacken school. She was there only on weekends, always alone, but she was happy to take the time to talk about the weather. Miss Alexandra was interested in Fjällbacka in the old days as well, and this was a topic that Eilert enjoyed discussing. She was nice to look at too. That was something he still appreciated, even though he was old now. Of course there had been a good deal of gossip about her, but once you started listening to women's chatter you wouldn't have much time for anything else.

About a year ago, she had asked him whether he might consider stopping in at the house as long as he was passing by on Friday mornings. The house was old, and both the furnace and the plumbing were unreliable. She didn't like coming home to a cold house on the weekends. She would give him a key, so he could just look in and see that everything was in order. There had been a number of break-ins in the area, so he was also supposed to check for signs of tampering with the doors and windows.

The task didn't seem particularly burdensome, and once a month there was an envelope with his name on it waiting in her mailbox, containing what was, to him, a princely sum. He also thought it was nice to feel useful. It was so hard to go around idle after he had worked his whole life.

The gate hung crookedly and it groaned when he pushed on it, swinging it in toward the garden path, which had not yet been shoveled clear of snow. He wondered whether he ought to ask one of the boys to help her with that. It was no job for a woman.

He fumbled with the key, careful not to drop it into the deep snow. If he had to get down on his knees, he'd never be able to get up again. The steps to the front porch were icy and slick, so he had to hold on to the railing. Eilert was just about to put the key in the lock when he saw that the door was ajar. In astonishment, he opened it and stepped into the entryway.

"Hello, is anybody at home?"

Maybe she'd arrived a bit early today. There was no answer. He saw his own breath coming out of his mouth and realized that the house was freezing cold. All at once he didn't know what to do. There was something seriously wrong, and he didn't think it was just a faulty furnace.

He walked through the rooms. Nothing seemed to have been touched. The house was as neat as always. The VCR and TV were where they belonged. After looking through the entire ground floor, Eilert went upstairs. The staircase was steep and he had to grab on hard to the banister. When he reached the upper floor, he went first to the bedroom. It was feminine but tastefully furnished, and just as neat as the rest of the house. The bed was made and there was a suitcase standing at the foot. Nothing seemed to have been unpacked. Now he felt a bit foolish. Maybe she'd arrived a little early, discovered that the furnace wasn't working, and gone out to find someone to fix it. And yet he really didn't believe that explanation. Something was wrong. He could feel it in his joints, the same way he sometimes felt an approaching storm. He cautiously continued looking through the house. The next room was a large loft, with a sloping ceiling and wooden beams. Two sofas faced each other on either side of a fireplace. There were some magazines spread out on the coffee table, but otherwise everything was in its place. He went back downstairs. There, too, everything looked the way it should. Neither the kitchen nor the living room seemed any different than usual. The only room remaining was the bathroom. Something made him pause before he pushed open the door. There was still not a sound in the house. He stood there hesitating for a moment, realized that he was acting a bit ridiculously, and firmly pushed open the door.

Seconds later, he was hurrying to the front door as fast as his age would permit. At the last moment, he remembered that the steps were slippery and grabbed hold of the railing to keep from tumbling headlong down the steps. He trudged through the snow on the garden path and swore when the gate stuck. Out on the pavement he stopped, at a loss what to do. A little way down the street he caught sight of someone approaching at a brisk walk and recognized Tore's daughter Erica. He called out to her to stop.

* * *

She was tired. So deathly tired. Erica Falck shut down her computer and went out to the kitchen to refill her coffee cup. She felt under pressure from all directions. The publishers wanted a first draft of the book in August, and she had hardly begun. The book about Selma Lagerlöf, her fifth biography about a Swedish woman writer, was supposed to be her best, but she was utterly drained of any desire to write. It was more than a month since her parents had died, but her grief was just as fresh today as when she received the news. Cleaning out her parents' house had not gone as quickly as she had hoped, either. Everything brought back memories. It took hours to pack every carton, because with each item she was engulfed in images from a life that sometimes felt very close and sometimes very, very far away. But the packing couldn't be rushed. Her apartment in Stockholm had been sublet for the time being, and she reckoned she might as well stay here at her parents' home in Fjällbacka and write. The house was a bit out of town in Sälvik, and the surroundings were calm and peaceful.

Erica sat down on the enclosed veranda and looked out over the islands and skerries. The view never failed to take her breath away. Each new season brought its own spectacular scenery, and today it was bathed in bright sunshine that sent cascades of glittering light over the thick layer of ice on the sea. Her father would have loved a day like this.

She felt a catch in her throat, and the air in the house all at once seemed stifling. She decided to go for a walk. The thermometer showed fifteen degrees below zero, and she put on layer upon layer of clothing. She was still cold when she stepped out the door, but it didn't take long before her brisk pace warmed her up.

Outside it was gloriously quiet. There were no other people about. The only sound she heard was her own breathing. This was a stark contrast to the summer months when the town was teeming with life. Erica preferred to stay away from Fjällbacka in the summertime. Although she knew that the survival of the town depended on tourism, she still couldn't shake the feeling that every summer the place was invaded by a swarm of grasshoppers. A many-headed monster that slowly, year by year, swallowed the old fishing village by buying up the houses near the water, which created a ghost town for nine months of the year.

Fishing had been Fjällbacka's livelihood for centuries. The unforgiving environment and the constant struggle to survive, when everything depended on whether the herring came streaming back or not, had made the people of the town strong and rugged. Then Fjällbacka had become picturesque and began to attract tourists with fat wallets. At the same time, the fish lost their importance as a source of income, and Erica thought she could see the necks of the permanent residents bend lower with each year that passed. The young people moved away and the older inhabitants dreamed of bygone times. She too was among those who had chosen to leave.

She picked up her pace some more and turned left toward the hill leading up to the Håkebacken school. As Erica approached the top of the hill she heard Eilert Berg yelling something she couldn't really make out. He was waving his arms and coming toward her.

"She's dead."

Eilert was breathing hard in small, short gasps, a nasty wheezing sound coming from his lungs.

"Calm down, Eilert. What happened?"

"She's lying in there! Dead."

He pointed at the big, light-blue frame house at the crest of the hill, giving her an entreating look at the same time.

It took a moment before Erica comprehended what he was saying, but when the words sank in she shoved open the stubborn gate and plodded up to the front door. Eilert had left the door ajar, and she cautiously stepped over the threshold, uncertain what she might expect to see. For some reason she didn't think to ask.

Eilert followed warily and pointed mutely toward the bathroom on the ground floor. Erica was in no hurry. She turned to give Eilert an inquiring glance. He was pale and his voice was faint when he said, "In there."

Erica hadn't been in this house for a long time, but she had once known it well, and she knew where the bathroom was. She shivered in the cold despite her warm clothing. The door to the bathroom swung slowly inward, and she stepped inside.

She didn't really know what she had expected from Eilert's curt statement, but nothing had prepared her for the blood. The bathroom was completely tiled in white, so the effect of the blood in and around the bathtub was even more striking. For a brief moment she thought that the contrast was pretty, before she realized that a real person was lying in the tub.

In spite of the unnatural interplay of white and blue on the body, Erica recognized her at once. It was Alexandra Wijkner, née Carlgren, daughter of the family that owned this house. In their childhood they had been best friends, but that felt like a whole lifetime ago. Now the woman in the bathtub seemed like a stranger.

Mercifully, the corpse's eyes were shut, but the lips were bright blue. A thin film of ice had formed around the torso, hiding the lower half of the body completely. The right arm, streaked with blood, hung limply over the edge of the tub, its fingers dipped in the congealed pool of blood on the floor. There was a razor blade on the edge of the tub. The other arm was visible only above the elbow, with the rest hidden beneath the ice. The knees also stuck up through the frozen surface. Alex's long blond hair was spread like a fan over the end of the tub but looked brittle and frozen in the cold.

Erica stood for a long time looking at her. She was shivering both from the cold and from the loneliness exhibited by the macabre tableau. Then she backed silently out of the room.

Afterward, everything seemed to happen in a blur. She rang the doctor on duty on her mobile phone, and waited with Eilert until the doctor and the ambulance arrived. She recognized the signs of shock from when she got the news about her parents, and she poured herself a large shot of cognac as soon as she got home. Perhaps not what the doctor would order, but it made her hands stop shaking.

The sight of Alex had taken her back to her childhood. It was more than twenty-five years ago that they had been best friends, but even though many people had come and gone in her life since then, Alex was still close to her heart. They were just children back then. As adults they had been strangers to each other. And yet Erica had a hard time reconciling herself to the thought that Alex had taken her own life, which was the inescapable interpretation of what she had seen. The Alexandra she had known was one of the most alive and confident people she could imagine. An attractive, self-assured woman with a radiance that made people turn around to look at her. According to what Erica had heard through the grapevine, life had been kind to Alex, just as Erica had always thought it would be. She ran an art gallery in Göteborg, she was married to a man who was both successful and nice, and she lived in a house as big as a manor on the island of Särö. But something had obviously gone wrong.

Erica felt that she needed to divert her attention, so she punched in her sister's phone number.

"Were you asleep?"

"Are you kidding? Adrian woke me up at three in the morning, and by the time he finally fell asleep at six, Emma was awake and wanted to play."

"Couldn't Lucas get up for once?"

Icy silence on the other end of the line, and Erica bit her tongue.

"He has an important meeting today, so he needed his sleep. Besides, there's a lot of turmoil at his job right now. The company is in a critical strategic stage."

Anna's voice was getting louder, and Erica could hear an undertone of hysteria. Lucas always had a ready excuse, and Anna was probably quoting him directly. If it wasn't an important meeting, then he was stressed out by all the weighty decisions he had to make, or his nerves were shot because of the pressure associated with being, in his own words, such a successful businessman. So all responsibility for the children fell to Anna. With a lively three-year-old and a baby of four months, Anna had looked ten years older than her thirty years when the sisters saw each other at their parents' funeral.

"Honey, don't touch that," Anna shouted in English.

"Seriously, don't you think it's about time you started speaking Swedish with Emma?"

"Lucas thinks we should speak English at home. He says that we're going to move back to London anyway before she starts school."

Erica was so tired of hearing the words "Lucas thinks, Lucas says, Lucas feels that . . ." In her eyes her brother-in-law was a shining example of a first-class shithead.

Anna had met him when she was working as an au pair in London, and she was instantly enchanted by the onslaught of attention from the successful stockbroker Lucas Maxwell, ten years her senior. She gave up all her plans of starting college, and instead devoted her life to being the perfect, ideal wife. The only problem was that Lucas was a man who was never satisfied, and Anna, who had always done exactly as she pleased ever since she was a child, had totally eradicated her own personality after marrying Lucas. Until the children arrived, Erica had still hoped that her sister would come to her senses, leave Lucas, and start living her own life. But when first Emma and then Adrian were born, she had to admit that her brother-in-law was unfortunately here to stay.

"I suggest that we drop the subject of Lucas and his opinions on child-rearing. What have auntie's little darlings been up to since last time?"

"Well, just the usual, you know . . . Emma threw a tantrum yesterday and managed to cut up a small fortune in baby clothes before I caught her, and Adrian has either been throwing up or screaming nonstop for three days."

"It sounds as though you need a change of scene. Can't you bring the kids with you and come up here for a week? I could really use your help going through a bunch of stuff. And soon we'll need to tackle all the paperwork too."

"Er, well . . . We were planning to talk to you about that."

As usual when she had to deal with something unpleasant, Anna's voice began to quaver noticeably. Erica was instantly on guard. That "we" sounded ominous. As soon as Lucas had a finger in the pie, it usually meant that there was something that would benefit him to the detriment of all others involved.

Erica waited for Anna to go on.

"Lucas and I have been thinking about moving back to London as soon as he gets the Swedish subsidiary on its feet. We weren't really planning to bother with maintaining a house here. It's no fun for you, either, having the hassle of a big country house. I mean, without a family and all . . ."

The silence was palpable.

"What are you trying to say?"

Erica twirled a lock of her curly hair around her index finger, a habit she'd had since childhood and reverted to whenever she was nervous.

"Well . . . Lucas thinks we ought to sell the house. It would be hard for us to hold on to it and keep it up. Besides, we want to buy a house in Kensington when we move back, and even though Lucas makes plenty of money, the cash from the sale would make a big difference. I mean, a house on the west coast in that area would go for several million kronor. The Germans are wild about ocean views and sea air."

Anna kept pressing her argument, but Erica felt she'd heard enough and quietly hung up the phone in the middle of a sentence. Anna had certainly managed to divert her attention, as usual.

She had always been more of a mother than a big sister to Anna. Ever since they were kids she had protected and watched over her. Anna had been a real child of nature, a whirlwind who followed her own impulses without considering the results. More times than she could count, Erica had been forced to rescue Anna from sticky situations. Lucas had knocked the spontaneity and joie de vivre right out of her. More than anything else, that was what Erica could never forgive.

By morning, the events of the preceding day seemed like a bad dream. Erica had slept a deep and dreamless sleep, but still felt as though she'd barely had a catnap. She was so tired that her whole body ached. Her stomach was rumbling loudly, but after a quick peek in the fridge she realized that a trip to Eva's Mart would be necessary before she was going to get any food to eat.

The town was deserted, and at Ingrid Bergman Square there was no trace of the thriving commerce of the summer months. Visibility was good, without mist or haze, and Erica could see all the way to the outer point of the island of Valö, which was silhouetted against the horizon. Together with Kråkholmen it bordered a narrow passage to the outer archipelago.

She met no one until she had walked halfway up Galärbacken. It was an encounter she would have preferred to avoid, and she instinctively looked for a possible escape route.

"Good morning." Elna Persson's voice chirped with unabashed sprightliness. "Well, if it isn't our little authoress out walking in the morning sun."

Erica cringed inside.

"Yes, I was just on my way down to Eva's to do a little shopping."

"You poor dear, you must be completely distraught after such a horrible experience."

Elna's double chins quivered with excitement, and Erica thought she looked like a fat little sparrow. Her woolen coat was shades of green and covered her body from her shoulders to her feet, giving the impression of one big shapeless mass. Her hands had a firm grip on her handbag. A disproportionately small hat was balanced on her head. The material looked like felt, and it too was an indeterminate moss-green color. Her eyes were small and deeply set in a protective layer of fat. Right now they were fixed on Erica. Clearly she was expected to respond.

"Yes, well, it wasn't very pleasant."

Elna nodded sympathetically. "Yes, I happened to run into Mrs. Rosengren and she told me that she drove past and saw you and an ambulance outside the Carlgrens' house, and we knew at once that something horrid must have happened. And later in the afternoon when I happened to ring Dr. Jacobsson, I heard about the tragic event. Yes, he told me in confidence, of course. Doctors take an oath of confidentiality, and that's something one has to respect."

She nodded knowingly to show how much she respected Dr. Jacobsson's oath of confidentiality.

"So young and all. Naturally one has to wonder

what could be the reason. Personally I always thought she seemed rather overwrought. I've known her mother, Birgit, for years, and she's a woman who has always been a bundle of nerves, and everyone knows that's hereditary. She turned all stuck-up, too, Birgit I mean, when Karl-Erik got that big management job in Göteborg. Then Fjällbacka wasn't good enough for her anymore. No, it was the big city for her. But I tell you, money doesn't make anyone happy. If that girl had been allowed to grow up here instead of pulling up roots and moving to the big city, things wouldn't have ended this way. I think they even packed the poor girl off to some school in Switzerland, and you know how things go at places like that. Oh yes, that sort of thing can leave a mark on a person's soul for the rest of her life. Before they moved away from here, she was the happiest and liveliest little girl one could imagine. Didn't you two play together when you were young? Well, in my opinion . . ."

Elna continued her monologue, and Erica, who could see no end to her misery, feverishly began searching for a way to extricate herself from the conversation, which was beginning to take on a more and more unpleasant tone. When Elna paused to take a breath, Erica saw her chance.

"It was terribly nice talking to you, but unfortunately I have to get going. There's a lot to be done. I'm sure you'll understand."

She put on her most pathetic expression, hoping to entice Elna onto this sidetrack.

"But of course, my dear. I wasn't thinking. All this must have been so hard for you, coming so soon after your own family tragedy. You'll have to forgive an old woman's thoughtlessness."

By this point Elna was almost moved to tears, so Erica merely nodded graciously and hurried to say good-bye. With a sigh of relief she continued walking to Eva's Mart, hoping to avoid any more nosy ladies.

But luck was not with her. She was grilled mercilessly by most of the excited residents of Fjällbacka, and she didn't dare breathe freely until her own house was within sight. But one comment she heard stayed with her. Alex's parents had arrived in Fjällbacka late last night and were now staying with her aunt.

Erica set the bags of groceries on the kitchen table and began putting away the food. Despite all her good intentions, the bags were not as full of staples as she had planned before she walked into the shop. But if she couldn't buy herself treats on a day as miserable as this, when could she? As if on signal, her stomach started growling. With a flourish, she plopped twelve Weight Watchers points onto a plate in the form of two cinnamon buns. She ate them with a cup of coffee.

It felt wonderful to sit and look at the familiar view outside her window, but she still hadn't gotten used to the silence in the house. She had been at home alone before, of course, but it wasn't the same thing. Back then there had been a presence, an awareness that somebody could walk through the door at any moment. Now it seemed as if the soul of the house had gone.

Papa's pipe lay by the window, waiting to be filled with tobacco. The smell still lingered in the kitchen, but Erica thought it was getting fainter each day.

She had always loved the smell of a pipe. When she was little she often sat on her father's lap and closed her eyes as she leaned against his chest. The smoke from the pipe had settled in all his clothing, and the scent had meant security in the world of her childhood.

Erica's relationship with her mother was infinitely more complicated. She couldn't remember a single time when she was growing up that she'd ever received a sign of tenderness from her mother; not a hug, a caress, or a word of comfort. Elsy Falck was a hard and unforgiving woman who kept their home in impeccable order but who never allowed herself to be happy about anything in life. She was deeply religious, and like many in the coastal communities of Bohuslän, she had grown up in a town that was still marked by the teachings of Pastor Schartau. Even as a child she had been taught that life would be endless suffering; the reward would come in the next life. Erica had often wondered what her father, with his good nature and humorous disposition, had seen in Elsy, and on one occasion in her teens she had blurted out the question in a moment of fury. He didn't get angry. He just sat down and put his arm around her shoulders. Then he told her not to judge her mother too harshly. Some people have a harder time showing their feelings than others, he explained as he stroked her cheeks, which were still flushed with rage. She refused to listen to him then, and she was still convinced that he was only trying to cover up what was so obvious to Erica: her mother had never loved her, and that was something she would have to carry with her for the rest of her life.

Erica decided on impulse to visit Alexandra's parents. Losing a parent was hard, but it was still part of the natural order of things. Losing a child must be horrible. Besides, she and Alexandra had once been as close as only best friends can be. Of course, that was almost twenty-five years ago, but so many of her happiest childhood memories were intimately associated with Alex and her family.

The house looked deserted. Alexandra's maternal aunt and uncle lived in Tallgatan, a street halfway between the center of Fjällbacka and the Sälvik campground. All the houses were perched high up on a slope, and their lawns slanted steeply down toward the road on the side facing the water. The main door was in the back of the house, and Erica did not hesitate before ringing the doorbell. The sound reverberated and then died out. Not a peep was heard from inside, and she was just about to turn and leave when the door slowly opened.

"Yes?"

"Hi, I'm Erica Falck. I'm the one who . . ."

She left the rest of her sentence hanging in midair. She felt foolish for introducing herself so formally. Alex's aunt, Ulla Persson, knew very well who she was. Erica's mother and Ulla had been active in the church group together for many years, and sometimes Ulla would come over on Sundays for coffee.

She stepped aside and let Erica into the entryway. Not a single light was lit in the entire house. Of course, it wouldn't be evening for several hours yet, but the afternoon dusk was beginning to descend and the shadows were growing longer. Muted sobs could be heard from the room straight down the hall. Erica took off her shoes and coat. She caught herself moving extremely quietly and cautiously because the mood in the house permitted nothing else. Ulla went into the kitchen and let Erica find her own way. When she entered the living room, the weeping stopped. On a sectional sofa in front of an enormous picture window,

Birgit and Karl-Erik Carlgren sat desperately holding on to each other. Both had wet streaks running down their faces, and Erica felt that she was trespassing in an extremely private space. Perhaps she shouldn't intrude. But it was too late to worry about that now.

She sat down cautiously on the sofa facing them and clasped her hands in her lap. No one had yet uttered a word since she entered the room.

"How did she look?"

At first Erica didn't understand what Birgit had said. Her voice was tiny, like a child's. Erica didn't know what to answer.

"Lonely," was what finally came out, and she regretted it at once. "I didn't mean . . ." The sentence faded away and was absorbed by the silence.

"She didn't kill herself!"

Birgit's voice all at once sounded strong and determined. Karl-Erik squeezed his wife's hand and nodded in agreement. They probably noticed Erica's skeptical expression, because Birgit repeated: "She didn't kill herself! I know her better than anyone, and I know that she would never be capable of taking her own life. She would never have had the courage to do it! You must realize that. You knew her too!"

She straightened up a bit more with each syllable, and Erica saw a spark light up in her eyes. Birgit was opening and closing her hands convulsively, over and over, and she looked Erica straight in the eye until one of them was forced to look away. It was Erica who yielded first. She shifted her gaze to look around the room. Anything to avoid fixing her eyes on the grief of Alexandra's mother.

The room was cozy but a bit overdecorated for Erica's taste. The curtains had been skillfully hung with enormous flounces matching the sofa pillows that had been sewn from the same floral fabric. Knickknacks covered every available surface. Hand-carved wooden bowls decorated with ribbons with cross-stitch embroidery shared the room with porcelain dogs with eternally moist eyes. What saved the room was the picture window. The view was wonderful. Erica wished that she could freeze the moment and keep looking out the window instead of being drawn into the grief of these people. Instead she turned her gaze back to the Carlgrens.

"Birgit, I'm really not sure. It was twenty-five years ago that Alexandra and I were friends. I really don't know a thing about her. Sometimes you just don't know someone as well as you think you do . . ."

Even Erica could hear how lame this sounded. Her words seemed to ricochet off the walls. This time Karl-Erik spoke up. He extricated himself from Birgit's convulsive grip and leaned forward as if wanting to make sure that Erica wouldn't miss one word of what he intended to say.

"I know it sounds as if we're denying what happened, and perhaps we're not presenting a very coherent impression right now. But even if Alex did take her own life for some reason, she would never, and I repeat *never*, have done it this way! You probably remember that Alex was always hysterically afraid of blood. If she got the slightest cut she was absolutely uncontrollable until someone put a bandage on it. Sometimes she even fainted when she saw blood. That's why I'm quite sure that she would have chosen some other method, like sleeping pills, for instance. There is no way in hell that Alex could have managed to take a razor blade and cut herself, first on one arm and then on the other. And then, it's like my wife says: Alex was fragile. She was not a courageous person. An inner strength is required for someone to decide to take her own life. She didn't have that kind of strength."

His voice was compelling. Even though Erica was still convinced that she was listening to the hope of two people in despair, she couldn't help feeling a flicker of doubt. When she thought about it, there was something that hadn't felt right when she stepped into that bathroom yesterday morning. Not because it would ever feel right to discover a dead body, but there was something about the atmosphere in the room that didn't really fit. A presence, a shadow. That was as close to a description as she could come. She still believed that something had driven Alexandra Wijkner to suicide, but she couldn't deny that something about the Carlgrens' stubborn insistence had struck a chord.

It suddenly occurred to her how much the adult Alex looked like her mother. Birgit Carlgren was petite and slender, with the same light-blonde hair as her daughter, except that instead of Alex's long mane she wore hers cut in a chic pageboy. Birgit was dressed all in black, and despite her sorrow she seemed aware of what a startling appearance she made, thanks to the contrast between light and dark. Tiny gestures betrayed her vanity. A hand carefully patting her coiffure, a collar straightened to perfection. Erica recalled that Birgit's wardrobe had seemed a veritable Mecca to eight-year-olds who loved to dress up, and her jewelry case had been the closest thing to heaven they could imagine in those days.

Next to Birgit, her husband looked ordinary. Far

from unattractive, but simply unremarkable. Karl-Erik Carlgren had a long, narrow face engraved with fine lines. His hairline had receded far up his scalp. He too was dressed all in black, but unlike his wife the color made him look even grayer. Erica could sense that it was time for her to leave. She wondered what she actually had wanted to accomplish by visiting them.

She stood up and the Carlgrens did too. Birgit gave her husband an urgent look, as if exhorting him to say something. Apparently it was something they had discussed before Erica arrived.

"We'd like you to write an article about Alex. For publication in *Bohusläningen*. About her life, her dreams—and her death. A commemoration of her life. It would mean a great deal to Birgit and me."

"But wouldn't you rather have something in *Göteborgs-Posten*? I mean, she did live in Göteborg, after all. And you do too, for that matter."

"Fjällbacka has always been our home, and it always will be. And that was true for Alex too. You can start by talking to her husband, Henrik. We spoke with him and he's willing to help. Of course you'll be compensated for all your expenses."

With that they apparently considered the subject closed. Without actually having accepted the assignment, Erica found herself standing outside on the steps, with the telephone number and address of Henrik Wijkner in her hand, as the door closed behind her. Even though she really had no desire to take on this task, to be perfectly honest the germ of an idea had begun to sprout in her writer's brain. Erica pushed away the thought and felt like a bad person for even thinking it, but it was persistent and refused to go away. An idea for a new book of her own, an idea that she had long been searching for, was right here in front of her. The account of a woman's path toward her destiny. An explanation of what had driven a young, beautiful, and obviously privileged woman to a self-inflicted death. She would not mention Alex's name, of course, but it would be a story based on what she could dig up about the path she had taken toward death. To date Erica had published four books, but they were all biographies about other prominent female authors. The courage to create her own stories had not yet emerged, but she knew that there were books inside her just waiting to be put down on paper. This one might give her the push she needed, the inspiration she'd been waiting for. The fact that she had once known Alex would only be to her advantage.

As a human being she writhed with repugnance at the thought, but as a writer she was jubilant.

The brush spread broad swathes of red across the canvas. He had been painting since dawn, and for the first time in several hours he now took a step back to look at what he had created. To the untrained eye it was merely large patches of red, orange, and yellow, irregularly arranged over the large canvas. For him it was humiliation and resignation re-created in the colors of passion.

He always painted using the same colors. The past shrieked and mocked him from the canvas, and now he went back to painting with growing frenzy.

After another hour he realized that he had earned the first beer of the morning. He took the can standing closest to him, ignoring the fact that he had flicked cigarette ashes into it sometime the night before. Flakes of ash stuck to his lips, but he eagerly downed the stale beer, then tossed the can to the floor after he had slurped the last drop.

His underwear, which was all he was wearing, was yellow in front from beer or dried urine, he couldn't tell which. Possibly a combination of the two. His greasy hair hung over his shoulders, and his chest was pale and sunken. The overall impression of Anders Nilsson was of a wreck, but the painting that stood on his easel showed a talent that was in sharp contrast to the artist's own degeneration.

He sank to the floor and leaned against the wall to face the painting. Next to him lay an unopened can of beer, and he liked the popping sound it made when he pulled the tab. The colors shrieked loudly at him, reminding him of something he had spent the greater part of his life trying to forget. Why in hell was she going to ruin everything now! Why couldn't she just let things be? That selfish fucking whore, she was thinking only of herself. Sweet and innocent as a bloody princess. But he knew what was beneath the surface. They were cast from the same mold. Years of mutual pain had shaped them, welding them together, yet suddenly she thought she could unilaterally change the order of things.

"Shit."

He roared and flung the half-full can of beer straight at the canvas. It didn't rip, which infuriated him even more. The canvas merely buckled and the can slid to the floor. The liquid sprayed across the painting, and red, orange, and yellow began to flow together, blending into new shades. He observed the effect with satisfaction.

He still hadn't sobered up after yesterday's twenty-four-hour binge. The beer did its work quickly despite his many years of hard drinking and his high tolerance for alcohol. He slowly sank into the familiar fog with the smell of old vomit hanging in his nostrils.

She had her own key to the apartment. In the hall, she carefully wiped off her shoes, although she knew it was a complete waste of time. Things were cleaner outdoors. She set down the bags of groceries and hung her coat neatly on a hanger. It wasn't a good idea to announce her arrival. By this time he had probably already passed out.

The kitchen to the left of the entryway was in its usual wretched state. Several weeks' worth of dirty dishes were stacked up, not only in the sink but on the table and chairs and even on the floor. Cigarette butts, beer cans, and empty bottles were everywhere.

She opened the door of the fridge to put in the food and saw that she was in the nick of time. It was completely empty. She spent several minutes putting things away, and then it was full again. She stood still for a moment, marshaling her strength.

The apartment was a small one-room. She was the one who had brought in the few pieces of furniture, but there wasn't much she could contribute. The room was dominated by the big easel next to the window. A shabby mattress was flung in one corner. She could never afford to buy him a regular bed.

At first she had tried to help him keep everything tidy, both the apartment and himself. She mopped, picked up after him, washed his clothes, and even gave him baths. Back then she still hoped that everything would turn around. That everything would blow over by itself. But that was many years ago now. Somewhere along the way she just couldn't face it anymore. Now she contented herself with seeing that at least he had food to eat.

She often wished that she still had the energy. Guilt weighed heavy on her shoulders and chest. In the past when she knelt down to wipe up his vomit, she had sometimes felt for a moment that she was paying off some of that guilt. But now she bore it without hope.

She looked at him as he lay slumped against the wall. A foul-smelling wreck, but with an incredible talent hidden behind that filthy exterior. Countless times she had wondered how things would have been if she had made a different choice that day. Every day for twenty-five years she had wondered how life would have turned out if she had acted differently. Twenty-five years is a long time to brood.

Sometimes she just let him lie there on the floor when she left. The cold had seeped in from outside, and the floor felt ice cold to her feet through the thin tights. She pulled on his arm that hung limp and lifeless at his side. He didn't respond. Wrapping both hands around his wrist, she dragged him toward the mattress. She tried to roll him onto it and shuddered a little when she pressed her hands against the slack flesh of his waist. After a bit of maneuvering she got most of his body onto the mattress. Since there was no blanket she took his jacket from the entryway and spread it over him. The effort made her pant, and she sat down. Without the strength in her arms that many years of cleaning had given her, she would never have managed this at her age. She was worried about what would happen on the day she could no longer physically cope with the effort.

A lock of greasy hair had fallen over his face, and she tenderly brushed it aside with her index finger. Life had not turned out the way she had imagined for either of them, but she would devote the rest of hers to preserving what little they had left.

People averted their eyes when she met them in the street, but not quickly enough that she didn't notice the look of pity. Anders was notorious in the whole town, and a permanent member of the local AA. Sometimes he would stagger through town when he was drunk, screaming abuse at everyone he met. He received the loathing and she received the pity. Actually, it should have been the other way around. She was the one who was loathsome, and Anders the one who deserved pity. It was her weakness that had shaped his life. But she would never again be weak.

She sat there for several hours, stroking his forehead. Sometimes he would stir in his sleep, but he was soothed by her touch. Outside the window life went on as usual, but inside that room time stood still.

Monday came with temperatures above freezing and clouds heavy with rain. Erica was always a careful driver, but now she drove a bit slower to give herself some leeway in case she happened to skid. Driving wasn't her strong suit, but she preferred the solitude of a car to being crowded into the E6 express bus or the train.

When she turned right onto the highway the condition of the road improved and she allowed herself to increase her speed a bit. She was supposed to meet Henrik Wijkner at noon, but she had left Fjällbacka early and had plenty of time for the trip to Göteborg.

For the first time since she saw Alex in that icy-cold

bathroom she thought about the phone conversation with Anna. She still had a hard time imagining that Anna would really go through with selling the house. It was their childhood home, after all, and their parents would have been upset if they knew. But anything was possible when Lucas was involved. It was because she could see how lacking in scruples he was that she even considered the likelihood. He kept sinking to ever lower depths, but this was far beyond almost anything he'd done before.

But before she seriously began worrying about the house, she ought to find out where she stood from a purely legal point of view. Until then, she refused to let Lucas's latest ploy get her down. Right now, she had to concentrate on the upcoming talk with Alex's husband.

Henrik Wijkner had sounded pleasant on the telephone, and he had already heard the news when she rang. Of course she could come over and ask him questions about Alexandra, since the memorial article was so important to her parents.

It would be interesting to see what Alex's home looked like, even though Erica wasn't eager to confront another person's grief. The meeting with Alex's parents had been heart-wrenching. As a writer, she preferred to observe reality from a distance. Study it from afar, safely and objectively. At the same time it would be an opportunity to get her first inkling of what Alex had been like as an adult.

From their first day at school Erica and Alex had been inseparable. Erica was tremendously proud that Alex had chosen her as a friend. Alex was like a magnet to all who came near her. Everyone wanted to be with Alex, yet she was totally oblivious to her popularity. She was withdrawn in a way that displayed a self-confidence which Erica now, as an adult, perceived as very unusual for a child. And yet Alex was open and generous and showed no sign of shyness despite her reserved manner. She was the one who chose Erica as her friend. Erica never would have dared approach Alex on her own. They were inseparable until the last year before Alex moved away and then vanished from her life for good. Alex had begun to withdraw more and more, and Erica spent hours alone in her room mourning for their lost friendship. Then one day when she rang the doorbell at Alex's house, nobody answered. Twenty-five years later Erica could still remember in detail the pain she felt when she realized that Alex had moved without even mentioning it to her, without saying good-bye. She still had no idea what had happened. Being a child, she'd put all the blame on herself and simply assumed that Alex had grown tired of her.

Erica maneuvered her way with some difficulty through Göteborg in the direction of Särö. She knew her way around the city after having studied there for four years, but back then she hadn't owned a car, so in that respect Göteborg was still a blank space on the map. If she could have driven on the bike paths things would have been much easier. Göteborg was a nightmare for an insecure driver, with plenty of one-way streets, circles with heavy traffic, and the stressful ringing of trams coming at her from every direction. It also felt as though all roads were leading to Hisingen, northwest of the city. If she took the wrong exit she was bound to end up there.

The directions that Henrik had given her were clear,

and she found the address on the first try, managing to stay out of Hisingen this time.

The house exceeded all her expectations. An enormous white villa from the turn of the last century, with a view of the water and a small gazebo that held the promise of warm summer nights to come. The garden, now hidden beneath a thick white mantle of snow, had been carefully laid out. Because of its sheer size, it would demand the tender care of a skilled gardener.

Erica drove down an avenue of willow trees and through a tall wrought-iron gate onto the gravel courtyard in front of the house.

Stone steps led up to a substantial oak door. There was no modern doorbell; instead she banged hard with a massive door knocker. The door was opened at once. She had almost expected to be greeted by a housemaid in a starched apron and cap, but instead she was received by a man she realized at once had to be Henrik Wijkner. He was unabashedly good-looking, and Erica was glad she had devoted a little extra effort to her appearance before she left home.

She stepped into a huge entrance hall and saw immediately that it was bigger than her entire apartment back in Stockholm.

"Erica Falck."

"Henrik Wijkner. We met last summer as I recall. At that restaurant down by Ingrid Bergman Square."

"Yes, that's right. At Café Bryggan. It seems like an eternity ago that we had summer. Especially considering this weather we're having."

Henrik muttered something polite in reply. He helped her off with her coat and showed her the way to a parlor off the hall. She sat down gingerly on a sofa. Even with her limited knowledge of antiques she could tell the sofa was old and probably very valuable. She said yes to Henrik's offer of coffee. As he puttered about with the coffee and they exchanged comments about the wretched weather, she watched him surreptitiously, concluding that he didn't look particularly bereaved. But Erica also knew that it might not mean anything. Different people had different ways of grieving.

He was casually dressed in perfectly pressed chinos and a sky-blue Ralph Lauren shirt. His hair was dark, almost black, and cut in a style that was elegant but not excessively fastidious. His eyes were dark brown and gave him a slightly South European look. She happened to prefer men who looked considerably more rough-and-tumble, but she couldn't help being affected by the attractive power of this man who looked as if he'd stepped right out of a fashion magazine. Henrik and Alex must have made a strikingly good-looking couple.

"What an incredibly lovely house."

"Thank you. I'm the fourth generation of Wijkners to live here. My paternal great-grandfather had the house built early in the last century and it's been in the family ever since. If these walls could talk . . ." He made a sweeping gesture and smiled at Erica.

"Well, it must feel strange to have so much of your family's history around you."

"Yes and no. But it is a great responsibility. In the footsteps of my ancestors and all that."

He chuckled softly and Erica didn't think he looked particularly weighed down by responsibility. She, however, felt helplessly out of place in this elegant room and struggled in vain to find a comfortable way to sit on the lovely but spartan sofa. Finally she perched on the very edge and carefully sipped her coffee, which was served in a small mocha cup. Her little finger twitched a bit but she resisted the impulse. The cups were perfect for crooking one's little finger, but she suspected that it would probably seem more of a parody than a sign of sophistication. She also struggled briefly when confronted with the plate of cakes on the table, but lost the battle in a duel with a thick slice of sponge cake. She estimated it at ten Weight Watchers points.

"Alex loved this house."

Erica had been wondering how to broach the real reason why she was sitting here. She was grateful when Henrik himself brought up the topic of Alex.

"How long did you live here together?"

"Ever since we were married, fifteen years. We met when we were both studying in Paris. She was reading art history, and I was trying to acquire enough knowledge about the business world to run the family empire. And I did, but just barely."

Erica strongly suspected that Henrik Wijkner had never done anything "just barely."

"Directly after the wedding we moved back to Sweden, to this house. My parents were both dead, and the house had stood empty for a couple of years while I was abroad, but Alex immediately began to renovate it. She wanted everything to be perfect. All the details in the house, all the wallpaper, rugs, and furniture, have either been here since the house was built and restored to its former appearance, or else they were purchased by Alex. She went around to, well, I don't know how many antiques dealers to find exactly the same items that were in the house when my great-grandfather lived here. She had stacks of old photographs to help her, and the result is fantastic. At the same time she was busy setting up her own gallery. I still don't understand how she found time to do everything."

"What was Alex like as a person?"

Henrik took his time before answering the question.

"Beautiful, calm, a perfectionist to her fingertips. She might have seemed vain to people who didn't know her, but that was because she didn't easily let anyone into her life. Alex was the sort of person one had to fight to get to know."

Erica was acutely aware of what he meant. Alex's air of remoteness was intriguing, but it marked her as stuck-up, even as a child. Yet the same girls who called her that often fought the hardest to sit next to her.

"How do you mean?"

Henrik looked out of the window and for the first time since she entered the Wijkner home, Erica thought she saw some feeling behind that charming exterior.

"She always went her own way. She didn't take anyone else into account. Not out of malice, there was nothing malicious about Alex, but out of necessity. The most important thing for my wife was to avoid getting hurt. Everything else, all other feelings, had to take a backseat to that priority. But the problem is, if you don't let anyone through the wall out of fear that they might be an enemy, then you end up locking out all your friends as well."

He fell silent. Then he looked at Erica. "She talked a lot about you."

Erica couldn't conceal her surprise. In view of the way their friendship had ended, Erica assumed that

Alex had turned her back on her and had never given her another thought.

"I vividly remember one thing she told me. She said that you were the last real friend she ever had. 'The last pure friendship.' That's exactly what she said. I thought it was a rather odd thing to say, but she never mentioned it again, and by that time I'd learned not to question her. That's why I'm telling you things about Alex that I've never told anyone else. Something tells me that despite all the years that have passed, you still had a place in my wife's heart."

"You loved her?"

"More than anything else in the world. Alexandra was my whole life. Everything I did, everything I said, revolved around her. The ironic thing is that she never even noticed. If only she had let me in, she wouldn't be dead today. The answer was always right in front of her nose, but she refused to see it. My wife had a strange mixture of cowardice and courage."

"Birgit and Karl-Erik don't think she took her own life."

"Yes, I know. They assume that I wouldn't believe she did it either, but to be honest, I don't quite know what I think. I lived with her for over fifteen years, but I never really knew her."

His voice was still dry and matter-of-fact. Judging by his tone of voice he could have been talking about the weather, but Erica realized that her first impression of Henrik couldn't have been more off the mark. The depth of his sorrow was enormous. He just didn't put it on public display the way Birgit and Karl-Erik Carlgren did. Perhaps because of her own experiences, Erica understood instinctively that he was not suffering merely from grief over his wife's death but also from forever losing the chance to get her to love him the way he loved her. It was a feeling with which she was intimately familiar.

"What was she afraid of?"

"I've asked myself that question a thousand times. I really don't know. As soon as I tried to talk to her about it she would shut the door, and I never managed to get in. It was as though she harbored a secret that she couldn't share with anyone. Does that sound odd? But because I don't know what that secret was, I can't say whether she was capable of taking her own life."

"How was her relationship with her parents and her sister?"

"Well, how should I describe it?" He thought for a long time before he replied. "Tense. As if they were all tiptoeing around one another. The only one who ever said what she thought was her little sister, Julia, and she's a very strange person in general. It always felt as if a whole different dialogue were going on underneath what was being said out loud. I don't quite know how to explain it. It was as if they were speaking in code, and someone had forgotten to give me the key."

"What do you mean when you say that Julia is odd?"

"As you probably know, Birgit gave birth to Julia quite late in life. She was already a good bit past forty, and it wasn't planned. So Julia has somehow always been the cuckoo in the nest. And it couldn't have been very easy to have a sister like Alex. Julia was not a pretty child. She hasn't grown any more attractive as an adult, and you know how Alex looked. Birgit and Karl-Erik have always been extremely focused on

Alex, and Julia was simply forgotten. Her way of dealing with it was to turn inward. But I like her. There's definitely something underneath her surly exterior. I only hope that someday someone will make the effort to find it."

"How has she reacted to Alex's death? What was their relationship like?"

"You'll probably have to ask Birgit or Karl-Erik about that. I haven't seen Julia in more than six months. She's studying to be a teacher up north in Umeå, and she doesn't like coming back here. She didn't even come home for Christmas last year. As far as her relationship with Alex goes, Julia has always worshiped her big sister. Alex had already started boarding school when Julia was born, so she wasn't home much, but whenever we visited the family Julia would follow her sister around like a puppy. Alex didn't like it much but she left her alone. Sometimes she could get angry at Julia and snap at her, but usually she just ignored her sister."

Erica felt that the conversation was nearing an end. In the pauses the silence in the house had been total, and she could sense that in the midst of all this luxury it had now become a lonely house for Henrik Wijkner.

Erica stood up and held out her hand. He took it in both of his, held it for a few seconds, then released it. He walked her to the door.

"I think I'll drive down to the gallery and look around a bit," she said.

"That's a good idea. Alex was incredibly proud of it. She built the business from the ground up, together with a friend from her student years in Paris, Francine Bijoux. Well, now her name is Sandberg. We used to socialize with Francine and her husband a good deal, although that became less frequent after they had children. Francine is probably at the gallery. I'll give her a ring and explain who you are. I'm sure she'll be glad to help out and tell you a bit about Alex."

Henrik held open the door for Erica. With a last thank you, she turned away from Alex's husband and walked to her car.

At the same moment that she got out of her car, the heavens opened up. The gallery was in Chalmersgaten, parallel to the main shopping street, Avenyn, but after half an hour of looking for a parking spot Erica resigned herself and parked at Heden. It wasn't so far away, really, but in the pouring rain it felt like six miles. And the parking fee was twelve kronor an hour. Erica could feel her mood sinking. Naturally she hadn't brought an umbrella with her, and she knew that her curly hair would soon look like a bad home perm.

She hurried across Avenyn and just managed to dodge the number 4 tram that came thundering in the direction of Mölndal. After passing Valand, where she had spent many an evening during her student years, she turned left into Chalmersgaten.

Galleri Abstract was on the left, with big display windows facing the street. A bell over the door pinged as she entered, and she saw that the space was much bigger than it looked from outside. The walls, floor, and ceiling were painted white so as not to distract from the works of art hanging on the walls.

At the far end of the gallery she saw a woman who looked unmistakably French. She exuded sheer elegance as she discussed a painting with a customer, gesturing eagerly as she talked.

"I'll be right there, please have a look around in the meantime." Her French accent sounded charming.

Erica took the woman at her word. With her hands clasped behind her back she walked slowly around the room as she looked at the artworks. As the gallery's name indicated, all the paintings were done in the abstract style. Cubes, squares, circles, and strange figures. Erica tilted her head and squinted, trying to see what the art aficionados saw. But it completely eluded her. Nope, still only cubes and squares like any five-year-old could produce, in her opinion. She would just have to accept that this was beyond her comprehension.

She was standing before a gigantic red painting with yellow, irregularly divided sections when she heard Francine come up behind her with heels clacking on the checkerboard floor.

"That one is certainly wonderful," said Francine.

"Yes, indeed. Exquisite. But to be honest, I'm not really at home in the world of art. I think Van Gogh's sunflowers are great, but that's about as far as my knowledge goes."

Francine smiled. "You must be Erica. Henri just rang and told me you were on your way here."

She held out a finely contoured hand. Erica hastily wiped off her own hand, still wet with rain, before she took Francine's.

The woman facing her was small and slender, with an elegance that Frenchwomen seem to have patented. Erica was five foot nine in her stocking feet, and she felt like a giant in comparison.

Francine's hair was raven-black. It was pulled back smoothly from her forehead and gathered in a chignon at the nape of her neck. She wore a form-fitting black dress.

The color was no doubt chosen in view of the death of her friend and colleague; she seemed more the type to dress in dramatic red, or perhaps yellow. Her makeup was light and perfectly applied, but it could not conceal the telling red rims of her eyes. Erica hoped that her own mascara wasn't running—no doubt a vain hope.

"I thought we ought to sit down and talk over a cup of coffee. The weather is very mild today. Let's go out back."

She led Erica toward a small room behind the gallery that was fully equipped with a refrigerator, microwave oven, and coffeemaker. The table was small and had room for only two chairs. Erica sat down and was instantly served a cup of steaming hot coffee by Francine. Her stomach protested after all the cups she had drunk when she was visiting Henrik. But she knew from experience, from the innumerable interviews she had conducted to dig up background material for her books, that for some reason people talked more easily with a coffee cup in their hand.

"From what I understood from Henri, Alex's parents asked you to write a commemorative article about her life."

"Yes. I've only seen Alex on brief occasions in the last twenty-five years, so I need to find out more about what she was like as a person before I can start writing."

"Are you a journalist?"

"No, I write biographies. I'm only doing this because Birgit and Karl-Erik asked me. And besides, I was the first one to find her, well, almost the first. And in some strange way I feel as though I need to do this to create another picture of Alex for myself, a living picture. Does that sound odd?"

"No, not at all. I think it's fabulous that you're taking so much trouble on behalf of Alex's parents—and Alex."

Francine leaned across the table and placed a well-manicured hand over Erica's.

Erica felt a warm blush spread across her cheeks and tried not to think of the draft of the book she'd been working on for large parts of the previous day.

Francine went on, "Henri also asked me to answer your questions with the utmost candor."

She spoke excellent Swedish. She rolled her R's softly, and Erica noticed that she used the French Henri rather than Henrik.

"You and Alex met in Paris?"

"Yes, we studied art history together. We ran into each other the very first day. She looked lost and I felt lost. The rest is history, as they say."

"How long have you known each other?"

"Let's see, Henri and Alex celebrated their fifteenth anniversary last fall so it would be . . . seventeen years. For fifteen of those years we've run this gallery together."

She fell silent and to Erica's astonishment lit a cigarette. For some reason she hadn't pictured Francine as a smoker. The Frenchwoman's hand shook a little as she lit the cigarette, and then she took a deep drag without taking her eyes off Erica.

"Didn't you wonder where she was?" Erica asked. "She must have been lying there a week before we found her."

It occurred to Erica that she hadn't thought to ask Henrik the same question.

"I know it sounds strange, but no, I didn't. Alex . . ."

She hesitated. "Alex always did pretty much as she liked. It could be incredibly frustrating, but I suppose I got used to it over the years. This wasn't the first time she was gone for a while. She usually popped up later as if nothing had happened. Besides, she did more than her share when she took care of the gallery all alone when I was on maternity leave. You know, in some way I still think the same thing is going to happen. That she's going to come walking in the door. But this time I know she won't." A tear threatened to spill from her eye.

"No, she won't." Erica looked down into her coffee cup to allow Francine to dry her eyes discreetly. "How did Henrik react whenever Alex simply vanished?"

"You've met him. Alex could do no wrong in his eyes. Henri has spent the past fifteen years worshiping her. Poor Henri."

"Why poor Henri?"

"Alex didn't love him. Sooner or later he would have been forced to realize that."

She stubbed out the first cigarette and lit another.

"You must have known each other inside out after so many years," said Erica.

"I don't think anyone really knew Alex. Although I probably knew her better than Henri did. He has always refused to take off his rose-tinted glasses."

"During our conversation Henrik hinted that in all the years of their marriage he felt as though Alex was hiding something from him. Do you know whether that's true? And if so, what it could be?"

"That was unusually perceptive of him. I may have underestimated Henri." She raised a finely shaped eyebrow. "To your first question I will answer yes: I've always known that she was carrying some sort of baggage. To the second question I must answer no: I don't have the faintest idea what it could be. Despite our long friendship there was always a point at which Alex would signal, 'so far, and no farther.' I accepted it, while Henri did not. Sooner or later it would have broken him. And it probably would have been sooner."

"Why is that?"

Francine hesitated. "They're going to do an autopsy on Alex, aren't they?"

The question took Erica by surprise.

"Yes, that's always done for a suicide. Why do you ask?"

"Because then I know that what I'm about to tell you will come out anyway. My conscience feels lighter, at least."

She stubbed out the cigarette carefully. Erica held her breath in tense expectation, but Francine took her time lighting a third cigarette. Her fingers didn't have the characteristic yellow discoloration of a smoker, so Erica suspected that she didn't usually chain-smoke like this.

"You must know that Alex has been going to Fjällbacka much more often for the past six months or so?"

"Yes, the grapevine works very well in small towns. According to the local gossip, she was in Fjällbacka more or less every weekend. Alone."

"Alone is not exactly the whole truth."

Francine hesitated again. Erica had to check her impulse to lean across the table and shake the woman to make her spit out whatever she was holding back. Her interest was definitely aroused.

"She had met someone there. A man. Well, it wasn't the first time that Alex had an affair, but somehow I got the feeling that this was different. For the first time in all the years we've known each other, she seemed almost content. And I know that she couldn't have taken her own life. Someone must have murdered her, I have no doubt about that."

"How can you be so sure? Not even Henrik could say for certain whether she might have committed suicide."

"Because she was pregnant."

Francine's reply caught Erica off guard.

"Does Henrik know about this?"

"I don't know. At any rate, it wasn't his child. They haven't lived together in that way for many years. And even when they did, Alex always refused to have a child with Henri. No matter how much he begged her. No, the child must have been fathered by the new man in her life—whoever he may be."

"She never said who he was?"

"No. As you probably realize by now, Alex was very sparing with her confidences. I have to admit that I was quite shocked when she told me about the child, but that's also one of the reasons why I'm absolutely sure she didn't kill herself. She was literally brimming with happiness and simply couldn't keep the news to herself. She loved that baby and never would have done anything to harm it, certainly not take its life. For the first time, I saw an Alexandra who had a zest for life. I think I would have grown quite fond of her." Her voice sounded sad. "You know, I also had a feeling that she intended to come to terms with her past. I don't know exactly how, but a few scattered remarks here and there gave me that impression."

The door to the gallery opened and they heard somebody stamping the wet snow from their shoes on the doormat. Francine got up.

"That's probably a customer. I have to go. I hope I've been of some help."

"Oh yes, I'm very grateful that you and Henrik have both been so frank. You've been a great help."

After Francine assured the customer that she would be right back, she showed Erica to the door. In front of an enormous canvas with a white square on a blue field they stopped and shook hands.

"Just out of curiosity, what would a painting like this go for? Five thousand, ten thousand?"

Francine smiled. "More like fifty."

Erica gave a low whistle. "So, there you see. Art and fine wine. Two areas that remain complete mysteries to me."

"And I can barely write a shopping list. We all have our specialties."

They laughed. Erica pulled her coat tighter even though it was still damp and headed out into the rain.

The rain had transformed the snow to slush, and she drove a bit below the speed limit just to be on the safe side. After wasting almost half an hour trying to get out of Hisingen, where she had ended up by mistake, she was now approaching Uddevalla. A dull rumble in her stomach reminded her that she had totally forgotten to eat all day. She turned off the E6 at the Torp shopping center north of Uddevalla and drove into McDonald's. She gulped down a cheeseburger as she sat in the parking lot and was soon back out on the highway. The whole time her thoughts were filled with the conversations she'd had with Henrik and Francine. What they had told her created an image of a woman who had built high defensive walls around herself.

What Erica was most curious about was who could be the father of Alex's baby. Francine didn't think that it was Henrik's, but no one could ever be completely sure what happened in other people's bedrooms, and Erica still reckoned it was a possibility. If not, the question was whether the father was the man that Francine hinted Alex had gone to meet every weekend in Fjällbacka, or whether she had a lover in Göteborg.

Erica had gotten the impression that Alex was leading some sort of parallel life. She did as she liked, without worrying about how it would affect those close to her, and Henrik in particular. Erica had the feeling that Francine had a hard time understanding how Henrik could accept a marriage under those conditions. She also thought that Francine disdained him for that reason. Yet Erica could understand all too well how these sorts of things happened. She had been observing Anna and Lucas's marriage for many years.

What depressed Erica most about Anna's inability to change her situation was that she couldn't help wondering whether she was part of the reason for Anna's lack of self-respect. Erica was five years old when Anna was born. From the first instant she saw her little sister she had tried to protect her from the reality she carried around with her like an invisible wound. Anna would never have to feel alone and rejected because of their mother's lack of love for her daughters. The hugs and loving words that Anna did not get from her mother, Erica supplied in abundance. She watched over her little sister with motherly concern.

Anna was an easy child to love. She was totally immune to the sadder aspects of life and took each moment as it came. Erica, who was old beyond her years and often upset, was fascinated by the energy with which her sister loved every minute of her life. Anna took Erica's anxieties in stride but seldom had the patience to sit on her lap or let herself be cuddled for very long. She grew up to be a wild teenager who did precisely whatever she pleased, an unflappable and self-centered girl. In moments of clarity, Erica admitted to herself that she had probably both protected and coddled Anna far too much. She was just trying to give her what she herself had never received.

When Anna met Lucas she became easy prey. She was enthralled by his surface charm but failed to see the stifling forces underneath. Slowly, very slowly, he broke down her joie de vivre and self-confidence by playing on her vanity. Now she sat in Östermalm like a lovely bird in a cage and did not have the power to realize her mistake. Every day Erica hoped that Anna of her own free will would reach out her hand and ask her for help. Until that day, Erica could do no more than wait and remain available. Not that she'd had any great luck with relationships herself. She had a long string of broken relationships and promises behind her; she was usually the one who had broken them off. There was something that snapped whenever she reached a certain point in a relationship. A feeling of panic so strong that she could hardly breathe; she had to clear out, lock and stock, without looking back. And yet, as long ago as she could remember, Erica had paradoxically yearned to have children and a family. She was now thirty-five and the years were slipping away from her.

Damn it, she had managed to repress the thought of Lucas all day long, but now he had gotten under her skin again, and she knew she would have to find out how vulnerable her position actually was. She was altogether too tired to deal with it now. It would have to wait till tomorrow. She felt an acute need to relax for the rest of the day, without thinking about either Lucas or Alexandra Wijkner.

She punched in a speed-dial number on her mobile.

"Hi, it's Erica. Are you two at home tonight? I thought I'd drop by for a while."

Dan gave a warm laugh. "Are we at home? Don't you know what tonight is?"

The silence that met her at the other end of the line was alarmingly total. Erica thought hard but couldn't recall that there was anything special about this evening. Not a holiday, nobody's birthday. Dan and Pernilla had been married in the summer, so it couldn't be their anniversary.

"No, I really have no idea. Tell me."

There was a deep sigh on the line and Erica realized that the big event had to be sports-related. Dan was an enormous sports fan, which sometimes caused a bit of friction between him and his wife, Pernilla. Erica had found her own way of retaliating for all the evenings she had to spend looking at some meaningless sporting event on TV when they were together. Dan was a fanatic follower of the Djurgården hockey team, so Erica had taken on the role of rabid AIK fan. Actually she was totally uninterested in sports in general and hockey in particular, and so it seemed to annoy Dan even more. What really got his goat was when AIK lost and she didn't seem to care.

"Sweden is playing Belarus!"

He sensed her lack of comprehension and heaved another deep sigh. "The Olympic Games, Erica, the

Olympics. Aren't you aware that such an event is going on. . . ?"

"Oh, you mean the football match? Yes, of course I know about that. I thought you meant that there was something special tonight *besides* that."

She spoke in an exaggerated tone, clearly showing she had no idea that there was a match tonight. She smiled because she knew Dan was literally tearing his hair out over such blasphemy. Sports were not a joking matter for him.

"But I'll come over and check out the match with you so I can see Salming crush the Russian defense . . ."

"Salming! Don't you know how many years it's been since he retired? You're kidding me, right? Tell me you're kidding."

"Yes, Dan, I'm kidding. I'm not that daft. I'll come over and check out Sundin, if that suits you better. Incredibly cute guy, by the way."

He sighed heavily yet again. This time because she had been sacrilegious enough to speak of such a giant in the hockey world in terms other than purely athletic.

"All right, come on over. But I don't want a repeat of last time! No yakking during the match, no comments about how sexy the players look in their shinguards, and above all, no questions about whether they're wearing jockstraps and if they wear underpants over them. Understood?"

Erica suppressed a laugh and said seriously, "Scout's honor, Dan."

He grunted. "You've never been a scout."

"No, precisely."

Then she pressed the off button on her mobile phone.

* * *

Dan and Pernilla lived in one of the relatively new row houses in Falkeliden. The houses stood in straight lines, climbing up along Rabekullen Hill, and they looked so much alike that it was almost impossible to tell one from the other. It was a popular area for families with children, mainly because the houses had no ocean view whatever and thus hadn't climbed to such dizzying prices as the neighborhoods closer to the sea.

The evening was much too cold to take a walk, but the car protested vehemently when she forced it up the icy hill, only moderately sanded. She turned into Dan and Pernilla's street with a deep sigh of relief.

Erica rang the doorbell, which instantly set off a tumultuous tramping of little feet inside, and a second later the front door was pulled open by a little girl in pajamas with feet—Lisen, Dan and Pernilla's youngest. Fury swelled up in Malin, the middle girl, who thought it was unfair that Lisen got to open the door for Erica, and the squabble didn't die down until Pernilla's firm voice was heard from the kitchen. Belina, the oldest girl, was thirteen, and Erica had seen her down by Acke's hot-dog kiosk surrounded by some downy-cheeked boys on mopeds when she drove past the square. Dan and Pernilla were certainly going to have their hands full with her.

After the girls each got a hug, they vanished as fast as they had appeared and left Erica to hang up her coat in peace and quiet.

Pernilla was out in the kitchen fixing dinner, with rosy cheeks and an apron with "Kiss the Cook" printed in huge letters on it. She looked to be in the midst of a critical stage in her preparations, and merely waved a bit distractedly at Erica before she turned back to her pots and pans, steaming and sizzling. Erica continued into the living room, where she knew she would find Dan, ensconced on the sofa with his feet on the glass coffee table and the remote control grasped firmly in his right hand.

"Hi! I see that the male chauvinist pig is relaxing while the missus toils by the sweat of her brow in the kitchen."

"Hey, Erica! Yeah, you know, if you just show them who wears the trousers in the family and run the house with an iron hand, you can whip most women into shape."

His warm smile belied his words, and Erica knew that whoever was running the Karlsson household, it certainly wasn't Dan.

She gave him a quick hug and settled down on the black leather sofa. She too put her feet up on the glass coffee table, feeling quite at home. They watched the news on channel 4 for a while in cozy silence, and Erica wondered, not for the first time, whether she and Dan could have had a life like this together.

Dan was her first great love and boyfriend. They were together all through high school and had been inseparable for three years. But they wanted different things out of life. Dan wanted to stay in Fjällbacka and work as a fisherman like his father and grandfather before him, while Erica could hardly wait to move away from the little town. She had always felt she was being asphyxiated here; for her the future lay elsewhere.

They had tried to stay together for a while, with Dan back in Fjällbacka and Erica in Göteborg, but their lives went in totally different directions. After a painful breakup, they had slowly managed to build a friendship that almost fifteen years later was still strong and close.

Pernilla came into Dan's life like a warm and comforting embrace when he was trying to get used to the idea that he and Erica had no future together. Pernilla was there when he most needed her, and she adored him in a way that filled part of the emptiness Erica had left behind. For Erica it had been a painful experience to see him with someone else, but she gradually realized that it was bound to happen sooner or later. Life went on.

Now Dan and Pernilla had three daughters together, and Erica thought that over the years they had built up a warm love for each other, even though she sometimes thought she noticed a restlessness in Dan.

At first it had not been entirely friction-free for Erica and Dan to continue their friendship. Pernilla had jealously watched over him, regarding Erica with deep suspicion. Slowly but surely Erica had managed to convince Pernilla that she wasn't after her husband, and even though they never became best friends, they had a relaxed and warm relationship with each other. Not least because the girls obviously adored Erica. She was even Lisen's godmother.

"Dinner is served."

Dan and Erica got up from their slouched position and went to the kitchen, where Pernilla had placed a steaming casserole on the table. Only two places were set, and Dan raised his eyebrows quizzically.

"I ate with the kids. Go ahead and eat while I put them to bed."

Erica felt ashamed that Pernilla had gone to so much

trouble for her sake, but Dan shrugged his shoulders and began nonchalantly shoveling down an enormous serving of what turned out to be a rich fish stew.

"How have you been, anyway? We haven't seen you in weeks."

His tone was concerned rather than accusatory, but Erica still felt a pang of guilty conscience that she had been so poor at keeping in touch recently. There had just been so much else to think about.

"Well, things are getting better. But now it looks as though there'll be a row over the house," said Erica.

"What do you mean?" Dan looked up from his plate in surprise. "You and Anna both love that house; you should be able to reach an agreement."

"Sure, we can. But you forget that Lucas is involved too. He smells money and probably can't stand to miss such an opportunity. He's never paid any attention to Anna's opinion before, and I don't understand why it should be any different this time."

"Damn it, if I could only get hold of him some dark night, he wouldn't be so bloody cocky afterward."

He pounded his fist emphatically on the table and Erica didn't doubt for a moment that he could give Lucas a real thrashing if he wanted. Dan had been powerfully built even in his teens, and the hard work on the fishing boat had built up his muscles even more, but a gentleness in his eyes belied his tough image. As far as Erica knew, he had never raised a hand to any living creature.

"I don't want to say too much yet, I don't really know what the situation will be. Tomorrow I'll ring Marianne, a lawyer friend, and find out what possibilities I have to prevent a sale, but tonight I'd rather not think about it. Besides, I've been through a lot in the past few days, and thoughts of my material possessions seem a bit petty."

"Yes, I heard about what happened." Dan paused. "What was it like to find someone dead like that?"

Erica contemplated what she should say.

"Sad and terrible at the same time. I hope I never have to experience anything like that again."

She told him about the article she was writing and about her conversations with Alexandra's husband and colleague. Dan listened in silence.

"What I don't understand is why she closed out the most important people in her life. You should have seen her husband, he absolutely adored her. But that's how it is with most people, I suppose. They smile and look happy but actually they feel burdened with all the worries and problems in the world."

Dan interrupted her abruptly.

"Erica, the game is starting in about three seconds and I would prefer an ice hockey match to your quasi-philosophical exegesis."

"No risk of that. Besides, I brought a book along in case the game is boring."

Dan had mayhem in his eyes before he noticed the teasing glint in Erica's eyes.

They made it back to the living room just in time for the face-off.

Marianne picked up at the first ring.

"Marianne Svan."

"Hi, it's Erica."

"Hi, it's been ages. How nice of you to call. How are you doing? I've been thinking a lot about you."

Once again Erica was reminded that she hadn't been paying enough attention to her friends lately. She knew that they were worried about her, but the past month she hadn't even managed to stay in touch with Anna. Yet she knew that they understood.

Marianne had been a good friend since their university days. They had studied literature together, but after almost four years of study Marianne realized that becoming a librarian was not her vocation in life, so she switched to law. Successfully, as it turned out, and she was now the youngest partner ever in one of the largest and most respected law firms in Göteborg.

"Well, under the circumstances I'm doing okay, I suppose. I'm starting to get a little order back in my life, but there are still plenty of things to deal with."

Marianne had never been much for small talk, and with her unerring intuition she could hear that Erica hadn't simply called to chat.

"So what can I do for you, Erica? I can hear there's something on your mind, so let's hear it."

"I'm really ashamed I haven't been in touch for so long, and now that I am calling it's because I need your help."

"Don't be silly. How can I help you? Is there some sort of problem with the estate?"

"Yes, you could certainly say that."

Erica was sitting at the kitchen table fidgeting with the letter that had come in the morning post.

"Anna, or rather Lucas, wants to sell the house in Fjällbacka."

"What do you mean?" Marianne's usual composure exploded. "Who the hell does he think he is? You love that house!"

Erica felt something suddenly snap inside her, and she burst into tears. Marianne instantly calmed down and started showering Erica with sympathy over the phone.

"So how are you really doing? Do you want me to come over? I could be there by tonight."

Erica's tears flowed even harder, but after a few moments of sobbing she calmed down enough to wipe her eyes.

"That's incredibly nice of you, but I'm okay. Really. It's just all been a bit too much lately. It was very traumatic to sort through Mama and Papa's things, and now I'm late with my book and the publisher is after me and then all this with the house . . . and to top it all off, last Friday I discovered my best friend from childhood, dead."

Laughter began bubbling inside her and with tears still in her eyes she began to laugh hysterically. It took her a while to recover.

"Did you say 'dead,' or did I hear you wrong?"

"Unfortunately you heard right. I'm sorry, it must sound terrible that I'm laughing. It's just been a bit too much. She was my best friend from when I was little, Alexandra Wijkner. She committed suicide in the bathtub of her family's house in Fjällbacka. You probably knew her, didn't you? She and her husband, Henrik Wijkner, apparently moved in the best circles in Göteborg, and those are the sorts of people you hobnob with these days, right?"

She smiled and knew that Marianne was doing the same at her end of the line. When they were both young students Marianne had lived in the Majorna district of Göteborg and fought for the rights of the working class. They were both aware that over the years she had been forced to think about completely different issues in order to fit in with the circles that came with her job at the venerable old law firm. Now it was chic suits and blouses with bows. It was the cocktail party in Örgryte that counted, but Erica knew that in Marianne that only served as a thin veneer over a rebellious temperament.

"Henrik Wijkner. Yes, I do know who he is. We even share some of the same acquaintances, but I've never had the opportunity to meet him. A ruthless businessman, so it's said. The type that could sack a hundred employees before breakfast without losing his appetite. His wife ran a boutique, I think?"

"A gallery. Abstract art."

Marianne's words about Henrik shocked her. Erica had always considered herself a good judge of people, and he seemed anything but her idea of a ruthless businessman.

She dropped the subject of Alex and started talking about the real reason she was calling.

"I got a letter today. From Lucas's attorney. They're summoning me to a meeting in Stockholm on Friday regarding the sale of Mama and Papa's house, and I'm completely clueless when it comes to the law. What are my rights? Do I even have any rights? Can Lucas really do this?"

She could feel her lower lip start to quiver again and took a deep breath to calm herself down. Outside the kitchen window the ice on the bay was glistening after the last couple of days of thawing rain, followed by freezing temperatures at night. She saw a sparrow land on the windowsill and reminded herself to buy a ball of suet to put out for the birds. The sparrow cocked its head inquisitively and pecked lightly at the window. After making sure that there wasn't anything edible being handed out, the bird flew off.

"As you know, I'm a tax attorney, not a family rights attorney, so I can't give you an answer straight off. But let's do this. I'll check with the experts in the office and ring you later today. You're not alone, Erica. We'll help you with this, I promise you."

It was great to hear Marianne's confident assurances, and when they said good-bye life seemed brighter, even though Erica actually knew no more than before she had called.

Restlessness set in almost at once. She forced herself to take up her work on the biography, but it was slow going. She had more than half of the book left to write, and the publishers were growing impatient because they hadn't received a rough draft yet. After filling up almost two pages she read through what she had written, saw it was crap, and quickly deleted several hours of work. The biography only made her feel depressed; the joy of working on it had vanished long ago. Instead, she finished writing the article about Alexandra and put it in an envelope addressed to *Bohusläningen* newspaper. Then it was time to ring Dan and rib him a bit about the near-fatal psychological wound he seemed to have suffered after Sweden's spectacular loss the night before.

Feeling content, Superintendent Mellberg patted his large paunch and debated whether to take a little nap. There was still almost nothing to do, and he didn't ascribe any great importance to the little there was.

He decided that it would be nice to doze for a moment so that his substantial lunch could be digested in peace and quiet. But he barely managed to close his eyes before a determined knocking announced that Annika Jansson, the station's secretary, wanted something.

"What the hell? Can't you see I'm busy?"

In an attempt to look busy he rummaged aimlessly among the papers lying in stacks on his desk, but succeeded only in tipping over a cup of coffee. The coffee flowed toward all the papers and he grabbed the closest thing he could find to wipe up the mess—which happened to be his shirttail, since it was seldom tucked into his trousers anymore.

"Damn it all, I'm the bloody boss of this place! Haven't you learned to show a little respect for your superiors and knock before you come barging in?"

She didn't feel like pointing out that she had actually done just that. With the wisdom born of age and experience, she waited calmly until the worst of his outburst was over.

"I presume you have something to tell me," Mellberg said, seething.

Annika answered in a restrained voice. "Forensic Medicine in Göteborg has been looking for you. Forensic Pathologist Tord Pedersen, to be precise. You can ring him at this number."

She held out a piece of paper with the number carefully printed on it.

"Did he say what it's about?"

Curiosity was giving him a tingling sensation in the pit of his stomach. They didn't hear from Forensic Medicine very often out here in the sticks. Perhaps there would be a chance for some inspired police work for a change.

He waved Annika away distractedly and clamped

the telephone receiver between his ear and shoulder. Then he eagerly began dialing the number.

Annika quickly backed out of the room and closed the door loudly behind her. She sat down at her own desk and cursed, as she had so many times before, the decision that had sent Mellberg to the tiny police station in Tanumshede. According to rampant rumors at the station, he had made himself unwelcome in Göteborg by abusing a refugee who was in his custody. That was clearly not the only mistake he had made, but it was the worst. His superior finally got fed up. An internal investigation had been unable to prove anything, but there was concern about what else Mellberg might do, so he was immediately moved to the post of superintendent in Tanumshede. Each and every one of the community's twelve thousand mostly law-abiding citizens served as a constant reminder to him of his demotion. His former superiors in Göteborg reckoned he wouldn't be able to do much damage there. Up until now this assessment had been correct. On the other hand, he wasn't doing much good, either.

Previously Annika had gotten on well at her job, but that was all over now with Mellberg as her boss. It wasn't enough that he was perpetually rude, he also saw himself as God's gift to women, and Annika was the one who suffered the brunt of it. Snide insinuations, pinches on the behind, and improper remarks were only a fraction of what she had to put up with at work nowadays. What she considered his most repulsive feature, however, was the atrocious comb-over he had constructed to hide his bald pate. He had let the remaining strands of hair grow out—his employees could only guess how long they must be—and then he

wound the hair around atop his head in an arrangement that most resembled an abandoned crow's nest.

Annika shuddered at the thought of how it must
look when not combed over. She was grateful that she
would never need to find out.

She wondered what Forensic Medicine wanted. Oh
well, she would find out soon enough. The station was
so small that any information of interest would spread
through the whole place within an hour.

Bertil Mellberg heard the phone ring as he watched
Annika retreat from his office.

A mighty good-looking woman, that one. Firm and
fine, but with curves in all the right places. Long blond
hair, nice high tits, and a substantial ass. Too bad she
always wore those long skirts and loose blouses. Maybe
he should point out that clothes a bit tighter might suit
her better. As the boss he was entitled to have opinions
on the way his staff dressed. Thirty-seven years old—
he knew that from checking her personnel file. A little
more than twenty years younger than himself, which
was precisely his taste. Let someone else deal with the
old ladies. He was man enough for the younger talent—mature and experienced, with an attractive stout-
ness, and surely no one could tell that his hair may have
thinned a bit over the years. He touched the top of his
head cautiously. All well, his hair was as it should be.

"Tord Pedersen."

"Yes, hello. This is Superintendent Bertil Mellberg,
Tanumshede police station. You were looking for me?"

"Yes, that's right. It's about the body we got in from
you. A woman by the name of Alexandra Wijkner. It
looked like suicide."

"Yes?" Mellberg's interest was definitely piqued.

"I performed the post-mortem yesterday and established that it was definitely not a suicide. Someone murdered her."

"Bloody hell!" In his excitement Mellberg tipped over his coffee cup again and the little that was left in it ran out across the desk. He used his shirttail as a rag again and got a new set of spots on it.

"How do you know that? I mean, what sort of proof do you have that it was murder?"

"I can fax the autopsy report over to you, but it's doubtful whether you would get much out of it. However, let me give you a summary of the most salient points. Just a moment while I put my glasses on," said Pedersen.

Mellberg heard him humming as he scanned the report. He waited eagerly for the information.

"All right, let's see. Female, thirty-five years old, good general physical condition. But you know all that already. The woman has been dead for about a week, but her body is nevertheless in very good condition, primarily thanks to the low temperature in the room where the body was found. The ice around the lower half of the body also helped preserve it.

"Deep incisions through the arteries of both wrists made with a razor blade, which was found at the scene. This was where I began to get suspicious. Both the incisions are the same depth and very straight, which is quite unusual. I would even venture to say that it never happens in a suicide. It's because people are either right-handed or left-handed. The incision on the left arm will be much straighter and more powerful for a right-handed person than the wound on the right. That's what happens when you're forced to use the 'wrong' hand, so to speak. I then examined the fingers on both hands and had my suspicion confirmed. The edge of a razor blade is so sharp that in most cases it leaves microscopic cuts on the hands. Alexandra Wijkner had nothing of the sort. This indicated that it was someone else who slashed her wrists, probably with the aim of making it look like suicide."

Pedersen paused, then went on. "The question I then asked myself was: how could a person do that without the victim putting up a struggle? The answer came with the toxicology report. The victim had residue of a strong sedative in her blood."

"What does that prove? Couldn't she simply have taken a sleeping pill?"

"Certainly, that's possible. But thankfully modern science has provided forensic medicine with a number of indispensable tools and methods. One of the tools is that today we can calculate extremely precisely the decay rates of various medications and even poisons. We ran the test several times on the victim's blood and each time reached the same conclusion: it would have been impossible for Alexandra Wijkner to slash her own wrists, since by the time her heart stopped due to loss of blood, she had already been unconscious for a long while. Unfortunately I can't give you any exact information about times; science hasn't progressed that far as yet. But there is absolutely no doubt that it was murder. I truly hope that you can handle this. You don't have many homicides in your area, I shouldn't think?"

Pedersen's voice expressed a good deal of doubt, which Mellberg instantly took as criticism directed at him personally.

"You're right that it's not something we have a lot of experience with here in Tanumshede. Fortunately, I've been assigned here only temporarily. My real workplace is at police headquarters in Göteborg. My long years of experience on the job mean we'll have no trouble handling even a murder investigation here. It will be a chance for the local authorities to see how real police work is done. It won't take long before the case is solved. Mark my words."

And with this pompous comment Mellberg knew that he had made it crystal clear to Pathologist Pedersen that he wasn't dealing with some greenhorn. Doctors always had to put on airs. Pedersen's part of the job was done, at any rate, and now it was time for a pro to take over.

"Oh, I almost forgot." The medical examiner was stunned by the conceit displayed by the policeman and had almost forgotten to tell him about two additional discoveries that he considered significant. "Alexandra Wijkner was in her third month of pregnancy, and she has also given birth before. I don't know whether this has any relevance for your investigation, but better too much information than too little, don't you think?" said Pedersen.

Mellberg merely snorted in reply, and after a few concluding pleasantries they hung up—Pedersen with a sense of doubt about the skill with which the murderer was going to be tracked, and Mellberg with revived spirits and a new feeling of eagerness. A preliminary examination of the bathroom had been done immediately after the body was found, but now he would have to see to it that Alexandra Wijkner's house was gone over one inch at a time.

2

He warmed a lock of her hair between his hands. Small ice crystals melted and made his palms wet. Carefully, he licked off the water.

He leaned his cheek against the edge of the bathtub and felt the cold bite into his skin. She was so beautiful. Floating there in the crust of ice.

The bond between them still existed. Nothing had changed. Nothing was different. They were two of a kind.

It took some effort to open up her hand so he could place his palm against hers. He laced his fingers with hers. The blood was dry and stiff, and small flakes stuck to his skin.

Time had never had any meaning when he was with her. Years, days, or weeks flowed together, becoming an amorphous entity in which the only thing that meant anything was this: her hand against his. That was why the betrayal had been so painful. She had made time meaningful again. That's why the blood would never flow hot through her veins again.

Before he left, he prised her hand back to its original position.

He did not look back.

Awakened from a deep and dreamless sleep, Erica at first could not identify the sound. By the time she realized that it was the shrill ring of the telephone that woke her, it had already rung many times. She jumped out of bed to answer it.

"Erica Falck." Her voice was no more than a croak. She cleared her throat loudly with her hand over the mouthpiece to get rid of the worst of the hoarseness.

"Oh, sorry, did I wake you? I beg your pardon."

"No, I was awake." The reply came automatically and Erica could hear how transparent it sounded. It was quite obvious that she was groggy, to say the least.

"Well, I'm sorry in any case. This is Henrik Wijkner. I just had a call from Birgit, and she asked me to contact you. Apparently she got a call this morning from a particularly rude police superintendent from the Tanumshede station. He more or less ordered her, in not very polite terms, to come down to the station. Evidently my presence was also desired. He didn't want to say what it was about, but we have an idea. Birgit is quite upset, and since neither Karl-Erik nor Julia is in Fjällbacka at the moment for various reasons, I wonder whether you could do me a big favor and go over to see her. Her sister and brother-in-law are at work, so she's at home alone at their house. It will be a couple of hours before I can get back to Fjällbacka, and I don't want her to be alone that long. I know it's a lot to ask, and we don't actually know each other that well, but I have no one else to turn to."

"Of course I'll go over to see Birgit. It's no problem. I just have to throw on some clothes. I can be over there in about fifteen minutes."

"That's fine. I'm eternally grateful to you. Really. Birgit has never been particularly stable, and I'd like someone to be with her until I make it back to Fjällbacka. I'll ring and tell her you're on the way. I'll be there sometime after noon, so we can talk more then. Once again—thank you."

Still with sleep in her eyes, Erica hurried into the bathroom to wash her face. She put on the clothes she'd been wearing the day before, and after running a comb through her hair and applying a little mascara, she was sitting behind the wheel of her car less than ten minutes later. It didn't take more than five minutes to drive to Tallgatan from Sälvik, so it was almost precisely a quarter hour after Henrik's call that she rang the doorbell.

Birgit looked as if she'd lost several pounds in the few days since Erica last saw her, and her clothes hung loosely on her body. This time they didn't go into the living room; instead, Birgit led her into the kitchen.

"Thank you for taking the time to come over. I get so nervous, and I just couldn't sit here worrying until Henrik arrived."

"He said you had a phone call from the police in Tanumshede?"

"Yes, this morning at eight a Superintendent Mellberg rang and told me that Karl-Erik, Henrik, and I were to come to his office at once. I explained that Karl-Erik had gone out of town on an urgent business matter, but that he would be back tomorrow. I asked if it was all right if we waited until then. That was not acceptable, as he expressed it, and so Henrik and I would have to do for the time being. The man was quite rude, and of course I rang Henrik at once. He said he'd come home as soon as he could. I probably sounded a bit upset, I'm afraid, and that's when Henrik suggested he would ring you and ask whether you could come over for a couple of hours. I really hope you don't think we're asking too much. You probably don't want to get even more involved in our family tragedy, but I didn't know where to turn. Besides, you were almost like a daughter in our house once upon a time, so I thought that maybe——"

"Think nothing of it. I'm happy to help. Did the police say what this was all about?"

"No, the superintendent didn't want to say a word. But I have an idea. Didn't I tell you that Alex didn't take her own life? Didn't I?"

Erica impulsively placed her hand over Birgit's.

"Dear Birgit, let's not draw any hasty conclusions. You may be right, but until we know for sure it's better that we don't speculate."

They spent two long hours sitting at the kitchen table. The conversation died out after only a short while, and the only thing that could be heard in the silence was the ticking of the kitchen clock. Erica drew circles with her index finger around the pattern on the slick surface of the oilcloth. Birgit was dressed neatly and her makeup was as immaculate as the last time Erica saw her. But now there was something indefinably tired and worn-out about Birgit, like a photograph whose edges were missing their crispness. The weight she had lost didn't suit her. Even last time she had bordered on skinny, and the weight loss had brought out new wrinkles around her eyes and mouth. Birgit was gripping her coffee cup so hard that her knuckles were white. If the long wait was tiresome for Erica, it had to be insufferable for her.

"I don't understand who would want to kill Alex." The words sounded like a pistol shot after the long silence. "She didn't have any enemies. She just lived a completely ordinary life together with Henrik."

"We don't know yet what this is about. It's no use speculating before we know what the police want," Erica said again. She interpreted the lack of a reply from Birgit as tacit agreement.

Just after twelve noon Henrik pulled into the little parking space in front of the house. They saw him through the kitchen window and got up with relief to put on their coats. When he rang the bell they were already waiting in the entryway, ready to go. Birgit and Henrik kissed each other lightly on one cheek and then the other. After that it was Erica's turn to receive the same greeting. She wasn't used to such mannerisms and was a bit worried that she would cause embarrassment by starting from the wrong side. But she handled the moment with no problem, and for a second she enjoyed the masculine scent of Henrik's aftershave.

"You're coming along, aren't you?"

Erica was already halfway to her car.

"Well, I don't know . . ."

"I'd really appreciate it."

Erica met Henrik's eyes over Birgit's head and with a silent sigh she got into the backseat of his BMW. This was going to be a long day.

The ride to Tanumshede took no more than twenty minutes. They chatted about the weather and the gradual depopulation of the countryside. Anything other than the reason for their imminent visit to the police station.

Erica sat in the backseat and wondered what she was doing there. Didn't she have enough of her own problems without getting involved in a murder, if that was what it turned out to be? That would also mean that her book idea was as good as worthless. She had already managed to outline a first draft, and now she might just as well toss the pages in the wastebasket. Oh well, at least it would force her to focus completely on the biography. Although with some small changes it might work out yet. In fact it might even be better. The murder angle could be a real plus.

She suddenly realized what she was sitting and doing. Alex was not some made-up character in a book that she could twist and turn however she wished. She was a real person who was loved by real people. Erica had loved Alex too. She looked at Henrik in the rearview mirror. He looked just as unmoved as before, despite the fact that in a few minutes he might be informed that his wife had been murdered. Wasn't it true that most murders were committed by someone within the victim's own family? Once again she was ashamed of her thoughts. With an effort she pushed aside that train of thought and saw with gratitude that they were finally there. Now she just wanted to get this over with so that she could go back to her comparatively trivial concerns.

The stacks of paper had grown to imposing heights on his desk. It was astonishing how a small community like Tanum could generate so many crime reports. Mostly petty matters, to be sure, but each report had to be investigated, and that's why he sat here with administrative duties worthy of an Eastern European bureaucracy. It wouldn't have been so bad if Mellberg helped out, instead of sitting on his fat ass all day long. But he had to do the boss's work too. Patrik Hedström sighed. Without a certain gallows humor, he would never have survived this long. Lately he'd begun to wonder whether this was really all there was to life.

The big event of the day would be a welcome interruption in the daily routine. Mellberg had asked him to sit in on the interview with the mother and husband of the woman who was found murdered in Fjällbacka. It wasn't that he didn't see the tragedy in the whole thing, or didn't feel for the victim's family. It was just that nothing exciting ever really happened in his job, and he couldn't help feeling a tingle of anticipation in his body.

At the police academy they had been trained in interview situations, but so far he'd only had a chance to try out his talents in that area in connection with stolen bicycles and domestic abuse. Patrik looked at the clock. Time to go over to Mellberg's office, where the conversation would take place. Technically it wasn't a matter of an official interview yet, but today's meeting was nonetheless important. He had heard through the grapevine that the mother kept claiming that the daughter couldn't possibly have killed herself. He was curious to hear what lay behind this claim, which had now turned out to be correct.

He gathered up his notebook, a pen, and a coffee cup and went down the corridor. With his hands full he had to use his elbows and feet to get the door open, so it wasn't until he put down his things and turned to face the room that he caught sight of her. His heart skipped a beat. He was ten years old again and trying to pull her pigtails. A second later, he was fifteen and trying to talk her into hopping onto his moped and going for a ride. He was twenty and had given up hope when she moved to Göteborg. After a quick mental calculation, he reckoned that it was at least six years ago since he had last seen her. She looked just the same. Tall and curvy, with hair curling to her shoulders in several shades of blonde that blended to a warm shade. Even as a little girl Erica had been vain, and he could see that she still placed great emphasis on the details of her appearance. Her face lit up with surprise when she saw him. But Mellberg was giving him a stern look to sit down, so he merely mimed a silent hello.

It was a tense group of people sitting before him. Alexandra Wijkner's mother was small and thin, with too much heavy gold jewelry for his taste. She was perfectly coiffed and extremely well-dressed but looked the worse for wear with dark circles under her eyes. Her son-in-law showed no such signs of grief. Patrik glanced through his background information. Henrik Wijkner, successful businessman in Göteborg and heir to a considerable fortune going back several generations. And it showed. Not because of the obviously expensive quality of his clothes or the scent of fancy aftershave that hovered in the room; it was something less definable. A self-confident assurance that he was entitled to a prominent place in the world, which came from never having lacked any advantages in life. Although Henrik looked tense, Patrik could tell that he always felt he had control of the situation.

Mellberg loomed behind his desk. He had actually managed to stuff his shirt into his trousers, but splotches of coffee stained the motley pattern of his

shirt. As he observed each of the participants in delib-
erate silence, his right hand straightened his comb-
over, which had slipped too far down on one side.
Patrik was trying not to look at Erica. Instead he concentrated on one of Mellberg's coffee stains.

"So. You are probably aware of why I called you
here." Mellberg made a long pause, for effect. "I am
Superintendent Bertil Mellberg, chief of Tanumshede
police station, and this is Patrik Hedström, who will
be assisting me during this investigation."

He nodded at Patrik, who was sitting a bit outside
the semicircle formed by Erica, Henrik, and Birgit in
front of Mellberg's desk.

"Investigation? She was murdered, for God's sake!"
Birgit leaned forward in her chair, and Henrik quickly
put a protective arm around her shoulders.

"Yes, we have confirmation that your daughter could
not have taken her own life. Suicide can be definitively
ruled out, according to the medical examiner's report.
Of course, I can't go into the details of the investigation, but the main reason we know she was murdered is
that, at the time her wrists were slashed, she could not
have been conscious. We found a large amount of sedative in her blood. While she was unconscious, some
person or persons apparently first put her in the bathtub, filled it with water, and then slashed her wrists
with a razor blade to try and make it look like suicide."

The curtains in the office were drawn against the
sharp midday sun. The mood in the room was double-
edged. Gloom was mixed with Birgit's obvious relief
that Alex had not committed suicide.

"Do you know who did it?" Birgit had taken a small
embroidered handkerchief from her handbag and care-

fully dried the corners of her eyes so as not to ruin her makeup.

Mellberg clasped his hands over his voluminous paunch and fixed his eyes on the people in front of him. He cleared his throat with authority.

"Perhaps the two of you might tell me that."

"Us?" Henrik's surprise sounded genuine. "How would we know that? This must be the work of a madman. Alexandra didn't have any enemies."

"So you say."

Patrik thought for an instant that a shadow passed across the face of Alex's husband. The next second it was gone, and Henrik was again his calm and controlled self.

Patrik had always harbored a healthy skepticism about men like Henrik Wijkner. Men who were born to succeed. Who had everything without ever having to lift a finger. Naturally Henrik seemed both pleasant and charming, but under the surface Patrik could sense currents that hinted at a more complex personality. He glimpsed ruthlessness behind the handsome features, and he wondered about the total lack of surprise on Henrik's face when Mellberg revealed that Alex had been murdered. Believing something is one thing, but hearing it stated as fact is quite another. That much he had learned in his ten years as a cop.

"Are we suspects?" Birgit looked as astounded as if the superintendent had changed into a pumpkin right before her eyes.

"The statistics speak for themselves in cases of murder. The great majority of perpetrators is usually found among the close family members. Now I'm not saying that's true in this case, but I'm sure you understand that we have to be quite certain. No stone will be left unturned, I can personally vouch for that. With my broad experience in murder cases"—another dramatic pause—"this will surely be resolved quickly. But I would like both of you to submit an account of your actions on the days leading up to the point in time when we suspect Alexandra was killed."

"And what point in time would that be?" asked Henrik. "The last of us to speak with her was Birgit, but none of us phoned her until Sunday, so the murder could even have occurred on Saturday. I did ring her around nine-thirty Friday night, but she often took a walk in the evening before bed, so I assumed that she might have been out walking."

"All the medical examiner can say is that she has been dead for approximately a week. Naturally we will check your statements about when you phoned her, but we have one piece of information that indicates she died sometime before nine o'clock on Friday night. At around six o'clock, which must have been just after she arrived in Fjällbacka, she rang a Lars Thelander about a furnace that wasn't working properly. He couldn't come right away, but promised to be there no later than nine that evening. According to his testimony it was precisely nine o'clock when he knocked on the door. No one came to the door, and after waiting for a while he drove back home. Our working hypothesis is therefore that she died sometime that evening after she arrived in Fjällbacka, since it seems unlikely that she would have forgotten that the repairman was coming to look at the furnace, considering how cold it was in the house."

His hair was slipping again, this time down the left side. Patrik noticed that Erica could hardly take her eyes from the spectacle. She was probably controlling an impulse to rush over and straighten his hair. Everyone at the station had been through that phase.

"What time did you say you talked to her?" Mellberg directed his question at Birgit.

"Well, I'm not quite sure." She thought for a moment. "Sometime after seven. About quarter past, or seventhirty, I think. We spoke briefly because Alex said she had a visitor." Birgit blanched. "Could it have been. . . ?"

Mellberg nodded solemnly. "Entirely possible, Mrs. Carlgren. But it's our job to find out, and I can assure you that we will put all our resources on the case. In our line of work the elimination of suspects is one of our primary tasks, so please write up an account of Friday evening."

"Do you want me to provide an alibi too?" Erica asked.

"I don't think that will be necessary. But we would like you to tell us everything you saw when you were inside the house, the day you discovered her. You can leave your written accounts with Assistant Hedström."

Everyone turned to look at Patrik, and he nodded in agreement. They began to get up.

"A tragic event, this. Particularly in view of the child."

They all turned their eyes to Mellberg.

"The child?" Quizzically, Birgit looked from Mellberg to Henrik and back.

"Yes, she was in the third month of pregnancy according to the medical examiner. Surely this can't have been a surprise to you, could it?"

Mellberg grinned and winked roguishly at Henrik. Patrik was utterly appalled by his boss's tactless behavior.

Henrik's face slowly lost all color until it looked like white marble. Birgit turned to stare at him in astonishment. Erica felt as if she were petrified.

"Were you two going to have a child? Why didn't you tell me? Oh, God."

Birgit pressed her handkerchief to her mouth and sobbed uncontrollably, without a thought for the mascara that now ran in rivulets down her cheeks. Henrik again put a protective arm around her, but over Birgit's head he met Patrik's gaze. It was obvious that he hadn't had a clue that Alexandra was pregnant. Judging by Erica's hopeless expression, however, it was clear that she did know.

"We'll talk about this when we get home, Birgit," said Henrik. He turned to Patrik. "I'll see to it that you receive written accounts about Friday evening. I suppose you'll probably want to interview us in more detail once you have them."

Patrik nodded affirmatively. He raised his eyebrows to give Erica a questioning look.

"Henrik, I'll be right there," she said. "I just have to speak with Patrik for a moment. We're old friends."

She lingered in the corridor as Henrik led Birgit out to the car.

"Imagine running into you here. That was a surprise," said Patrik. He rocked nervously back and forth on his heels.

"Yes, if I'd thought about it I would have remembered that you work here, of course."

She was twisting the handle of her purse between her fingers and looking at him with her head cocked a little to one side. All her small gestures were so familiar to him.

"It's been a long time. I'm sorry I couldn't come to the funeral. How are you coping, you and Anna?"

Despite her height she looked small all of a sudden, and he resisted the urge to caress her cheek.

"We're doing all right. Anna drove home right after the funeral, but I've been here a couple of weeks now, trying to clean up the house. It's not easy."

"I heard that a woman in Fjällbacka had discovered the victim, but I had no idea it was you. That must have been horrible. The two of you were friends when you were kids, weren't you?"

"Yes. I don't think I'll ever be able to erase that sight from my mind. Well, I have to run now, they're waiting for me in the car. Maybe we could get together sometime. I'm going to be here in Fjällbacka for a while yet."

She was already on her way down the hall.

"How about dinner, Saturday night?" he said. "At my house, eight o'clock? I'm in the book."

"Sure, that sounds nice. See you at eight, then." She backed out through the door.

As soon as she was out of sight he did a little improvised dance in the corridor, to the great astonishment of his colleagues. But his joy was spoiled a bit when he realized how much work it would take to get his house in presentable shape. After Karin left him, he hadn't really felt like dealing with the housework.

He and Erica had known each other since birth. Their mothers had been best friends since childhood and were as close as two sisters. Patrik and Erica played together a lot when they were small, and it was no exaggeration to say that Erica was his first love. In fact, he believed he was born in love with Erica. There had always been such a natural quality about his feelings for her. As far as Erica was concerned, she had merely taken his puppy-like admiration for granted. Not until she moved to Göteborg did he realize that it was time to put his dreams on the shelf. He had fallen in love with others since then, of course. And when he married Karin he was utterly convinced that they would grow old together, but Erica was always in the back of his mind. Sometimes months would pass without thinking about her; sometimes he thought about her several times a day.

The piles of paper had not been miraculously reduced while he was gone. With a deep sigh he sat down at his desk and picked up the page on top. The work was monotonous enough that he could ponder the menu for Saturday at the same time. Dessert, in any case, was already decided. Erica had always loved ice cream.

He awoke with a nasty taste in his mouth. It had been a real blowout yesterday. His buddies had come over in the afternoon and together they had kept drinking until the small hours. A vague memory of the police stopping by at some point last night hovered just beyond his reach. He tried to sit up but the whole room spun around and he decided to stay where he was for a while.

His right hand was aching, and he raised it toward the ceiling to look at it. The knuckles were severely scraped and full of coagulated blood. Damn, there must have been a bit of a dustup last night, that's why the cops showed up. More and more of his memory began to return. It was the guys who had brought up the subject of the suicide. One of them had started talking a bunch of shit about Alex. "Upper-class bitch" and "society cunt" were words he had used about her. Anders had short-circuited, and after that he remembered only a red haze of rage as he started bashing the guy in a drunken fury. Sure, he had called her a few names himself when he was most furious at her betrayal. But that wasn't the same thing. The others didn't know her. He was the only one who had the right to judge her.

The telephone rang with a shrill sound. He tried to ignore it but decided it was less bothersome to get up and answer the phone than to let the noise keep slicing into his brain.

"Yes, this is Anders." He was slurring his words.

"Hi, it's Mama. How are you doing?"

"I feel like shit." He slid down the wall to sit on the floor. "What the hell time is it?"

"It's almost four in the afternoon. Did I wake you?"

"Nope." His head felt disproportionately large and kept threatening to fall down between his knees.

"I was in town shopping earlier. There's a lot of talk about something that I want you to know about. Are you listening?"

"Yeah, damn it, I'm listening."

"Apparently Alex didn't commit suicide. She was murdered. I just wanted you to know."

Silence.

"Anders, hello? Did you hear what I said?"

"Yeah, sure, I heard you. What did you say? Was Alex . . . murdered?"

"Yes, that's what they're saying in town, anyway. Apparently Birgit was down at Tanumshede police station and got the news today."

"Oh, shit. Look, Mama, I've got a lot to do. We'll talk later."

"Anders? Anders?"

He had already hung up.

With an enormous effort he showered and got dressed. After taking two Tylenols he felt more like a human being. The vodka bottle in the kitchen tried to tempt him, but he refused to give in. He had to be sober right now. Well, relatively sober, at least.

The phone rang again. He ignored it. Instead he took a phone book out of the cabinet in the hall and quickly found the number he was looking for. His hands were shaking as he punched in the number. It seemed to ring a hundred times.

"Hi, it's Anders," he said when the receiver on the other end was finally picked up. "No, don't hang up, damn it. We have to talk . . . well, you don't have that much of a fucking choice, I have to tell you . . . I'll be at your place in fifteen minutes. And you'd better fucking be there . . . I don't give a shit who else is there, fuck it! Don't forget who has the most to lose here . . . That's bullshit. I'm going now. See you in fifteen minutes."

Anders slammed down the receiver. After taking a couple of deep breaths, he pulled on his jacket and went out. He didn't bother to lock the door. The phone in the apartment started ringing furiously again.

Erica was exhausted when she got back to the house. There was a strained silence in the car during the trip home, and Erica understood that Henrik was facing a difficult choice. Should he tell Birgit that he wasn't the father of Alexandra's child, or should he keep quiet and hope that it didn't come out during the investigation? Erica didn't envy him and couldn't say how she would have acted in his situation. The truth wasn't always the best solution.

It was already getting dark, and she was grateful that her father had put in outdoor lamps that turned on automatically when anyone approached the house. She had always been terribly afraid of the dark. When she was little, she thought it was something she would grow out of, because adults couldn't be afraid of the dark, could they? But she was thirty-five years old, and she still looked under the bed to make sure that nothing was lurking there in the dark. How pathetic.

When she had turned on all the lights in the house, she poured herself a big glass of red wine and curled up on the wicker sofa on the veranda. The darkness was impenetrable, but she still stared straight ahead, though with unseeing eyes. She felt lonely. There were so many people grieving for Alex, people who had been affected by her death. But Erica had only Anna now. Sometimes she wondered whether even Anna would miss her.

She and Alex had been so close as girls. When Alex began to withdraw, and finally disappeared completely when she moved, it felt as though the world had ended for Erica. Alex was the only person she'd had to herself, and except for her father the only one who really cared about her.

Erica put her glass of red wine down on the table so forcefully that she almost broke the base off the glass. She felt altogether too restless to sit still. She had to do something. It was no use to pretend that Alex's death had not affected her deeply. What bothered her most of all was that the image of Alex conveyed by family and friends did not jibe at all with the Alex she had known. Even if people change on the path from childhood to adulthood, there is still a core of personality that remains intact. The Alex they had described to her was a complete stranger.

She got up and put on her coat again. Her car keys were in her pocket, and at the last moment she took a flashlight and stuffed it into the other pocket of her coat.

The house at the top of the hill looked deserted in the violet light from the streetlamp. Erica parked the car in the lot behind the school. She didn't want anyone to see her going into the house.

The bushes on the property offered a welcome cover as she cautiously sneaked up to the veranda. She hoped their old habits persisted and raised the doormat. There was the spare key to the house, hidden in exactly the same place as twenty-five years ago. The door creaked a little when she opened it, but she hoped that none of the neighbors had heard anything.

It was eerie stepping into the shadowy house. Her fear of the dark made it hard for her to breathe, and she forced herself to take some deep breaths to calm her nerves. She thankfully remembered the flashlight in her coat pocket and said a silent prayer that the batteries were good. They were. The light from the flashlight made her feel a bit calmer.

She played the beam of light over the living room on the first floor. She didn't know what she was looking for here in the house. She hoped that no neighbor or passerby would see the light and call the police.

The room was lovely and airy, but Erica noticed that the brown and orange seventies furniture that she remembered from her childhood had been replaced by light pieces of clean-lined Scandinavian design, made of birch. She understood that Alex had set her mark on the house. Everything was in perfect order, which created a desolate impression. There wasn't a single crease on the sofa or even a magazine laid out on the coffee table. She saw nothing that seemed worth examining more closely.

She recalled that the kitchen lay beyond the living room. It was big and roomy and immaculate, disturbed only by a lone coffee cup in the dish rack. Erica returned to the living room and went upstairs. She turned right at the top of the stairs and entered the master bedroom. Erica remembered it as Alex's parents' bedroom, but now it was obviously Alex and Henrik's room. It, too, was tastefully decorated but with a more exotic flavor. The fabrics were chocolate-brown and magenta, and there were African wooden masks on the walls. The room was spacious with a high ceiling, which allowed a large chandelier to hang properly. Alexandra had apparently resisted the temptation to decorate her house from top to bottom with marine details, something that was common in the houses of summer residents. Everything from curtains adorned with shells to paintings of complicated knots sold like hotcakes in the small summertime shops in Fjällbacka.

Unlike the other rooms that Erica looked in, the bedroom seemed lived-in. Small personal items lay scattered here and there. On the nightstand lay a pair of glasses and a book of poems by Gustaf Fröding. A pair of stockings were flung on the floor and some pullover sweaters were laid out on the bedspread. This was the first time Erica felt that Alex really had lived in this house.

Erica began cautiously looking through drawers and cabinets. She still didn't know what she was searching for and felt like a voyeur as she rummaged among Alex's lovely silk underwear. But just as she decided to move on to the next drawer she heard something rustle on the bottom.

All of a sudden she paused with her hand full of lace-trimmed panties and bras. She clearly heard a sound from downstairs through the stillness in the house. A door being carefully opened and closed. Erica looked all around her in panic. The only hiding places in the room were under the bed or in one of the wardrobes covering one wall. All at once she felt claustrophobic. She couldn't move until she heard footsteps on the stairs; instinctively she crept over to the closest wardrobe. The door opened without a creak, thank God, and she quickly climbed in among the clothes and closed the door behind her. She had no chance to see who had entered the house, but she could clearly hear footsteps coming closer and closer. The person stopped for a moment outside the bedroom door before coming in. She suddenly realized that she was holding something in her hand. Without thinking she had grabbed whatever it was that rustled in the drawer. She cautiously put it in her jacket pocket.

She scarcely dared breathe. Her nose started to itch and she desperately tried to wiggle it to relieve the problem. She was in luck; it stopped.

The intruder was searching the bedroom. It sounded as if he or she were doing about the same thing Erica was doing before she was interrupted. Drawers were pulled out, and Erica knew that the wardrobes were next. Her panic rose. Beads of sweat formed on her brow. What could she do? The only solution she saw was to squeeze as far back behind the clothes as possible. She was lucky to have stepped into a wardrobe with several long coats in it, and she cautiously squeezed in among them and draped them in front of her. She hoped the two ankles sticking out of a pair of shoes on the floor wouldn't be noticed.

It took a while for the person to go through the bureau. She inhaled a musty smell of mothballs, sincerely hoping they had done their job so that no bugs were creeping around here in the dark. She also hoped that it wasn't Alex's killer out there, only a few feet away. But who else would have reason to sneak around in Alex's house, thought Erica, choosing to ignore the fact that she had no written invitation either.

All at once the door to the wardrobe was opened and Erica felt a gust of fresh air against the exposed skin of her ankles. She held her breath.

The wardrobe didn't seem to be hiding any secrets or valuables—at least not for the person who was doing the searching—and the door was closed again almost at once. The other doors were opened and closed just as quickly, and the next moment she heard the footsteps going out the bedroom door and down the stairs. She didn't dare step out of the wardrobe until a good while after she heard the front door carefully closing. It was wonderful to be able to breathe at last without being acutely conscious of each breath.

The room looked the same as when Erica came in. Whoever the visitor was, the search had been careful and had left no traces. Erica was fairly convinced that it wasn't a burglar. She took a closer look at the wardrobe she had hidden inside. When she retreated to the far corner she had felt something hard pressing against the back of her calves. She swept aside the clothes and saw that what she had felt was a large canvas. It stood with the back facing her. She lifted it out carefully and turned it around. It was an incredibly beautiful painting. Even Erica could see that it had been done by a talented artist. The motif was a naked Alexandra, lying on her side with her head resting on one hand. The artist had chosen to use warm colors, which gave Alex's face an impression of peace. She wondered why such a beautiful painting had been put in the back of a wardrobe. Judging from the picture, Alex had nothing to be ashamed of. Her body was just as perfect as the painting. Erica couldn't shake off the feeling that there was something familiar about it. There was something obvious that she'd seen before. She knew that she had never seen this particular painting, so it had to be something else. The space in the lower right corner lacked a signature, and when she turned it over there was nothing there but "1999," which must have been the year the painting was done. She carefully put the painting back in its place at the back of the wardrobe and closed the door.

She looked around the room one last time. There was something she couldn't really put her finger on. Something was missing, but for the life of her she couldn't think what it was. Oh well, it would probably come to her later. She didn't dare stay in the house any longer. She put back the key where she had found it. She didn't feel safe until she was back in her car with the motor running. That was enough excitement for one evening. A stiff cognac would soothe her soul and drive off some of her uneasiness. Why in the world had she decided to drive over there and snoop around? She felt like slapping her forehead at her own stupidity.

When she pulled into the driveway at home she saw that scarcely an hour had passed since she left. That surprised her. It had felt like an eternity.

* * *

Stockholm was putting on its best face. And yet Erica felt as though a gloomy cloud were hovering over her. Normally she would have been overjoyed at the sunshine that glittered on Riddarfjärden as she drove across Västerbron. Not today. The meeting was set for two o'clock. She had been mulling over things all the way from Fjällbacka, trying in vain to come up with a solution. Unfortunately Marianne had made her legal position very clear. If Anna and Lucas insisted on selling the house, she would have to go along with it. Her only alternative was to buy them out at half the market value of the house, and with the prices that houses in Fjällbacka were bringing, she didn't have even a fraction of that amount. Of course she wouldn't be left holding the baby if the house were sold. Her half could bring in as much as a couple of million kronor, but she didn't care about the money. No money in the world could replace the loss of the house. She felt sick at the idea of some Stockholmer, who thought a brand-new sailor's cap would transform him into a coastal dweller, ripping out the lovely veranda on the front and putting in a picture window. And nobody could say that she was exaggerating. She'd seen it happen time and time again.

Erica turned in at the attorney's office in Runebergsgatan in Östermalm. The building was magnificent with its marble façade lined with columns. She checked herself in the mirror in the lift one last time. Her attire was carefully selected to fit in with the milieu. This was the first time she had been here, but she could easily picture what sort of attorneys Lucas would hire. In a gesture of feigned civility he had pointed out that, of course, she could bring along her own attorney. Erica had chosen to come alone. She simply could not afford an attorney.

Actually, she had wanted to meet Anna and the children before the meeting, maybe have a bite to eat with them. Despite her bitterness over Anna's actions, Erica had decided to do her utmost to keep their relationship alive.

Anna didn't seem to share her point of view, excusing herself by saying that it would be too stressful. It was better that they meet at the attorney's office. Before Erica could suggest that they could see each other afterward instead, Anna beat her to the punch and said that she had to rush off and meet a girlfriend after the meeting. Hardly a coincidence, Erica thought. It was obvious that Anna wanted to avoid her. The question was whether it was on her own initiative or whether Lucas refused to permit Anna to meet Erica while he was at work and had no chance to supervise.

Everyone was already there when she came in. They observed her solemnly as she put on a fake smile and offered her hand to greet Lucas's two attorneys. Lucas merely nodded hello, while Anna ventured a weak wave behind his back. They all sat down and began the negotiations.

The whole thing didn't take very long. The attorneys explained in a dry and businesslike manner what Erica already knew. That Anna and Lucas were perfectly within their rights in demanding the sale of the house. If Erica could buy them out for half the market value, then she was entitled to do so. If she could not or would not, then the house would be put up for sale as soon as a value was set by an independent appraiser.

Erica looked Anna straight in the eye.

"Do you really want to do this? Doesn't the house mean anything to you? Imagine what Mama and Papa would have thought if they knew you were going to sell it as soon as they were gone. Is this really what *you* want, Anna?"

Out of the corner of her eye she saw Lucas frown at her emphasis on *you*.

Anna looked down and picked some invisible flecks of dust off her elegant dress. Her blonde hair was tightly pulled back in a ponytail.

"What are we going to use that house for? Old houses are just a lot of trouble, and think of all the money we could get out of it. I'm sure that Mama and Papa would have appreciated it if one of us took a practical view of the matter. I mean, when would we use the house? Lucas and I would rather buy a summer place in the Stockholm archipelago so we have something closer. What are you going to do with that house anyway?"

Lucas smiled scornfully at Erica as he patted Anna on the back with phony concern. She still hadn't dared meet Erica's gaze.

Once again, Erica was struck by how tired her little sister looked. She was thinner than usual, and the black dress she wore was loose around the bust and waist. She had dark circles under her eyes, and Erica thought she saw a blue shadow under the powder on her right cheekbone. Her rage at the powerlessness of the situation hit her with full force and she fixed her eyes on Lucas. He returned her gaze with composure. Having come directly from work, he was wearing his professional uniform: a graphite-gray suit with a blinding white shirt and a shiny dark-gray tie. He looked elegant and sophisticated. Erica was sure that many women found him attractive. But she thought he had a cruel streak that acted like a filter over his facial features. His face was angular with sharp cheekbones and firm jawline. This was accentuated even more because he always combed his hair straight back from his high forehead. He didn't look the typical ruddy Englishman; he was more like a Norwegian with light-blond hair and icy blue eyes. His upper lip was curved and full like a woman's, giving him an indolent, almost decadent expression. Erica noticed that his eyes drifted down to her décolletage, and she instinctively pulled her jacket closed. He registered her reaction, which annoyed her. She didn't want him to see that he had any sort of effect on her.

When the meeting was finally over, Erica simply turned on her heel and walked out the door without bothering to say any polite words of farewell. As far as she was concerned, everything had been said that could be said. She would be contacted by someone who would come to appraise the house, and then the house would be put on the market as soon as possible. No amount of persuasion had done any good. She had lost.

She had sublet her apartment in Vasastan to a pleasant couple studying for their doctorates, so she couldn't go back there. Since she didn't feel like setting off on the five-hour drive to Fjällbacka for a while, she parked the car in the garage at Stureplan and went over to sit in Humlegårdsparken. She needed to collect her thoughts. The peacefulness in the lovely park that felt like an oasis in the middle of Stockholm offered just the right meditative atmosphere she needed.

Snow must have just fallen over the city; the grass was still white. In Stockholm, it only took a day or two for snow to turn into a dirty-gray slush. She placed her mittens on a park bench and then sat down on them as protection under her seat. Urinary tract infections were nothing to play around with; that was the last thing she needed right now.

She let her thoughts drift as she watched the crowd of people rushing by on the path. It was the middle of the lunch rush. She had almost forgotten how stressed the mood could be in Stockholm. Everyone was always in a rush, chasing after something they never really could catch. She suddenly longed for Fjällbacka. She probably hadn't realized how much she had settled in there over the past few weeks. Certainly she'd had a lot to deal with, but at the same time she'd discovered a peace inside herself that she never found in Stockholm. If you were alone in Stockholm, you were completely isolated. In Fjällbacka you were never alone, which could be both good and bad. People cared about their neighbors and kept tabs on them. Sometimes it could go too far; Erica didn't care for all the gossip, but as she sat here watching the bustle of the city she felt that she could never return to this.

Like so many times recently, her thoughts turned to Alex. Why had she driven to Fjällbacka every weekend? Who was she meeting there? And the ten-thousand-krona question: who was the father of the child she was expecting?

All at once, Erica remembered the piece of paper she had stuffed into her jacket pocket as she stood in the dark in the wardrobe. She didn't understand how she could have forgotten about it when she got home the day before yesterday. She felt in her right-hand pocket and pulled out a wrinkled sheet of paper. With fingers that had grown stiff without mittens, she carefully unfolded the paper and smoothed it out.

It was a copy of an article from *Bohusläningen*. There was no date, but based on the typeface and a black-and-white picture, she could see that it wasn't recent. Judging from the photo, it dated from the seventies. She easily recognized both people in the picture and the story recounted in the article. Why had Alex saved this article at the bottom of a bureau drawer?

Erica stood up and put the article back in her pocket. There was no answer to be found here. It was time to go home.

The funeral was tasteful and reverential. Fjällbacka Church was far from full. Most people hadn't known Alexandra but were there merely to satisfy their curiosity. Family and friends sat in the front pews. Besides Alex's parents and Henrik, Erica recognized only Francine. She had a tall blond man next to her in the pew, who Erica assumed was her husband. Otherwise, there weren't many friends. They filled only two rows of pews, confirming Erica's image of Alex. She had certainly had numerous acquaintances, but few close friends. There were only a few curiosity-seekers scattered here and there in the rest of the church.

Erica had taken a seat up in the balcony. Birgit had caught sight of her outside the church and invited her to sit with them. She had politely declined. It would have felt hypocritical to sit there among family and friends. Alex was actually a stranger to her.

Erica squirmed on the uncomfortable pew. All through their childhood she and Anna had been dragged to church on Sundays. For a child, it had been terribly boring to sit through long sermons and hymns whose melodies were hopelessly difficult to learn. To amuse herself Erica had made up stories in her head. Numerous sagas about dragons and princesses had been composed here without ever being committed to paper. In Erica's teenage years, her church attendance was much less frequent because of her vehement protests. When she did go along, the sagas were replaced by stories with a more romantic theme. Ironically enough, she actually had this forced church attendance to thank, or blame, for her choice of profession.

Erica still hadn't embraced any type of religion; for her a church was a beautiful building steeped in traditions, nothing more. The sermons of her childhood had prompted no desire to accept a faith. They often dealt with hell and sin; they lacked the bright belief in God that she knew existed but had never personally experienced. Much had changed. Now a woman stood before the altar, dressed in a pastor's robes, and instead of eternal damnation she spoke of light, hope, and love. Erica wished that this view of God had been offered to her when she was growing up.

From her hidden place in the balcony, she saw a young woman sitting next to Birgit in the first pew. Birgit was holding the woman's hand in a convulsive grip, and occasionally she leaned her head on her shoulder. Erica thought she recognized her. The young woman must be Julia, Alex's little sister. She was too far away for Erica to see her face, but she noticed that Julia seemed to flinch at Birgit's touch. Julia withdrew her hand each time Birgit took it, but her mother either pretended not to notice or was truly unaware of her daughter's reaction, due to the state she was in.

Sunshine flowed in through the high stained-glass windows. The pews were hard and uncomfortable, and Erica felt the beginning of a dull ache in her lower back. She was grateful that the ceremony was relatively short. When it was over she sat there and looked down on the people slowly wandering out of the church.

Outdoors the sun was almost unbearably bright in a cloudless sky. A procession of people walked down the little hill to the churchyard and the newly dug grave where Alex's coffin would be buried.

Until her parents' funeral, she had never thought about how burials were done in the winter, when the ground was frozen. Now she knew that an area was heated so that the ground could be dug up. An area just big enough to hold all the coffins that were to be interred.

On the way to the site that had been selected for Alex's grave, Erica passed her parents' grave. She was last in the procession and stopped for a moment by the headstone. A thick strip of snow lay on the edge and she carefully swept it off. With one last look at the grave she hurried toward the small group that was gathered a bit farther on. At least the rubberneckers had stayed away from the burial ceremony; now only family and friends were left. Erica had felt unsure of whether she should come along, but at the last moment she decided that she wanted to follow Alex to her final resting place.

Henrik stood in front with his hands stuck deep in his coat pockets, head bowed and eyes fixed on the coffin that was slowly covered with flowers. Mostly red roses.

Erica wondered if he too was looking around and thinking that the child's father might be among the group gathered at the grave.

When the coffin was lowered into the ground Birgit

let out a long, drawn-out sigh. Karl-Erik was resolute and dry-eyed. It took all his strength to hold Birgit upright, both physically and emotionally. Julia stood a bit away from them. Henrik had been right in his description of Julia as the family's ugly duckling. Unlike her big sister, she was dark-haired with short tresses clumsily cut in what could hardly be called a hairstyle. Her features were coarse, with deeply set eyes peering out from beneath bangs that were much too long. She wore no makeup, and her skin showed clear signs of severe acne during her teens. Birgit looked even smaller and more fragile than usual standing next to Julia. Her younger daughter was more than four inches taller, with a broad, heavy, shapeless body. Fascinated, Erica watched the series of conflicting emotions that raced like whirlwinds across Julia's face. Pain and rage alternated at lightning speed. No tears. She was the only one who hadn't placed a flower on the casket, and when the ceremony was over she quickly turned her back on the hole in the ground and headed back toward the church.

Erica wondered how relations had been between the sisters. It couldn't have been easy, always being compared with Alex, always drawing the short straw. Julia's turned back was a rebuff as she quickly put more distance between herself and the rest of the group. Her shoulders were hunched in a dismissive gesture.

Henrik came up to Erica.

"We're going to have a small reception afterward. We'd be happy if you came."

"Well, I don't really know," said Erica.

"You could stop by for a little while at least."

She hesitated. "Well, okay. Where is it? At Ulla's house?"

"No, we considered having it there but finally decided on Birgit and Karl-Erik's house. Despite what happened there, I know that Alex loved that house. We all have happy memories from there, so what better place to remember her? Even though I understand that it might be a bit tough for you. You don't have such pleasant memories from your last visit, I mean."

Erica blushed in shame at the thought of what had really been her last visit. Quickly, she looked away.

"It'll be fine," she said.

She drove her own car and parked again in the lot behind the Håkebacken school. The house was already full when she went in, and she wondered if she should turn around and go home. The moment for that came and passed; when Henrik came over and took her jacket, it was too late to change her mind.

It was crowded around the dining room table, where a buffet of savory quiches was laid out. Erica chose a big piece with shrimp and quickly moved to a corner of the room, where she could eat and watch the rest of the party in peace and quiet.

The party seemed unusually upbeat in view of the occasion. The undertone was feverishly cheerful. When she looked at the people around her, they all seemed to be wearing strained expressions as they conversed. The thought that Alex had been murdered hovered just beneath the surface.

Erica scanned the room, looking from one face to the next. Birgit was sitting on the edge of the sofa, wiping her eyes with a handkerchief. Karl-Erik stood behind her with one hand placed awkwardly on her shoulder and a plate of food in the other. Henrik was working the room like a pro. He went from one group to another, shaking hands, nodding in reply to condolences, reminding people that there was also coffee and cake. In every respect he was the perfect host. As if he were at a cocktail party, instead of his wife's funeral reception. The only thing that showed what an effort it was for him was the deep breath he took and a brief moment of hesitation, as if to gather new strength before he went on to the next group.

The only person who was behaving out of sync with everyone else was Julia. She had sat down on the windowsill on the veranda. One knee was drawn up and she was staring out to sea. Anyone who tried to approach her with a little kindness or some words of sympathy was firmly rebuffed. She ignored all attempts at conversation and kept staring out at the big expanse of whiteness.

Erica felt a light touch on her arm and gave an involuntary start so that a little coffee splashed onto her plate.

"Excuse me, I didn't mean to startle you." Francine was smiling.

"Oh, that's okay. I was just thinking."

"About Julia?" Francine nodded toward the figure in the window. "I saw you watching her."

"Yes, I must admit that she interests me. She's so totally cut off from the rest of the family. I can't figure out whether she's grieving for Alex or whether she's been cast out for some reason I don't understand."

"Probably nobody understands Julia. But she couldn't have had an easy time of it. The ugly duckling growing up with two beautiful swans. Always shoved aside and ignored. It wasn't that they were outright mean to her, she was just—unwanted. Alex, for example, never mentioned her during the time we lived in France. I was very surprised when I moved to Sweden and discovered that Alex had a little sister. She talked about you more than she talked about Julia. You must have had a very special relationship, didn't you?"

"I don't know, actually. We were children. Like all kids of that age, we were blood sisters and never wanted to be separated and all that. But if Alex hadn't moved away, the same thing probably would have happened to us. The same thing that happens to other little girls who grow up and turn into teenagers. We would have fought over the same boyfriends, had different taste in clothes, ended up on different rungs of the social pecking order, and abandoned one another for different friends who better suited the phase we were in—or wanted to be in. But sure, Alex had a big influence on my life, even as an adult. I don't think I've ever been able to shake off that feeling of being betrayed. I always wondered whether I was the one who said or did something wrong. She just retreated more and more and then one day she was gone. When we met again as adults, she was a stranger. In some odd way it feels as though now I'm getting to know her again."

Erica thought about the book pages that were piling up at home. So far she only had a collection of impressions and episodes mixed with her own thoughts and reflections. She didn't even know how she would shape the material; all she knew was that it was something she had to do. Her writer's instinct told her that this was a chance to write something genuine, but where the boundary lay between her needs as a writer and her personal connection to Alex, she had no idea. The sense of curiosity that was crucial to writing something also impelled her to seek the answer to the riddle of Alex's death on a much more personal level. She could have chosen to dismiss Alex and her fate, turn her back on the whole sad clan surrounding Alex and devote herself to her own affairs. Instead she was standing in a room full of people she really didn't know.

It suddenly occurred to her that she had almost forgotten the painting she found in Alex's wardrobe. Now she realized why the warm tones used to depict Alex's nude form on the canvas were so familiar. She turned to Francine.

"You know, when I met you at the gallery . . ."

"Yes?"

"There was a painting right by the door. A big canvas all in warm colors—yellows, reds, oranges . . ."

"Yes, I know the one you mean. What about it? Don't tell me you're a collector?" Francine smiled.

"No, but I'm wondering—who painted it?"

"Well, that's a very sad story. The painter's name is Anders Nilsson. He's actually from here in Fjällbacka. It was Alex who discovered him. He's incredibly talented. Unfortunately he's also a serious alcoholic, which apparently will ruin his chances as an artist. Today it's not enough to hand in your paintings to a gallery and hope for success. As an artist you also have to be clever at marketing yourself. You need to show up at openings, go to functions, and live up to the image of an artist in every respect. Anders Nilsson is a drunken wino who isn't fit for civilized company. We sell a painting now and then to customers who know talent when they see it, but Anders will never be a big star in the firmament of art. To be completely crass about it, he'd have the most potential if he drank himself to death. Dead painters have always been a hit with the general public."

Erica gave the delicate creature in front of her a look of astonishment.

Francine saw her expression and added, "I didn't mean to sound so cynical. It just burns me up that someone can have so much talent and squander it on booze. Tragic is only his first name. He was lucky that Alex discovered his paintings. Otherwise the only ones who would have enjoyed them would be the winos of Fjällbacka. And I have a hard time believing that they're capable of appreciating the finer aspects of art."

One piece of the puzzle was in place, but Erica couldn't for the life of her see how it fit with the rest of the pattern. Why did Alex have a nude portrait of herself painted by Anders Nilsson hidden in her wardrobe? One explanation was that it was intended as a present for Henrik, or maybe for her lover, and that Alex had commissioned the portrait from an artist whose talent she admired. Yet it didn't quite ring true. There had been a sensuality and sexuality about the portrait that belied a relationship between strangers. There was some sort of bond between Alex and Anders. On the other hand, Erica was well aware that she was no art connoisseur, and her gut feeling could be all wrong.

A murmur spread through the room. It began in the group closest to the front door and rippled through the rest of the guests. Everyone's eyes turned toward the door, where a highly unexpected guest was making a grandiose entrance. When Nelly Lorentz stepped through the door, the others held their breath from sheer astonishment. Erica thought of the newspaper article she'd found in Alex's bedroom. She could feel how all the apparently disconnected facts were spinning around in her head without making any sense.

Since the early fifties, the continued livelihood of Fjällbacka had waxed or waned with the Lorentz cannery. Almost half of the able-bodied residents of Fjällbacka were employed at the factory, and the Lorentz family was regarded as royalty in the little town. Since Fjällbacka wasn't exactly a hotbed of high society, the Lorentz family was in a class all by itself. From their elevated position in the enormous villa at the top of the hill they looked down on Fjällbacka with guarded superiority.

The factory was started in 1952 by Fabian Lorentz. He came from a long line of fishermen and was expected to follow in his forefathers' footsteps. But the stock of fish was running out, and young Fabian was both ambitious and intelligent, with no intention of scraping by on the same meager earnings of his father.

He started the cannery with his two bare hands, and when he died in the late seventies he left his wife, Nelly, both a robust business and a considerable fortune. Unlike her husband, who was very well liked, Nelly Lorentz had a reputation for being haughty and cold. She never showed herself in town anymore, but like a queen held audiences for those specially invited. So it was a sensation of a high order to see her step through the door. This was going to provide grist for the gossip mill for months to come.

It was so quiet in the room that you could have heard a pin drop. Mrs. Lorentz graciously allowed Henrik to help her off with her fur coat, and she entered the living room on his arm. He led her over to the sofa in the middle where Birgit and Karl-Erik were sitting, as she briefly nodded a greeting to a select few of the other guests. When she reached Alex's parents the conversation finally started up again. Small talk about this and that as everyone strained to hear what was being said over by the sofa.

One of those who had graciously been granted a nod was Erica. Due to her quasi-celebrity status she had apparently been found worthy, even prompting an invitation to come to tea with Nelly Lorentz after her parents' death. Erica had politely declined, giving as an excuse that she was still in mourning.

With curiosity, she now regarded Nelly as she formally offered her deepest sympathies to Birgit and Karl-Erik. Erica doubted that there was even a scrap of sympathy in her skinny body. She was very thin, with knotty wrists that stuck out of her well-tailored dress. She must have starved herself her whole life to be so fashionably slender, not realizing that what can be lovely with the natural roundness of youth is not as attractive once age has taken its toll. She had a sharp and angular face that was surprisingly smooth and free of wrinkles, which made Erica suspect that the scalpel had helped to put nature on the right track. Her hair was her most handsome attribute. It was thick and silvery gray, done up in an elegant French twist, but combed back so tightly that the skin of her forehead was pulled up a little, giving her a slightly surprised look. Erica estimated Nelly's age to be a bit over eighty. It was rumored that in her youth she'd been a dancer, and that she'd met Fabian Lorentz when she was part of a ballet company at a theater in Göteborg where no upper-class girls would dare show their faces. Erica thought she caught a glimpse of a dancer's training in the graceful way she still moved. But according to the official story, she'd never been near a dance school but was the daughter of a consul from Stockholm.

After a few minutes of hushed conversation, Nelly left the grieving parents and went out on the veranda to sit with Julia. No one gave the slightest indication that they found this quite strange. They went on with their conversations, keeping a watchful eye on the odd pair.

Erica once again stood alone in the corner after Francine left to continue mingling. From there, she could watch Julia and Nelly undisturbed. For the first time that day Erica saw a smile spread across Julia's face. She hopped down from the windowsill and sat next to Nelly on the rattan sofa, and there they sat with their heads close together, whispering.

What could such a mismatched pair have in common? Erica cast a look in Birgit's direction. The tears had finally stopped streaming down her cheeks. She fixed her gaze on her daughter and Nelly Lorentz with a look of naked horror on her face. Erica decided to accept that invitation from Mrs. Lorentz after all. It might be interesting to have a little chat with her in private.

With a great sense of relief she finally left the house on the hill, glad to breathe in the invigorating winter air once more.

Patrik felt a little nervous. It was a long time since he had made dinner for a woman. A woman, moreover, for whom he felt a strong attraction. Everything had to be perfect.

He hummed as he sliced cucumbers for the salad. After much agony and pondering, he had finally decided on fillet of beef. Now it was trimmed and in the oven, almost done. The gravy was sputtering on the stove, and he could feel his stomach growling from the aroma.

It had been a hectic afternoon. He hadn't been able to leave work as early as he had hoped, so he had to clean the house in record time. He hadn't really been aware of the extent to which he had let the house go to pot since Karin left him, but when he saw it with Erica's eyes, he realized that it was going to take a serious effort.

It felt a little embarrassing to have fallen into the typical bachelor's trap with untidy surroundings and nothing in the fridge. He hadn't really understood what a big burden Karin had carried at home. He took the neat, well-kept home for granted and didn't give a thought to how much work it required to keep it in order. There was a lot he had taken for granted.

When Erica rang the doorbell he flung off his apron and glanced in the mirror to check his hair. Although he'd put gel in it, it was as unruly as ever.

Erica looked fantastic, as always. Her cheeks were a warm pink from the cold, and her blond hair curled thickly over the collar of her down jacket. He gave her a brief hug, allowing himself to shut his eyes for a moment and inhale the scent of her perfume. Then he let her into the warm house.

The table was already set, and they started in on the appetizer while they waited for the entree to be done. Patrik surreptitiously watched as she tasted with plea-sure the avocado stuffed with shrimp. Not really a dif-ficult dish; hard to ruin.

"I never would have thought that you could rus-tle up a three-course dinner," Erica said as she took another bite of the avocado.

"No, I can hardly believe it myself. But—*skål* and welcome to Restaurant Hedström."

They clinked glasses and sipped at the chilled white wine. Then they ate for a while in companionable silence.

"How have you been?" Patrik peered at Erica from under the hair hanging into his eyes.

"I've probably had better weeks."

"Why did you come with them to the interview? It must have been quite a few years since you've had any contact with either Alex or her family."

"Yes, it's probably been about twenty-five years or so. I'm not quite sure why I came. I feel as though I've just been sucked into a whirlpool, and I don't know whether I can escape, or whether I even want to. I think Birgit sees me as a reminder of better days. Plus I'm an outsider, so maybe I represent some sort of security." Erica paused. "Have you made any progress?"

"I'm sorry, I can't say anything about the case."

"No, I understand. Pardon me, I wasn't thinking."

"No problem. But I thought you might be able to help me. You've seen the family a good deal now, plus you know them from before. Could you tell me a little about your impressions of the family and what you know about Alex?"

Erica put down her silverware and tried to sort out her own impressions in the order she wanted to present them to Patrik. She told him everything she'd found out, along with her impressions of the people in Alex's life. Patrik listened attentively even as he got up and cleared away the appetizer and brought out the entree. Now and then he would interject a question. He was astonished at all the information Erica had uncovered in such a short time. And after she also told him what she knew about Alex from the past, the woman who until now had been merely a murder victim was suddenly transformed into someone with a face and personality.

"I know that you can't talk about the case, Patrik, but can you tell me if the police have any leads? Any ideas at all about who could have murdered her?"

"No, I have to say that we haven't gotten very far in the investigation. A minor breakthrough, anything at all, would be extremely welcome about now." He sighed and circled his finger around the edge of his wineglass.

Erica hesitantly said, "I may have something that could be of interest." She reached for her handbag and began digging around in it. She pulled out a piece of paper which she handed to him across the table. Patrik took it and unfolded it. He read what it said with interest, but raised a questioning eyebrow when he was done.

"What does this have to do with Alex?"

"That's what I was wondering too. I found this article in a bureau drawer, hidden beneath Alex's underwear."

"What do you mean, you 'found' it? When did you have a chance to go through her bureau drawers?"

He saw her blush and wondered what she was hiding.

"Well, one night I went to the house and snooped around a little."

"You did what?"

"Yes, I know. You don't have to say it. It was really stupid, but you know how I am. Act first and think later." She was talking fast in order to ward off any additional reproaches. "In any case, I found this paper in Alex's drawer and managed to take it with me."

He refrained from asking how she could "manage" to take the item with her. It was better not to know.

"What do you think it could mean?" asked Erica. "An article about a disappearance twenty-five years ago. What connection could that have with Alex?"

"What else do you know about this?" asked Patrik, waving the article.

"Factually, no more than what's in the article. That Nils Lorentz, son of Fabian and Nelly Lorentz, disappeared without a trace in January of 1977. No body was ever found. On the other hand, there has been a good deal of speculation over the years. Some people think that he drowned and the body washed out to sea. Other rumors say that he embezzled a large amount of money from his father and then fled the country. What I heard was that Nils Lorentz was not a nice person, so most people leaned toward the latter alternative. He was the only son, and Nelly apparently spoiled him rotten. She was inconsolable after he disappeared, and Fabian Lorentz never got over the loss. He died of a heart attack about a year later. The only heir to the fortune is now a foster son they took in about a year before Nils vanished. Nelly adopted him a couple of years after her husband died. Well, that's just a small sampling of the local gossip. I still don't understand how this could have any bearing on Alex's death. The only dealings the families ever had with each other were when Karl-Erik worked in the office at the Lorentz cannery when Alex and I were little, before they moved to Göteborg. But that was over twenty-five years ago."

Erica suddenly remembered one other link. She told Patrik about Nelly's appearance at the funeral reception and how she had devoted almost all her attention to Julia.

"I have no idea how any of this could be connected to the article. But there must be something. Francine, Alex's partner in the gallery, also mentioned that she thought Alex wanted to come to terms with the past somehow. That was as much as Francine knew, but I think it makes sense. Call it woman's intuition or whatever you like, but I have a feeling that there's a connection."

She was a little ashamed because she knew she hadn't told Patrik the whole truth. There was one more small but very strange piece of the puzzle that she was keeping to herself. At least until she knew more.

"Well, I certainly can't argue with a woman's intuition. Would you like a little more wine?"

"Yes, please." Erica looked around the kitchen. "A nice place you have here. Did you decorate it yourself?"

"No, I can't take credit for that. It was Karin who was the decorating talent."

"Oh right, your wife, Karin. What happened between the two of you, actually?"

"Well, it was really the same old story. Girl meets dance-band singer in a waist-length jacket. Girl falls in love. Girl divorces her husband and moves in with the dance-band singer."

"You're kidding!"

"Unfortunately I'm not. It was bad enough that she dumped me. But she left me for Leif Larsson, popular singer and heart-throb in 'Leffes,' the most famous dance band in Bohuslän. The man with the prettiest hockey girlfriend on the west coast. Yep, there's not much you can do to compete with a man in tasseled loafers."

Erica looked at him wide-eyed.

Patrik smiled. "Well, that's probably a somewhat exaggerated version, but something along those lines."

"But that must have been terrible. It couldn't have been easy for you."

"I felt sorry for myself for quite a while, but it's okay now. Not good, but okay."

Erica changed the subject. "The news about Alex's pregnancy was like a bomb going off." She stared hard at Patrik, and he had a feeling that there was something more behind her apparently innocent remark.

"In any case, it seemed she hadn't shared the good news with her husband," Erica said.

Patrik waited silently for her to go on. After a moment Erica appeared to have decided to continue down that path, but she spoke in a low voice, still sounding hesitant.

"According to her best friend, Henrik isn't the father of the child."

Patrik raised an eyebrow and whistled, but still said nothing in the hope of more information from Erica.

"Francine told me that Alex had met someone here in Fjällbacka. And she drove here every weekend to see him. According to Francine, Alex had never wanted to have children with Henrik, but it was different with this man. She was overjoyed about the baby, and that's why Francine insisted so strongly that her death wasn't suicide. In her view, Alex was happy for the first time in her life."

"Did she know who the man was?"

"No, she didn't. Alex kept that information to herself."

"But why would her husband put up with her driving to Fjällbacka every weekend without him? Did he know that she was meeting someone here?"

Patrik took another sip of wine and felt his cheeks beginning to flush. Whether from the wine or from Erica's presence, he wasn't quite sure.

"Apparently they had a quite unusual relationship. I met Henrik in Göteborg and I got the feeling that their lives ran on parallel tracks that seldom crossed. It's also impossible to say what he knows or doesn't know, from the short conversation that I had with him. That man has a stone face. I think that whatever he knows, he's very careful to keep it to himself."

"That type of person can sometimes be like a pressure cooker. The steam builds and builds, and one day it explodes. Do you think that's what might have happened? That one day the rejected husband had enough, and he killed the unfaithful wife?" Patrik asked.

"I don't know, Patrik. I really don't know. But now I think we should drink more than our share of wine and talk about all sorts of things, as long as it doesn't have to do with murder and sudden death."

He willingly agreed and raised his glass in a toast.

They moved to the sofa and spent the rest of the evening talking comfortably about everything else under the sun. She told him about her life, about the fuss over the house and her grief over her parents. He told her about his anger and feeling of failure after his divorce, and about the frustration of finding himself at square one again, just as he was starting to feel ready for children and a family, ready to believe that he and Karin would grow old together.

Even the brief pauses in the conversation felt comfortable, and it was at those moments he had to keep himself from leaning forward and kissing Erica. He refrained, and the opportunity passed.

3

He was watching when they carried her out. He wanted to wail and throw himself over her covered body. Keep her forever.

Now she was truly gone. Strangers were going to poke and dig at her body. None of them would see her beauty the same way he had.

For them she would only be a piece of meat. A number on paper, without life, without fire.

With his left hand he stroked the palm of his right hand. Yesterday it had caressed her arm. He pressed his palm against his cheek and tried to feel her cold skin on his face.

He felt nothing. She was gone.

Blue lights were flashing. People were rushing back and forth, in and out of the house. Why were they in a hurry? It was already too late.

No one saw him. He was invisible. He had always been invisible.

It didn't matter. She had seen him. She could always see him. When she fixed her blue eyes on him he felt that he was seen.

Now there was nothing left. The fire had been put out long ago. He stood in the ashes and watched as *his life was carried off, covered by a yellow hospital blanket. At the end of the road there were no choices. He had always been aware of that, and now the hour had finally arrived. He had been longing for it. He embraced it.*

She was gone.

Nelly had sounded a bit surprised when Erica called. For a moment, Erica wondered whether she was making a mountain out of a molehill, although she still couldn't help thinking that it was very odd for Nelly to show up at Alex's funeral reception. Not to mention the way she had talked almost exclusively to Julia. It's true that Karl-Erik had worked for Fabian Lorentz as the factory's office manager until the family moved to Göteborg, but as far as Erica knew they had never associated socially. The Carlgrens were far below the Lorentz family's requirements for acceptable social class.

The drawing room she was ushered into was exquisitely beautiful. The view stretched from the harbor at one end to the open horizon beyond the islands at the other. On a winter day like this, when the sunshine was reflecting off the snow-covered ice, the view could compete with even the sunniest summertime panorama.

They sat down on an elegant sofa group and Erica was served small canapés from a silver tray. They were fantastic, but she tried to control her appetite so she wouldn't look unrefined. Nelly ate only one. Afraid to add a gram of flesh to those knobby bones.

The conversation flowed slowly but politely. In the long pauses between the words, only the ticking of a clock could be heard along with the dainty slurping as they sipped their hot tea. They kept the topics of conversation neutral. The flight of young people from Fjällbacka. The lack of work. How distressing it was that more and more of the lovely old homes were being bought up by tourists and turned into summer houses. Nelly talked a little about how it used to be, when she came to Fjällbacka as a young woman, newly married. Erica listened attentively, politely asking a question now and then.

It felt as if they were circling around the subject they both knew that they would have to broach sooner or later.

It was Erica who finally got up the courage.

"Well, the last time we saw each other it was under rather sad circumstances."

"Yes, so tragic. Such a young woman."

"I didn't realize that you knew the Carlgrens so well."

"Karl-Erik worked for us for many years, and of course we met his family on numerous occasions. It seemed only right to express my condolences in person." Nelly lowered her eyes. Erica saw that her hands were fidgeting nervously in her lap.

"I got the impression that you also knew Julia. She wasn't even born when the Carlgrens lived in Fjällbacka, was she?"

No more than a stiffening of her back and a slight movement of her head indicated that Nelly found the question uncomfortable. She waved a hand covered with gold jewelry.

"No, Julia is a new acquaintance. But I think she's a very enchanting young lady. Yes, I know that she may not have the same outer beauty as Alexandra, but unlike her sister, she has a strength of will and a courage that makes me view her as considerably more interesting than her foolish sibling."

Nelly clapped her hand to her mouth. Besides the fact that, for an instant, she forgot she was talking about a dead person, for a fraction of a second she had revealed a crack in her façade. What Erica saw in that brief moment was pure hatred. Why would Nelly Lorentz hate a woman she could hardly have met except when Alex was a child?

Before Nelly had a chance to smooth over her faux pas, the telephone rang. With obvious relief, she excused herself and went to answer it.

Erica took the opportunity to snoop around the room. It was beautiful but impersonal. The invisible hand of an interior decorator hovered over the entire room. Everything was color coordinated down to the smallest detail. Erica couldn't help comparing it with the simplicity of the furnishings in her parents' house. There nothing had been included for the sake of appearances; all the objects had been purchased over the decades based on their usefulness. Erica thought that the beauty of worn and personal items far surpassed this polished showroom. The only personal thing Erica could find was a row of family portraits on the mantelpiece. She leaned forward and studied them intently. They seemed to be in chronological order from left to right, beginning with a black-and-white portrait of an elegant couple in their wedding finery. Nelly was really radiantly beautiful in a white sheath dress that hugged her figure, but Fabian looked uncomfortable in his tuxedo.

In the next photo the family had grown; Nelly was holding a baby in her arms. At her side, Fabian still looked stiff and serious. Then there was a long row of portraits of children at various ages, sometimes alone, sometimes together with Nelly. In the last picture in the row, Nils Lorentz looked to be about twenty-five. The son who had vanished. After the first portrait of the whole family, it was as though Nils and Nelly were the only members left. Although perhaps Fabian wasn't so eager to be in the picture and instead stood behind the camera. Photos of Jan, the adopted son, were conspicuous in their absence.

Erica turned her attention to a desk in one corner of the room. Made of dark cherrywood, with lovely inlays that Erica traced with her finger, it was completely bare and looked as if it served no other function than decoration. She was tempted to peek in the drawers but wasn't sure how long Nelly would be gone. The phone conversation was apparently taking some time, but she could come back into the room at any moment. The wastebasket attracted Erica's attention instead. There were some crumpled papers in it. She took out the paper ball on top and gently smoothed it out. She read it with growing interest. Even more astonished than before, she carefully replaced it in the wastebasket. Nothing in this story was what it seemed.

She heard someone clear his throat behind her. Jan Lorentz was standing in the doorway, his eyebrows raised quizzically. She wondered how long he'd been standing there.

"Erica Falck, isn't it?"

"Yes, that's right. And you must be Nelly's son, Jan?"

"Also correct. Pleased to meet you. You're a bit of a topic of conversation here in town, you should know."

He gave her a big smile and came toward her with outstretched hand. She took it reluctantly. Something about him made the small hairs on her arms stand up. He held her hand a bit too long. She resisted the impulse to pull it back.

He looked as though he'd come directly from a business meeting, wearing a well-pressed suit and with a briefcase in his hand. Erica knew that he was the one who ran the family business. And very successfully.

He wore his hair slicked back, with a touch too much gel. His lips were a little too full and fleshy for a man, and his eyes were lovely with long dark lashes. If it hadn't been for a square, powerful jaw with a deep cleft in his chin, he probably would have looked rather feminine. As it was, the mixture of angularity and luxuriance gave him a slightly odd appearance; it was impossible to say whether he was attractive or not. Personally, Erica found him repellent, but she based that opinion more on a feeling she got in the pit of her stomach.

"So, Mother has finally managed to entice you here. You've been high on the wish list ever since you published your first book, I must tell you."

"I see. Well, I understand it's been received as the event of the century here. Your mother has invited me before, but the time didn't seem right until now."

"I heard about your parents. Very tragic. I really must express my sincere condolences."

He managed a sympathetic smile, but the emotion never reached his eyes.

Nelly came back into the room. Jan bent over to kiss his mother on the cheek. She let him do it with an indifferent expression.

"How nice for you, Mother, that Erica could finally come to visit. You've been looking forward to this for a long time."

"Yes, it's very nice indeed."

She sat down on the sofa. A grimace of pain swept across her face and she grabbed her right arm.

"Mother, what is it? Are you in pain? Shall I fetch your pills?"

Jan leaned forward and placed his hands on her shoulders, but Nelly brusquely shook them off.

"No, there's nothing wrong with me. Just the aches and pains of age, that's all. Nothing to worry about. Shouldn't you be at the factory, by the way?"

"Yes, I just dashed home to pick up some papers. Well, I suppose I should leave you ladies alone. Don't overexert yourself, Mother, remember what the doctor said . . ."

Nelly merely snorted in reply. Jan's face showed a concern and sympathy that seemed genuine. But Erica could swear that she saw a tiny smile at the corners of his mouth when he left the room and turned to look at them for a second.

"Don't ever get old. With each year that passes, the old Viking idea of jumping off a cliff to one's death looks better and better. The only thing to hope for is that you get so senile that you think you're twenty years old again. That would be fun to relive." Nelly gave a bitter smile.

It didn't seem like a particularly amusing topic of conversation. Erica muttered something in reply and then changed the subject.

"In any case it must be a comfort to have a son who can carry on the family business. From what I understand, Jan and his wife live here with you."

"A comfort. Yes, perhaps it is."

Nelly glanced quickly at the photographs on the

mantelpiece. She said nothing more, and Erica didn't dare ask any questions.

"Enough about me and my family. Are you working on a new book? I must say that I loved your last one about Karin Boye. You make the people come so alive somehow. Why is it that you only write about women?"

"At first it was more of an accident, I think. I wrote my dissertation at the university about great female Swedish authors and became so fascinated by them that I wanted to find out more about who they were as individuals. I began, as you probably know, with Anna Maria Lenngren, since I knew the least about her. Things have just snowballed from there. Right now I'm writing about Selma Lagerlöf, and I'm coming up with a lot of interesting angles."

"Haven't you ever thought about writing something, what should I say . . . non-biographical? You have such a flair for language and it would be so interesting to read something fictional by you."

"Of course I've had some thoughts in that direction." Erica tried not to look guilty. "But at the moment I'm swamped with the Lagerlöf project. After that we'll see what happens."

She glanced at the clock. "Speaking of my writing . . . unfortunately I really have to get going. Even though there's no time clock in my profession, it's important to maintain discipline. I must go home and write my daily quota. Thank you so much for tea— and the delicious canapés."

"Think nothing of it. It was delightful to have you here."

Nelly rose graciously from the sofa. Now there was no sign of her aches and pains.

"I'll see you out. In the old days our maid, Vera, would have done that, but times change. Maids aren't fashionable anymore, and besides hardly anyone can afford one. I would have liked to have kept her on, since we can afford it, but Jan refused. He doesn't want strangers in the house, he says. Although it's all right for her to come and clean once a week. Well, it's not always easy to make sense of you young people."

Evidently they had now reached a new level of familiarity, because when Erica offered her hand in farewell, Nelly ignored it and kissed her lightly on both cheeks instead. Erica now knew instinctively which side to begin on. She was starting to feel quite sophisticated and almost at home in the more refined drawing rooms.

Erica hurried home. She hadn't wanted to tell Nelly the real reason for her departure. She looked at her watch. Twenty to two. At two o'clock the real estate agent was coming to look at the house prior to putting it up for sale. Erica gnashed her teeth at the thought that somebody was going to walk around poking and prodding at the house, but there was nothing for it but to let events take their course.

She had left the car at home, and she picked up her pace to get there in time. Although he could just as well wait, she thought, slowing down. Why should she rush?

Happier thoughts crept into her mind. Dinner on Saturday at Patrik's place had far exceeded her expectations. For Erica he had always seemed like a nice but slightly annoying younger brother, even though they were the same age. She had still expected Patrik to be the same irritating boy. Instead she had found a mature, warm, and humorous man. He didn't look half bad, she had to admit. She wondered how soon she could decently ask him over to dinner—just returning the invitation, that is.

The last hill up to the Sälvik campground looked deceptively level; it was a long, slow incline. She was panting heavily when she turned off to the right and went up the last small slope to the house. When she reached the top she stopped short. A big Mercedes was parked in front of the house, and she knew exactly who the registered owner was. She'd thought that the day's activity couldn't be any more trying than it already was. She was wrong.

"Hello, Erica." Lucas was leaning against the front door with his arms crossed.

"What are you doing here?"

"Is that any way to welcome your brother-in-law?" His Swedish had an accent but was grammatically perfect.

Lucas mockingly spread out his arms as if to give her a hug. Erica ignored the gesture. She could see that that was precisely what he'd expected. She'd never made the mistake of underestimating Lucas. That's why she always observed a great deal of caution when she was in his presence. She wanted more than anything to walk right up to him and slap his grinning face, but she knew that could start something that she might regret.

"Answer my question. What are you doing here?"

"If I'm not mistaken . . . hmmm . . . let's see, exactly one quarter of all this is mine."

He gestured toward the house, but he might as well have been pointing at the whole world, his self-assurance was so vast.

"Half is mine and half is Anna's. You have nothing to do with this house."

"You may not be very well versed in the community property code, seeing as you haven't succeeded in finding anyone stupid enough to get hitched with you, I mean. But according to that law, a married couple shares everything equally. Even ownership in a house by the sea."

Erica was well aware that this was the case. For a brief moment she cursed her parents who had not been farsighted enough to guarantee that the house was solely owned by their daughters. They had known what sort of man Lucas was, but they probably hadn't reckoned that they had so little time left. No one likes to be reminded of his own mortality, and like so many other people they had postponed that sort of decision.

She chose not to take the bait and object to his pejorative comment about her marital status. She would rather be an old maid for the rest of her life than make the mistake of marrying someone like Lucas.

He went on, "I wanted to be here when the real estate agent arrived. It never hurts to check up on one's net worth. We want everything to go smoothly, now don't we?"

He smiled that infernal smile of his again. Erica unlocked the front door and pushed past him. The agent was late, but she hoped he would show up soon. She didn't like the prospect of being alone with Lucas.

He entered the house after her. She hung up her jacket and began puttering about the kitchen. The only way she could handle him was to ignore him. She heard him walking about the house, inspecting it. It couldn't be more than the third or fourth time he'd been inside. The beauty of simplicity was not something that Lucas appreciated, nor had he ever shown the slightest interest in visiting Anna's family. Their father couldn't stand his son-in-law, and the feeling was mutual. When Anna and the children came to visit, they came alone.

She didn't like the way Lucas was walking around touching things in the house—the way he was touching the furniture and the decorative objects. Erica had to repress a desire to walk behind him with a dustrag and wipe off everything he had touched. With relief she saw a gray-haired man in a big Volvo turn into the driveway. She hurried to open the door for him. Then she went into her office and closed the door. She didn't want to watch him go around looking at her childhood home and assessing its weight in gold. Or price per square foot.

The computer was already on. The file was open, waiting for her to get back to work. She had been up early for a change and had gotten a lot done. She had written four pages that morning for her draft of the book about Alex, and now she went back and read through them. She still had a number of problems with the form of the book. At first, when she'd thought that Alex's death was suicide, she'd considered writing a book to answer the question "why?" It would have been more of a biography. Now the material was increasingly taking on the form of a crime novel, a genre to which she'd never felt particularly attracted. It was people—their relationships and psychological motivations—that she was interested in; she thought that was something most crime novels had to give up in favor of bloody murders and cold shivers running down the spine. She hated all the clichés they used; she wanted to write about something that was genuine. Something that attempted to describe why someone could commit the worst of all sins—to take the life of another human being. So far she had written down everything in chronological order, reproducing word-for-word what was said to her, and mixing in her own observations and conclusions. She would have to pare down that material. Tighten it up to get as close to the truth as possible. How Alex's nearest and dearest might react was not something she had wanted to consider yet.

She regretted not telling Patrik everything about her visit to the house where Alex had died. She should have told him about the mysterious visitor and about the painting she found hidden in the wardrobe. And about the feeling she had that something was missing, something that had been in the room when she first went inside. She couldn't stand to ring him now and admit that there was more to tell. But if the right occasion presented itself, she would tell him the rest, she promised herself that.

She could hear Lucas and the real estate agent walking around in the house. He must have thought she was behaving quite strangely, barely saying hello and then rushing off and locking herself in her office. The agent wasn't to blame for the situation in which she found herself, so she decided to grit her teeth and display some of the good manners she had been taught.

When she came into the living room, Lucas was in the midst of describing in effusive terms the magnificent light let in by the big mullioned windows. Strange, Erica didn't know that creatures that crept out from under a rock would appreciate sunlight. She had a vision of Lucas as a big, shiny beetle; she just wished she could have eradicated him from her life with a simple stamp of her boot heel.

"Please excuse my rudeness just now. I had some urgent business to tend to."

Erica smiled broadly and held out her hand to the agent, who introduced himself as Kjell Ekh. He assured her that he was in no way offended. Selling houses was a very emotional affair. If she only knew what stories he could tell . . . Erica smiled wider and even permitted herself a sly little flutter of her lashes. Lucas looked at her suspiciously. She ignored him.

"Well, don't let me interrupt. How far did you get?"

"Your brother-in-law was just showing me your lovely living room. It's very tasteful, I must say. Quite beautiful with the light coming in through the windows."

"Yes, it is lovely, isn't it. Too bad about the draft."

"The draft?"

"Yes, unfortunately the windows are not properly sealed, so when the least wind blows you have to make sure you're wearing your warmest woolen socks. But it's nothing that replacing all the windows couldn't fix."

Lucas glared at her furiously, but Erica pretended not to notice. Instead she took Kjell by the arm; if he'd been a dog he would have been eagerly wagging his tail by this point.

"You've seen the upstairs, I take it, so perhaps we should continue down to the cellar. And don't worry about the moldy smell. As long as you're not allergic, there's no danger. I practically lived down there, and it didn't hurt me any. The doctors have assured me that my asthma has no connection with the mold."

As the finishing touch she broke into a coughing fit so violent that she bent in half. Out of the corner of her eye she saw Lucas's face take on a much redder hue. She knew that her exaggerated claims would be exposed in a closer inspection of the house. But until then, it was some small consolation to be able to annoy Lucas a bit.

Kjell looked very relieved when he got outside in the fresh air again, after being shown all the cellar's good points by an enthusiastic Erica. Lucas was silent and passive during the rest of the tour. With a pang of uneasiness she wondered whether she'd carried her childish prank a little too far. He knew that a real appraisal would show that none of the "drawbacks" of the house that she had revealed would have any substance, but she had attempted to make him a laughingstock. And that was something that Lucas Maxwell could not tolerate. With a slight feeling of dread Erica saw the agent drive off, waving happily, after promising that they would be contacted by a certified appraiser who would go through the house from attic to cellar.

Lucas followed her into the hallway. The next second she felt herself plastered to the wall, with Lucas's hand in a brutal grip around her throat. His face was no more than half an inch from hers. The anger she saw there made her understand for the first time why it was so hard for Anna to get out of her relationship with Lucas. What Erica saw was a man who let no obstacle stand in his way. She stood stock still, much too afraid to move.

"Don't you ever, ever do that again, do you hear me? Nobody makes a fool of me like that without consequences, so watch your step!"

He snarled the words so fiercely that he sprayed her face with saliva. She had to resist the impulse to wipe his spittle from her face. Instead, she stood as motionless as a pillar of salt, silently praying he would get out of her house and go away. To her astonishment he did just that. He released his grip on her throat and turned on his heel to head for the door. But just as she was about to heave a deep sigh of relief, he spun around and with a single step was in front of her again. Before Erica could react, he grabbed her by the hair and pressed his mouth to hers. Lucas forced his tongue between her lips and at the same time took such a tight hold on her breast that she felt the underwire of her bra cut into her skin. With a smile he turned, headed for the door, and vanished into the winter cold. Not until Erica heard his car start and drive off did she dare move. She sank down onto the floor with her back to the wall and wiped the back of her hand across her mouth in disgust. His kiss had somehow seemed more threatening than his stranglehold; she felt herself starting to shake. With her arms wrapped around her legs she leaned her head on her knees and wept. Not for her own sake, but for Anna's.

Monday mornings were not associated with pleasant feelings in Patrik's world. He didn't begin to turn into a real human being until eleven o'clock. So he woke from an almost trancelike state when the hefty stack of papers landed on his desk with a thunk. The awakening was brutal. In one stroke, the pile of documents had doubled, and he let out a groan.

Annika Jansson gave him a mischievous smile and asked innocently, "Didn't you say you wanted everything that's been written about the Lorentz family over the past years? Here I do a magnificent job digging up every single word ever written about them, and what do I get as payment for my efforts? A groan. How about your eternal gratitude instead?"

Patrik smiled. "My eternal gratitude isn't good enough for you, Annika. If you weren't already married I would marry you and cover you in mink and diamonds. But since you broke my heart and insisted on keeping that lout of a husband of yours, you'll have to settle for a simple thank-you instead. And my eternal gratitude, of course."

To his great delight he saw that he'd almost succeeded in making her blush this time.

"All right, now you've gone one step too far. Why do you want to look through all this? What's it got to do with the murder in Fjällbacka?"

"No idea, to tell you the truth. Let's call it woman's intuition."

Annika raised her eyebrows. She decided that she probably wouldn't get any more out of him for the moment. But she was curious. Everyone knew the Lorentz family, even in Tanumshede, and if they were somehow involved with a murder it would be a sensation, to say the least.

Patrik looked up as she closed the door. An incredibly efficient woman. He sincerely hoped that she could stand to be under Mellberg's command. It would be a great loss for the station if she decided one day that she'd had enough. He forced himself to focus on the stack of papers Annika had placed before him. After quickly leafing through them, he could tell that it was going to take him the rest of the day to read all the material. He leaned back in his chair, put his feet up on the desk and picked up the first article.

Six hours later, he massaged his weary neck and felt his eyes itching and stinging. He had read the articles in chronological order, starting with the oldest newspaper clip first. It was fascinating reading. A lot had been written about Fabian Lorentz and his successes over the years. The great majority of it was positive, and for a long time life seemed to have dealt Fabian a winning hand. The company took off with astonishing speed. Fabian seemed to be a very talented, if not to say a brilliant, businessman. His marriage to Nelly was reported in the society columns with accompanying photos showing the handsome couple in evening attire. Then photos of Nelly and her son, Nils, began appearing in the papers. Nelly seemed to have been unflagging in her work for various charity and society events, and Nils was always at her side—often with a frightened expression and his hand securely held in his mother's.

Even when he reached his teens and should have been a bit more reluctant to be seen with his mother in public, he was unfailingly there by her side, now with her arm tucked under his and with a proud expression on his face. Patrik thought he looked extremely proprietary. Fabian was seen less and less often; he was mentioned only when news of some big business deal was reported.

One article was different from the others and caught Patrik's attention. *Allers* had a whole feature about Nelly in the mid-seventies when she took in a foster child, a boy who came from a "tragic family background," as the *Allers* reporter described it. The article showed Nelly, carefully made up and dressed to the nines in her elegant living room, with her arm around a boy of twelve. He had a defiant and sulky expression on his face. When the picture was snapped he looked as if he were about to shake off her bony arm. Nils, who was then a young man in his mid-twenties, was standing behind his mother, and he wasn't smiling either. Serious and ramrod straight in a dark suit and slicked-back hair, he seemed to blend in to the elegant atmosphere completely, while the younger boy stuck out like a sore thumb.

The article was full of praise about the sacrifice and great social contribution Nelly was making by taking in this child. It was hinted that the boy had been involved in some terrible tragedy in his childhood, a trauma that Nelly was quoted as saying she had helped him overcome. She was confident that the healthy and loving environment they were offering him would heal the boy and turn him into a productive human being. Patrik found himself feeling sorry for the boy. What naïveté.

About a year later, the glamorous society photos and enviable "at-home-with" reports were replaced by big black headlines: "Heir to Lorentz family fortune missing." For several weeks the local newspapers trumpeted the news, and it was even considered important enough for the *Göteborgs-Posten* to report. The eye-catching headlines were accompanied by an abundance of more or less well-founded speculations about what might have happened to young Lorentz. Every conceivable and inconceivable alternative was aired—he had embezzled his father's entire fortune and was now in an undisclosed location living the life of luxury. Or he had taken his own life because he discovered that he was not actually the son of Fabian Lorentz, who had made it clear that he didn't intend to let a bastard inherit his considerable fortune. Most of these rumors were not published in so many words, merely intimated discreetly. But anyone who had the least bit of sense could easily read between the lines.

Patrik scratched his head. For the life of him he couldn't understand how he was going to link a disappearance from twenty-five years ago to the current murder case, but he had a strong feeling that there was a connection.

He rubbed his eyes wearily and continued going through the stack of papers, now nearing the bottom. After a while, with no new information about Nils's fate, public interest had begun to flag and the disappearance was seldom mentioned anymore. Even Nelly made the society columns only rarely after that; she wasn't written about even once during the nineties. Fabian's death in 1978 had prompted a large obituary in *Bohusläningen*, with the usual rhetoric about being a pillar of society, and that was the last time he was mentioned.

Their adopted son, Jan, however, was in the papers more and more frequently. After Nils vanished, he became the sole heir to the family business, and when he turned twenty-one he stepped in at once as CEO. The company had continued to flourish under his leadership, and now it was he and his wife, Lisa, who were constantly written up in the society columns.

Patrik paused. A paper had fluttered to the floor. He bent down to pick it up and began reading with interest. The article was over twenty years old. It provided Patrik with a great deal of interesting information about Jan and his life before he ended up with the Lorentz family. Disturbing information, but fascinating. His life had changed radically when he became part of the Lorentz family. The question was whether Jan himself had changed just as radically.

Patrik resolutely gathered up all the papers and tapped the stack on the desk to even out the edges. He pondered what he should do now. So far he had no more than his—and Erica's—intuition to go on. He leaned back in his office chair, put his feet up on the desk, and clasped his hands behind his head. With his eyes closed, he tried to create some sort of order in his thoughts so he could weigh one alternative against another. Closing his eyes was a mistake. Ever since their dinner on Saturday, all he could see was Erica.

He forced himself to open his eyes and focused instead on the depressing light-green concrete of the wall. The police station was from the early seventies, and presumably designed by someone who specialized in government institutions, with their predilection for ninety-degree angles, concrete, and dirty green paint. He had tried to liven up the office a bit with a couple of potted plants in the window and some framed pictures on the walls. When he was married he had kept a photo of Karin on his desk. Even though the desk had been dusted many times since then, he still thought he could see a mark where it had stood. He obstinately set his penholder in that spot and quickly went back to weighing his options. What should he do about the material he had in front of him?

There were really only two courses of action. The first was to investigate this lead on his own, which would mean doing it in his free time. Mellberg always saw to it that his workload was enough to make him run about like a scalded rat all day long. He actually hadn't managed to look at the articles during work hours, but only because of a rebellious desire to make trouble. He would have to pay for it by working a good part of the evening. He wasn't very eager to spend the little free time he had doing the work Mellberg had assigned to him, so option two should at least be tried.

If he went to Mellberg and presented the matter the

right way, perhaps he could get permission to follow up on these leads during working hours. Mellberg's vanity was his weak point, and if it was massaged correctly he might be able to win his consent. Patrik was aware that the superintendent viewed the case of Alex Wijkner as a guaranteed return ticket to the Göteborg force. Based on all the rumors he'd heard, Patrik believed that Mellberg had burned all his bridges, but he still might be able to exploit the man's vanity for his own ends. If he could exaggerate the connection to the Lorentz family a little, perhaps hint that he'd received tips that Jan was the father of Alex's child, it might get Mellberg to go along with him. Not particularly ethical perhaps, but he felt deep in the pit of his stomach that the connection to Alex's death could be found in the piles of papers in front of him.

With one fluid motion, he took down his feet from the desk and shoved back the chair so hard that it continued backward on its wheels and banged into the wall behind him. Patrik picked up all the photocopies and went down to the other end of the bunker-like corridor. Before he could change his mind he pounded hard on Mellberg's door and thought he heard him say, "Come in."

As always he was shocked at how a man who did absolutely nothing could manage to amass such a huge amount of paper. Stacks of paper covered every inch of his desk. In the window, on all the chairs, and above all on the desk, thick piles of paper were collecting dust. The bookshelf behind the superintendent was sagging with binders, and Patrik wondered how long it had been since the documents had seen the light of day. Mellberg was on the telephone but waved for Patrik to come in. Patrik wondered in amazement what was going on. Mellberg was beaming like a star in the window on Christmas Eve. It's a good thing his ears are in the way, thought Patrik, or that smile would wrap all the way around his head.

Mellberg's half of the phone conversation was terse.

"Yes.

"Yes, of course.

"Not at all.

"Yes, that's obvious.

"You did the right thing.

"Heavens no.

"Yes, thank you so much, ma'am, I promise to get back to you."

In triumph, he slammed the receiver down in the cradle, making Patrik jump in his chair.

"That's the way to do things!"

Mellberg continued beaming like a jovial Santa Claus. It occurred to Patrik that this was the first time he'd ever seen Mellberg's teeth. They were astonishingly white and regular. Almost a little too perfect.

Mellberg gave him an expectant look, and Patrik gathered that he wanted him to ask what was going on. Obediently he did so, but he didn't expect the answer he received.

"I've got him! I've got Alex Wijkner's murderer!"

Mellberg was so beside himself with excitement that he didn't notice that his comb-over had slipped down over one ear. For once Patrik was not struck by a desire to giggle at the sight. He ignored the fact that the superintendent had used the pronoun "I" indicating that he had no intention of sharing any glory with his coworkers. Instead Patrik leaned forward with his elbows on his knees and asked earnestly, "What do you mean? Have we got a breakthrough in the case? Who was that you were talking to?"

Mellberg raised his hand to stop the barrage of questions and then leaned back in his chair and clasped his hands over his stomach. This was a moment he intended to milk to the last drop.

"Well, Patrik, when you've been in this profession as long as I have, then you know that breakthroughs aren't something you get; they're something you earn. Due to my extensive experience and skill, as well as my hard work, there has indeed been a breakthrough in the case. A certain Dagmar Petrén rang and passed on some interesting observations that she'd made just before the body was discovered. Yes, I'd even venture to say *significant* observations, which will eventually lead to our putting a dangerous killer behind bars."

Impatience tingled like tiny pinpricks inside of Patrik, but he had sense enough to know that all he had to do was wait Mellberg out. Eventually he would get to the heart of the matter. Patrik only hoped that it would happen before he took retirement.

"Yes, I recall a case we had in Göteborg, autumn of 1967 . . ."

Patrik sighed and prepared himself for a long wait.

She found Dan where she expected to find him. He was moving the pieces of equipment on the boat as easily as if they were sacks filled with cotton. Huge, fat rolls of rope, seamen's sacks, and enormous fenders. Erica enjoyed watching him work. In a hand-knit sweater, cap, and gloves and with white vapor steaming out of his mouth with each breath, he looked as though he fit right in with the tableau behind him. The sun was high in the sky and the light reflected off the snow on deck. The silence was absolute. He worked efficiently and purposefully, and Erica could see that he was loving every minute of it. This was his true element. The boat, the sea, the islands in the background. She knew that in his mind he was picturing how the ice would start to break up and how the *Veronica* would head off for the horizon at full speed. Winter was merely one long waiting period. It had always been hard for people living on the coast. In the old days, if the summer was good they would salt down enough herring to make it through the winter. If not, they would have to find another way to survive. Like so many of the coastal fishermen, Dan couldn't live on fishing alone, so he had gone to night school. He now worked as a substitute Swedish teacher at the high school in Tanumshede a couple of days a week. Erica thought he was a very talented teacher, but his heart was here, not in the classroom.

He was fully absorbed with his work on the boat. She padded along on light feet so she could watch for a while without disturbing him until he noticed her standing there on the wharf. She couldn't help comparing him to Patrik. In appearance they were completely different. Dan's hair was so blond that during the summer months it turned almost white. Patrik's dark hair was the same color as his eyes. Dan was muscular while Patrik was more of a lanky type. But in terms of personality they could have been brothers. The same calm, gentle manner, with a quiet humor that always surfaced at the right moments. Actually it had never occurred to her before how alike they were in temperament. In a

way that pleased her. Since breaking up with Dan she
had never been truly happy in a relationship. All these
years she had either looked for or ended up in relationships with men of a totally different type. "Immature," Anna had pointed out. "You're trying to raise
boys instead of finding a grown man, so it's no wonder
that the relationships never work out," Marianne had
said. Maybe they were right. But the years were slipping away, and she had to admit that she was starting
to feel a bit panicky. The death of her parents was also
a brutal wake-up call to examine what she was missing
in her life. Then last Saturday night the subject had suddenly led her to think about Patrik Hedström.

Dan's voice interrupted her musings. "Well hello,
how long have you been standing there?"

"Oh, just a little while. I thought it would be interesting to see how you work."

"Yeah, it's certainly not the way you make your living. You get paid to sit on your backside and make
things up all day long. Ridiculous."

They both smiled. It was an old familiar subject for
their bantering.

"I brought along something good to warm you up."
Erica waved the basket she held in one hand.

"Oh, why the luxury treatment? What do you want
now? My body? My soul?"

"No thanks, you can keep both of them. Even
though I'd call the latter wishful thinking in your
case."

Dan took the basket she handed to him and then
helped her over the railing with a steady hand. She
almost fell on her backside but was saved by Dan's firm
grip around her waist. Together they brushed the snow

off the lid of one of the fish-packing cases. They sat down on top of their mittens, carefully laid out on the cases, and began unpacking the basket. Dan smiled in delight when he opened the thermos of hot chocolate and the salami sandwiches neatly wrapped in foil.

"You're a gem," he said with his mouth full of salami sandwich.

They sat in silence for a while, devoting all their attention to the food. It was peaceful to sit there in the morning sun, and Erica pushed away her guilt about her lack of work discipline. She had been working hard on the manuscript for the past week and thought she deserved a little time off.

"Have you heard anything more about Alex Wijkner?"

"No, the police investigation doesn't seem to be making any headway."

"Well, according to what I heard in town, you have special access to inside information."

Dan gave her a teasing smile. Erica never stopped being amazed at the speed and efficiency of the grapevine. She had no idea how the rumor of her meeting with Patrik could have already spread through town.

"No idea what you're talking about."

"Right. So, how far did the two of you get? Go for a test drive yet, or what?"

Erica whacked him across the chest with her arm but couldn't help laughing.

"No, I didn't take him on a 'test drive.' I don't really know if I'm interested or not. Or rather, I *am* interested, but I don't know if I want to let it go further than that. Assuming that *he's* interested, that is. Which may not be the case at all."

"In other words, you're chicken."

Erica hated the way Dan was almost always right. Sometimes she thought he knew her too well.

"Yes, I'm feeling a little insecure, I must admit."

"Well, you're the only one who can decide to take the chance. Have you thought about how it might feel if it actually worked out?"

She had given it some thought. Many times over the past few days. But at this point the question was extremely hypothetical. All they'd done was have dinner together, after all.

"Well anyway, I think you should go for it. Nothing ventured, nothing gained, and all that . . ."

Erica quickly changed the subject. "Apropos Alex, I happened to find something odd."

"Oh yeah, what's that?" Dan's voice was full of curiosity.

"Well, I was in her house a couple of days ago and found an interesting piece of paper."

"You were *what*?"

Erica didn't feel like replying and just waved off his shocked response.

"It was a copy of an old article about Nils Lorentz's disappearance. Do you have any idea why Alex would have kept an article twenty-five years old hidden at the bottom of her underwear drawer?"

"Her underwear drawer! Erica, what the hell!"

She held up a hand to halt his protests and continued calmly. "My intuition tells me that this has something to do with why she was murdered. I don't know how, but it smells fishy to me. Besides, somebody came into the house and rummaged around while I was there. Maybe that person was looking for the article."

"Are you crazy?" Dan just stared at her, gaping. "What the hell business is it of yours? It's the police's job to figure out who murdered Alex." His voice climbed to a falsetto.

"Yes, I know. You don't have to shout, there's nothing wrong with my hearing. I'm fully aware that it's really none of my business, but first of all, I've already been involved through her family, and second, we were actually very close at one time, and third, I'm having a hard time forgetting about the whole thing since I was the one who found her."

Erica omitted telling Dan about the book. Somehow it always sounded more crass and cold-blooded when she said it out loud. She also thought that Dan was overreacting, but he had always been incredibly solicitous of her. She had to admit that it didn't sound awfully smart to be running around in Alex's house, considering the circumstances.

"Erica, promise me you'll drop all this." He put his hands on her shoulders and forced her to face him. His clear eyes were unusually steely for Dan.

"I don't want anything to happen to you, and if you keep poking about in this I'm afraid you're going to get in over your head. Let it go."

Dan's grip on her shoulders tightened as he stared into her eyes. Erica opened her mouth to reply, dismayed at Dan's reaction, but before she could say anything she heard Pernilla's voice from up on the wharf.

"So, the two of you are having a cozy time, I see."

Her voice had a coldness that Erica had never heard before. Her eyes were flashing and she kept clenching and unclenching her hands. Both of them had frozen at the sound of Pernilla's voice; Dan's hands were still on

Erica's shoulders. Like lightning, as if he'd burned himself, he snatched his hands away and stood at attention.

"Hello, dear. Did you finish early today? Erica just came by with a little lunch and wanted to talk for a while."

Dan jabbered on frenetically and Erica looked back and forth between him and Pernilla in astonishment. Erica hardly recognized her. Pernilla gave her a look of pure hatred. Her hands were clenched so hard that her knuckles turned white, and for an instant Erica wondered if she was going to attack her. She didn't know what was going on. It had been years and years since they'd cleared the air about her and Dan. Pernilla knew that they no longer had feelings for each other, or at least Erica thought she knew. Now she was no longer sure. The question was, what had brought on this reaction? She looked back and forth from Dan to Pernilla. A silent power struggle was going on, and Dan seemed to be losing. There was nothing more for Erica to say, and she decided it would be best to slip away quietly and let them handle it on their own.

She hastily gathered up the cups and thermos and put them back in the basket. When she walked down the wharf, she could hear Dan and Pernilla's agitated voices breaking through the silence.

4

He was indescribably lonely. The world was empty and cold without her, and there was nothing he could do to thaw the cold. The pain had been easier to bear when he could share it with her. After she vanished it was as if he had to endure both their pain, and it was more than he thought he could bear. He dragged himself through the days minute by minute, second by second. Reality outside him did not exist; all he had was the consciousness that she was gone forever.

The guilt could be divided up into equal bits and portioned out among the guilty. He did not intend to bear it all alone. He had never intended to bear it alone.

He looked at his hands. How he hated his hands. They carried both beauty and death—an incompatible duality that he had learned to live with. Only when he caressed her had his hands been entirely good. His skin against her skin had driven away all the evil, forced it to flee for a while. At the same time they had nourished each other's hidden wish. Love and death, hatred and life. Opposites that turned them into moths flying in circles closer and closer to the flame. She was burned first.

He felt the heat from the fire on the back of his neck. It was close now.

She was tired. Tired of cleaning up other people's filth. Tired of her joyless existence. One day followed another with no differentiation. She was tired of bearing the guilt that weighed her down day in and day out. Tired of waking up each morning and going to bed each night and wondering how Anders was doing.

Vera put the coffee on the stove to boil. The ticking of the kitchen clock was the only sound to be heard. She sat down at the kitchen table to wait for the coffee to be ready.

She had spent today cleaning at the Lorentz family's house. The house was so big that it took all day. Sometimes she missed the old days. Missed the security of going to the same place to work, the status that went along with being the housekeeper for the wealthiest family in northern Bohuslän. But she didn't always feel that way. Most often she was glad that she didn't have to go there every day. That she no longer needed to bow and scrape to Nelly Lorentz. The woman she hated beyond all rhyme and reason. And yet Vera had continued to work for her, year in and year out, until time finally caught up with her. Housekeepers went out of style. For over thirty years, she had lowered her eyes and muttered "yes, thank you, Mrs. Lorentz, certainly, Mrs. Lorentz, right away, Mrs. Lorentz," at the same time as she repressed a desire to put her strong hands around Nelly's frail neck and squeeze until that woman breathed no more. Sometimes the desire had been so overwhelming that she hid her hands underneath her apron so that Nelly wouldn't see how they shook.

The kettle whistled to signal that the coffee was ready. With an effort Vera got up and straightened her back before she took out a battered old cup and poured the coffee. The cup was the last remnant of the wedding service they had received from Arvid's parents when they got married. It was fine Danish porcelain. A white background with blue flowers that had scarcely lost any color at all over the years. Now this cup was the only piece left. When Arvid was alive they had used the dishes as their good porcelain, but after his death it didn't seem to make much sense to distinguish between the everyday and special occasions. Normal wear and tear had taken their toll over the years, and the rest Anders had smashed during an attack of delirium more than ten years ago. This last cup was her most prized possession.

She sipped the coffee with pleasure. When there were just a few drops left, she poured the coffee into the saucer and drank it with a lump of sugar between her teeth so the coffee filtered through. Her legs were tired and sore after a whole day of cleaning; she had propped them up on the chair in front of her for a little relief.

The house was small and simple. Here she had lived for almost forty years, and here she intended to stay until the day she died. It wasn't actually very practical. The house stood high up on a steep hill, and she often had to stop and catch her breath several times on her way home. It was also much the worse for wear and looked shabby and run-down both inside and out. The location was good enough that she could get a pretty penny if she sold the house and moved into an apartment instead, but the thought had never entered her mind. She would rather it rot away around her than move. Here she had lived with Arvid, after all, those few happy years of their marriage. In that bed in the bedroom she had slept outside her parents' house for the first time. Her wedding night. In that same bed Anders had been conceived. And when she was very pregnant and couldn't lie in any other position but on her side, Arvid had crept close to her and lain behind her back, caressing her belly. In her ear he had whispered words about how their life together was going to be. About all the children who would grow up in their house. All the happy laughter that would fill this house in the years to come. And when they grew old and the children had moved out, they would sit in their rocking chairs in front of the fireplace and talk about what a wonderful life they'd had together. They were in their twenties back then, incapable of imagining what was waiting for them beyond the horizon.

It was at this kitchen table she'd been sitting when she got the news. Constable Pohl had knocked on the front door with his cap in hand, and as soon as she saw him she knew what was coming. She had held her finger to her lips to stop him from speaking, and instead motioned him to come into the kitchen. She waddled after him, in her ninth month of pregnancy, and slowly and methodically made a pot of coffee. As they waited for the coffee to boil, she had sat staring at the man across the table. He, for his part, could not look at her. Instead, he let his eyes wander around the walls as he compulsively tugged at his collar. Not until they each had a cup of steaming hot coffee before them did she gesture to the constable to continue. She herself had not yet uttered a word. She listened to a humming sound in her head that grew louder and louder. She saw the constable's mouth moving, but not a word penetrated the cacophony in her head. She didn't need to hear. She knew that Arvid now was on the bottom of the sea, swaying in time with the seaweed. No words could change that. No words could chase away the clouds that now gathered in the sky until all that was visible was a murky gray.

Vera sighed as she sat now at the kitchen table, many years later. Others who had lost loved ones said that the image of them faded as the years passed. For her it had been just the opposite. The image of Arvid grew clearer and clearer; sometimes she saw him so clearly before her that the pain felt like an iron band around her heart. The fact that Anders was the spitting image of Arvid was both a curse and a blessing. She knew that if Arvid had lived, the evil never would have happened. He had been her strength; with him beside her she could have been as strong as she should have been.

Vera gave a start when the telephone rang. She had been deeply immersed in old memories and didn't like being disturbed by the shrill ring of the phone. She had to lift her legs down from the chair where they had gone to sleep. Then she hobbled to the phone that was out in the hall.

"Mama, it's me."

Anders was slurring his words, and from years of experience she knew precisely what stage of intoxication he was in. About halfway to passing out. She sighed.

"Hello, Anders. How's it going?"

He ignored the question. She'd had countless conversations like this.

Vera could see herself in the hall mirror as she stood with the receiver to her ear. The mirror was old and worn, with dark spots on the glass; she thought how much she was like that mirror. Her hair was shabby and gray, with its original dark color still visible here and there. She always combed her hair straight back and cut it herself with nail scissors in front of the bathroom mirror. No sense throwing money away on a hairdresser. Her face was furrowed and wrinkled with years of worry. Her clothes matched her appearance: almost colorless but practical, most often gray or green. Many years of hard work and a lack of interest in food had prevented her from becoming stout like many other women her age. Instead she looked wiry and strong. Like a workhorse.

She suddenly registered what Anders was saying on the other end of the line and looked away from the mirror in shock.

"Mama, there are police cars outside. It's a hell of an escort. It must be me they're after. It has to be. What the hell should I do?"

Vera heard his voice getting more frantic; his panic was rising with each syllable. An icy cold spread through her body. In the mirror she saw that she was holding the phone with white knuckles.

"Don't do anything, Anders. Just wait there. I'm coming."

"Okay, but hurry for God's sake. This isn't the usual way the cops arrive, Mama, they usually come in one car. Now there are three cars outside with all their blue lights and sirens going. Damn . . ."

"Anders, listen to me now. Take a deep breath and calm down. I'm going to hang up now and I'll be there as quick as I can."

She could hear that she'd managed to calm him a little, but as soon as she hung up she threw on her coat and ran out the door, not bothering to lock it.

She ran across the parking lot beyond the old taxi stand and took the shortcut behind the loading dock of Eva's Mart. She had to slow down after that, and it took her almost ten minutes to reach the apartment house where Anders lived.

She got there in time to see two husky policemen lead him away in handcuffs. A shriek surged up in her chest, but she forced it back when she saw all the neighbors hanging out their windows like snooping vultures. There was no way she was going to give them more of a show than what they had already witnessed. Her pride was all she had left. Vera hated the gossip that she knew clung to her and Anders like chewing gum. There was always a lot of whispering going on, and now it would gather speed. She knew what they were going to say: "Poor Vera, first her husband drowns and then her son ruins his life with booze. And she's such a dependable person." Yes, she knew exactly what they were going to say. But she also knew that she would do everything in her power to limit the damage. She just couldn't break down now. Then everything would collapse like a house of cards. Vera turned to the closest police officer, a small blonde woman Vera thought looked ill-suited to the severe police uniform. She still hadn't gotten used to the newfangled arrangement that women could apparently do any job they liked.

"I'm Anders Nilsson's mother. What's happening here? Where are you taking him?"

"Unfortunately I can't give you any information. You'll have to check with the police station in Tanumshede. They're taking him there under arrest."

Her heart sank with every word. She understood that it wasn't about a drunken fight this time. The police cars began driving off one by one. In the last one she saw Anders sitting between two officers. He turned around as they pulled away and looked at her until they drove out of sight.

Patrik saw the car with Anders Nilsson drive off in the direction of Tanumshede. The massive police presence had been a little overdone, he thought. But Mellberg wanted a show, so there was a show. Extra resources from Uddevalla had been called in to assist in the arrest. In Patrik's opinion the only result was that, of the six men present, it was a waste of time for at least four of them.

A woman was still standing in the car park, gazing after the police cars.

"The perp's mother," said Senior Constable Lena Waltin from the Uddevalla police, who had also stayed behind to help Patrik search Anders Nilsson's apartment.

"You know better, Lena—he's not a 'perp' before he's found guilty and convicted. Until then he's just as innocent as the rest of us."

"I sure as hell doubt that. I'd bet a year's salary that he's guilty."

"If you're so sure, then you would bet more than such a negligible sum."

"Ha ha, very funny. Joking with a cop about salary is like tripping a cripple, for God's sake."

Patrik had to agree. "No, there's probably not much to expect. Shall we go up?"

He saw that Anders's mother was still standing there gazing after the squad cars, even though they had long since disappeared from view. He felt genuinely sorry for her and considered for a moment going over to offer some words of solace. But Lena pulled on his sleeve and motioned toward the entrance to the building. He sighed, shrugged his shoulders, and followed her inside to execute the search warrant.

They tried the door to Anders Nilsson's apartment. It was unlocked and they could walk straight into the hall. Patrik looked around and sighed for the second time in a minute. The apartment was in sad shape, and he wondered how they would ever find anything of value in this mess. They stepped over empty bottles in the hall and surveyed the living room and kitchen.

"Damn." Lena shook her head in disgust.

They took thin plastic gloves out of their pockets and pulled them on. In silent agreement, Patrik started in the living room while Lena took the kitchen.

It was a slightly schizophrenic feeling to be in Anders Nilsson's living room. Filthy, filled with trash, and with an almost total lack of furniture and personal objects, it looked like a classic crash pad for a drunk. And Patrik had seen plenty of those during his years on the force. But he had never been inside a drunk's apartment where the walls were covered with art. The paintings were so close together that they completely filled the walls, from three feet above the floor all the way to the ceiling. It was an explosion of color that made Patrik's eyes hurt, and he had to stifle an impulse to put up his hand to shield them. The paintings were abstract, painted only in warm colors, and they struck Patrik like a kick in the stomach. The feeling was so physical that he had to fight to stand upright. He had to force himself to turn away from the paintings because they seemed to be jumping off the walls at him.

Cautiously he began looking through Anders's things. There wasn't that much to look at. For a moment Patrik felt very grateful for the privileged life he led in comparison. His own problems all at once seemed very small. It fascinated him that the human will to survive was so strong that despite the complete absence of any quality of life, one still chose to go on, day after day, year after year. Was there any cause for rejoicing left in a life like Anders Nilsson's? Did he ever experience the emotions that made life worth living: joy, anticipation, happiness, elation? Or was everything merely a stop on the way to the next shot of alcohol?

Patrik went through everything in the living room. He felt the mattress to see if anything was hidden inside, pulled out the drawers in the only cabinet and checked underneath. He carefully unhooked all the paintings one by one and looked behind them. Nothing. Absolutely nothing aroused his interest. He went out to the kitchen to see whether Lena had had better luck.

"What a pigsty. How the hell can anybody live like this?"

With a disgusted expression she went through the contents of a rubbish bin that she emptied onto a newspaper.

"Have you found anything interesting?" Patrik asked.

"Yes and no. I found some receipts in the trash. The list of calls on the telephone bill might be something to look at more closely. Otherwise the rest just seems to be garbage." She pulled off her plastic gloves with a snap. "What do you say? Should we call it a day?"

Patrik looked at the clock. They had already been there for two hours, and it was dark outside.

"Yes, it doesn't seem we'll get much further today. How are you getting home? Do you need a lift?"

"I brought my own car, so I'm okay. Thanks anyway."

They left the apartment with relief, careful not to leave it in the same unlocked state as when they arrived.

The streetlights were lit when they came out to the parking lot. It had begun to snow lightly while they were inside, and they both had to brush a good deal of snow from their windshields. When Patrik drove off toward the OK Q8 gas station he felt something rise to the surface in his mind, something that had been gnawing at him all day. In the silence of his car, alone with his thoughts, he had to admit that something didn't feel right about the arrest of Anders Nilsson. He wasn't confident that Mellberg had asked the right questions when he interviewed the witness, which had caused Anders to be brought in to the station. Perhaps he ought to take a closer look at the matter. In the middle of the intersection by the gas station Patrik made up his mind. He turned the wheel hard and headed into the center of Fjällbacka instead of toward Tanumshede. He hoped that Dagmar Petrén would be at home.

Erica was thinking about Patrik's hands. She usually looked first at a man's hands and wrists. She thought that hands could be incredibly sexy. They shouldn't be small, but they didn't need to be as big as toilet seat lids either. Just big enough and sinewy, without hair, vigorous and supple. Patrik's hands were just right.

She forced herself out of her daydreams. It was futile, to say the least, to think about feelings that so far she only felt as a light quiver in her stomach. And it wasn't even certain how long she would be here in these parts. When the house was sold there would be nothing to keep her here, and then her apartment in Stockholm would be waiting for her, along with the life she had there with her friends. These weeks spent in Fjällbacka would be, in all probability, only a brief interlude in her life. Considering all of those things, it would be stupid to build romantic castles in the air regarding an old childhood friend.

Erica looked out at the twilight that was beginning to settle over the horizon, despite the fact that it was no later than three in the afternoon, and sighed deeply. She was huddled up in a big, loose-fitting sweater that her father used to wear at sea on cold days. She warmed her chilly hands by pulling them far up inside the long sleeves and twisting the ends together. At the moment she was feeling a little sorry for herself. There didn't seem to be much to be happy about just now. Alex dead, the hassle with the house, Lucas, the book that was heavy going—it all weighed like a huge burden on her chest. Besides, she felt that she still had a lot to deal with after her parents' death, both practically and emotionally. In recent days, she hadn't been able to face continuing the cleanup, and there were half-full trash bags and cartons all over the house. Inside her there were also half-full spaces, with loose threads and unresolved knots of emotion.

All afternoon she had been pondering the scene she witnessed between Dan and Pernilla. She simply couldn't make sense of it. It was so long ago that there had been any friction between herself and Pernilla; it had all been cleared up for years now. In any case, that was what Erica had thought. So why had Pernilla reacted the way she did? Erica contemplated ringing Dan, but she didn't really dare in case Pernilla answered the phone. She couldn't face another conflict right now, so she decided not to think about it anymore. She would let it rest and hope that Pernilla had simply gotten up on the wrong side of the bed and that everything would have blown over by the next time they met. And yet the scene kept on gnawing at her. It was no random fit of temper on Pernilla's part; it was something that went much deeper. But for the life of her, she couldn't work out what it could be.

This delaying of the work on her book was stressing her out, and she decided to relieve her conscience and write for a while. She sat down at the computer in her workroom and realized that she would have to take her hands out of the sweater's warmth in order to work. Things went sluggishly at first, but after a while she worked up both some creative steam and some body heat. She envied the writers who could keep to a strict discipline in their writing. She had to force herself to sit down and write every time. Not out of laziness but because of a deep-seated fear that she might have lost her ability since the last time she wrote anything. That she might sit there with her fingers on the keys and her eyes fixed on the screen and nothing would happen. There would just be emptiness, the words wouldn't come, and she would realize that she was never going to put a single sentence on paper again. Each time that did not happen was a relief. Now her fingers were flying over the keyboard and she had written over two pages in only an hour. After another three pages, she felt she had earned a reward and allowed herself to spend a while on the book about Alex.

The cell was very familiar. It wasn't the first time he had sat there. Drunken nights with vomit on the floor was an everyday occurrence during the periods when things were really bad. Although this time it was different. This time it was serious.

He lay down on his side on the hard cot, curled up in a fetal position and rested his head on his hands to avoid the feeling of plastic sticking to his face. Cold shivers ran through him from a combination of the cold in the cell and the alcohol deprivation in his body.

The only thing he'd been told was that he was suspected of murdering Alex. Then they shoved him into the cell and told him to wait. What else did they think he was going to do in this cold place? Teach courses in life drawing? Anders smiled wryly to himself.

His thoughts wandered dully since there was nothing to rest his eyes on. The walls were painted light green over worn concrete with gray spots where the paint had flaked off. In his thoughts, he painted the walls in bold colors. A brushstroke of red here, one of yellow there. Strong swathes that quickly obliterated the worn green color. In his mind's eye the room was soon a blazing cacophony of colors, and only then could he focus his thoughts.

Alex was dead. That wasn't a thought he could flee

from even if he wanted to; it was an irrefutable fact. She was dead, and his future was dead with her.

Soon they would come to get him. Drag him away. They would shove him roughly, taunt him, tear at him, until the truth lay there naked and shivering before them. He couldn't stop them. He didn't even know if he wanted them to be stopped. There was so much he no longer knew. Not that he'd known very much before. There was little that had enough power to cut through the redemptive fog of alcohol. Only Alex. Only the knowledge that she was breathing the same air somewhere, thinking the same thoughts, feeling the same pain. That was the only thing that had always had enough power to worm its way past, under, over, around the treacherous fogs that did their best to bury all his memories in merciful darkness.

His legs began to fall asleep as he lay stretched out on the cot, but he ignored the signals from his body and stubbornly refused to budge from the spot. If he moved, he might lose control over the colors that covered the wall and have to stare at bare ugliness again.

In more lucid moments, he could see some humor, or at least irony, in it all. The fact that he was born with an insatiable need for beauty, at the same time that he was condemned to a life of filth and squalor. Perhaps his fate was already written in the stars when he was born, perhaps his fate was rewritten on that ill-fated day.

If only. Many times his thoughts had run in circles around this "if," playing with the thought of what his life would have been like *if*. Maybe a good and honorable life, with family, a home, and art as a source of joy instead of despair. Children playing in the garden outside his studio while fragrant aromas wafted from the kitchen. The very height of a Carl Larsson idyll, with a rosy glow around the edges of the fantasy. And Alex was always in the midst of this tableau. Always in the center, with him like a planet circling round and round her.

His fantasies always made him feel warm inside, but suddenly the warm image was replaced with a cold one, with bluish tones and icy chill. He knew this image well. For many nights he'd been able to study it in peace and quiet so that he knew it down to the smallest detail. The blood was what he feared the most. The red, which stood in sharp contrast to the blue. Death was also there, as usual. He lurked along the edges, rubbing his hands in delight. Waiting for him to make his move, do something, anything at all. The only thing he could do was pretend not to see Death. Ignore him until he disappeared. Perhaps then the image could regain its rosy glow. Perhaps Alex could once again smile at him, the smile that tugged and tore at his guts. But Death was a much too familiar companion to be ignored. It was many years now that they had known each other, and the acquaintance had not grown more pleasant with the years. Even in the brighter moments he had shared with Alex, Death had wedged in between them, insistent, importunate.

The silence in the cell was comforting. In the distance he could hear the sound of people moving about, but they seemed so far away that they might be in another world. Not until he heard one of the sounds approaching did he snap out of his dream state. Footsteps in the corridor, steadily approaching his cell door. The rattle of the lock and then the door swung open and the fat little superintendent appeared in the doorway. Listlessly, Anders swung his legs over the edge of the cot and put his feet on the floor. Time for interrogation. Might as well get it over with.

The bruises had begun to fade enough that she could try covering them with a good layer of powder. Anna looked at her face in the mirror. She looked worn and harried. Without makeup she could clearly see the blue contours under her skin. One eye was still a bit blood-shot. Her blonde hair was dull and lifeless and in need of a trim. She hadn't gotten around to booking a new appointment with the hairdresser; she simply never had the energy. All her strength went into taking care of the children's daily needs and seeing to it that she kept her head up. How did things ever get to this point?

She pulled back her hair in a tight ponytail and laboriously got dressed as she tried to avoid moving in a way that would make her ribs hurt. Before, he used to be careful to hit her only in places that could be hidden by clothing, but during the past six months he had stopped being careful and had repeatedly struck her in the face.

But the beating wasn't the worst of it. It was having always to live under the threat of future blows, waiting for the next time, the next fist. The cruelest thing was that he was well aware of this and played on her fear. He would raise his hand to strike her and then switch over to a caress and a smile. Sometimes he hit her for no apparent reason. Right out of the blue. Not because he needed much of a reason, but in the middle of a dis-cussion about what to buy for dinner, or which TV program they should watch, his fist might suddenly fly out and catch her in the stomach, on the head, on her back, or wherever else he aimed. Then he would continue the conversation without for a moment losing his train of thought, as if nothing had happened, as she lay on the floor gasping for breath. It was the feeling of power that he enjoyed.

Lucas's clothes lay scattered all over the bedroom; she arduously picked up the clothes, one by one, and hung them up on hangers or put them in the laundry basket. When the bedroom was once again in perfect order she went to check on the children. Adrian was sleeping peacefully on his back with his pacifier in his mouth. Emma sat playing quietly in her bed, and Anna stood a moment in the doorway watching her. She was so much like Lucas. The same determined, angular face and ice-blue eyes. The same stubbornness.

Emma was one of the reasons she couldn't stop loving Lucas. Not loving him would feel like denying a part of Emma. He was a part of their daughter, and because of that, a part of Anna as well. He was also a good father to the children. Adrian was still too little to understand, but Emma worshiped Lucas, and Anna simply couldn't take her away from her father. How could she take the children away from half of their security, rip up everything that was familiar and important to them? Instead she had to try to be strong enough for all of them; then they would be able to get through this. Things weren't like that in the beginning. Things could be good again. As long as she was strong. After all, he told her that he really didn't want to hit her, that it was for her own good, because she didn't do what she was supposed to do. If only she could make more of an effort, be a better wife. She didn't understand him, he said. If only she could find what made him happy, if only she could do the right things so that he didn't have to be so disappointed in her all the time.

Erica didn't understand. Erica with her independence and her solitude. Her courage and her overwhelming, stifling solicitude. Anna could hear the contempt in Erica's voice, and it drove her mad. What did she know about the responsibility for keeping a marriage and a family going? About carrying a load on her shoulders that was so heavy she could barely stand upright. The only thing Erica had to worry about was herself. She'd always been such a know-it-all. Her excessive maternal concern for Anna had sometimes threatened to suffocate her. She had felt Erica's restless, watching eyes following her everywhere, when all she wanted was to be left in peace. What did it matter if their mother never managed to care for them? They had Papa, at least. One out of two wasn't so bad. The difference between her and Erica was that she accepted things, while Erica was always trying to find a reason. More often than not, Erica also turned the questions inward and tried to find the reason inside herself. That was why she had always exerted herself too much. Anna, on the other hand, chose not to exert herself at all. It was easier not to worry, to go with the flow and take one day at a time. That was why she felt such bitterness toward Erica. She worried and fretted over her younger sister, coddling her, and that made it even harder for Anna to close her eyes to the truth and the people around her. Moving out of her parents' house had been so liberating. When she then met Lucas soon afterward, she thought she had finally found the only person who could love her just as she was and, above all, respect her need for freedom.

She smiled bitterly as she cleaned the table after

Lucas's breakfast. Freedom? She no longer even knew how to spell the word. Her life consisted of the space inside this apartment. It was only the children who made it possible for her even to breathe, the children and the hope that if she found the right formula, the right answer, then everything could be the way it used to be.

In slow motion she placed the lid on the butter dish, put the cheese in a plastic bag, inserted the dirty dishes in the dishwasher, and wiped off the table. When everything was shiny and clean, Anna sat down on one of the kitchen chairs and looked around the room. The only sound was Emma's childish prattle from the nursery, and for a few minutes Anna allowed herself to enjoy a little peace and quiet. The kitchen was bright and airy, decorated in a tasteful combination of wood and stainless steel. They had spared no expense on the appliances, which meant that Philippe Starck and Poggenpohl were the dominant brand names. Anna herself had wanted a cozier kitchen, but when they moved into the lovely five-room apartment in Öster-malm she knew better than to air her views.

Erica's concern over the house in Fjällbacka was something she couldn't even consider. Anna couldn't afford to be sentimental, and the money they would get from the sale of the house might mean a new start for her and Lucas. She knew that he wasn't happy with his job here in Sweden and wanted to go back to London; that was where he thought the action and the career opportunities were. He viewed Stockholm as a backwa-ter, careerwise. And even though he made a good, even excellent, salary at his present job, the windfall from the house in Fjällbacka, combined with the money they had already saved, would buy them a residence in London that was consistent with their social standing. That was important to Lucas, so it became important to her. Erica would get along all right. She had only herself to think of; she had a job and an apartment in Stockholm. The house in Fjällbacka would only serve as a summer cottage. The money would help her out as well—a writer made no money to speak of, and Anna knew that Erica sometimes went through hard times. She would soon realize that this was for the best. For both of them.

Adrian's shrill voice came from the children's room, and her brief respite was over. No sense sitting and fretting. The bruises would go away as they always did, and tomorrow was another day.

Patrik felt inexplicably lighthearted and took the stairs to Dagmar Petrén's house two at a time. But when he was almost to the top he had to catch his breath, bending over with his hands on his knees. He certainly wasn't twenty years old anymore. The woman who opened the door definitely wasn't either. He hadn't seen anything so little and wrinkled since the last time he opened a bag of prunes. Stooped and hunched as she was, she hardly came up much past his waist, and Patrik was afraid she'd snap in two in the slightest breeze. But the eyes that looked up toward him were as clear and alert as a young girl's.

"Don't stand there puffing, son. Come in and have a cup of coffee."

Her voice was surprisingly powerful, and Patrik suddenly felt like a schoolboy as he followed her obediently inside. He resisted a strong urge to bow and struggled to maintain the snail's pace so as not to run over Mrs. Petrén. Inside the door he stopped short. Never in his entire life had he seen so many Santa Clauses. Every-where, on every available surface, there they were. Big ones, little ones, old ones, young ones, winking ones, and gray ones. He felt his brain go into overdrive to handle all the sensory input flowing toward him.

"What do you think? Aren't they magnificent!"

Patrik didn't know quite what to say, and after a moment he managed to stammer a reply.

"Yes, absolutely. Fantastic."

He gave Mrs. Petrén an anxious look to see whether she could hear that his words didn't really match his tone of voice. To his amazement she gave him a rogu-ish smile that made her eyes flash.

"Don't worry, boy. I'm well aware that it's not really your taste, but when one gets old it involves cer-tain responsibilities, you understand."

"Responsibilities?"

"One is expected to show a bit of eccentricity to be interesting. Otherwise one is simply a sad old crone, and no one wants that, you know."

"But, why gnomes?"

Patrik still didn't quite understand. Mrs. Petrén explained it to him as if she were speaking to a child.

"Well, the best thing, you see, is that one only needs to put them up once a year. The rest of the year I can keep the place nice and tidy. Then there's the advan-tage that it brings a pack of children running up here at Christmastime. And for an old crone who doesn't have many visitors, it's a joy to the soul when the lit-tle creatures come and ring my bell to see the Santas."

"But how long do you keep them up, Mrs. Petrén? We're in the middle of February now."

"Well, I start putting them up in October and then

take them down around April. Although you must realize that it probably takes a week or two to put them up and take them down."

Patrik had no difficulty at all visualizing that it would take time. He tried doing a quick calculation in his head, but his brain hadn't really recovered from the shock of the whole scene. Instead he turned to Mrs. Petrén with a direct question.

"How many do you actually have here?"

The reply was instant. "One thousand four hundred and forty-three, no excuse me, one thousand four hundred and forty-two—I happened to break one yesterday. And one of the nicest ones at that," said Mrs. Petrén with a sad expression.

But she pulled herself together, her eyes flashing again. With astonishing strength she tugged on Patrik's sleeve and more or less dragged him to the kitchen, where in contrast there was not a Santa to be seen. Patrik discreetly smoothed out his jacket but had a feeling that she would have grabbed hold of his ear instead if she could reach that high.

"We'll sit here. One gets a bit testy always having a bunch of old men around one. Here in the kitchen they're banned."

He sat down on the hard kitchen bench after all his offers of assistance were brusquely refused. Steeling himself at the thought of some thin, wretched boiled coffee, his mouth fell open for the second time at the sight of the huge, stainless-steel, hypermodern coffee brewer enthroned on the worktop.

"What would you like? Cappuccino? Café au lait? Maybe a doppio espresso—you look like you could use it."

Patrik managed only a nod. Mrs. Petrén was apparently enjoying his amazement.

"What did you expect? An old percolator from forty-three and hand-ground beans? No, just because I'm an old crone doesn't mean that one can't enjoy the good things in life. I got this from my son as a Christmas present a couple of years ago, and it's always running, I can tell you that. Sometimes there's a queue of old ladies from the neighborhood waiting to have a drop."

She tenderly patted the machine, which was now sputtering and fizzing as it whipped up milk to an airy froth.

As the coffee was being prepared, one fantastic pastry after another materialized on the table in front of Patrik. Not a Finnish pin roll or Karlsbad kruller as far as the eye could see; instead big cinnamon buns, stunning muffins, sticky chocolate biscuits, and fluffy meringue cakes were set out as Patrik's eyes grew bigger and bigger. His mouth started watering so much that saliva threatened to run out the corners of his mouth. Mrs. Petrén chuckled when she saw the expression on his face, and sat down across from him on one of the Windsor chairs. She served them each a cup of hot, aromatic, freshly brewed coffee.

"I understand that it's the girl in the house across the way that you want to talk to me about. Well, I already spoke with your superintendent and told him what little I know."

With an effort Patrik detached himself from the sticky bun he had just sunk his teeth into. He had to clean his front teeth with his tongue before he could open his mouth.

"Yes, Mrs. Petrén, perhaps you would be so kind as

to recount what you said? Is it all right if I turn on the tape recorder, by the way?"

He pressed the red button on the tape recorder and made sure to chew thoroughly while waiting for her reply.

"Yes, of course you may. Well, it was Friday, the twenty-second of January, at six thirty. And please don't be so formal. It makes me feel ancient."

"How can you be so sure of the date and time? It's been a couple of weeks since then."

Patrik took another bite.

"Well, you see, it was my birthday that day, so my son and his family were here. We had cake and they brought me presents. Then they left just before the six-thirty news on channel 4, and that was when I heard a devil of a row outside. I rushed to the window that faces out back and over by the lass's house, and that's when I saw him."

"Anders?"

"Anders the painter, yes. Drunk as a lord he was, standing there yelling like a madman and banging on the door. Finally she let him in and then it was quiet. Well, he may have kept yelling, I don't know anything about that. It's impossible to hear what goes on inside these houses."

Mrs. Petrén noticed that Patrik's plate was empty, so she pushed over the tray of cinnamon buns to tempt him. He didn't need a great deal of persuasion. He quickly helped himself to one on top.

"And you're quite sure, Mrs. Petrén, that it was Anders Nilsson? No doubts on that point?"

"Oh no, I'd know that rascal anywhere. He used to come over at all hours, and if he wasn't here then he'd be down with the drunks on the square. I never did understand what he had to do with Alexandra Wijkner. That girl had class, I have to tell you. Both good-looking and well-brought-up. When she was little she'd often come over for juice and buns. She used to sit right there on the bench, often together with Tore's little girl, what was her name now. . . ?"

"Erica," said Patrik with his mouth full of cinnamon bun, and he felt a tingle in the pit of his stomach just from saying her name.

"Erica, that's right. She was a nice girl too, but there was something special about Alexandra. She had a radiance about her. But then something happened . . . she stopped coming by and hardly ever said hello. A couple of months later they moved to Göteborg, and then I didn't see her until she started coming here on weekends a couple of years ago."

"Weren't the Carlgrens ever here during the years in between?"

"No, never. But they kept the house in order. Painters and carpenters would come by, and Vera Nilsson came twice a month to clean."

"And you have no idea, Mrs. Petrén, what happened before the Carlgrens moved to Göteborg, what might have changed Alex, I mean? No fight in the family or anything like that?"

"There were rumors, of course, there always are here, but nothing I'd put much store in. Even though plenty of folks here in Fjällbacka claim to know most of what's going on with everyone else, one thing you should be clear about: nobody ever knows what goes on inside the four walls of anyone else's home. That's why I won't speculate about it either. It serves no purpose. Look, take another pastry, you still haven't tasted my meringue dreams."

Patrik patted his stomach and found that yes, there was a tiny little nook that he might be able to fill with a meringue dream.

"Did you see anything else after that? Did you notice when Anders Nilsson left, for example?"

"No, I didn't see him anymore that evening. But I did see him go into the house several times in the following week. That was odd, I must say. From what I heard in town she was already dead by then. So what in all the world could he have been doing in there?"

That was precisely what Patrik was wondering. Mrs. Petrén gave him an inquiring look. "So, did you enjoy those?"

"Probably the best pastries I've ever tasted, Mrs. Petrén. How is it that you can rustle up a tray of pastries just like that? I mean, I didn't ring more than fifteen minutes before I came here. You would have had to be as fast as Superman to bake all these goodies."

She basked in the compliment and tossed her head proudly.

"For thirty years, my husband and I ran the pastry shop here in Fjällbacka, so one hopes one has learned something over the years. Old habits are hard to break, so I still get up at five in the morning and bake every day. What doesn't go to the kids and old ladies who come to visit, I feed to the birds. And then it's always fun to try new recipes. There are so many modern baked goods that are so much better than those dry old Finnish pin rolls we used to bake tons of in the old days. I find recipes in the food magazines, and then I modify them to my liking."

She gestured at an enormous stack of food magazines on the floor next to the kitchen bench—there was everything from *Amelia Mat* to *Allt om mat*, several years' worth. Judging by the price per issue, Patrik suspected that Mrs. Petrén must have saved a pretty penny during her years at the pastry shop. He had a bright idea.

"Do you know whether there was any connection between the Carlgren family and the Lorentz family, besides the fact that Karl-Erik worked for them? Did they ever get together socially, for example?"

"Goodness gracious, the Lorentzes getting together with the Carlgrens? No, my friend, that would only have happened if there were two Thursdays in one week! They didn't move in the same circles. The fact that Nelly Lorentz—according to what I heard—showed up at the funeral reception at the Carlgrens' house, I'd have to call that quite a sensation, nothing less!"

"But what about the son? The one who disappeared, I mean. Did he ever have anything to do with the Carlgrens, as far as you know?"

"No, one would hope not. A nasty boy he was. Always trying to nick pastries behind one's back in the pastry shop. But my husband taught him a lesson when he caught him red-handed. That boy got the scolding of his life. Then, of course, Nelly came rushing over here to tell us off. She threatened to call the police on my husband. Well, he put a stop to that when he told her that there were witnesses to the pilfering, so she could go right ahead and ring the public prosecutor."

"But no connection to the Carlgrens, as far as you know, then?"

She shook her head.

"Well, it was just a thought on my part," said Patrik.

"Next to the murder of Alex, Nils's disappearance is probably the most dramatic thing that's ever happened here, and one never knows. Sometimes the most interesting coincidences turn up. So, I don't think I have any other questions, so I'll just say thanks for the coffee. Tremendously good pastry, I must say. I'll have to eat salad for a few days." He patted his stomach.

"Oh, you shouldn't have to eat rabbit food. You're still a growing boy."

Patrik chose to accept the compliment, instead of pointing out that at thirty-five only his waistline was still growing. He got up from the kitchen bench but had to sit right down again. It felt like he had a ton of concrete in his stomach, and a wave of nausea rose up in his throat. On second thought, it hadn't been such a good idea to stuff himself with all these pastries.

He tried to squint a bit as he walked through the living room, and all one thousand four hundred forty-two Santas winked and glittered at him.

Walking out to the door took as long as it had to come in. He had to restrain himself from running around Mrs. Petrén as he shuffled behind her toward the front door. She was a feisty old woman, no doubt about it. She was also a reliable witness, and with her testimony it was only a matter of time before they would be able to add another couple of pieces to the puzzle and build a watertight case against Anders Nilsson. For the time being, it was mostly circumstantial evidence, but it looked as though the murder of Alexandra Wijkner was now solved. Yet he had an uneasy feeling in his stomach, to the extent he could feel anything besides pastry. It was a feeling that the simple solutions were not always the correct ones.

It was magnificent to breathe fresh air, which somewhat relieved the nausea. He was just thanking Mrs. Petrén once more and turning to go when she pressed something into his hand before he pulled the door closed. He looked to see what it was. It was a shopping bag from ICA stuffed full of pastries—and a little Santa Claus. He grabbed his stomach and groaned.

"Well now, Anders, things aren't looking so good for you."

"Oh yeah?"

"Oh yeah—is that all you have to say? You're sitting up to your neck in shit if you haven't realized that! Have you realized that?"

"I didn't do anything."

"Bullshit! Don't you sit there and shovel bullshit right in my face. I know you murdered her, so you might as well confess and save us all some trouble. If you save me trouble, you'll save yourself trouble. Do you get what I'm talking about?"

Mellberg and Anders were sitting in the only interrogation room at Tanumshede police station, and unlike American cop shows, there was no one-way glass wall through which his colleagues could watch the interrogation. Which suited Mellberg just fine. It was completely against regulations to be alone with a subject under interrogation, but what the hell, as long as he delivered, nobody would care about any stupid regulations. And Anders hadn't asked for an attorney or anyone else to be present, so why should Mellberg insist?

The room was small and sparsely furnished, with bare walls. The only furniture was a table and two chairs, now occupied by Anders Nilsson and Bertil Mellberg.

Anders was leaning back nonchalantly in his chair, with his hands folded in his lap and his long legs stretched out under the table. Mellberg stood leaning halfway over the table with his face as close to Anders's as he could stand, in view of the suspect's anything but minty-fresh breath. But it was close enough for tiny drops of saliva to spray in Anders's face when Mellberg spat out his words. Anders didn't bother to wipe his face. He chose to pretend that the superintendent was merely an annoying fly, so insignificant that it wasn't even worth swatting away.

"Both you and I know that you were the one who murdered Alexandra Wijkner. Tricked her into taking sleeping pills, put her in the bathtub and slit her wrists, and then calmly watched as she bled to death. So why don't we just make this easy on both of us? You confess and I'll write it down."

Mellberg felt very pleased with what he regarded as a powerful start to the interrogation. He sat down on the chair and clasped his hands over his big paunch. He waited. No response from Anders. His head continued to droop forward, his hair concealing any facial expression. A twitch at the corner of Mellberg's mouth revealed that indifference was not what he considered his preamble deserved. After waiting in silence a bit longer, he slammed his fist on the table to try to rouse Anders out of his torpor. No reaction.

"What the hell, you fucking drunk! Do you think you can get out of this by sitting there and not saying a word? Then you've ended up in the hands of the wrong cop, I can tell you that. You're going to tell me the truth if we have to sit here all day!"

The sweat stains under Mellberg's arms were growing larger with each syllable.

"You were jealous, weren't you? We found some paintings you did of her, and it's quite obvious that you were fucking each other. And to dispel any further doubt, we also found your letters to her. Your sickly sweet, pathetic love letters. Jesus, what fucking crap. What did she see in you, anyway? I mean, just look at you. You're filthy and disgusting and as far from any Don Juan as you could get. The only explanation would have to be that she was some kind of pervert. That she was turned on by filth and revolting old drunks. Did she take on the other winos in Fjällbacka too, or were you the only one she serviced?"

Quick as a weasel Anders was on his feet. He launched himself across the table and had his hands around Mellberg's neck.

"You fuck, I'm going to kill you, you cop son of a bitch!"

Mellberg tried in vain to prise off Anders's hands. His face got redder and redder, and his hair fell out of its nest and hung down over his right ear. From sheer astonishment Anders loosened his grip on Mellberg's neck, and the superintendent was able to take a deep breath. Anders fell back in his chair and glowered at Mellberg.

Mellberg had to cough and clear his throat to recover his voice. "Don't you ever do that again! Do you hear me, never! Now you're going to sit still, damn it, or I'll toss you in a cell and throw away the key, do you hear me?"

Mellberg sat back down on his chair but kept his eyes vigilantly on Anders. There was a hint of fear in Mellberg's eyes that wasn't there before. He discovered that his meticulously arranged hairdo had suffered a real blow, and with a practiced motion he swung the hair up onto the shiny patch in the middle of his scalp, at the same time as he tried to pretend that nothing had happened.

"Now, back to business. So you had a sexual relationship with the victim, Alexandra Wijkner?"

Anders muttered something into his lap.

"Excuse me, what did you say?" Mellberg leaned forward across the table with his hands clasped in front of him.

"I said we loved each other!"

The words echoed and bounced off the bare walls. Mellberg gave Anders a contemptuous smile.

"Okay, so you loved each other. Beauty and the beast loved each other. How touching. So how long did you 'love' each other, then?"

Anders mumbled something incomprehensible again, and Mellberg had to ask him to repeat it.

"Since we were kids."

"Oh, I see, okay. But I assume that you weren't screwing like rabbits since you were five, so let me reformulate that question: how long did you have a sexual relationship? How long was she shagging you on the side? How long did you dance the horizontal tango? Do I have to go on, or have you managed to understand the question?"

Anders glared with hatred at Mellberg but made a great effort to stay calm.

"I don't know, off and on over the years. I don't really know, I didn't check off the dates on the calendar." He picked at some invisible threads on his trousers. "She wasn't here very much back then, so it wasn't that often. Mostly I just painted her. She was so beautiful."

"What happened the night she died? Was it a lovers' quarrel? Didn't she want to put out? Or was it the fact that she was knocked up that made you so mad? Sure, that must have been it. She was knocked up and you didn't know whether it was your kid or her husband's. She probably threatened to make life hell for you too, didn't she?"

Mellberg felt extremely pleased with himself. He was convinced that Anders was the killer, and if he just pushed hard enough on the right buttons he would undoubtedly get a confession out of him. No doubt about it. Then Göteborg would beg and plead for him to come back to the force. They would probably try to tempt him with a promotion and a higher salary if he kept them on the hook for a while. He rubbed his belly in pleasure and only now noticed that Anders was staring at him wide-eyed. His face was white, empty of all blood. His hands were twitching in spasms. When Anders raised his head and for the first time looked straight at Mellberg, the superintendent saw that his lower lip was quivering and his eyes were full of tears.

"You're lying! She couldn't have been pregnant!" Snot was dripping from his nose, and Anders wiped it on his sleeve. He gave Mellberg an almost imploring look.

"What do you mean? Condoms aren't a hundred percent safe, you know. She was in her third month, so don't try to get all dramatic on me. She was knocked up and you know very well how it happened. Whether it was you or her high-class husband who delivered the goods, well, we'll never know, will we? It's a man's curse, I have to tell you. I've been close to getting nailed a few times, but no fucking bitch has ever got me to sign any papers." Mellberg chuckled.

"Not that it's any of your business, but we hadn't had sex in over four months. Now I don't want to talk to you anymore. Take me back to my cell, because I don't intend to say another word."

Anders gave a big snuffle and the tears kept threatening to spill over. He leaned back in the chair with his arms crossed and glared spitefully from under his mop of hair at Mellberg, who heaved a deep sigh but acquiesced.

"All right, we'll continue in a couple of hours. And just so you know—I don't believe a fucking word of what you're saying! Go think about that while you sit in your cell. The next time we talk I want a complete confession from you."

He remained sitting there for a while after Anders was led away to his cell. The stinking drunk hadn't confessed. Mellberg thought it was utterly incredible. But his trump card was still unplayed and intact. The last time Alexandra Wijkner had been heard alive was at a quarter past seven on Friday, January twenty-second, exactly one week before she was found dead. On that occasion she had talked to her mother on the phone for five minutes and fifty seconds, according to Telia, the phone company. That also matched the time frame indicated by the medical examiner. Thanks to the neighbor, Dagmar Petrén, he had testimony that Anders Nilsson visited the victim not only on that very evening, just after six-thirty, but that he was also seen going into the house on several occasions during the following week. *And by that time Alexandra Wijkner lay dead in the bathtub.*

A confession would have made Mellberg's work considerably easier, but even if Anders turned out to be obstinate, Mellberg felt sure that he would be able to get a conviction. Not only did he have the testimony from Mrs. Petrén, but on his desk he also had a report on the search of Alex Wijkner's house. Most interesting were the data from the scrupulous examination of the bathroom where she was found. Not only had a footprint been found in the coagulated blood on the floor that matched a pair of shoes confiscated in Anders's apartment, but Anders's fingerprints had also been found on the victim's body. Not as clear as they would have been on a hard, even surface, but still clear and identifiable.

He hadn't wanted to use all his options today, but at the next interrogation he would bring out the big guns. And damn if he wouldn't crack this bastard then.

Pleased with himself, Mellberg spat on his palm and smoothed back his hair with saliva.

The telephone call interrupted her just as she was typing up an account of her conversation with Henrik Wijkner. Annoyed, Erica took her hands off the keyboard and reached for the phone.

"Yes?" She sounded more irritated than she had intended.

"Hello, it's Patrik. Am I interrupting you?"

Erica sat bolt upright in her chair and regretted that she hadn't sounded nicer when she answered.

"No, absolutely not. I'm just sitting here writing, and I was so into what I was doing that I jumped when the phone rang, so I might have sounded a bit . . . but you're not bothering me at all, it's quite all right, I mean . . ."

She slapped her forehead when she heard herself rambling on like a fourteen-year-old girl on the phone. Time to pull herself together and control those hormones, she thought. This is ridiculous.

"Well, I'm in Fjällbacka and just thought I'd see if you were at home and whether I could drop by for a while."

He sounded self-confident, manly, secure, and calm, and Erica felt even more idiotic for stammering like a teenager. She looked down at what she was wearing, which today consisted of a slightly dirty jogging suit. At the same time she felt her hair. Yep, just as she feared. Her hair was pulled into a knot on top of her head with loose strands sticking out in every direction. The situation could almost be called disastrous.

"Hello, Erica—are you still there?" Patrik sounded puzzled.

"Uh yes, I'm still here. I just thought it sounded like your mobile dropped the call."

Erica slapped her forehead for the second time in about ten seconds. God in heaven, you'd think she was a beginner at this.

"Hello-o-o, Erica—can you hear me? Hello?"

"Uh, of course I can. Come on over. Just give me fifteen minutes, because I'm busy . . . uh . . . writing a very important part of my book that I'd like to finish first."

"Sure, no problem. Are you sure I'm not bothering you? I mean, we're seeing each other tomorrow night so—"

"No, absolutely not. I'm sure. Just give me fifteen minutes."

"Okay. See you then."

Erica carefully put down the receiver and took a deep breath full of anticipation. Her heart was beating so hard that she could hear it. Patrik was on his way to her place. Patrik was on . . . She gave a start as if someone had tossed a bucket of cold water on her, and jumped out of her chair. He was going to be here in fifteen minutes and she looked like she hadn't washed or combed her hair in a week. She went upstairs two steps at a time as she pulled the jogging sweatshirt over her head. In the bedroom she wriggled out of her sweatpants, tripped, and almost fell on her face.

In the bathroom she washed under her arms and sent a silent prayer of thanks that she had shaved her underarms when she showered this morning. She dabbed perfume on her wrists, between her breasts, and at her throat where she felt her pulse beating so strong beneath her fingers. She threw open the wardrobe and tossed most of the contents on the bed before she managed to decide on a simple black Filippa top and matching tight black skirt that came down to her ankles. She looked at the clock. Ten minutes left. Bathroom again. Powder, mascara, lip gloss and a light eye shadow. No need for rouge, her face was red enough already. The effect she was going for was the fresh, unpainted look, and with every year that passed it seemed to take more and more makeup to achieve.

The doorbell rang. As she cast one last look in the mirror she realized in panic that her hair was still up in a slovenly topknot, held in place with a neon-yellow elastic. She ripped off the elastic and with a brush and a little mousse she managed to make her hair look presentable. Another ring, more insistent this time, and she hurried downstairs but stopped halfway to catch her breath and compose herself for a second. With the coolest expression she could muster, she opened the door with a big smile.

* * *

His finger was shaking a little as he pressed the door-bell. He'd been about to turn around several times and phone her with some excuse, but the car practically drove itself toward Sälvik. Of course he remembered where she lived and automatically took the tight curve to the right on the hill before the campground on the way up to her house. Although it was only afternoon it was black as night out, but the streetlights were bright enough that he could glimpse a view of the sea. All at once he understood how Erica felt about her parents' house. He also understood the pain she must feel at the thought of losing it. And he realized the impossibility of his feelings for her. She and Anna would sell the house and then there would be nothing to keep Erica in Fjällbacka. She would move back to Stockholm, and a provincial cop from Tanumshede wouldn't make much of an impression compared with the lounge lizards of Stureplan. He plodded with Moloch-like steps up to the front door and rang the bell.

No one came to the door, so he rang the doorbell again. This was definitely starting to feel like a bad idea, not the way he had first imagined on the way from Mrs. Petrén's house. He simply couldn't resist calling Erica since she was so close. But he was beginning to regret the whole thing as soon as she answered the phone. She sounded so busy, even irritated when he rang. Oh well, it was too late to worry about that now. The chime of the doorbell echoed for the second time through the house.

He could hear someone coming down the stairs. The footsteps paused for a moment before they continued the rest of the way to the door. The door opened and there she stood with a big smile. She took his breath away. He couldn't understand how she always managed to look so fresh. Her face was bare of any makeup, with the natural beauty that he found most attractive in a woman. Karin had never dreamed of showing her face without makeup, but Erica looked so amazing in his eyes that he couldn't imagine anything that could possibly improve her appearance.

The house looked exactly the same as always, the way he remembered it from his visits as a child. Here the furniture and the house had been allowed to age together with dignity. Wood and white paint predominated, with light-colored fabrics in blue and white that harmonized with the aging patina of the furniture. She had lighted candles to drive away the winter darkness. The whole place breathed calm and tranquillity. He followed Erica out to the kitchen.

"Would you like some coffee?"

"Yes, please. Oh, and I brought these." Patrik handed over the bag of pastries. "Although I should really take some back to the station. I'm sure there's enough for everybody, and then some."

Erica peeked into the plastic bag. She smiled. "I see you've been visiting Mrs. Petrén."

"Yep. And I'm so full I can hardly move."

"A charming old lady, don't you think?"

"Incredible. If I were around ninety-two I'd marry her."

They smiled at each other.

"So, how are you doing?"

"Fine, thanks."

A moment of silence made them both squirm. Erica poured coffee into two cups and then poured the rest into a table thermos.

"Let's sit on the veranda."

They took their first sips and the silence no longer felt uncomfortable, but rather pleasant. Erica sat on the wicker sofa across from him. He cleared his throat.

"How's it going with the book?"

"Good, thanks. And what about you? How's the investigation going?"

Patrik thought for a moment and decided to tell her a little more than he actually should. Erica was already involved anyway, and he couldn't see that it would hurt any.

"It looks like we've probably solved it. We actually have a suspect in custody. He's being interrogated right now, and the evidence is as watertight as it could possibly be."

Erica leaned forward with an inquisitive expression. "Who is it?"

Patrik hesitated a moment. "Anders Nilsson."

"So it was Anders after all. Strange, but that doesn't feel quite right."

Patrik was inclined to agree with her. There were simply too many loose ends that couldn't be tied up by Anders's arrest. But the physical evidence from the murder scene and the testimony of witnesses—that he was in the house not only just before the time Alex was presumably murdered, but also on a number of other occasions after she was killed—didn't leave much room for doubt. And yet . . .

"Well, I suppose it's over then. Funny, I thought I'd feel more relieved. What about the article I found? The one about Nils's disappearance, I mean. How does that fit into the picture if Anders is the killer?"

Patrik shrugged his shoulders and raised his hands, palms up.

"I just don't know, Erica. I don't know. Maybe it had nothing to do with the murder. Pure coincidence. In any case there's no reason to rummage through everything anymore. Alex took her secrets with her to the grave."

"And the baby she was expecting? Was it Anders's?"

"Who knows? Anders's, Henrik's . . . Your guess is as good as mine. I really wonder what got those two together. Talk about odd couples. It's true that there's nothing unusual about people having someone on the side, but Alexandra Wijkner and Anders Nilsson? I mean, I find it hard to believe that he could get anyone in bed, and Alexandra Wijkner was . . . well, cute as hell is the only thing I can think of to describe her."

For a moment Patrik thought he saw a furrow form between Erica's eyebrows, but the next second it was gone and she was her usual polite, agreeable self. At least he imagined as much. She was just opening her mouth to say something when the theme song from an ice-cream commercial was heard from the hall. Both Patrik and Erica gave a start.

"It's my mobile," Patrik said. "Excuse me for a moment."

He rushed out to the hall to take the call, and after rummaging in his jacket pocket he took out his mobile.

"Patrik Hedström.

"Hmm . . . okay . . . I get it . . . Well, then we're back at square one again. Yeah, I know. Oh, so he said that? Well, you couldn't have known about that. Okay, Superintendent, see you later." He flipped his phone closed with a decisive click and went back to Erica.

"Throw on a jacket and let's take a ride."

"Where to?" Erica gave him a quizzical look with the coffee cup halfway to her mouth.

"There's new information about Anders's involvement. It looks like we have to cross him off the suspect list."

"Really? But where are we going?"

"Both you and I could feel that there was something wrong about this. You found the article about Nils's disappearance at Alex's house, and there may be more things to find there."

"But didn't the police already go through the house?"

"Sure, but I'm not sure we were looking for the right things. I just want to test an idea I have. Come on."

Patrik was already halfway out the door. Erica had to throw on her jacket and run after him.

The house looked small and dilapidated. It was beyond her comprehension that people could live like this. That anyone could endure such a dreary and gray existence, so—impoverished. But that was the way of the world. Some were rich and some were poor. Nelly thanked her lucky stars that she belonged to the former category and not the latter. It wasn't in her nature to be poor. A woman like her was made for furs and diamonds.

The woman who opened the door had probably never even seen a real diamond. Everything about her was gray and brown. Nelly viewed with disgust Vera's shabby cardigan and the chapped hands holding it closed over her breast. Vera said nothing, just stood in the doorway.

After nervously looking around, Nelly finally had

to say, "Well, are you going to invite me in, or shall we stand here all day? I'm sure neither you nor I wants anyone to see me visiting you, am I right?"

Vera still said nothing, just backed into the hallway so that Nelly could come in.

"We have to talk, you and I, don't we?"

Nelly elegantly removed the gloves she always wore outdoors and took a look around the house with distaste. The hallway, the living room, the kitchen, and a small bedroom. Vera walked behind her with her eyes cast down. The rooms were dark and dismal. The wallpaper had long since seen its best days. No one had bothered to take up the linoleum to reveal the hardwood floors underneath, as most people did with old houses these days. But everything was shiny clean and neat. No dirt in the corners, only a depressing hopelessness that permeated the house from floor to ceiling.

Nelly sat down cautiously on the very edge of the old wing chair in the living room. As if she were the one who lived there, she motioned to Vera to take a seat on the sofa. Vera obeyed, also sitting on the very edge. She didn't make a sound, but her hands nervously fidgeted in her lap.

"It's important that we continue to keep this to ourselves. You understand that, don't you?" Nelly's voice was urgent. Vera nodded as she kept her eyes on her lap.

"Well, I can't say that I feel sorry about what happened to Alex. She got what she deserved, and I think you'll agree with me about that. That hussy was going to come to grief sooner or later, I've always known that."

Vera reacted to Nelly's words by casting a hasty glance up at her, but she still didn't say a word. Nelly felt a great contempt for this plain, sad woman, who didn't seem to have even an ounce of will left in her body. Typical working class, with her downcast eyes. Not that she thought it should be otherwise, but she still couldn't help feeling scorn for these people without class, without style. What irritated her most of all was that she was dependent on Vera Nilsson. But no matter what it cost, she had to secure Vera's silence. It had worked before, and it would have to work again.

"It's unfortunate that things turned out as they did, but now it's even more important that we don't do anything hasty. Everything must continue as before. We can't change the past, and there's no reason to drag old rubbish out into the open."

Nelly opened her handbag, took out a white envelope, and placed it on the coffee table.

"Here's a little something to make your budget go a little further. Come on, take it."

Nelly pushed the envelope toward her. Vera didn't pick it up but only stared at it.

"I'm sorry things have turned out this way with Anders. It might even be the best thing that could have happened to him. There's not much alcohol to be had in prison, I mean."

Nelly understood at once that she'd gone too far. Vera slowly got up from the sofa and with a shaking finger pointed toward the front door.

"Get out!"

"Now now, dear little Vera, you mustn't take it—"

"Get out of my house! Anders isn't going to prison, and you can take your filthy money and go to hell, you fucking bitch! I know exactly where someone like you comes from, and it doesn't matter how much perfume you try to pour over it. The smell of shit is still there!"

Nelly shrank back at the naked hatred in Vera's eyes. Her fists were clenched and she stood erect, staring straight into Nelly's eyes. Her whole body seemed to be shaking with years of pent-up rage. There was no trace of the subservience she had displayed before, and Nelly began to feel very uncomfortable in this situation. Talk about overreacting! All she had done was speak the truth. A person ought to be able to stand a little truth. She hurried toward the door.

"Get out of here and don't ever show your face here again!"

Vera as good as chased her out of the house, and just before she slammed the door she threw the envelope out. Nelly had to laboriously stoop down and pick it up. Fifty thousand wasn't something one left lying on the ground, no matter how humiliating it was to see the neighbors pulling their curtains aside. They watched as she practically groveled in the gravel. What an ingrate! Well, Vera would probably show a little more humility when her money ran out and nobody would hire her as cleaning woman anymore. Her job at the Lorentz home was definitely over, and it probably wouldn't take much to make her other jobs dry up as well. Nelly would see to it that Vera came crawling on her bare knees to the welfare office before she was done with her. No one insulted Nelly Lorentz with impunity.

It felt like walking through water. His limbs were heavy and stiff after the night spent on the cot in jail, and his head was full of cotton for want of alcohol. Anders looked around the apartment. The floor was covered with the dirt of police boots tramping about.

But he hardly cared. A little dirt in the corners had never bothered him.

He took a six-pack of strong beer out of the fridge and flopped down on the mattress in the living room. Leaning on his left elbow, he opened the beer with his right hand and greedily took long, deep swallows until the can was empty to the last drop. Then he tossed it in a wide arc through the living room. It landed with a clank on the floor in the far corner. With his most acute need temporarily quenched, he lay down on the mattress with his hands clasped behind his head. His eyes stared unseeing at the ceiling as he allowed himself to sink for a while into memories from long ago. It was only in the past that he could sometimes find a little respite for his soul. Between these brief moments when he allowed himself to reminisce about better days, the pain would cut through his heart with ceaseless intensity. It amazed him that past events could feel simultaneously so remote and so near.

In his memory the sun was always shining. The asphalt felt warm on his bare feet, and his lips were still salty from swimming in the sea. Oddly enough he could never remember anything but summertime. No winters. No overcast days. No rain. Only sunshine from a clear blue sky and a light breeze that broke the shining mirror of the sea.

Alex in her light summer dresses that clung to her legs. Her hair that she refused to cut, so it hung blond and straight all the way down to the small of her back. Sometimes he could even recall her fragrance so strongly that he felt it in his nostrils, tickling and awakening a sense of longing. Strawberries, salt water, shampoo with timothy grass. Sometimes mixed with a smell of sweat that was not at all unpleasant as they raced their bicycles or climbed the rocky hills until their legs gave out. Then they might lie on their backs at the top of Veddeberget, with their feet pointing out to sea and their hands clasped on their stomachs. Alex in the middle between them, with her hair spread out and her eyes looking up at the sky. On rare, precious occasions she would take their hands in hers and for a moment it was as if they were one instead of three.

They were careful not to let anyone ever see them together. That would ruin the magic. The spell would be broken and they would no longer be able to keep reality at bay. Reality was something that had to be warded off at all costs. It was ugly and gray and had nothing to do with the sun-drenched dream-world they could construct when they were together. Reality was nothing they ever spoke about. Instead their days were filled with frivolous games and frivolous conversation. Nothing could be taken seriously. Then they could pretend that they were invulnerable, unconquerable, unreachable. Each of them alone was nothing. Together they were the Three Musketeers.

The grown-ups were only peripheral dream creatures, mere extras who moved about in their world without affecting them. Their mouths moved, but no sound came out. They made gestures and faces that supposedly had meaning but seemed stilted and meaningless, taken out of context.

Anders smiled faintly at the memories, but slowly he was forced out of his catatonic dream state. Nature called, and he was once again back in his own anxiety. He got up to take care of the problem.

The toilet was located below a mirror covered with

dust and dirt. When he relieved his bladder he caught
a glimpse of himself in the glass, and for the first time
in many years he saw himself the way other people saw
him. His hair was greasy and matted. His face was
pale with a sickly gray hue to his skin. Years of neglect
had given him a couple of gaps in his front teeth, which
made him look decades older than he actually was.

The decision was made without his really being aware
of it. As he fumbled to do up his fly, he understood what
the next step would have to be. The look in his eyes was
resolute when he went into the kitchen. After searching
through the drawers he found a big kitchen knife that
he wiped off on his trouser leg. Then he went into the
living room and began methodically taking down the
paintings from the walls. One by one, he lifted down
the paintings that were the result of many years' work.
Those he had kept and hung up were only the ones he
was most satisfied with. He had thrown out many others because they didn't really pass muster in his eyes.
Now the knife slashed through the canvas of one painting after another. He worked slowly and with a steady
hand, slicing the paintings into thin strips until it was
impossible to see what they had once depicted. It was
surprisingly hard work to cut through the canvases, and
when he was done beads of sweat lined his brow. The
room looked like a battlefield of colors. Strips of canvas
covered the living room floor, and frames gaped empty
like toothless gums. He looked around in satisfaction.

"How do you know that it wasn't Anders who murdered Alex?" asked Erica.

"A girl who lives in the same building as Anders saw
him coming home just before seven o'clock, and Alex

talked to her mother at quarter past. It would have been impossible for him to make it back there in such a short time. Which means that Dagmar Petrén's testimony can only tie him to the house while Alex was still alive."

"But what about the fingerprints and footprints you found in the bathroom?"

"Those don't prove that he murdered her, only that he was in the house after she died. In any case it's not enough to hold him in custody any longer. Mellberg will no doubt bring him in again; he's still convinced that Anders is the killer, but for the time being he has to release him, otherwise an attorney could make mincemeat of him. I've always thought that something didn't feel quite right, and this confirms it. Anders is still under suspicion, but there are enough question marks that there's reason to keep looking."

"And that's why we're on the way to Alex's house? What is it you hope to find there?" asked Erica.

"I don't really know. I just feel that I need to get a clearer picture of how things happened."

"Birgit said that Alex couldn't talk to her because she had a visitor. If it wasn't Anders, then who was it?"

"Well, that's the question, isn't it?"

Patrik was driving a bit too fast for Erica's taste. She was holding on tight to the handle over the door. He almost missed the turnoff by the sailing club and turned right at the very last second, which meant he was a hairsbreadth from taking out a fence as they zipped past.

"Are you afraid that the house might not be there if we don't get there fast?" Erica gave him a wan smile.

"Oops, sorry. I just got a little excited."

He slowed down considerably, and on the last bit of

road to Alex's house Erica dared let go of the handle. She still didn't understand why he wanted her to come along, but she had agreed. It might provide some information for her book.

Outside the door Patrik stopped with a sheepish look on his face.

"I forgot that I don't have a key. I'm afraid we won't be able to get in. Mellberg wouldn't appreciate it if one of his cops was caught red-handed climbing in through a window."

Erica gave a deep sigh and bent down to feel under the mat. With a mocking smile she held up the key to Patrik and then opened the door and let him go in first.

Someone had gotten the furnace started again; the temperature inside was now considerably warmer than outside, and they took off their coats and hung them on the rack by the stairs leading to the top floor.

"Now what do we do?" Erica crossed her arms and gave Patrik a questioning look.

"Some time after quarter past seven, when she was talking to her mother on the phone, Alex ingested a large quantity of sedatives. There was no sign that anyone broke in, so in all probability that means that she had a visit from someone she knew. Someone who then had the opportunity to give her the sedatives. How did this someone manage to do that? Well, they must have had something to eat or drink together."

Patrik was pacing up and down in the living room as he spoke. Erica sat down on the sofa and watched with interest.

"Actually," he stopped pacing and raised an index finger in the air, "the medical examiner was able to tell us what she last ate, based on the contents of her stomach.

What did Alexandra eat on the evening of the murder? According to the ME, her stomach contained fish casserole and cider. In the rubbish bin was found an empty packet of Findus fish casserole, and there was an empty cider bottle on the worktop, so that seems to match. What seems a bit strange is that in the fridge there were two large beef fillets, and in the oven there was a frozen potato dish. But the oven was not on, and the potato dish was still raw. There was also a bottle of white wine on the worktop. It was opened, and about five ounces were gone. That corresponds to about one glass."

Patrik measured the amount between his thumb and index finger.

"But there was no wine in Alex's stomach?" Erica was leaning forward with interest, resting her elbows on her knees.

"No, precisely. Since she was pregnant she must have drunk cider instead of wine, but the question is, who drank the wine?"

"Were there any dirty dishes?"

"Yes, there was a plate, a fork, and a knife with remnants of fish casserole on it. There were also two glasses in the sink. One glass was full of fingerprints— Alex's. But there were no prints on the other glass."

He stopped pacing and sat down in the easy chair facing Erica, stretching out his long legs and clasping his hands on his stomach.

"Which must mean that someone wiped off the fingerprints on the glass," said Erica.

She was feeling incredibly intelligent as she sat there coming up with deductions, and Patrik was polite enough to try to look as though he hadn't already thought of all this before.

"Yes, that's what it looks like. Since the inside of the glasses had been rinsed out we found no residue of sedative in either of them, but my guess is that Alex drank it in her cider."

"But why would she eat fish casserole all alone if she had a smashing dinner of beef fillets for two under way in the kitchen?"

"Yes, that's the question, all right. Why would a woman abandon a feast and instead heat up something in the microwave?"

"Because she planned a romantic dinner for two, but her date never showed up."

"That's my guess too. She waited and waited, but finally gave up and tossed something from the freezer into the microwave. I completely understand. It's not much fun eating beef fillet by yourself."

"Anders actually came here for a visit, so it could hardly be him she was waiting for. How about the child's father?" said Patrik.

"Yes, that seems the most plausible. How tragic. Here she's prepared the world's greatest dinner and put wine in the fridge to cool, maybe to celebrate the baby, what do I know, and then he doesn't show up. So she sits here waiting and waiting. The question is, who came over instead?"

"We can't rule out the person she was waiting for," said Patrik. "He could have still shown up later than expected."

"Yes, that's true. Oh, this is so frustrating! If only the walls could talk." Erica looked around the room.

It was a very lovely room. It felt new and fresh. When she sniffed the air she could even smell a hint of paint. The paint on the walls was one of Erica's favorite colors, light blue with a hint of gray, crisply contrasted with the white of the window frames and furniture. A sense of calm filled the room, making her want to lean her head back against the sofa and close her eyes. She had seen this sofa at the House boutique in Stockholm, but on her income she could only dream about it. It was big and puffy and sort of flowed over all the edges. New furniture was mixed with antiques in an especially tasteful blend. Alex must have found the antiques during her work restoring the house in Göteborg. Most of the antique furniture was in the Gustavian style of the 1770s–80s. Erica thanked IKEA for the fact that she could even identify the style. She had often wished that she could buy a couple of pieces from their series of reproductions based on precisely this style. She gave a deep, envious sigh and then reminded herself why they were here. That quickly quashed any feeling of envy.

"So what you're saying is that someone she knew, her lover or somebody else, came here and they had a glass together and then this someone put a sedative in Alex's cider glass," Erica said.

"Yes, that's the most plausible scenario."

"And then what? What do you think happened after that? How did she end up in the bathtub?"

Erica burrowed even deeper into the sofa and propped her feet up on the coffee table. She really had to save up for a sofa like this! For a moment the thought occurred to her that if they sold her parents' house she would have enough money to buy any furniture she wanted. She instantly pushed that thought away.

"I think that the killer waited until Alex fell asleep, undressed her, and dragged her into the bathroom."

"Why do you think the killer dragged her and didn't carry her into the bathroom?"

"The autopsy report showed that she had scrape marks on her heels and bruises under her upper arms."

Patrik sat bolt upright in the easy chair and gave Erica a hopeful look. "Could I try something?"

Erica said skeptically, "It depends on what it is."

"I was thinking you could play murder victim."

"Oh, thanks a lot. Do you really think my acting talents can handle such a stretch?" She laughed but willingly stood up.

"No, no, sit back down. The likely scenario is that they sat here and Alex fell asleep on the sofa. So could you please collapse into a lifeless heap?"

Erica grunted but did her best to act like an unconscious person. When Patrik began pulling on her she opened one eye and said, "I hope you're not thinking of taking my clothes off too."

"Oh no, absolutely not, I wouldn't, I hadn't intended to, I mean . . ." he stammered and blushed.

"That's cool, I was only kidding. Go ahead, murder away."

She felt him drag her onto the floor after first shoving aside the coffee table a bit. He started by trying to drag her by her wrists, but when that didn't work very well he grabbed her under her armpits and dragged her toward the bathroom. All at once she felt extremely conscious of her weight. Patrik must think that she weighed half a ton. She tried to cheat a little and push so she wouldn't feel so heavy, but received a reprimand from Patrik. Oh, why hadn't she followed the Weight Watchers diet a little more strictly the past few weeks? To be honest, she hadn't even tried to follow it; instead she had devoted herself to unrestrained comfort eating. To top it off her pullover rode up when Patrik dragged her, and a treacherous spare tire threatened to spill out of her waistband. She tried to suck in her stomach by taking a deep breath, but was forced to exhale after only a second.

The tiled floor in the bathroom was cold against her back and she shivered involuntarily, but not only from the cold. When Patrik had dragged her all the way over to the bathtub, he carefully set her down.

"Well, that went smoothly enough. Rather heavy, but not impossible. And Alex weighed less than you do."

Thanks a lot for that, Erica thought as she lay on the floor discreetly trying to pull her sweater down over her stomach.

"Now all the killer had to do was get her into the tub."

He made a move to lift Erica's feet, but she got up quickly and brushed herself off.

"No, Patrik, I refuse to go along with that. I've already got enough bruises for one day. And I'm not getting in that bathtub where Alex was found, that's one thing for damn sure!"

He reluctantly accepted her protests and they left the bathroom and went back to the living room.

"After the killer got Alex into the tub it was a simple matter to run the water and then slit her wrists with a razor blade from a bag in the medicine cabinet. Then all the killer had to do was clean up after himself. Rinse out the glasses and wipe off the fingerprints from one of them. Meanwhile Alex slowly bled to death in the bathroom. Terribly, terribly coldhearted."

"And the furnace? Was it already off when she arrived in Fjällbacka?"

"Yes, it seems so. Which was lucky for us. It would have been much harder to gather any evidence from the body if it had been in room temperature for a whole week. For example, it would probably have been impossible to distinguish Anders's fingerprints."

Erica shuddered. The thought of taking fingerprints off a corpse was a little too macabre for her taste.

Together they searched the rest of the house. Erica took time to go through Alex and Henrik's bedroom more thoroughly, since her previous visit had been so rudely interrupted. But she found nothing else. The feeling that something was missing lingered, and it irritated her that she couldn't think of what it was. She decided to tell Patrik; he was just as frustrated as she was. To her satisfaction she also saw that he looked quite uneasy when she told him about the intruder and how she had been forced to hide in the wardrobe.

Patrik heaved a sigh and sat down on the edge of the big four-poster bed, trying to help her figure out what it was she was searching for in her memory.

"Was it something small or something big?"

"I don't know, Patrik, probably something small, otherwise I would have noticed it, don't you think? If the four-poster bed was gone, for instance, I would probably have noticed it." She smiled and sat down next to him.

"But where in the room was it? By the door? Over by the bed? On the bureau?"

Patrik fingered a little scrap of leather he found on Alex's nightstand. It looked like some sort of club insignia, with an inscription burned into the leather in a childish hand: "T.T.M. 1976." When he turned it over he saw some indistinct spots of what looked like old dried blood. He wondered where it had come from.

"I don't know what it was, Patrik. If I did I wouldn't be sitting here tearing out my hair."

She glanced at him in profile. He had wonderfully long, dark eyelashes. His beard stubble was perfect. Just long enough to be felt as light sandpaper against the skin, but short enough not to scratch uncomfortably. She wondered how it would feel against her skin.

"What is it? Have I got something on my face?"

Patrik wiped his mouth nervously. She quickly looked away, embarrassed that he had caught her staring at him.

"It's nothing. A little crumb of chocolate. It's gone now."

There was a moment's silence.

"Well, what do you say—we're not going to get any farther now, do you think?" Erica said at last.

"No, probably not. But listen, ring me as soon as you think of what's missing. If it's important enough for someone to come here to find, it must be important to the investigation as well."

They locked up carefully, and Erica placed the key back under the mat.

"Would you like a ride back?"

"No thanks, Patrik. I'll enjoy the walk."

"See you tomorrow night then." Patrik shifted from one foot to the other, feeling like an awkward fifteen-year-old.

"Okay, I'll see you at eight. Come hungry," Erica said.

"I'll try. But I can't promise anything. Right now it doesn't feel like I'll ever be hungry again." Patrik laughed as he patted his stomach and nodded at Dagmar Petrén's house across the street.

Erica smiled and waved as he drove off in his Volvo. She could already feel anticipation churning inside of her, mixed with insecurity, anxiety, and outright fear.

She started for home but hadn't gone more than a few yards before she stopped short. An idea had come out of nowhere, and it had to be tested before she could let it go. With determined steps she went back to the house, took the key from under the mat, and entered the house again, after first carefully kicking the snow off her shoes.

What should a woman do who was waiting for a man who never showed up for a romantic dinner? She should ring him, of course! Erica said a prayer that Alex had a modern telephone and hadn't fallen for the trendiness of a '50s Cobra phone or still had some old Bakelite model. She was in luck. A brand-new Doro hung on the wall in the kitchen. With trembling fingers she pushed the button for the last number called and crossed her fingers that nobody had used the phone since Alex's death.

The phone rang and rang. After seven rings she was about to hang up, but then the voicemail switched on. She listened to the message but hung up before the beep. Her face pale, Erica slowly replaced the receiver. She could almost hear the clatter in her head as the pieces of the puzzle fell into place. Suddenly she knew precisely what it was that was missing from the bedroom upstairs.

Mellberg was seething with rage. He strode through the station in a fury. If they could have, the employees at Tanumshede police station would have taken cover under their desks. But grown-ups didn't do that, so they had to suffer through a whole day of fiery oaths, reprimands and general abuse. And Annika had to bear the brunt of it. Even though she'd developed a tough hide during the months since Mellberg had become boss, for the first time in a long time she felt on the verge of tears. By four o'clock she'd had enough. She left work and stopped at Konsum to buy a large tub of ice cream. Then she went home, turned on Glamour TV and let the tears run down into the chocolate ice cream. It was just one of those days.

It drove Mellberg crazy that he'd been forced to release Anders Nilsson from jail. He felt in every bone of his body that Anders was Alex Wijkner's killer, and if he'd only had more time alone with him he would have wrung the truth out of him. Instead he'd been forced to release Anders because of a fucking witness who said she saw him come home just before *Separate Worlds* started on TV. That placed him at home in his apartment by seven o'clock, and Alex had talked with Birgit at a quarter past. Bloody hell.

Then there was that young cop, Patrik Hedström. Kept spouting a bunch of wild ideas that it was somebody other than Anders Nilsson who murdered the woman. No, if there was anything he'd learned in all his years in the police, it was that everything was most often exactly what it appeared to be. No hidden motives, no complicated plots. Just riffraff that made life unsafe for honest citizens. Find the riffraff and you find the perpetrator, that was his motto.

He hit the number of Patrik's mobile.

"Where the hell are you?" No pleasantries needed here. "Are you sitting around gathering navel lint somewhere, or what? Down here at the station we're working. Overtime. I don't know if that's a phenomenon you're familiar with. If not, I can fix it so you no longer have to worry about that either. Not here, at any rate."

He felt a bit better in the pit of his stomach when he'd had a chance to put some pressure on that young whippersnapper. You had to keep them on a short leash, or those young cocks would get too full of themselves.

"I want you to drive down and talk to a witness who places Anders Nilsson at home at seven o'clock. Press her, twist her arm a little and see what you can find out . . . yes, NOW, damn it."

He slammed down the receiver, grateful for the circumstances in life that put him in a position to make other people do the dirty work. Suddenly, life seemed considerably brighter. Mellberg leaned back in his chair, pulled open the top drawer, and took out a packet of chocolate balls. With his short sausage-like fingers he took one out of the packet and blissfully stuffed the whole thing in his mouth. When he finished chewing it he took another. Hard-working men like himself needed fuel.

Patrik had already turned off toward Tanumshede via Grebbestad when Mellberg rang. He pulled into the entrance to the Fjällbacka golf course and turned the car around. He gave a deep sigh. It was getting to be late afternoon and he had plenty to do back at the station. He shouldn't have stayed so long in Fjällbacka, but being with Erica exerted a particularly strong attraction on him. It felt like being sucked into a magnetic field; he had to use both strength and willpower to pull himself free. Another deep sigh. This could only end one way. Badly. It wasn't so long ago that he finally got over the breakup with Karin, and now he was already going full speed ahead toward new pain. Talk about self-destructive. The divorce had taken over a year to process. He had spent many nights in front of the TV staring blankly at high-quality shows like *Walker, Texas Ranger* and *Mission Impossible*. Even *TV Shopping* had felt like a better alternative than lying alone in the double bed, tossing and turning, while images of Karin in bed with another man flickered past like a bad soap opera. And yet the attraction he felt for Karin in the beginning was nothing compared to the attraction he now felt for Erica. Logic whispered malevolently in his ear: won't the fall be that much greater?

He drove much too fast, as usual, in the last tight curves before Fjällbacka. This case was starting to get on his nerves. He took out his frustration on the car and was in real mortal danger when he sped around the last curve before the hill down to the place where the old silo once stood. Now it was torn down and instead there were houses and boathouses built in the old-fashioned style. Prices were around a couple of million kronor per house; he never ceased to be amazed at how much money people must have to be able to buy a summer house at those prices.

A motorcyclist appeared out of nowhere in the curve and Patrik had to swerve in panic. His heart was pounding fast and he braked to a bit below the posted speed limit. That was a close call. A check in the rearview mirror assured him that the biker was still on his machine and could continue his journey.

He kept going straight ahead, past the minigolf course and up to the intersection by the gas station. There he turned left to the apartment houses. He reflected one more time over how horribly ugly the buildings were. Brown and white constructions from the sixties, like big square blocks tossed near the southern entrance to Fjällbacka. He wondered about the rationale of the architect who designed them. Had he gone in for making the buildings as ugly as possible, as an experiment? Or did he just not care? Apparently, they were the result of the frenzy to build a million housing units in the sixties. "Homes for all." Too bad they didn't say: "Beautiful homes for all."

He parked in the lot and went into the first entrance. Number five. The stairwell to Anders's apartment, but also the apartment of the witness Jenny Rosén. They lived two flights up. He was puffing hard when he reached the right landing, reminded that he'd been getting far too little exercise and way too much coffee cake lately. Not that he'd ever been a paragon of physical training, but it had never been this bad before.

Patrik stopped for a second outside Anders's door and listened. Not a sound to be heard. Either he wasn't home or he was passed out.

Jenny's door was on the right, and directly opposite from Anders. She had exchanged the standard nameplate for her own made out of wood, with the names Jenny and Max Rosén in ornate script with decorative roses winding around the plate. So she was married.

She had rung the police station with her testimony early this morning, and he hoped she would still be at home. She hadn't been when they knocked on all the doors in the stairwell yesterday, but they had left a card and asked her to ring the police station. That's why it wasn't until today that they got the information about Anders's return home on the Friday evening when Alex died.

The doorbell echoed in the apartment, followed at once by a loud shriek from a child. Footsteps could be heard in the hall, and Patrik felt rather than saw someone looking at him through the peephole in the door. A safety chain was unhooked and the door opened.

"Yes?"

A woman with a one-year-old child was standing there. She was very thin with bleached blond hair. From the color of her roots, her natural hair color must have been somewhere between dark brown and black, which was confirmed by a pair of nut-brown eyes. She wore no makeup and looked tired. She had on a pair of worn jogging trousers with baggy knees and a T-shirt with a big Adidas logo on the front.

"Jenny Rosén?"

"Yes, that's me. What's this about?"

"My name is Patrik Hedström and I'm from the police. You put in a call to us this morning, and I'd like to talk with you a little about the information you gave."

He spoke in a low voice so he wouldn't be heard in the apartment across the landing.

"Come in." She stepped aside to let him in.

The apartment was small, a one-room, and there was definitely no man living there. None older than one year at any rate. The apartment was an explosion in pink. Everything was pink. Rugs, tablecloths, curtains, lamps, everything. Rosettes were once again a popular motif, and they were on lamps and candlesticks in a profusion that was both lavish and superfluous. On the walls were pictures that further emphasized the romantic disposition of the occupant. Soft-focus female faces with birds fluttering past. Even a picture of a crying child hung over the bed.

They sat down on a white leather sofa, and thank goodness she didn't offer him coffee. He'd had plenty of that today. She set the child on her lap, but he squirmed out of her grasp. So she put him on the floor, where he toddled about on his still unsteady legs.

Patrik was struck by how young the woman was. She couldn't be out of her teens, he guessed about eighteen. But he knew that it wasn't unusual for girls in small towns to have one or two children before the age of twenty. Since she called the boy Max, he concluded that the father didn't live with them. That wasn't unusual either. Teenage relationships often couldn't survive the stress of a baby.

He pulled out his notebook.

"So it was Friday the week before last, the twenty-second, that you saw Anders Nilsson come home at seven o'clock? How is it that you're so sure of the time?"

"I never miss *Separate Worlds* on TV. It starts at seven and it was just before that when I heard a lot of commotion outside. Nothing unusual, I must say. It's always rather lively over at Anders's place. His drinking buddies come and go at all hours, and sometimes the police show up as well. But I still went to check through the peephole in the door, and that's when I saw him. Drunk as a lord, he was trying to unlock his door, but the keyhole would have had to be a foot wide for him to find it. He finally got the door open and went inside, and that's when I heard the theme song for *Separate Worlds* and hurried back to the TV."

She was chewing nervously on a lock of her long hair. Patrik saw that her nails were bitten down to the quick. There were traces of hot pink nail polish on what was left of her nails.

Max had steadily worked his way around the coffee table in the direction of Patrik and now took triumphant possession of his trouser leg.

"Up, up, up," he chanted, and Patrik gave Jenny a questioning look.

"Sure, pick him up. He obviously likes you."

Patrik awkwardly lifted the boy onto his knee and gave him his bunch of keys to play with. The child beamed like the sun. He gave Patrik a big smile and showed two front teeth that looked like little grains of rice. Patrik gave him a big smile back. He felt a quavering in his chest. If things had turned out differently he could have had a boy of his own on his knee by this time. He cautiously stroked Max's downy head.

"How old is he?"

"Eleven months. He keeps me busy, you'd better believe."

Her face lit up with tenderness when she looked at her son, and Patrik saw at once how sweet she was behind the tired exterior. He couldn't even imagine how much work it must take to be a single parent at her age. She should be out partying and living life with her friends. Instead she spent her evenings changing diapers and keeping house. As if to illustrate the tensions within her, she took a cigarette out of a packet lying on the table and lit it. She took a deep, pleasurable drag and then held out the packet to Patrik. He shook his head. He had definite views about smoking in the same room as a baby, but it was her business, not his. Personally he couldn't understand how anyone could sit and suck on something that smelled as bad as a cigarette.

"So couldn't he have come home and then gone out again?"

"The walls are so thin in this building that you can hear a pin drop out on the landing. Everyone who lives here knows exactly who comes and goes—and when. I'm quite sure that Anders didn't go out again."

Patrik realized that he wouldn't get much further. Out of curiosity he asked, "What was your reaction when you heard that Anders was suspected of murder?"

"I thought it was bullshit."

She took another deep drag and blew the smoke out in rings. Patrik had to restrain himself from saying anything about the dangers of secondhand smoke. On his knee Max was fully occupied with sucking on his keyring. He held it between his chubby little fingers and occasionally looked up at Patrik as if to thank him for lending him this fantastic toy.

Jenny went on, "Sure, Anders is a fucking wreck, but he could never kill anyone. He's a decent guy. He rings my bell and asks to bum a cigarette now and then, and whether he's sober or pissed he's always decent. I've even let him babysit Max a few times when I had to run out to the market. But only when he was completely sober. Never otherwise."

She stubbed out the cigarette in an overflowing ashtray.

"Actually there's nothing bad about any of the winos here. They're just unfortunate devils, drinking away their lives together. The only people they're hurting is themselves."

She tossed her head to get the hair out of her face and reached for the cigarette packet again. Her fingers were yellow from nicotine, and this cigarette obviously tasted as good to her as the first one. Patrik was starting to feel smoked out and didn't think he'd get any more useful information from Jenny. Max protested at being lifted down and handed back to his mother.

"Thanks for the help. We'll probably have occasion to come back again."

"Well, I'm always here. I'm not going anywhere."

The cigarette now lay smoldering in the ashtray and the smoke curled toward Max, who squinted his eyes in annoyance. He was still chewing on the keys and gave Patrik a look as if challenging him to try to take them. Patrik gave a cautious pull, but the rice-grain teeth were amazingly strong. By this time the keys were covered in drool, and it was hard to get a real grip on them. He tentatively pulled a little harder and got an angry grunt in reply. Jenny, used to handling such situations, took a firm grip and managed to extract the keys and hand them to Patrik. Max shrieked at the top of his lungs to show his displeasure at how the situation had turned out. Holding the keyring between his thumb and index finger, Patrik discreetly tried to wipe it off on his trouser leg before he stuffed it back in his pocket.

Jenny and a screaming Max followed him to the door. The last thing Patrik saw before the door closed were big tears running down the boy's round cheeks. Again he felt an ache somewhere deep in his heart.

The house was too big for him now. Henrik wandered from room to room. Everything in the house reminded him of Alexandra. She had loved and cared for every inch of this house. Sometimes he had wondered if it was for the sake of the house that she had married him. It wasn't until he had brought her home that their relationship had turned serious, for her. As for him, he'd been serious since the first time he saw her at a university meeting for foreign students. Tall and blonde, she had an aura of aloofness that attracted him more than anything else in his whole life. He'd never wanted anything as much as he wanted Alex. And he was used to getting whatever he wanted.

His parents had been far too preoccupied with their own lives to have time to put any energy into his. The hours that weren't taken up by the business had been devoured by endless social events. Charity balls, cocktail parties, dinners with business associates. Henrik had to sit nicely at home with the nanny. What he remembered most about his mother was the smell of her perfume when she kissed him good-bye, in her thoughts already on her way to some elaborate party. As compensation he had only to point at something and he would have it. Nothing material had ever been denied him, but it was given with indifference, the same way one absentmindedly scratches a dog that begs for attention.

Alex had been the first thing in Henrik's life that he couldn't have just for the asking. She was inaccessible and contrary and therefore irresistible. He had courted her stubbornly and intensely. Roses, dinners, presents, and compliments. No effort had been spared. And she had reluctantly let herself be courted and led into a relationship. Not under protest—he never could have coerced her—but with indifference. It wasn't until he took her home to Göteborg that first summer and they walked into the house here on the island of Särö that she began to take an active interest in the relationship. She responded to his embraces with a newfound intensity, and he was happier than ever before. They were married that same summer in Sweden after knowing each other for only a few months. After they returned to France for one last year of college and graduation, they returned to the house on Särö for good.

Now that he thought back, he realized that the only time he'd seen her really happy was when she was refurbishing the house. He sat down in one of the big Chesterfield easy chairs in the library, leaned his head back and closed his eyes. Images of Alex flickered past like in an old Super 8 film. He felt the leather cool and taut under his hands and followed the winding path of an age crack with his index finger.

What he remembered best were her different smiles. When she found a piece of furniture for the house that was exactly what she'd been looking for, or when she cut away old wallpaper with a knife and found the old original wallpaper in good condition underneath, then her smile was big and genuine. When he kissed her on the nape of her neck, or caressed her cheek, or told her how much he loved her, she would also smile— sometimes. But not always. Her smile then was a smile he came to hate, a distant, preoccupied smile. Afterward, she would always turn away, and he could see her secrets wriggling like little snakes just beneath the surface.

He had never asked any questions. Out of sheer cowardice. He'd been afraid to start a chain reaction whose consequences he was not prepared to handle. It was better at least to have her physically by his side, with the hope that she would one day be his completely. He was prepared to risk that he might never have everything, but at least he'd be sure of keeping a part of her. A fragment of Alex was enough. That's how much he loved her.

He looked around the library. The books that covered all the walls and which she had laboriously tracked down in the antiquarian bookshops of Göteborg were only for show. Except for college textbooks he couldn't recall ever seeing her read a book. Perhaps she had enough of her own pain and didn't need to read about other people's.

What was hardest for him to accept was the pregnancy. Whenever he brought up the question of children she would shake her head vehemently. She didn't want to bring children into a world that looked like this one, she had told him.

He'd accepted the fact that there was another man. Henrik knew that Alex wasn't driving so eagerly to Fjällbacka every weekend to be alone, but he could live with that. Their own sex life had been dead for more than a year. He could live with that too. Even her death he could learn to live with, over time. What he couldn't accept was that she was ready to bear another man's child but had refused to bear his. That was what haunted him at night. In a sweat he would toss and turn between the sheets with no hope of sleep. He had developed dark circles under his eyes and lost several pounds. He felt like an elastic band that was stretched and stretched and sooner or later would reach a point where it broke with a snap. So far, he had grieved without tears, but now Henrik Wijkner leaned forward, put his face in his hands, and wept.

5

The accusations, the harsh words, the insults all ran off him like water. What were several hours of insults compared with years of guilt? What were several hours of insults compared with life without his ice princess?

He laughed at the pathetic attempts to make him accept the blame. He saw no reason to do that. As long as he saw no reason to do so, they would not be successful.

But perhaps she had been right. Perhaps the day of reckoning was finally here. Unlike her, he knew that the judgment would not be clothed in human flesh. The only thing that could pass judgment on him was something that was greater than humanity, greater than the flesh, but equal to the soul. *The only thing that can judge me is the one who can see my soul*, he thought.

It was strange the way completely opposite emotions could be combined into a whole new feeling. Love and hate became indifference. Vengeance and forgiveness became decisiveness. Tenderness and bitterness became sorrow, so great that it could crush a man. For him she had always been a remarkable mixture of light and darkness. A Janus face that alter-

nately judged and understood. Sometimes she covered him with hot kisses despite his repulsiveness. Sometimes she reviled and hated him for the same reason. There was no rest or peace to be found in opposites.

The last time he saw her was the time he loved her most. Finally she was completely his. Finally she belonged to him totally, to do with as he pleased. To be loved or hated. Without the chance of once again countering his love with her indifference.

Before it had been like loving a veil. An elusive, transparent, seductive veil. The last time he saw her the veil had lost its mystique and all that remained was the flesh. But that made her accessible. For the first time he thought that he could know who she was. He had touched her stiff, frozen limbs and felt the soul that was still thrashing inside its frozen prison. Never had he loved her as much as he did then. Now it was time to meet his fate, eye to eye. He hoped that fate would prove to be forgiving. But he didn't believe it would.

The telephone woke her. To think that people couldn't ring at a sensible hour.

"Erica Falck."

"Hi, it's Anna." Her tone was wary. With good reason, Erica thought.

"Hi." Erica didn't intend to let her off easily.

"How's it going?" Anna was treading softly on a minefield.

"Fine, thanks. How about you?"

"Thanks, things are going fine. How's the book coming?"

"It's a little up and down. But it's progressing, at least. Everything all right with the kids?" Erica decided to throw her a sop, at least.

"Emma has a bad cold, but Adrian's colic seems to be improving. So now I get to sleep an hour a night anyway."

Anna laughed but Erica thought she heard an undertone of bitterness.

There was a moment of silence.

"You know, we have to talk about this thing with the house."

"Yes, I think so too." Now it was Erica's turn to sound bitter.

"We have to sell it, Erica. If you can't buy us out then we'll have to sell it."

When Erica didn't reply, Anna babbled on nervously. "Lucas has talked to the real estate agent, and he thinks we should set the asking price at three million. Three million, Erica, can you imagine that? With a million and a half as your share you could write in peace and quiet without having to worry about finances. It can't be easy for you to make a living as a writer. What sort of printings do you have for each book? Two thousand? Three thousand? And you probably don't make too many kronor per book, do you? Don't you understand, Erica, this is your big chance too. You've always talked about wanting to write a novel. With this money you can take the time. The agent thinks we should wait to show the house until at least April or May to get the most interest, but once we list it the house should sell in a couple of weeks. You understand that we have to do this, don't you?"

Anna's voice sounded imploring, but Erica wasn't in a sympathetic mood. Her discovery from the day before had kept her awake and worrying half the night. She felt betrayed and grumpy in general.

"No, I don't understand it, Anna. This is our parents' home. We grew up here. Mama and Papa bought this house when they were newlyweds. They loved this house. And I do too, Anna. You can't do this."

"But the money—"

"I don't give a shit about the money! I've managed fine so far, and I intend to continue doing so." Erica was so angry now that her voice was shaking.

"But Erica, you must understand that you can't

make me keep the house if I don't want to. Half of it is mine, after all."

"If you were the one who wanted to do this, I'd think it was very, very sad, but I would accept your point of view. The problem is that I know that it's somebody else's opinions I'm hearing. Lucas is the one who wants to do this, not you. The question is whether you even know what you want. Do you?"

Erica didn't bother waiting for Anna's reply. "And I refuse to let my life be controlled by Lucas Maxwell. Your husband is a big fucking shithead! And you bloody well ought to come over here and help me go through Mama and Papa's things. I've been at it for weeks, trying to organize everything, and I'm only halfway done. It's not fair that I have to do it all by myself! If you're so tied to the stove that you aren't even allowed to help with your parents' estate, then you ought to give serious thought to whether this is how you want to live the rest of your life."

Erica slammed down the phone so hard that it almost flew off the nightstand. She was so furious she was shaking.

In Stockholm Anna was sitting on the floor with the phone in her hand. Lucas was at work and the children were asleep, so she had taken the opportunity to ring Erica now that she had some time to herself. It was a conversation she'd been putting off for several days, but Lucas had been nagging her to ring Erica about the house. Finally she gave in.

Anna felt torn into a thousand pieces, all being pulled in different directions. She loved Erica and she also loved the house in Fjällbacka. What Erica didn't understand was that she had to put her own family first. There was nothing she was not prepared to do or sacrifice for her children, and if that meant keeping Lucas happy at the cost of her relationship with her big sister, then so be it. Emma and Adrian were the only reason she got up in the morning, the only reason to continue living in this world. If she could only make Lucas happy, everything would work out. She knew that. It was because she was so difficult and didn't do what he wanted that he was forced to be so hard on her. If she could give him this gift, sacrifice her parents' home for him, then he would understand how much she was prepared to do for him and her family. And everything would be good again.

But somewhere deep inside her a voice was saying something entirely different. Anna hung her head and wept, and with her tears she drowned out that faint voice. She left the phone lying on the floor.

Erica kicked off the covers in annoyance and swung her legs over the edge of the bed. She regretted her hard words to Anna, but she was already in a bad mood, and lack of sleep had made her lose her head completely. She tried ringing Anna back to try to patch things up, but got a busy signal.

"Shit!"

She gave the stool in front of the vanity table an undeserved kick, but instead of feeling better Erica stubbed her toe so badly that she hopped about howling on one foot, holding her sore toe. She was very doubtful that even childbirth could be this painful. When the pain finally ebbed away she got onto the scale against her better judgment.

She knew that she shouldn't, but the masochist inside her forced her to find out for sure. She took off the T-shirt she slept in. It always added a few extra ounces, and she even wondered whether her underpants would make any difference. Probably not. She stepped on with her right foot first but kept some of her weight on the left foot that was still on the floor. Gradually she transferred her weight to the right foot, and when the needle reached 132 pounds she wished she could let it stay there. But no. When she finally put all her weight on the scale, it mercilessly read 150. Okay. As she had feared, over two pounds worse. She had guessed about one, but the scale showed over four pounds more than the last time she weighed herself, which was on the morning she found Alex.

Since then, she had felt it was very, very unnecessary to weigh herself. Not because she hadn't noticed from her waistband that she had gained weight, but up until the moment when she saw it in black and white, denial was a welcome companion. Dampness in the closet or shrinkage due to excessive washing temperature had served her well as excuses countless times in the past. Right now it merely felt hopeless, and she had a good mind to cancel dinner that evening with Patrik. When she saw him she wanted to feel sexy and pretty and thin, not bloated and fat. She gloomily looked at her stomach and tried sucking it in as far as she could. Useless. She looked at herself in profile in the full-length mirror and tried instead to pooch out her stomach as much as she could. There, that's the image that matched how she felt right now.

With a sigh, she pulled on a pair of loose jogging trousers with a forgiving stretch waistband and put on the same T-shirt she'd slept in. She promised herself that on Monday, she'd do something about her weight again. Starting now was no good, she'd already planned to serve a three-course dinner tonight and she had to admit: if you want to dazzle a man with your cooking, then cream and butter are essential ingredients. Besides, Monday was a good day to start a new life. For the hundred-thousandth time she made a solemn promise to herself that on Monday she would start exercising and stay on her Weight Watchers diet. But not today.

A bigger problem was the reason why she'd almost worried herself sick since yesterday. She had turned over all the options, pondering what she should do, but without coming up with any solution. She suddenly knew something that she sincerely wished she had never found out.

The coffee began to smell good from the coffee-maker, and life seemed a shade brighter. Amazing what a little of that hot beverage could do. She poured a cup and drank it black with great enjoyment as she stood by the kitchen worktop. She had never been much for breakfast; that would save her a few calories for this evening.

When the doorbell rang she was so startled that she spilled a little coffee on her T-shirt. She swore out loud, wondering who it could be at this hour of the morning. She glanced at the kitchen clock. Eight-thirty. She set down the cup and opened the door. There on the porch stood Julia Carlgren slapping her arms to keep warm.

"Hi." Erica's voice was inquisitive.

"Hi." Then silence from Julia.

Erica wondered what Alex's little sister was doing

on her front porch so early on a Tuesday morning, but her good breeding asserted itself and she asked Julia to come in.

Julia tramped briskly inside, hung up her coat and scarf, and preceded Erica into the living room.

"Do you think I could have a cup of that wonderful coffee I smell?"

"Oh, sure, I'll get you one."

Safely out of Julia's sight in the kitchen, Erica poured a cup of coffee and rolled her eyes. Something wasn't quite right with that girl.

Erica handed the cup to Julia and asked her to have a seat on the wicker sofa on the veranda. They drank their coffee in silence. Erica decided to wait her out. Julia was going to have to broach the subject herself and explain why she was here. It took a couple of tense minutes before Julia spoke.

"Are you living here now?"

"No, actually. I live in Stockholm but I'm here straightening out everything with the house."

"Yes, I heard. I'm sorry."

"Thank you. My condolences to you too."

Julia gave an odd little laugh that Erica found surprising and misplaced. She recalled the document she had found in the wastebasket at Nelly Lorentz's house and wondered how the pieces fit together.

"You're probably wondering why I'm here." Julia looked at Erica with her strange, steady gaze. She blinked very seldom.

It struck Erica again how diametrically opposite she was to her big sister. Julia's skin was pitted with acne scars, and her hair looked as if she'd cut it herself with nail scissors. Without a mirror. There was something unhealthy about the way she looked. A sickly pallor had settled like a dirty gray film over her skin. Nor did she appear to share Alex's interest in clothes. Her outfits looked as though they had been bought in shops catering to little old retired ladies. Her clothes were as far from the style of the day as they could get without crossing the line to become masquerade costumes.

"Do you have any photos of Alex?"

"Excuse me?" Erica was startled by the direct question. "Photos? Yes, I suppose I do. Quite a few, even. Papa loved taking pictures, and he took a lot of us when we were kids. Alex was over here so often that she's probably in a lot of the pictures."

"Could I see them?" Julia gave Erica a reproachful look, as if admonishing her for not going to fetch the photos already. Grateful for any excuse to escape Julia's penetrating gaze for a moment, Erica went to get the photo albums.

The albums were in a chest up in the attic. She hadn't had a chance to clean there yet, but she knew exactly where the chest was. All the family photographs were stored inside; she had shuddered at the thought of sitting down to go through them. A large part of the photos were in unsorted piles, but she knew that the ones she was looking for had been carefully put into albums. She paged through them systematically, starting at the top of the stack. In the third album she found what she was looking for. The fourth album also had pictures of Alex, and clutching both albums she cautiously climbed down the attic stairs.

Julia was sitting in exactly the same position as before. Erica wondered whether she had moved at all while she was gone.

"Here's something that should interest you."

Erica was out of breath. She dropped the thick photo albums on the coffee table so hard that dust flew.

Julia eagerly began looking through the first album while Erica sat down next to her on the sofa to describe what was in the pictures.

"When was this one taken?"

Julia was pointing at the first photo she found of Alex, two pages into the album.

"Let me see. This must be . . . 1974. Yes, I think that's right. We were about nine then, I think."

Erica ran a finger over the photo and felt a strong sense of melancholy in her stomach. It was so long ago. She and Alex stood naked in the garden on a warm summer day. If she remembered correctly they had been naked because they were running back and forth through the water spraying from the garden hose. What seemed a bit odd about the picture was that Alex was wearing winter mittens.

"Why does she have mittens on? This looks like it's in July or something." Julia turned an astonished face to Erica, who laughed at the memory.

"Your sister loved those mittens and insisted on wearing them, not only all winter long but also for large parts of the summer. She was as stubborn as a mule, and nobody could convince her to put away those darn disgusting mittens."

"She knew what she wanted, didn't she?"

Julia looked at the picture in the album with an almost tender expression. The next second it was gone, and she impatiently moved on to the next page.

The photos felt like relics from another lifetime for Erica. It was so long ago, and so much had happened since then. Sometimes it felt as if the childhood years with Alex were only a dream.

"We were more like sisters than friends. We spent all our waking hours together, and we often slept over at each other's house too. Every day we used to compare notes on what was for dinner and then we picked the house with the best food."

"In other words, you often ate here." For the first time a smile crept onto Julia's lips.

"Yes, say what you will about your mother, she could never have made a living on her cooking."

One particular photo caught Erica's eye. She touched it gently. It was an incredibly lovely photograph. Alex was sitting in the stern of Tore's boat, laughing boisterously. Her blonde hair was flying around her face, and the silhouette of all of Fjällbacka was spread out behind her. They must have been on their way out for a day of sunshine and swimming on the skerries. There had been many such days. Her mother had not come along, as usual. She had always blamed a host of small matters she had to attend to, and chose to stay home. That's how it always was. Erica could easily count on the fingers of one hand the excursions that had included her mother, Elsy. She chuckled when she saw a picture of Anna from the same boat trip. As usual, she was playing monkey; in this picture she was hanging daringly outside the railing and making faces at the camera.

"Your sister?"

"Yes, my little sister, Anna."

Erica's tone was curt, indicating that she didn't want to discuss that subject any further. Julia got the message and kept paging through the album with her short fat fingers. Her nails were bitten to the quick. On some of her fingers she had bitten the nail so much that sores formed around the edges. Erica forced her gaze away from Julia's wounded fingers and looked instead at the pictures flipping past in her hands.

Toward the end of the second album Alex was suddenly no longer included in the pictures. It was quite a sharp contrast. Before she was on every page; now there were no more pictures of her. Julia carefully stacked the albums on the coffee table and leaned back in the corner of the sofa with her coffee cup in her hands.

"Would you like some fresh coffee? That must be cold by now."

Julia looked at her cup and saw that Erica was right. "Yes, if there's more I'll take some, thanks."

She handed over her cup to Erica, who was happy for a chance to stretch her legs a bit. The wicker sofa was lovely to look at, but after sitting on it a while both her back and her bottom were protesting. Julia's back seemed to share this opinion, since she got up and followed Erica into the kitchen.

"It was a nice funeral. Lots of friends for the reception at your place as well."

Erica stood with her back to Julia and poured fresh coffee into their cups. A noncommittal murmur was the only reply she got. She decided to be a little nosy.

"It looked as though you and Nelly Lorentz were quite well acquainted. How do you happen to know each other?"

Erica held her breath. The paper she had found in the wastebasket at Nelly's house made her very curious about Julia's answer.

"Papa worked for her." The reply came reluctantly from Julia. She put a finger in her mouth without even seeming to be conscious of it and began gnawing at it frantically.

"Yes, but that must have been long before you were born," said Erica. She was still fishing for information.

"I had a summer job at the cannery when I was younger," said Julia.

Her replies still came like pulling teeth. She stopped biting her nails only long enough to answer.

"You looked like you were getting along well."

"Well, I suppose that Nelly sees something in me that nobody else does." Her smile was bitter and introspective. All at once Erica felt great sympathy for Julia. Life as the ugly duckling must have been hard. She said nothing, and after a while the silence forced Julia to go on.

"We were here every summer, after all. The summer after tenth grade Nelly rang Papa and asked if I'd like to earn a little extra and work in the office. I could hardly turn it down, so after that I worked there every summer until I started at the teachers' college."

Erica understood that this answer left a good deal unsaid. But it would have to do. She also understood that she wouldn't get much more out of Julia about her relationship with Nelly. They sat down on the sofa on the veranda again and drank a few sips of coffee in silence. Both of them gazed blankly out across the ice that stretched toward the horizon.

"It must have been hard for you when Mama and Papa and Alex moved away." It was Julia who spoke first.

"Yes and no. We were no longer playing with each

other by then, so of course it was sad, but it wasn't as dramatic as if we'd still been best friends."

"What happened? Why did you stop hanging out together?"

"If I only knew."

Erica was astonished that the memory could still hurt so much. That she could still feel the loss of Alex so strongly. So many years had passed since then, and it was probably the rule rather than the exception that childhood best friends often slipped away from each other. Maybe it was because there had never been any natural ending and above all no explanation. They didn't have a disagreement, Alex didn't find a new best friend; none of the reasons why a friendship usually dies. She simply withdrew behind a wall of indifference and vanished without saying a word.

"Did you have a fight about something?"

"No, not that I know of. Alex just lost interest somehow. She stopped ringing me and stopped asking if we should think up something to do together. If I asked her to do something she wouldn't say no, but I could tell that she was utterly uninterested. So finally I stopped asking."

"Did she have new friends she hung around with?"

Erica wondered why Julia was asking all these questions about her and Alex, but she had nothing against reviving old memories. She might be able to use them in the book.

"I never saw her with anyone else. At school she always kept to herself. And yet . . ."

"What?" Julia leaned forward eagerly.

"I still had a feeling that there was someone. But I could be wrong. It was just a feeling."

Julia nodded thoughtfully. Erica had the feeling that she had merely confirmed something that Julia already knew.

"Excuse me for asking, but why do you want to know so much about when Alex and I were kids?"

Julia avoided looking her in the eye. Her answer was evasive.

"She was so much older than I was, and she'd already left the country by the time I was born. Besides, we were really different. I don't think I ever really got to know her. And now it's too late. I looked for pictures of her at home, but we have hardly any. So I thought of you."

Erica felt that Julia's reply contained so little truth as to qualify as a lie, but she reluctantly accepted it.

"Well, I have to get going now. Thanks for the coffee."

Julia got up abruptly and went to the kitchen to put her coffee cup in the dish tub. She was suddenly in a big hurry to leave. Erica walked her to the door.

"Thanks for letting me see the pictures. It meant a lot to me."

Then she was gone.

Erica stood in the doorway a long time watching her walk away. A gray and shapeless figure who hurried down the street with her arms held tight to her body as protection from the biting cold. Erica slowly closed the door and went back inside where it was warm.

It was a long time since Patrik had felt so nervous. The feeling he had in the pit of his stomach was wonderful and frightening at the same time.

The pile of clothes on the bed grew as he tried on

yet another outfit. All the clothes he put on felt too old-fashioned, too sloppy, too dressy, too square, or simply too ugly. Besides, most of the trousers were uncomfortably tight around the waist. With a sigh he tossed another pair of trousers on the pile and sat down in his shorts on the edge of the bed. He immediately lost all sense of anticipation for the evening and instead got a serious touch of good old anxiety. Maybe it would be better if he rang and canceled.

Patrik lay back on the bed and looked up at the ceiling with his hands clasped behind his head. He still owned the double bed that he and Karin had shared, and now he stroked his hand over her side of the bed in a fit of sentimentality. It was not until recently that he had begun rolling over onto her side in his sleep. Actually, he should have bought a new bed as soon as she moved out, but he hadn't been able to face it.

Despite all the sadness he felt when Karin left him, he'd sometimes wondered if it really was Karin he was missing, or whether he missed the illusion he'd had of marriage as an institution. His father had left his mother for another woman when he was ten years old. The divorce that followed had been heartrending, exploiting him and his little sister, Lotta, as the primary weapons. He had promised himself that he would never be unfaithful, but above all that he would never ever get a divorce. If he got married it would be for life. So when he and Karin got married five years ago in Tanumshede Church, he didn't doubt for a second that it would last forever. But life seldom turns out the way one thinks it will. She and Leif had been meeting behind his back for over a year before he caught them. So fucking classic.

He had come home early from work one day because he wasn't feeling well, and there they were in the bedroom. In the bed he was lying in right now. Maybe there was a masochist somewhere inside of him. How else could he explain why he hadn't gotten rid of the bed long ago? Although now it was all in the past. It no longer mattered.

He heaved himself up out of bed, still unsure if he wanted to go over to Erica's house tonight or not. He wanted to. And he didn't want to. With one blow an attack of low self-esteem had swept away the sense of anticipation he'd been feeling all day, even all week. But it was too late to decline, so he didn't have much choice.

When he finally found a pair of chinos that fit well around the waist and put on a freshly ironed blue shirt, he felt all at once a little better. And he began looking forward to the evening again. A touch of gel made his hair look suitably disheveled, and after giving his reflection in the mirror a good-luck wave, he felt ready to go.

It was pitch black out although it was only seven-thirty, and a light snowfall made visibility poor as he drove back to Fjällbacka. He had left in good time and didn't need to hurry. His thoughts of Erica were briefly pushed aside by the events of recent days at work. Mellberg hadn't been pleased when Patrik could do no better than substantiate that the witness, Anders's neighbor Jenny, seemed positive about what she had seen. Anders actually did seem to have an alibi for the critical time period. This may not have provoked the same degree of anger in Patrik as it had in Mellberg, but he couldn't deny that he felt a certain hope-

lessness. Two weeks had passed since they had found
Alex's body, and they didn't feel any closer to a solution than they were then.

What was important now was not to lose heart
completely. They had to regroup and start over from
the beginning. Every lead, every bit of testimony had
to be gone over with new eyes. Patrik made a list in his
head of what he needed to work on tomorrow. The top
priority was to find out who was the father of the child
Alex was expecting. There must be someone in Fjällbacka who had seen or heard something about who
she was meeting on weekends. Not that it could be
ruled out that Henrik might be the father, and Anders
was always a possible candidate too. Although somehow Patrik didn't think that Anders was someone
Alex would consider a suitable candidate to father her
child. He thought that what Francine had told Erica
was much closer to the truth. There was someone in
her life who was very, very important. Someone who
was important enough that she would be happy to
have a child with him—something that she could not,
or would not, want with her husband.

Her sexual relationship with Anders was also something he wanted to find out more about. What did a
society woman from Göteborg have in common with
a down-and-out drunk? Something told him that if
he discovered how their paths had crossed, he would
find many of the answers he was seeking. Then there
was the article about Nils Lorentz's disappearance.
Alex had been a child back then. Why was she saving
a twenty-five-year-old newspaper clipping hidden in a
bureau drawer? There were so many threads that were
so tangled together. He felt as if he were staring at

one of those pictures where everything looks like incoherent dots, until you relax your eyes in just the right way and a shape suddenly emerges with unexpected clarity. The only thing was, he couldn't find that perfect position to make the dots form a pattern. In his weaker moments he sometimes wondered if he was a good enough cop to find it. Perhaps a murderer would escape because he wasn't competent enough.

A deer bounded out in front of the car and Patrik was yanked abruptly out of his gloomy thoughts. He hit the brake and managed to miss the deer's rump by an inch or so. The car skidded on the slick road and didn't stop for a couple of long, terrifying seconds. Then he leaned his head on his hands, which were still gripping the steering wheel, and let his pulse return to normal. He sat like that for a couple of minutes. Then he drove on toward Fjällbacka, but it took a mile or two at a creeping pace before he dared speed up.

When he drove up the sanded hill in Sälvik toward Erica's house, he was five minutes late. He parked the car behind hers in the driveway and grabbed the bottle of wine he had brought as a gift. A deep breath and a last check of his hair in the rearview mirror and he was ready.

The pile of clothes on Erica's bed was about as big as Patrik's, maybe even a bit bigger. Her wardrobe was beginning to look empty, and hangers were rattling on the rod. She gave a deep sigh. Nothing fit quite right. The extra weight that had sneaked up on her in the past week meant that no garment sat the way she would have liked. Weighing herself that morning was something she still cursed and regretted bitterly. Erica gave herself a critical look in the full-length mirror.

The first dilemma had arisen after her shower when, like her favorite literary heroine, Bridget Jones, she was faced with the decision of which panties to choose. Should she wear a beautiful, lace-trimmed thong, for the slim eventuality that she and Patrik ended up in bed? Or should she put on the substantial and terribly ugly panties with the extra support for tummy and backside, which would increase her chances that they might end up in bed at all? A hard choice, but considering the extent of her belly's bulge she decided after much deliberation on the support variety. Over them she would wear pantyhose with a tummy-flattening panel. In other words, the heavy artillery.

She glanced at the clock and realized that it was time to decide. After another look at the pile on the bed she pulled out from the bottom the first outfit she had tried on. Black was slimming, and the classic, knee-length dress in a Jackie Kennedy style was flattering to the figure. A pair of pearl earrings and her wristwatch would be her only jewelry, and she let her hair fall loosely over her shoulders. She looked at her profile again in the mirror and held in her stomach as a test. All right—with the combined help of support panties, pantyhose, and slightly restricted breathing she looked downright acceptable. The extra pounds were not altogether a bad thing, she had to admit. She would have preferred to do without the ones that ended up on her belly, but the ones distributed to her breasts made a not entirely uneven cleavage stand out in her décolletage. With a little help from a padded push-up bra, of course, but such aids were virtually universal nowadays. And the bra she was wearing was of the very latest technology, with gel in the cups, which gave her bust a true-to-life movement. Splendid testimony to the advancement of science in the service of humanity.

Trying on all those clothes along with the emotional stress had made her sweat, and with a deep sigh she washed under her arms again. Her makeup took almost twenty minutes to perfect. By the time she was ready, she realized all the primping had taken a bit too long and that she ought to have started cooking long ago. She quickly tidied up the bedroom. It would have taken far too much time to hang up all the clothes, so she simply picked up the whole pile, dumped it on the floor of the wardrobe and shut the door. Just in case, she made the bed and looked around the room to make sure that no unused panties lay about the floor. A pair of dirty everyday panties from Sloggi could dampen any man's desire.

Out of breath she rushed down to the kitchen. All the stress made her feel utterly at a loss. She didn't have any idea where to start.

Erica forced herself to stand still and take a deep breath. There were two recipes lying on the table in front of her, and she tried to plan the time needed for each of them. She was no master chef, but a fairly decent cook, and she had found the recipes after digging through back issues of *Elle Gourmet*. The appetizer would be potato pancakes with crème fraîche, lumpfish caviar, and finely chopped red onions. For the entree she had planned fillet of pork baked in puff pastry with a port wine sauce and mashed potatoes, and for dessert Gino with vanilla ice cream. Thankfully she'd already prepared it that afternoon, so she could cross that off her list. She decided to start by putting the potatoes on to boil. Then she would grate raw potatoes for the appetizer.

She concentrated on her work for an hour and a half and jumped when the doorbell rang. The time had gone a little too fast, and she hoped that Patrik wasn't roaring hungry since the food would take a while before it was ready.

Erica was halfway to the door when she noticed that she still had her apron on. The bell rang again as she struggled to undo the granny knot she had tied at her back. She finally got it undone, pulled the apron over her head, and tossed it on a chair in the hall. She ran her hand over her hair, reminded herself to hold in her stomach, and took a deep breath before she opened the door with a smile.

"Hi, Patrik. Welcome! Come in."

They hugged briefly and Patrik handed her a bottle of wine wrapped in aluminum foil.

"Oh, thank you, how nice!"

"Yes, they recommended this one at the State Liquor Store. Chilean wine. Robust and round with a trace of red berries and a hint of chocolate, supposedly. I'm no wine connoisseur, but they usually know what they're talking about."

"I'm sure it's excellent." Erica gave a warm laugh and put down the bottle on the old hall bureau for a moment so she could help Patrik off with his jacket.

"Come in. I hope you're not starving. As usual, my planning was much too optimistic, so it'll be a while before dinner is ready."

"No problem, I'm fine."

Patrik followed Erica into the kitchen with the wine.

"Can I help with anything?"

"Yes, you can take a corkscrew from the top drawer and open a bottle of wine for us. Perhaps we could start by tasting the wine you brought?"

He obeyed willingly. Erica set two large wineglasses for them on the worktop and then began stirring pots and checking the progress of what was in the oven. The fillet of pork had a good way to go, and when she poked the potatoes they were still only half cooked. Patrik handed her one of the wineglasses, now full of deep-red wine. She swirled the glass lightly to release the wine's aroma, stuck her nose deep into the glass, and then inhaled with her mouth closed. The warm oak fragrance of the wine was sucked in through her nostrils and seemed to propagate all the way down to her toes. Delightful. She tasted it cautiously, letting the wine roll around as she sucked in a little air through her mouth. The taste was just as pleasant as the aroma, and she could tell that Patrik had spent a significant sum on this bottle.

Patrik gave her an expectant look.

"Fantastic!"

"Yes, I realized last time that you knew about these things. Unfortunately I couldn't tell the difference between a wine in a box for fifty kronor and a wine that cost thousands."

"Sure you could. But it's all a matter of habit as well. And you have to take the time to really taste a wine instead of guzzling it down."

Shamefaced, Patrik looked at the glass of wine he had in his hand. A third of it was already gone. He carefully tried to imitate Erica's method of tasting the wine when she turned her back to check something on the stove. It did seem to taste like a whole new wine. He let a sip of wine roll around in his mouth the same way he had seen Erica do it, and suddenly distinctly different tastes appeared. He even thought he could sense a faint hint of chocolate, dark chocolate, and a rather strong taste of red berries, red grapes perhaps, mixed with a little strawberry. Incredible.

"How's it going with the investigation?" Erica made an effort to ask the question casually, but she waited anxiously for the reply.

"I think we're back at square one, so to speak. Anders has an alibi for the time of the murder, and we don't have a lot else to go on right now. Unfortunately we may have made a classic mistake. We allowed ourselves to feel too certain that we had the right person and stopped investigating other possibilities. Although I have to agree with the superintendent that Anders is perfect in the role of Alex's killer. A drunk who for some inexplicable reason is having a sexual relationship with a woman who, according to all the rules, should be far, far out of reach of a wino like Anders. A crime of jealousy with the inevitable outcome, when his improbable luck finally runs out. His fingerprints are all over the body and in the bathroom. We even found his footprint in the pool of blood on the floor."

"But isn't that proof enough?"

Patrik swirled his wine and looked thoughtfully down into the red eddies that formed in the glass.

"If he hadn't had an alibi it might have been enough. But now he does have one for what we think is the probable time of the murder. And as I said before, it doesn't prove anything except that he was in the bathroom *after* the murder. A small but important difference if we want an indictment that will hold up."

The aroma spreading through the kitchen was wonderful. Erica took the potato pancakes she had sautéed a while ago out of the fridge and put them in the oven to warm up. She set out two appetizer plates, opened the refrigerator again and took out a container of crème fraîche and a jar of lumpfish caviar. The onions were chopped and ready in a bowl on the worktop. She was intensely aware of how close Patrik was standing.

"So, Erica, have you heard anything more about the house?"

"Yes, unfortunately. The real estate agent rang yesterday and proposed that we show the house during the Easter holiday. He said that Anna and Lucas apparently thought that was a brilliant idea."

"It's still a couple of months until Easter. A lot can happen before that."

"Yes, I can always hope that Lucas has a heart attack or something. No, pardon me, I didn't say that. It's just that it makes me so mad!" She closed the oven door a bit too hard.

"Oi, be kind to the appliances."

"I'm probably just going to have to get used to the fact and start planning what to do with all the money I make from the sale. Although I have to admit, I always thought I'd feel happier if I became a millionaire."

"You don't have to worry about becoming a millionaire. With the taxes in this country, you'll probably have to spend the majority of your profit on financing terrible schools and ever worse health care. Not to mention the incredibly, fantastically, totally underpaid police force. We'll probably eat into a good share of your fortune, you'll see."

She couldn't help laughing. "Well, that would be

wonderful. Then I won't have to worry about whether to buy a mink or a blue fox coat. Patrik, believe it or not, the appetizer is ready now."

She took a plate in each hand and led Patrik into the dining room. She had pondered whether they should sit in the kitchen or in the dining room, and she finally decided on the dining room with its lovely wooden drop-leaf table, which looked even lovelier by candle-light. And she hadn't skimped on the candles. Nothing was more flattering to a woman's appearance than candles, she'd read somewhere.

The table was set with silverware and linen servi-ettes, as well as Rörstrand plates for the entree. It was her mother's finest, the white Rörstrand china with the blue trim. She remembered how careful her mother had always been with those plates. They were only taken out on very special occasions. Which did not include the children's birthdays or anything else that had to do with them, Erica thought bitterly. The ordi-nary china at the kitchen table was good enough for them. But when the pastor and his wife, or the vicar, or the deacon came to dinner, then there was no end to all the fuss. Erica forced herself back to the present and set the appetizer plates across from each other on the table.

"It looks delicious." Patrik sliced off a piece of potato pancake, added a healthy dollop of onions, crème fraîche and caviar on his fork, and managed to lift it halfway to his mouth before he noticed that Erica was sitting there with her wineglass raised along with one eyebrow. Shamefaced, he put down the fork and switched to his wineglass.

"*Skål* and welcome."

"*Skål.*"

Erica smiled at his faux pas. It was refreshing in comparison with the men she'd dated in Stockholm, who were all so well brought up and knowledgeable about etiquette that they could have been clones. Compared to them Patrik felt like the real deal, and as far as she was concerned he could eat with his fingers if he wanted to; it wouldn't bother her. Besides, he looked terribly cute when he blushed.

"I had an unexpected visitor today."

"Oh? Who was that?"

"Julia."

Patrik gave Erica a surprised look. She was pleased to see that he seemed to have a hard time tearing himself away from the food.

"I had no idea you knew each other," he said.

"We don't, really. Alex's funeral was actually the first time we met. But this morning she was standing at my door."

"What did she want?"

Patrik scraped his plate clean so eagerly that it looked like he was trying to scrape the color off the porcelain.

"She asked me to show her pictures from when Alex and I were kids. The family apparently doesn't have many photographs, according to Julia, and she took a chance that I might have more. Which I do. Then she asked me a lot of questions about when we were kids and things like that. The people I've talked to said that the sisters weren't very close, which is not so odd considering the age difference, and now she wants to find out more about Alex. Get to know her. Anyway, that's the impression I got. Have you met Julia, by the way?"

"No, I haven't yet. But from what I heard they aren't, or weren't, very similar," said Patrik.

"No, God no. They're more like complete opposites, at least in appearance. They both seem to be introverts, even though Julia has a sullenness that I don't think Alex had. Alex seemed more, how should I put it . . . indifferent, based on what I heard from the people I talked to. If anything, Julia seems angry. Or maybe even furious. I get the impression that there's rage bubbling and fizzing just below the surface. Rather volcanic. A dormant volcano. Does that sound stupid?"

"No, I don't think so. I imagine that as an author you have to have a feeling for people. A knowledge of human nature."

"Oh, don't call me an author. I don't think I've earned that title yet."

"Four books published and you don't consider yourself an author?"

Patrik looked downright uncomprehending and Erica tried to explain what she meant.

"Well, four biographies, working on the fifth. I don't mean to denigrate it, but for me an author is someone who writes something from her own heart and her own brain, and doesn't just describe someone else's life. The day I write something that comes from me, then I can call myself an author."

She was suddenly struck by the fact that this wasn't the whole truth. Looked at superficially, according to that definition there was no difference between the biographies she'd written about historical personalities and the book that she was writing about Alex. It was also about another person's life. And yet somehow it *was* different. First, Alex's life had run at a tangent to her own in a quite obvious way, and second, she could express some of her own views in this book. Within the framework of actual events she could even steer the book's soul. But she couldn't explain that to Patrik. Nobody could know that she was writing a book about Alex.

"So Julia came here and asked a bunch of questions about Alex. Did you have a chance to ask her about Nelly Lorentz?"

Erica waged an intense battle with herself and finally decided that she couldn't in good conscience withhold this information from Patrik. Maybe he'd be able to draw conclusions from it that she couldn't. It was the one small but vital piece of the puzzle she had chosen not to reveal when she went to dinner at his place. But since she hadn't gotten much further with it, she saw no reason to keep quiet any longer. But first she had to serve the entree.

She bent over to take his plate, making sure to lean forward a bit more than usual. She intended to make the most of the trump cards she had. Judging by Patrik's face she had just shown herself to be holding three aces. So far her Wonderbra had proved to be worth the 500 kronor she had invested, even though it had left a sizable dent in her pocketbook.

"Let me get that." Patrik took the plates from her and followed her into the kitchen. She drained the water from the potatoes and put him to work mashing them. She reheated the gravy one last time and tasted it. A splash of port and a generous dollop of butter and it was ready to be served. No light cream in this dish! Then all that was left was to take the baked pork fillet out of the oven and slice it. It looked perfect. Light pink in the middle, but without the red juice that signaled the meat was underdone. For the vegetable dish she had selected steamed sugar peas, which she put in the same Rörstrand bowl with the mashed potatoes. They both helped carry in the food. She let Patrik serve himself before she dropped the bomb.

"Julia is the sole heir to Nelly Lorentz's fortune."

Patrik was just taking a sip of wine and apparently it went down the wrong way, because he coughed and grabbed his chest. Tears sprang to his eyes from the discomfort.

"Excuse me, what did you say?" Patrik asked in a strained voice.

"I said that Julia is the sole heir to Nelly's fortune. It's in Nelly's will," Erica said calmly, pouring Patrik some water to calm his cough.

"Do I dare ask how you know this?"

"Because I snooped in Nelly's wastebasket when she invited me over for tea."

Patrik had another coughing fit and gave Erica an incredulous look. As he drained his entire water glass in one gulp, Erica went on.

"There was a copy of her will in the wastebasket. It clearly and explicitly stated that Julia Carlgren would inherit Nelly Lorentz's fortune. Yes, Jan gets a share, but Julia gets all the rest."

"Does Jan know this?"

"I have no idea. But I would guess he does—no, he probably *doesn't* know."

Erica continued as she ate.

"I actually asked Julia when she was here how she happened to know Nelly Lorentz so well. Naturally I got a nonsense answer. Something about her having a summer job at the cannery for a couple of years. I don't doubt that the part about her working there is true, but she left out the rest of the truth. It was quite obviously a subject that she really didn't want to talk about."

Patrik looked pensive. "Do you realize that makes two very ill-matched pairs in this story? I would even call them improbable pairs. Alex and Anders, and Julia and Nelly. What is the lowest common denominator? If we find the link I think we'll find the solution to everything."

"Alex. Isn't Alex the lowest common denominator?"

"No," said Patrik, "I think that's a little too simple. It's something else. Something we can't see, or that we don't understand."

He waved his fork excitedly. "And then we have Nils Lorentz. Or to be more precise, his disappearance. You were living in Fjällbacka then, what do you remember about it?"

"I wasn't very old then, and nobody tells a kid anything. But what I do remember is that it was all very hush-hush."

"Hush-hush?"

"Yes, you know, conversations that stopped when I came into the room. Grown-ups talking in low voices. 'Shh, don't let the children hear' and comments like that. In other words all I know is that there was a lot of talk at the time about Nils's disappearance. But I was too young. I wasn't told anything."

"Hmm, I'm going to have to dig a little deeper into this. It's going on my list of things to do tomorrow.

But right now I'm having dinner with a woman who's not only beautiful but also a fantastically good cook. A *skål* to the hostess."

He raised his glass and Erica felt all warm inside from the compliment. Not so much because of what he said about the meal but because he'd called her beautiful. Imagine how much easier everything would be if we could read each other's minds, she thought. This whole charade would be unnecessary. Instead she sat here hoping that he would give her the slightest little hint that he was interested. It was fine to throw yourself out there and take a chance when you were a teenager, but with the years it felt as if her heart had grown less and less elastic. The efforts required were greater and the damage to one's self-confidence bigger each time.

After Patrik had helped himself to three more servings and they had long since stopped talking about sudden death and switched to discussing dreams, life, and various world problems, they moved to the veranda to give their stomachs a break before dessert. They sat at opposite ends of the sofa and sipped their wine. Bottle number two was almost empty, and both of them could feel the effect. Their limbs were heavy and warm and their heads felt as if they were wrapped in lovely soft cotton. The night outside the windows was pitch black with not a single star to light up the sky. The dense darkness outside made them feel as though they were wrapped in a big cocoon, completing the illusion that they were the only people on earth. Erica couldn't recall ever feeling so content, so at home in her own existence. She made a sweeping gesture with the hand holding her wineglass, managing to encompass not only the whole veranda but the whole house.

"Can you believe that Anna would want to sell all this? It's not just that this is the most beautiful house in the whole world, there's history in these walls. And I don't mean only Anna's and my history, but the histories of those who lived here before us. Did you know that a sea captain had this house built for his family in 1889? Captain Wilhelm Jansson. The story is actually very sad, like so many other stories in this town. He built the house for himself and his young wife, Ida. They had five children in five years, but during the sixth childbirth Ida died. In those days single fathers were unheard of, so Captain Jansson's unmarried older sister moved in and took charge of the children while he sailed the Seven Seas. His sister Hilda was not the best choice for foster mother. She was the most religious woman for several counties around, and that's saying a lot considering how religious everyone was here. The children could hardly move without being accused of sinning, and the beatings they received from Hilda were administered with a God-fearing and stern hand. Today she would probably be called a sadist, but in those days it was totally acceptable to hide such propensities under the guise of religion.

"Captain Jansson wasn't home often enough to see how badly the children were faring, even though he must have had his suspicions. But like most men he considered child-rearing to be women's work, and he felt that he was fulfilling his fatherly duties by seeing to it that they had a roof over their heads and food on the table. Until he came home one day, and discovered that the youngest girl, Märta, had gone for a week with a broken arm. Then Hilda was given the boot and the captain, who was a man of action, searched among the unmarried women of the area for a suitable new foster mother for his children. He made a good choice. Within two months he had married a solid daughter of peasant stock, Lina Månsdotter, and she took the children to her heart as if they were her own. She and the captain also had seven more together, so it must have been awfully crowded here. If you look carefully you can see traces of those kids. Little nicks and dents and worn spots. All over the house."

"So how did your father come to buy the house?"

"Over the years the Jansson siblings were scattered with the wind. Captain Jansson and his Lina, who had grown very fond of each other, passed away. The only one left in the house was the eldest son, Allan. He never married and when he grew old he couldn't keep up the house by himself, so he decided to sell. Papa had just married Mama, and they were looking for a home. Papa told us that he fell in love with the house on the spot. He didn't hesitate for a second.

"When Allan sold the house to Papa, he also passed on the story to him. The history of the house and his own family. It was important to him, he said, that Papa knew whose feet had worn the old wooden floors. He also left some documents behind. Letters that Captain Jansson had sent from every corner of the world, first to his wife Ida, then to Lina. He also left the horsewhip that Hilda had used to punish the children. It still hangs down in the cellar. Anna and I used to go down there and touch it sometimes when we were small. We had heard the story about Hilda, and we used to try to imagine how the rough straws of the whip would feel on our bare skin. We felt sorry for the little children who were treated so badly."

Erica looked at Patrik. She went on, "Now you understand why my heart breaks at the thought of selling this house. If we sell this house we'll never ever get it back again. It's irrevocable. It makes me sick to think that some rich Stockholmer would stomp in here and start sanding the floors and put up new wallpaper with little shells on it, not to mention the panoramic window that would go up here in the veranda faster than I can say 'tasteless.' Who would care about preserving the pencil marks that are left on the inside of the pantry doors, where Lina each year marked how tall the children had grown? Who would care about reading the letters in which Captain Jansson tried to describe how it looked in the South Seas for his two wives who had hardly been out of the parish? Their history would be erased and then this house would be only . . . a house. Any old house. Charming, but without a soul."

She could hear that she was babbling, but for some reason it was important to her that Patrik understood. She looked at him. He was watching her intently and she flushed under his gaze. Something happened. An instant of absolute understanding, and before she knew what was happening Patrik was sitting next to her, and after a second of hesitation he pressed his lips to hers. At first she only sensed the taste of wine on both their lips, but then she sensed the taste of Patrik. She cautiously opened her mouth and felt the tip of his tongue seeking hers. Her whole body felt electric.

After a while it became unbearable, and Erica got up, took him by the hand, and without a word led him up to the bedroom. They lay down on the bed and kissed and caressed each other. After a while Patrik gave her a questioning look and then began unbuttoning the back of her dress. She gave her silent assent by starting to unbutton his shirt. She realized at once that the undergarments she'd chosen were not the ones she wanted to show to Patrik the first time. God only knew that the pantyhose she had on weren't the world's sexiest undergarment. The question was how she could get out of them and the support panties without Patrik seeing them. Erica sat up abruptly.

"Excuse me, I just have to go to the toilet."

She rushed to the bathroom and looked around feverishly. She was in luck. There was a pile of clean wash in the laundry basket that she hadn't had time to put away. She laboriously wriggled out of the tight pantyhose and put them and the old-lady pants in the laundry basket. Then she pulled on a pair of thin white lace panties that would go well with her bra. She pulled her dress down over her backside and carefully checked herself in the mirror. Her hair was disheveled and curly and her eyes had a feverish look. Her mouth was redder than normal and slightly swollen from all the kissing. She actually looked rather sexy, she thought. Although without the support panties her belly didn't look as flat as she liked. She sucked it in and instead thrust out her bust as she went in to Patrik, who was still lying on the bed just as she had left him.

Their clothes began disappearing, with more and more of them landing in a pile on the floor. The first time wasn't as fantastic as it always is in romance novels; it was more of a mixture of strong feelings and embarrassing awareness. At the same time that their bodies reacted explosively to each other's touch, they were acutely aware of their nakedness, conscious of little imperfections, worried that embarrassing sounds might arise. They were clumsy and unsure of what the other person might like and dislike. Not sure enough of each other yet that they dared put their thoughts into words. Instead they used small guttural sounds to indicate what worked and what might need to be adjusted. But the second time it was better. The third time it was quite acceptable. The fourth time was very good and the fifth time was fantastic. They fell asleep, curved around each other like spoons. The last thing Erica noticed before she fell asleep was Patrik's arm safely around her breast and his fingers laced in hers. She fell asleep with a smile on her lips.

Patrik's head was splitting into bits. His mouth was so dry that his tongue stuck to the roof of his mouth, but at some time there must have been saliva in it, because against his cheek he felt a wet spot of drool on the pillow. It felt like someone was holding down his eyelids and fighting his attempts to open his eyes. After a couple of strenuous attempts he finally got them open.

He saw a vision before him. Erica was lying on her side, turned toward him, with her blond hair curled around her face. She seemed to be dreaming, because her eyelashes were fluttering and her eyelids were twitching. Patrik thought he could lie here like this and look at her forever, without ever tiring of what he saw. His whole life if need be. Erica gave a start in her sleep but returned quickly to her steady breathing. It was true that this was like riding a bike. And by that he didn't mean only the sex act, but also the feeling of loving a woman. During the dark, gloomy days and the nights he had thought it impossible that he would ever feel like this again. Now it felt impossible *not* to feel like this.

Erica stirred restlessly and he saw that she was about to resurface. She too struggled to get her eyelids open. But when she did, he was astonished all over again at how blue her eyes were.

"Good morning, sleepyhead."

"Good morning."

The smile that spread across her face made him feel like a millionaire.

"Did you sleep well?" Erica said.

Patrik looked at the alarm clock's glowing numerals. "Yes, the two hours I slept were wonderful. Although the waking hours before that were probably even more wonderful."

Erica merely smiled in reply.

Patrik suspected that his breath smelled like a viper's, but he still couldn't resist leaning forward and kissing her. The kiss became deeper and an hour raced by. Afterward Erica lay on his left arm drawing circles with her finger on his chest. She looked up at him.

"Did you think when you came over that we'd end up in bed?"

He thought about it a moment before he answered, and put his right hand behind his head while he was thinking.

"No-o-o, I can't say that I thought it would happen. But I hoped it would."

"Me too. Hoped, I mean, not thought."

Patrik deliberated for a moment about how bold he should be, but with Erica in his arms he felt he could dare anything.

"The difference is that you started hoping quite

recently, didn't you? Do you know how long I've been hoping this would happen?"

She gave him a puzzled look. "No, how long?"

Patrik paused for effect. "As long as I can remember. I've been in love with you as long as I can remember." Now that he'd said it out loud, he heard how true it sounded.

Erica stared at him wide-eyed. "You're kidding! And here I've gone around worrying whether you were even the slightest bit interested in me! And now you tell me that you were mine for the taking."

Her tone was lighthearted, but he saw that she was a bit shaken by what he'd said.

"Well, it's not as if I've been celibate or living in an emotional desert my whole life. Of course I've been in love with other women too, Karin for example. But you've always been special. I always felt something here every time I saw you." He pressed his hand to a spot above his heart. Erica took his hand, kissed it, and put it against her cheek. That gesture told him everything.

They spent the morning getting to know each other. When Erica asked Patrik how he liked to spend his free time, his reply elicited a frustrated groan.

"No-o-o-o-o! Not another sports fan! Why oh why can't I find a guy who's smart enough to realize that it's an entirely normal pastime to chase a ball across a lawn—if you're five! Or at least a guy who might question what use it is to humanity if someone can jump seven feet in the air over a crossbar."

"Eight feet plus."

"What do you mean, eight feet plus?" said Erica in a voice that showed she wouldn't be very interested in the answer.

"The guy who jumps the highest in the world, Soto-mayor, jumps eight feet and one inch. Women jump around seven feet."

"Yeah, yeah, whatever." She gave him a suspicious look. "Do you get the Eurosport channel?"

"Yep."

"Canal+, not for the films but for the sports?"

"Yep."

"TV1000, same reason?"

"Yep. Although to be accurate, I get TV1000 for another reason besides sports."

Erica gave him a playful swat on the chest. "Have I forgotten anything?"

"Yep, TV3 has a lot of sports."

"My sport-fool radar is really well-developed, I have to say. I spent an incredibly boring evening at my friend Dan's house last week, watching Olympic hockey. I just don't understand how anyone can think it's interesting to see guys in gigantic padding chase around after a little black thingamabob."

"In any case it's a lot more fun and more productive than spending a whole day running from one clothing boutique to another."

In reply to this blatant attack on her greatest vice in life, Erica wrinkled her nose and made a face at Patrik. Then she saw how his eyes suddenly took on a glazed look.

"Damn." He sat up straight in bed.

"Pardon me?"

"Damn, shit, bloody hell."

Erica looked at him wide-eyed.

"How the hell could I miss something like that?" He struck his forehead several times with his hand.

"Hello, Earth to Patrik! Would you please tell me what you're talking about?"

Erica waved her hands in front of him. Patrik lost his focus for a moment when he saw how the gesture made her naked breasts jiggle. Then he hopped briskly out of bed, naked as a newborn, and rushed downstairs. He came back up with a couple of newspapers in his hand, sat down on the bed, and started leafing through them frantically. By this time Erica had given up trying to get any answers and merely watched him with interest.

"Aha!" Patrik shouted in triumph. "What luck that you didn't toss your old TV listings."

He waved the paper in front of Erica. "Sweden vs. Canada!"

Still silent, Erica made do with raising a very puzzled eyebrow.

Impatient, Patrik tried to explain. "Sweden beat Canada in an Olympic match. On Friday, January twenty-second. On TV4."

She still looked at him without expression. Patrik sighed.

"All ordinary programs were canceled because of the match. Anders couldn't have come home at the same time as *Separate Worlds* that Friday, because it was canceled. Do you understand?"

Slowly, it dawned on Erica what he was saying. Anders no longer had an alibi. Even though it was tenuous, the police would still have a hard time getting past it. Now they could bring Anders in again, based on the evidence they already had. Patrik nodded with satisfaction when he saw that Erica understood.

"But you don't think that Anders is the killer, do you?" said Erica.

"No, of course not. But for one thing, sometimes I can be wrong, even though I know you have a hard time believing that." He winked at her. "And for another thing, if I'm not mistaken, I'll bet that Anders knows considerably more than he's told us. Now we have a chance to press him a lot harder."

Patrik began hunting around the bedroom for his clothes. They were strewn here and there, but most alarming was that he discovered he still had his socks on. He quickly pulled on his trousers and hoped that in the heat of passion Erica hadn't noticed the socks. It was hard to look like a sex god with white tube socks embroidered with "Tanumshede IF."

Suddenly it felt like there was no time to lose, and he dressed with fumbling fingers. On his first attempt to button his shirt he got it wrong, and he swore when he had to undo all the buttons and start over. Patrik realized all at once how his rash behavior must look, and he sat down on the edge of the bed, took Erica's hands in his, and gazed steadily into her eyes.

"I'm sorry to rush off like this, but I have to. I just want you to know that this has been the most wonderful night of my life and I can hardly wait until the next time we see each other. Do you want to see me again?"

What they had shared still felt fragile and delicate, and he held his breath waiting for her reply. She nodded.

"Then I can come back here when I finish work?"

Erica nodded again. He leaned forward and kissed her.

When he left she was sitting on the bed with her knees pulled up and the covers wrapped loosely around her body. The sun was shining in through the little round window, creating the illusion of a halo around her blonde head. It was the most beautiful thing he'd ever seen.

The snow was wet and stubbornly seeped through Bengt Larsson's thin loafers. His shoes were more suited to summer weather, but alcohol was an effective way to deaden the cold. And faced with the choice between buying a pair of winter shoes or a whole liter of schnapps, the decision was easy.

The air was so clear and clean and the light so delicate on this early Wednesday morning that Bengt had a feeling in his breast that he hadn't had in a long time. It was alarmingly like a sense of peace, and he wondered what it was about a normal Wednesday morning that could call forth such a peculiar sensation. He stopped and breathed in the morning air with his eyes closed. Imagine if his life could be full of mornings like this.

It was clear to him when he had come to the fork in the road. He knew precisely what day his life had taken its unhappy turn. He could even tell you what time it was. Actually he'd had all the usual excuses. There was no abuse to blame it on. No poverty, hunger, or emotional deficiencies either. The only thing he had to blame was his own stupidity and an excessive faith in himself. Naturally there was a girl involved too.

He was seventeen years old, and back then there was nothing he did that didn't involve a girl. But this girl was special. Maud, with her exuberant blondeness and feigned modesty, who played on his ego like a well-tuned violin. "Dear Bengt, I just have to have . . ." "Dear Bengt, couldn't you get me a . . ." She had held the leash and he had obediently let himself be led by the nose. Nothing was ever enough for her. He saved all the money he earned and bought her fine clothes, perfumes, everything she wanted. But as soon as she got whatever it was she'd been so eagerly begging for, she tossed it aside and begged for something else, which was the only thing that could make her happy.

Maud had been like a fever in his blood. Without noticing it the wheels had gradually begun to turn faster and faster until he no longer knew what was up or down. When he turned eighteen, Maud had decided that she wanted to ride around with him in no less than a Cadillac convertible. It cost more than he made in a whole year, and he lay awake night after night as he racked his brain, trying to figure out how to get the money. While he was going through this agony Maud would pout and hint in more and more obvious terms that if he didn't get the car, there were certainly other guys who could treat her the way she deserved to be treated. Then jealousy was added to the torment of those sleepless, anxious nights, and finally he couldn't stand it any longer.

On September 10, 1954, at precisely two o'clock in the afternoon, he went into the bank in Tanumshede, armed with an old army pistol his father had kept at home for years, and wearing a nylon stocking over his head. Nothing had gone right. The bank tellers had tossed banknotes into the bag he brought with him, but not nearly as much as he had hoped. Then one of the customers, the father of a classmate of his, recognized Bengt despite the nylon stocking. Within an hour the police were at his parents' apartment and found the bag of money under the bed in his room. Bengt never forgot the expression on his mother's face. She had been dead now for many years, but her eyes still haunted him whenever the alcoholic gloom kicked in.

Three years in prison had killed all hope of a future. When he got out Maud was long gone. He didn't know where, and he didn't care. All his old friends had gone on to secure jobs and family life and didn't want anything to do with him. His father had been killed in an accident while Bengt was inside, so he moved in with his mother. With cap in hand he tried to find work, but was met by rejection everywhere he went. No one wanted to hire him. What finally drove him to seek his future in the bottom of a bottle were all the looks that kept following him.

For someone who had grown up in the close-knit confines of a small town where everyone says hello to each other on the street, the feeling of being frozen out was just as painful as physical torture. He had thought about moving away from Fjällbacka, but where would he go? It was easier to stay and let himself sink into a blissful alcoholic torpor.

He and Anders had found each other at once. Two poor fucks, they used to say, laughing bitterly. Bengt harbored an almost fatherly affection for Anders and felt greater sorrow over his fate than over his own. He often wished that he could have done something to turn Anders's life in a different direction. But because he also knew the seductive siren song of alcohol, he knew how impossible it was to tear yourself away from the demanding lover that booze had become over the years. She demanded everything and gave nothing back. All he and Anders could do was give each other a little consolation and companionship.

The path up to the front door of Anders's building had been carefully sanded. So Bengt didn't have to tread cautiously because of the bottle in his inside pocket, as he had done many times during the hard winter just past, when the ice lay shiny and slick all the way to the stairs.

The two flights up to Anders's apartment were always a challenge. There was no lift. Several times he had to stop to catch his breath, and twice he made sure to take a bracing swig from the bottle in his inside pocket. When he finally stood outside the door to Anders's apartment he was panting hard. He leaned against the doorjamb for a moment before he opened the door, which he knew Anders never locked.

It was quiet in the apartment. Maybe Anders wasn't home. If he was sleeping it off, his deep breathing and snuffling snores could usually be heard all the way out in the hall. Bengt looked in the kitchen. Nobody there, except for the normal colonies of bacteria. The bathroom door stood wide open, and there too it was empty. When he turned the corner he had a horrible feeling in the pit of his stomach. The sight in the living room made Bengt stop short. The bottle he was holding in his hand fell to the floor with a heavy clunk, but it didn't break.

The first thing he saw was the feet dangling freely a bit above the floor. The naked feet swung slightly, swaying back and forth. Anders had trousers on but nothing on his upper body. His head hung at an odd angle. His face was swollen and discolored, and his tongue looked too big for his mouth as it stuck out between his lips. It was the saddest sight Bengt had ever seen. He turned and quietly left the apartment, but not before he picked up the bottle from the floor. He tried to find something inside himself to grab hold of, but found only emptiness. Instead he grasped at the only lifeline he knew. He sat down on the threshold of Anders's apartment, put the bottle to his mouth, and cried.

It was doubtful whether he had a legal blood alcohol content, but Patrik wasn't worrying about that right now. He drove a little slower than usual for safety's sake, but since he was dialing numbers on his mobile and talking on the phone, it was debatable how much help that was to traffic safety.

His first call was to TV4, which confirmed that *Separate Worlds* had been canceled on Friday the twenty-second because of the hockey match. Then he rang Mellberg, who not unexpectedly was overjoyed to hear the news. He demanded that Anders immediately be brought back in. With his third call, Patrik got the backup he requested and drove straight toward the residential complex where Anders lived. Jenny Rosén must have simply mixed up the days. Not an uncommon occurrence among witnesses.

Despite his excitement at a possible break in the case, Patrik couldn't really focus on the task. His thoughts kept returning to Erica and the night they had just spent together. He caught himself grinning like a fool from ear to ear, and his hands involuntarily drummed little rhythms on the steering wheel. He turned on the radio to an oldies station and got Aretha Franklin with "Respect." The upbeat Atlantic sound fit his mood perfectly and he turned up the volume. At the refrain he sang along at the top of his lungs and danced as best he could from a sitting position. He thought he sounded damned good, at least until the radio cut out and he heard only his own voice roaring "R-E-S-P-E-C-T." His eardrums reverberated, but not in a good way.

The entire past night felt like an intoxicated dream, and it wasn't only because of the amount of wine they had drunk. It was as though a veil or hazy curtain of emotion, love, and sex had settled over those night-time hours.

He was reluctantly forced to put aside his thoughts of yesterday as he turned into the lot at the residential complex. The backup patrol cars had arrived unusually fast. They must have been in the vicinity. He saw two cars with blue lights flashing and frowned slightly. Typical that they would misconstrue the instructions. He'd asked for *one* car, not two. As he approached he saw that there was an ambulance behind the police cars. Something wasn't right.

He recognized Lena, the blonde policewoman from Uddevalla, and went over to her. She was talking on a mobile phone, but as he approached she signed off. He heard "Bye" and she stuffed the phone into a holder she wore on her belt.

"Hi, Patrik."

"Hi, Lena. What's going on?"

"One of the winos found Anders Nilsson hanged in his apartment." She nodded in the direction of the main door. Patrik got an ice-cold feeling in his stomach.

"You haven't touched anything?"

"No, what do you think we are? I just talked to dispatch in Uddevalla and they're sending over a team to examine the crime scene. We also talked to Mellberg so I assumed you came because he rang you."

"No, I was on the way over here anyway to bring Anders in for more questioning."

"But I heard he had an alibi?"

"Yes, that's what we thought, but it just fell apart so we were going to bring him back in."

"Well, this is fucking bad luck then. What the hell do you think it means? I mean, the probability that there would suddenly be two murderers here in Fjällbacka must be almost zero. He must have been killed by the same person who killed Alex Wijkner. Do you have any other suspects besides Anders?"

Patrik pulled himself together. It was true that this changed everything, but he still wasn't ready to draw the same conclusions as Lena, that Anders had been killed by the same person who murdered Alex. Of course it was almost statistically impossible. There hadn't been a murder here in decades, and suddenly two separate killers were on the loose. But he wasn't prepared to rule out the impossible either.

"Well, let's go up so I can have a look. Then you can tell me what you've found out so far. How did the call come in, for instance?"

Lena led the way, entering the stairwell ahead of him.

"Well, as I said it was one of Anders's alky pals who found him, Bengt Larsson. He came over this morning so they could start drinking and get a head start on the day. He usually just walks right in, and that's what he did today. When he entered the apartment he found

Anders hanging by a rope tied to the hook for the ceiling lamp in the living room."

"Did he call it in right away?"

"Actually no. He sat on the threshold of the apartment and drowned his sorrows in a bottle of Explorer vodka. But then a neighbor happened to come out of his apartment and in passing asked Bengt how things were going. That's when he blurted out what he had seen. Then the neighbor rang us. Bengt Larsson is too drunk to be questioned in more detail, so I just sent him off to your drunk tank."

Patrik silently wondered why Mellberg hadn't rung to tell him about all the action, but resigned himself to the fact that the ways of the superintendent were most often utterly inscrutable.

Patrik took the stairs two at a time and passed Lena. When they reached the second floor the door was wide open and he saw people moving about inside the apartment. Jenny was standing in the doorway to her apartment with Max in her arms. When Patrik went over to them, Max waved his chubby little hands in delight and showed his gap-toothed smile.

"What's going on?" Jenny took a firmer grip on Max, who was doing his best to wriggle out of her arms.

"We're not sure yet. Anders Nilsson is dead, but we don't know much more. Did you see or hear anything unusual?"

"No, I can't recall anything special. The first I heard was when my next-door neighbor started talking to somebody here in the stairwell. After a while the police cars arrived and an ambulance, and there was a hell of a commotion out here."

268 CAMILLA LÄCKBERG

"But nothing special earlier today, or last night?"
Patrik was still fishing.

"No, not a thing."

Patrik let it drop for the time being. "Okay, thanks
for your help, Jenny."

He smiled at Max and let him grab hold of his finger, something that was apparently hysterically funny
because Max laughed so hard he looked like he might
choke. Reluctantly Patrik tore himself loose and backed
slowly in the direction of Anders's apartment while he
kept waving at Max and saying bye-bye.

Lena stood in the doorway of the apartment with
a mocking smile on her lips. "Need one of your own,
don't you?"

To his dismay Patrik felt himself blush, something
that only made Lena smile even more. He muttered
something unintelligible in reply.

She preceded him into the apartment, saying over
her shoulder, "Well, you know, all you have to do is
ask. I'm free and single and I've got a biological clock
ticking so loud I can hardly sleep at night."

Patrik knew she was joking, that was Lena's usual
flirty banter, but he still couldn't help blushing even
more. He didn't reply, and when they entered the living room they both lost any urge to smile.

Someone had cut Anders's body down from the
rope it had been hanging from, and now he lay on
the living room floor. Right above him hung the stub
of the rope, sliced off about four inches from the
hook. The rest of the rope was around Anders's neck
in a noose, and Patrik could see the deep, angry red
wound on his neck where the rope had bit into the
skin. What always bothered him the most about dead

people was the unnatural facial color. Strangulation
caused a nasty bluish-purple hue which gave the victim a very odd look. Patrik also recognized the thick,
swollen tongue sticking out between Anders's lips as
normal for victims who were strangled or suffocated.
Even though his experience with murder victims was
limited, to say the least, the police got their share of
suicides each year, and he'd helped cut down three of
them during his career.

But when Patrik looked around the living room
there was one thing that quite clearly distinguished
this scene from the suicides by hanging that he'd
seen. There was no possibility that Anders could have
climbed up and put his head through the noose tied to
the ceiling. No chairs or tables were anywhere near.
Anders had swung freely in the middle of the room
like a macabre human mobile.

Unused to homicide scenes as he was, Patrik cautiously moved in a wide circle around the body.
Anders's eyes were open, staring rigidly into space.
Patrik couldn't help leaning forward and closing the
dead man's eyes. He knew that he shouldn't have any
sort of contact with the body before the ME arrived—
actually the body shouldn't even have been cut down—
but something in those staring eyes set all his nerves
on edge. It felt as though the eyes were following him
around the room.

The room seemed unusually desolate. Then he
noticed that all the paintings had been taken down
from the walls. Only big ugly marks were left where
the paintings had once hung. Otherwise the room was
just as shabby as he remembered it from the last time he
was here, but then the paintings had somehow lighted

up the room. They had given Anders's home a certain
air of decadence by combining filth with beauty. Now
the place just looked dirty and disgusting.

Lena was talking nonstop on her mobile. After one
conversation in which Patrik only heard her swearing
in single syllables, she slapped shut the lid of her little
Ericsson phone and turned to him.

"We're getting reinforcements from Forensic Medicine for crime scene investigation. They're leaving
Göteborg now. We can't touch anything. I suggest we
wait outside for safety's sake."

They went out on the landing and Lena carefully
closed and locked the door. The cold was piercing
when they stepped outside the main door; Lena and
Patrik stamped their feet in place.

"Where's Janne right now?" Patrik was asking
about Lena's partner, who should have been with her
in the car.

"He's TCC'ing today."

"TCC'ing?" Patrik looked quizzical.

"Taking care of a sick child. TCC. Thanks to all the
cutbacks there was nobody who could step in on short
notice, so I had to come alone when we got the call."

Patrik nodded, not really paying attention. He was
inclined to side with Lena. There was a lot to suggest
that it was one and the same killer they were searching for. Drawing hasty conclusions was definitely one
of the riskiest things a cop could do, but the odds of
there being two different murderers in this little town
were infinitesimally low. Add to that the fact that there
were strong connections between the two victims and
the odds were even lower.

Lena and Patrik knew that the trip from Göteborg

would take at least an hour and a half, maybe two, so they sat in his car and turned on the heat. They also turned on the radio, and for a long time they sat listening to happy-go-lucky pop music. It was a welcome distraction from the reason for their long wait. After an hour and forty minutes they saw two police cars drive into the parking lot, and they got out to meet their reinforcements.

"Please, Jan, can't we get our own house? I saw that one of the houses at Badholmen is for sale. Couldn't we drive down and take a look at it? It has the most fantastic view, and there's a little boathouse too. Please?"

Lisa's whining voice made his sense of irritation grow. Her voice almost always did these days. Being married to her would be a lot more pleasant if she had the sense to shut up and just look pretty. Lately not even her big, firm breasts and round ass had managed to convince him that she was worth all the trouble. Her babbling had only accelerated, and in moments like this he bitterly regretted giving in to her nagging about getting married.

Lisa was working as a waitress at Röde Orm in Grebbestad when he first laid eyes on her. All his friends had practically drooled when they saw her plunging neckline and long legs, and he decided on the spot that he had to have her. He usually got what he wanted, and Lisa proved to be no exception. He wasn't bad-looking, but what usually nailed the final decision was when he introduced himself as Jan Lorentz. Mentioning his last name normally brought a gleam to a woman's eyes, and from then on it was all systems go.

He had been obsessed with Lisa's body in the beginning. He couldn't get enough of her, and he effectively closed his ears to all the stupid comments she kept making in her shrill voice. The envious looks from other men when he showed up with Lisa on his arm also increased her attractiveness in his eyes. At first her little hints that he should make an honest woman out of her fell on deaf ears. To be quite frank, her stupidity had begun to chip away at her appeal. But what finally clinched his decision to make her his wife was Nelly's vehement opposition to the whole idea. She loathed Lisa from the first moment she saw her and never missed an opportunity to make her views known. A childish wish to rebel had put Jan in his present predicament, and he cursed his own stupidity.

Lisa was pouting as she lay on her stomach on their big double bed. She was naked and doing her best to look seductive, but he was no longer interested. He knew that she was waiting for an answer.

"You know we can't move away from Mama. She isn't well, and she could never take care of this big house by herself."

He turned his back to Lisa, knotting his tie in front of the big mirror on her dressing table. In the mirror he saw Lisa frown in annoyance. It wasn't a very becoming look.

"Why doesn't the old bitch have enough sense to move into some nice old folks' home instead of being a burden on her family? Doesn't she understand that we have a right to our own lives? Instead, we have to take care of her day in and day out. And what enjoyment does she get from sitting on all that money? I bet you she loves watching us demean ourselves, crawling after the little crumbs that roll off her table. Doesn't she understand how much you do for her? You slave away at that company and spend the rest of the time babysitting her. The old hag won't even let us have the best rooms in the house as thanks for our help. We have to live in the cellar while she lolls about in the drawing rooms."

Jan turned and gave his wife a cold look. "Didn't I tell you not to talk about my mother that way?"

"Your mother." Lisa snorted. "You can't think that she really looks on you as a son, Jan. You'll never be more than a charity case for her. If her darling Nils hadn't disappeared, you would probably have been tossed out on your ear sooner or later. You're nothing more than a temporary stand-in, Jan. Who else would slave away practically twenty-four hours a day for her for nothing? The only thing you have is a promise that when she croaks, you get all the money. First of all, the bitch will probably live to be at least a hundred, and second, I bet she's willed the money to a home for abandoned dogs and is laughing her head off at us behind our backs. Sometimes you're just so fucking dumb, Jan."

Lisa rolled over onto her back and studied her well-manicured nails. With ice-cold calm Jan took a step toward Lisa where she lay on the bed. He squatted down, wound the long blonde hair hanging off the edge of the bed around his hand, and began pulling slowly, harder and harder, until she grimaced in pain. He put his face right up to hers, so close that he could feel her breath on his face, and snarled in a low voice: "Don't you ever, ever call me dumb, you hear me? And believe me, the money will be mine some day. The only question is, whether you'll be around long enough to enjoy it."

With satisfaction he saw a spark of fear ignite in her eyes. He watched her stupid but primitively sly brain process the information and conclude that it was time to change tactics. She stretched out on the bed, pouting and cupping her hands around her breasts. She circled her finger around her nipples until they hardened and then purred, "Forgive me, that was stupid of me, Jan. You know how I am. I talk without thinking sometimes. Is there any way I can make it up to you?"

She sucked suggestively on her index finger and then slipped her hand down to her crotch.

Jan reluctantly felt his body respond and decided that at least there was one thing he could use her for. He undid his tie.

Mellberg scratched his crotch meditatively without noticing the expression of disgust that this gesture aroused in the faces of the people who sat gathered before him. In honor of the day he had put on a suit, even though it was a bit too tight, but he blamed that on the dry cleaners, who must have screwed up and run it at too high a temperature. He didn't have to weigh himself to know that he'd put on an ounce or two since he was a young recruit, but he thought that buying a new suit was a waste of money. Good quality was timeless. He couldn't help it if the idiots at the dry cleaners couldn't do their job properly.

He cleared his throat to get everyone's full attention. The chatter and scraping of chairs ceased, and all eyes turned toward him as he sat behind his desk. Chairs had been gathered and arranged in a semicircle in front of him. Mellberg looked at everyone in silence with a solemn expression. This was a moment he intended to milk as much as possible. He noticed with a frown that Patrik looked exhausted. Naturally the staff did what they liked in their free time, but considering it was the middle of the workweek one ought to expect that they observe moderation in the form of partying and alcohol. Mellberg effectively repressed the memory of the half bottle he himself had downed yesterday evening. He made a mental note to have a talk with Patrik in private about the station's alcohol policy.

"As you all know, at this time another murder has occurred in Fjällbacka. The probability that there are two killers is very low, so I think we can proceed from the assumption that the same person who murdered Alexandra Wijkner also murdered Anders Nilsson."

He enjoyed the sound of his own voice and the zeal and interest he saw in the faces before him. He was in his true element. He was born to do this.

Mellberg went on. "Anders Nilsson was found this morning by Bengt Larsson, one of the victim's drinking buddies. He had been hanged, and according to preliminary information from Göteborg, he'd been there at least since yesterday. Until we have more precise information this will be the hypothesis from which we'll be working."

He liked the feel of the word "hypothesis" rolling off his tongue. The group before him was not particularly large, but in his mind it was many times bigger and the interest was impossible to misconstrue. It was his words and orders they were all waiting for. He looked about with pleasure. Annika was typing eagerly on a laptop computer, with a pair of reading glasses perched on the tip of her nose. Her ample feminine curves were clothed in a well-tailored yellow jacket with matching skirt; he gave her a wink. That would have to do. Best not to scare her off. Next to her sat Patrik, who looked as if he were going to fall apart at any moment. His eyelids were heavy and his eyes clearly bloodshot. Mellberg decided he would really have to have a talk with him at the earliest opportunity. After all, one had the right to demand a certain semblance of professionalism from one's subordinates.

Besides Patrik and Annika, there were another three employees from the Tanumshede police station. Gösta Flygare was the eldest at the station. He devoted all his energy to doing as little as possible until retirement, which was now only a couple of years off. After that he would devote all his time to his grand passion—golf. He had started playing ten years ago when his wife died of cancer, and weekends suddenly felt much too long and desolate. Sport had soon become like a poison in his blood. He now regarded his job, in which he had never been terribly interested in the first place, only as a disruptive element that prevented him from being out on the golf course.

Despite the fact that his salary was meager, he had managed to save enough to buy an apartment on the Costa del Sol in Spain. Soon he'd be able to devote the summer months to playing golf in Sweden and the rest of the year he could spend on the courses in Spain. Although, he had to admit, these murders had succeeded in arousing his interest for the first time in ages. But not so much that he wouldn't rather play eighteen holes right now if the season had permitted it.

Next to him sat the station's youngest member. Martin Molin elicited varying degrees of parental instincts in all of them. They took turns acting as invisible crutches for him at work, although they were careful that he never notice anything. They only gave him assignments that a child could do, and they went over and corrected everything he wrote before his reports reached Mellberg's desk.

He had graduated from the Police Academy no more than a year ago. Everyone was astonished that he'd been able, first of all, to immerse himself in the difficult booking procedures and second, complete his training and pass the exam. But Martin was pleasant and good-natured, and despite his naïveté, which made him totally unsuitable for police work, they all reckoned that he couldn't do any great damage here in Tanumshede. So they gladly helped him over all obstacles. Annika in particular had taken him under her wing and sometimes, to everyone's great amusement, she showed her feelings by spontaneously pressing him to her large bosom in a bear hug.

On those occasions Martin's fiery red hair, which always stood on end, and his equally red freckles competed with the color of his face. But he worshiped Annika and had spent many evenings visiting her and her husband when he needed to ask advice about being unlucky in love—which he always was. His innocence and amiability seemed to make him an irresistible magnet for women who ate men for breakfast and then spat out the remains. But Annika was always there to listen, patch up the shreds of his self-confidence, and then send him back out into the world, in the hope that one day he would find a woman who could appreciate this gem of a man, hiding beneath the freckled exterior.

The last member of the group was also the least popular. Ernst Lundgren was a big-time ass kisser who never missed a chance to promote himself, preferably at the expense of others. No one was surprised that he was still single. He was a far from attractive man. Even though uglier men than he had found a partner thanks to a helpfully pleasant personality, Ernst lacked this attribute completely. That's why he was now living with his old mother on a farm six miles south of Tanumshede. Rumor had it that his father, who was notorious in the area as an alcoholic and highly aggressive man, had received a helping hand from his wife when he fell from the hayloft and landed on a pitchfork. That was many years ago now, but the rumor was revived whenever people had nothing more exciting to talk about. In any case, it was true that only a mother could love Ernst, since his buck teeth, straggly hair, and big ears were accompanied by a choleric disposition and a self-promoting manner. Right now he was hanging on Mellberg's every syllable as though his words were pearls, and he took every opportunity to shush the others testily if they dared make the slightest noise to distract attention from Mellberg's speech. He eagerly raised his hand like a schoolboy to ask a question.

"How do we know that Anders wasn't murdered by the drunk, who later merely pretended to discover him this morning?"

Mellberg gave Lundgren an appreciative nod.

"A very good question, Ernst, very good. But as I said, we're going on the assumption that it's the same person who killed Alex Wijkner. Just to be safe, though, we'll check out Bengt Larsson's alibi for yesterday."

Mellberg pointed with his pen to Lundgren as he scanned the rest of the group.

"This is the sort of alert thinking we need to solve this case. I hope you will all listen and learn from Ernst. You have a long way to go before you reach his level."

Ernst modestly lowered his eyes, but as soon as Mellberg turned his attention elsewhere, he couldn't resist casting a triumphant look at his colleagues. Annika snorted loudly and stared back without blinking in response to the angry look Lundgren gave her.

"Now where was I?"

Mellberg hooked his thumbs under the braces he was wearing under his jacket and spun around on his chair. He ended up facing the whiteboard that had been set up on the wall behind him to track the case of Alex Wijkner. A similar whiteboard had now been put up next to it, but the only thing on it was a Polaroid photo taken of Anders before the ambulance attendants cut down his body.

"So, what do we know so far? The body of Anders Nilsson was found this morning, and according to the preliminary report, he'd been dead since sometime yesterday. He was hanged by one or more persons unknown, presumably more than one because it would take considerable strength to lift up a full-grown man high enough to hang him from the ceiling. What we don't know is how they went about it. There are no signs of a struggle, either in the apartment or on Anders's body. No bruises to indicate rough handling of the body, either before or after death occurred. These are only preliminary data, as I said, but we expect confirmation as soon as the autopsy is complete."

Patrik waved his pen. "How soon do we expect to get the autopsy results?"

"Apparently they have a whole pile of bodies waiting, so unfortunately I haven't been able to get any information as to when the report will be ready."

Nobody looked surprised.

"We also know that there's a clear connection between Anders Nilsson and our first murder victim, Alexandra Wijkner."

Now Mellberg stood up and pointed at the photo of Alexandra that was in the middle of the first whiteboard. They had received the picture from her mother, and once again they were all struck by how beautiful she had been in life. It made the picture next to it, of Alexandra in the bathtub with a bluish, pale face and frost in her hair and eyelashes, look even more horrible.

"This ill-matched pair had a sexual relationship. Anders himself admitted it and we also have certain evidence, as you know, to support his claim. What we don't know is how long it lasted, how they got involved with each other, and above all why a beautiful society woman would choose as her bed partner a filthy and generally repulsive alcoholic. Something is fishy here, I can smell it."

Mellberg tapped his index finger a couple of times on the side of his bulbous red nose.

"Martin, you're assigned to dig deeper into this. Above all you need to press Henrik Wijkner a lot harder than we've done so far. That guy knows more than he's admitting, I'm sure of it."

Martin nodded eagerly, taking notes for dear life. Annika gave him a tender, motherly look over the tops of her reading glasses.

"Unfortunately, this brings us back to square one as far as suspects in the first murder are concerned. Anders seemed very promising in that role, but now the case has taken a whole different turn. Patrik, you'll have to review all the material that we have on the Wijkner murder. Check and double-check every detail. Somewhere in that material there's a lead we missed."

Mellberg had heard that line on a TV cop show and memorized it for future use.

Gösta was now the only one who hadn't been given an assignment. Mellberg looked at his list and thought for a moment.

"Gösta, you go and talk with Alex Wijkner's family. Maybe they know something else they haven't told us about. Ask them about her friends and enemies, her childhood, her personality, everything. Whatever you can think of. Talk to both parents and the sister, but make sure you talk to them one at a time. You get the most out of people that way, in my experience. Just coordinate with Molin, who'll be talking to the husband."

Gösta winced under the burden of a concrete assignment and sighed in resignation. Not because it would take time away from golf in the middle of this bitter cold winter, but in the past few years he'd almost gotten used to not needing to do any real work. He had perfected the art of looking busy while he played solitaire on his computer to kill time. The burden of having to produce some concrete results weighed on him. His peace and quiet were over. He probably wouldn't even be paid overtime. He'd be happy if he even got reimbursed for the gas back and forth to Göteborg.

Mellberg clapped his hands and shooed them off.

"All right, let's get going. We can't sit on our backsides if we want to solve this thing. I reckon you're going to work harder than you've ever worked before, and as far as days off are concerned, you can forget about that until this is over. Until then your time belongs to me. Get moving."

If any of them had anything against being shooed off like little children, nobody said a word. They got up, took the chairs they'd been sitting on in one hand and their notebooks and pens in the other. Only Ernst Lundgren stayed behind, but Mellberg uncharacteristically was in no mood for flattery, so he shooed him off as well.

It had been a very productive day. Certainly it was a big disappointment that his prime suspect for the Wijkner murder had turned out to be a blind alley. But at least one plus one was considerably more than two. One murder was an event, two murders were a sensation for such a small district. If before he was reasonably sure of getting a one-way ticket to the center of the action when he solved the Wijkner case, he was now dead certain that if he wrapped up both murders in a neat package, they would beg and plead for him to come back to Göteborg.

With these bright prospects within reach, Bertil Mellberg leaned back in his chair, stuck his hand into the third drawer, took out a Mums-Mums chocolate-dipped meringue biscuit, and popped the whole thing blissfully into his mouth. Then he clasped his hands behind his head, closed his eyes and decided to take a little nap. After all, it was almost lunchtime.

* * *

After Patrik left, Erica had tried to sleep for a couple of hours without success. All the feelings jostling inside her made her toss back and forth in bed. A smile kept sneaking over her lips. There ought to be a law against being this happy. The feeling of well-being was so strong that she hardly knew what to do with herself. She lay on her side and rested her right cheek on her hands.

Everything felt brighter today. Everything felt easier to deal with. Alex's murder, the book that her publisher was impatiently waiting for and that wasn't really flowing properly, her grief for her parents, and not least the sale of her childhood home. All felt easier to bear today. The problems hadn't gone away, but for the first time she felt truly convinced that her world wasn't about to collapse and that she could handle any difficulties that came her way.

Imagine what a difference a day makes, twenty-four little hours. Yesterday at this time she had woken up with a weight on her chest. Woken to a loneliness she couldn't manage to look beyond. Now it seemed as though she could still physically feel Patrik's caresses against her skin. Physically was actually the wrong word, or too limited a word.

With her entire being she felt that her loneliness had been replaced by a sense of being two. The silence in the bedroom was now peaceful where it had felt threatening and unending before. Of course she already missed him, but she was secure in the knowledge that wherever he was, he was thinking of her.

Erica felt as if she had taken a mental broom and resolutely swept away all the old cobwebs in the corners and all the dust that had accumulated in her mind. But this new clarity also made her realize that she could no longer flee from what had been occupying her thoughts the past few days.

Ever since the true identity of the father of Alex's child had appeared like blazing letters in the sky for Erica, she had dreaded the confrontation. She was still not looking forward to it. But the new strength that she felt inside made it possible to come to grips with the dilemma, instead of pushing it aside. She knew what she had to do.

She took a long shower in scalding hot water. Everything felt like a new beginning this morning, and she wanted to meet it completely clean. After the shower and a glance at the outdoor thermometer, she dressed warmly and said a prayer that she could get the car started. She was in luck. It started on the first try.

During the drive Erica thought about how she should bring up the subject. She practiced a few opening lines but each sounded lamer than the last, so she decided to ad-lib. She didn't have that much to go on, but her gut told her that she was right. For a fraction of a second she considered ringing Patrik and telling him about her suspicions, but she quickly vetoed that idea, deciding that she had to check it out herself first. There was too much at stake.

The road to her destination was short, but it felt as if it took an eternity. When she turned into the lot below the Badhotel, Dan waved happily from the boat. She had guessed that he would be here. Erica waved but didn't smile back. She locked the car and with her hands in the pockets of her light-brown duffel coat, she sauntered over toward Dan and the boat. The day was hazy and gray, but the air smelled fresh. She took a couple of deep breaths to try to dispel the last traces of haze in her head, caused by last night's copious wine intake.

"Hi, Erica."

"Hi."

Dan kept working on his boat but looked happy to have company. Erica glanced around a little nervously for Pernilla; she was still worried about the look Dan's wife had given them last time. But in light of what she now knew, she suddenly understood it much better.

For the first time Erica saw how beautiful the worn old fishing boat was. Dan had taken it over after his father, and he had cared for it with real tenderness. Fishing was in his blood, and it was his great sorrow in life that this occupation could no longer feed a family. Naturally he got on well in his role as teacher at Tanum School, but fishing was his true calling in life. He couldn't help smiling whenever he worked on the boat. The hard work didn't bother him, and he kept the winter cold at bay by wearing layers of clothing. He hoisted a heavy roll of line onto his shoulder and turned toward Erica.

"What the hell is this? No treats today? I hope you don't intend to make a habit of it."

A lock of his blond hair hung down from under the knit cap. He looked big and strong, standing in front of her like a massive pillar. He radiated strength and happiness, and it pained her that she would have to puncture that joy. But if she didn't do it, someone else would. The police, in the worst case. She convinced herself that she was doing him a favor, but she knew she was entering an emotional gray zone. The main reason was that she personally wanted to know. She had to find out.

Dan went up to the bow with the roll of line, tossed

it onto the deck, and came back to Erica, who was leaning against the railing in the stern.

Erica gazed unseeing out at the horizon. "I purchased my love for money, for me there was naught else to have."

Dan laughed and finished the verse: "Sing lovely you soft burring strings, sing lovely of my only love."

Erica wasn't smiling.

"Is Fröding still your favorite poet?"

"Always has been, always will be. The kids at school claim they're going to puke if they read any more Fröding, but in my opinion it's impossible to read too much of his poetry."

"Yes, I still have that collection of his that you gave me when we were together."

She was speaking to his back now, because Dan had turned around to move some crates of nets that were lying against the opposite railing. She continued relentlessly.

"Do you always give that book to your girlfriends?"

He stopped short with his chores and turned to Erica with a shocked expression.

"What do you mean? You got one and yes, Pernilla got one, although I doubt that she ever bothered to read it."

Erica saw an uneasy expression on his face. She gripped the railing she was leaning against a little harder with her mitten-clad hands and looked him straight in the eye.

"And Alex? Did she get a copy too?"

Dan's face turned the same color as the snow on the icy bay behind him, but she also saw an expression of relief quickly slide over it.

"What do you mean? Alex?"

He was not yet ready to capitulate.

"I told you last time that I was in Alex's house one evening last week. What I didn't tell you was that someone came into the house while I was there. Someone who came straight up to the bedroom and took something away. At first I couldn't think of what it was, but then I checked the last call that Alex made from home. It was to your mobile, and that's when I remembered what was missing from the room. I have the exact same book at home."

Dan didn't say a word, so she continued. "It wasn't hard to work out why someone would take the trouble to go into Alex's house and then steal something as simple as a poetry book. There's a dedication in it, isn't there? A dedication that would point straight to the man who was her lover?"

" 'With all my love I surrender my passion—Dan.' "

He declaimed it in a voice full of emotion. Now it was his turn to stare vacantly at the water. He sat down abruptly on a crate on deck and tore off his cap. His hair stuck out in all directions. He pulled off his gloves and ran his hands through his hair. Then he looked straight at Erica.

"I couldn't let it get out. What we had together was madness. An intense and all-consuming madness. Not something that we could let collide with our real lives. We both knew that it had to end."

"Were you supposed to meet on the Friday she died?"

A muscle twitched in Dan's face at the reminder. After Alex died he must have pondered countless times what would have happened if he had actually shown up. Whether she still would have been alive.

"Yes, we were supposed to meet that Friday evening. Pernilla was going to visit her sister in Munkedal with the kids. I thought up some excuse about feeling out of sorts and preferring to stay at home."

"But Pernilla didn't go, did she?"

There was a long silence.

"Yes, Pernilla went but I stayed at home. I turned off my mobile, and I knew she'd never dare ring the phone at the house. I stayed away because I was afraid. I didn't dare look her in the eye and tell her it was over. Even though I knew she realized that it would have to happen sooner or later, I was afraid to be the one who took that step. I thought that if I could slowly start backing away, she'd get tired of things and break it off with me. Very manly, don't you think?"

Erica knew that the hardest part was yet to come, but she had to go on. Better that he heard it from her.

"But Dan, she didn't understand that it had to end. She envisaged a future with you. A future where you left your family and she left Henrik and the two of you lived happily ever after."

He seemed to shrink with each word, and the worst was yet to come.

"Dan, she was pregnant. With your child. Apparently, she had intended to tell you about it that Friday night. She'd prepared a feast and put champagne on ice."

Dan couldn't look at her. He tried to fix his gaze out in the distance, but tears began to flow, making everything run together in a mist. Grief welled up from somewhere deep inside him, and tears started running down his cheeks. He began to sob, and he kept having to wipe his nose with his gloves to stop the snot from running down. Finally, he put his head in his hands and gave up all attempts to wipe off his face.

Erica squatted down next to him and put her arms around him to console him. But Dan shook her off. She knew that he'd have to get himself out of the hell he was in on his own. So she waited him out with her arms crossed until the tears came more slowly and he seemed to be able to breathe again.

"How do you know she was pregnant?" The words came in a stammer.

"I was with Birgit and Henrik at the police station when they told us."

"Do they know it wasn't Henrik's child?"

"I'm sure Henrik knows, but Birgit doesn't; she thinks Henrik is the father."

Dan nodded. It seemed to console him a little that her parents didn't know.

"How did you meet?"

Erica wanted to turn away his thoughts from his unborn child, if only for a moment, to give him a little breathing space.

He smiled bitterly. "Really classic. Where do people meet each other in Fjällbacka at our age? Having a beer at Galären, of course. We saw each other across the room and it was like being kicked in the stomach. I've never felt so attracted to a woman before."

Erica felt a tiny, tiny twinge of jealousy at those words.

Dan went on. "We didn't do anything then, but a couple of weekends later she called on my mobile. I drove over to see her. Then it just sort of snowballed from there. Stolen hours when Pernilla was away somewhere. Not that many nights, in other words; it was usually during the day that we met."

"Weren't you afraid that the neighbors would see you when you went to Alex's house? You know how fast gossip travels here."

"Sure, I did think about that. I used to climb over the fence in the backyard and then go in through the cellar entrance. To be quite honest, that was probably a good part of the excitement between us as well. The danger and the risk."

"But didn't you understand how much you were risking?"

Dan was fidgeting with his cap and kept his eyes fixed on the deck as he talked.

"Of course I did. On one level. But on another I felt invulnerable. Other people might get caught, but not me. Isn't that how it always is?"

"Does Pernilla know?"

"No. Not in so many words, anyway. But I think she suspects something. You saw how she reacted when she saw us here. That's how she's been the past few months—jealous and watchful. I'm sure she senses that something is going on."

"You know you have to tell her about it now."

Dan shook his head vehemently. Tears welled up in his eyes again.

"That won't work, Erica. I can't do it. It wasn't until this thing with Alex that I really understood how much Pernilla means to me. Alex was a passion, but Pernilla and the kids are my life. I can't do it!"

Erica leaned forward and put her hand over Dan's. Her voice was calm and clear and showed nothing of the agitation she felt inside.

"Dan, you have to. The police need to be informed, and you have a chance now to tell Pernilla about it in your own way. Sooner or later the police will figure it out by themselves, and then you won't have a chance to explain to Pernilla the way you want to. Then you'll no longer have any choice. And you said yourself that she probably knows or at least suspects something. Maybe it would even be a relief for both of you if you talked about it. Clear the air."

She saw that Dan was listening and taking in what she said. She could also feel that he was shaking.

"But what if she leaves me? What if she takes the kids and leaves me, Erica? Where will I go then? I'm nothing without them."

A tiny, tiny voice inside Erica whispered cruelly that he should have thought of that earlier, but stronger voices drowned it out and said that the time for recriminations was past. There were more important matters to take care of right now. She leaned forward, put her arms around him, and ran her hands over his back to comfort him. At first his sobs intensified, then ebbed away. When he freed himself from her embrace and wiped away the tears she saw that he had decided not to postpone the inevitable.

As she drove away from the wharf she looked at him in the rearview mirror, standing motionless on his beloved boat with his eyes fixed on the horizon. She crossed her fingers that he would find the right words. It wasn't going to be easy.

The yawn felt like it came all the way from his toes and spread through his whole body. Patrik had never been so tired in his life. Nor had he ever been so happy.

It was difficult to focus on the huge piles of paperwork lying in front of him. A homicide generated incredible amounts of documents, and his job now was to go through everything in detail to find that one tiny piece of the puzzle that could propel the investigation forward. He rubbed his eyes and took a deep breath to gather energy for the task.

Every ten minutes, he had to get up from his chair to stretch, get some coffee, hop a little in place, or whatever would make him stay awake and focused for a little while longer. Several times his hand had strayed toward the telephone to ring Erica, but he checked himself. If she was as tired as he was, she was probably still in bed asleep. He hoped she was. He intended to keep her awake as long as possible tonight too, if he had anything to say about it.

One stack of papers had grown since he last went through them—the documents containing information on the Lorentz family. Annika, assiduous as always, had apparently kept digging for old articles and items mentioning the family, and then placed the papers neatly in the stack on Patrik's desk. He worked methodically, refreshing his memory by turning over the stack and working up from the bottom so that he first read the articles he'd read before. Two hours later, there was nothing that had set his imagination in motion. Despite a strong feeling that he was missing something, it still seemed to elude him.

The first really interesting new information came a good way down in the pile. Annika had inserted an article about a case of arson in Bullaren, about thirty miles from Fjällbacka. The article was dated 1975 and had been given almost a whole page in *Bohusläningen*. The house had burned down the night of the sixth of July 1975 in an explosionlike event. When the fire was extinguished there was almost nothing left of the house except ashes, but the remains of two human bodies had been found. The bodies turned out to be Stig and Elisabeth Norin, the couple who owned the house. Miraculously their ten-year-old son had managed to escape the fire. He was discovered in one of the outbuildings. The circumstances surrounding the fire were considered suspicious according to *Bohusläningen*, and the police called it arson.

The article was fastened with a paper clip to a folder, and inside Patrik found the police report. He was still perplexed at what the article had to do with the Lorentz family until he opened the folder and saw the name of the Norins' ten-year-old son. The boy was named Jan. The folder also contained a report from social services in which his foster-home placement with the Lorentz family was mentioned. Patrik gave a low whistle. It was still uncertain what this might have to do with Alex's death, or with the murder of Anders for that matter, but something began to stir at the edges of Patrik's consciousness. Shadows which faded and dissolved as soon as he tried to focus on them, but which indicated that he was on the right track. He made a mental note about this and then continued his laborious scrutiny of the material on his desk.

His notebook was slowly filling up. His handwriting was so sprawling that Karin always teased him that he should have been a teacher instead, but he could read it all right, and that was the main thing. Some to-do items took shape, but most dominant among the notes were all the questions that the material had generated, marked with big black question marks. Who was Alex waiting for when she made the fancy dinner? Who was the man she was meeting in secret? And whose child was she expecting? Could it be Anders's, even though he had denied it? Or was there someone they hadn't yet managed to identify? Why would a woman like Alex, with her looks, class, and money, have an affair with someone like Anders? Why had Alex saved an article about Nils Lorentz's disappearance in a bureau drawer?

The list of questions grew longer and longer. Patrik was on the third page before he got into the matter of Anders's death. The stack of paper on Anders was much smaller so far. But the documents would start piling up soon enough. For the moment there were only about ten documents, including the one confiscated during the search of Anders's apartment. The biggest question concerning Anders was the way he had died. Patrik underlined this question several times with furious black strokes. How did the killer or killers lift Anders up to the hook in the ceiling? The autopsy would provide more answers, but from what Patrik had seen there were no marks of a struggle on the body, precisely as Mellberg had pointed out at this morning's run-through. Someone who is unconscious feels incredibly heavy, and Anders would have had to be lifted up a good distance for someone to fasten the rope to the hook.

He was actually leaning toward the possibility that Mellberg might be right for once—that more than one person had been on the scene. Although that didn't seem to agree with what happened when Alex was killed. Yet Patrik could swear that it was the same killer they were looking for. After his initial doubt he was now more and more certain that this was true.

He looked at the papers they'd found in Anders's apartment and fanned them out in front of him on the desk. Stuck between his teeth he had a pencil that he had chewed beyond recognition. His mouth felt full of yellow flakes from the pencil. He spat out a few and tried to pick the rest of the flakes from his tongue. It was no use. Now they were stuck to his fingers instead. He flicked them a couple of times to try to dislodge them but gave up and turned his attention back to the papers fanned out on his desk. None of the pages seemed to arouse his interest, so he picked up Anders's telephone bill as a starting point. Anders made very few calls, but with all the fixed charges the total was still rather high. The details were still attached to the phone bill, and Patrik sighed when he realized that now he would have to do a little old-fashioned leg-work. Even though he didn't think this was the right day for boring, routine tasks.

He systematically rang one number after another on the list. He soon saw that Anders only called very few numbers. But one number stood out. It didn't appear at all near the top of the list, but after it popped up the first time, it was the most frequently occurring number. Patrik dialed the number and let it ring.

He was just about to hang up after eight rings when he heard an answering machine switch on. The name at the other end made him sit bolt upright in his chair, which made his thigh muscles stretch painfully because he had propped his legs on his desk. He swung his legs to the floor and massaged a tight muscle on the inside of his right thigh.

Patrik replaced the receiver before the beep ended, indicating that one could leave a message. He drew a circle around one of the notes on his notepad, and after thinking for a moment he placed another call. One task he wanted to deal with himself, but the other he could leave for Annika. With his notes in hand he went into her office. She was typing intently on her keyboard, with her computer glasses perched on the end of her nose. She gave him a questioning look.

"You're coming to offer your help, to lighten my unreasonably heavy workload, right?"

"Well, that wasn't quite what I had in mind." Patrik grinned.

"No, I didn't think so." Annika gave Patrik a feigned look of exasperation. "So, what does this have to do with my incipient ulcer?"

"Just one very tiny request." Patrik indicated how small it was by measuring a half inch between his thumb and forefinger.

"All right, let's hear it."

Patrik pulled up a chair and sat down at Annika's desk. Her office, despite being extremely small, was without exception the most pleasant at the station. She had brought in lots of plants that seemed to be healthy and thriving. That ought to qualify as a minor miracle, since the only light in the room came through the window facing the foyer. The cold concrete walls were covered with pictures of Annika and her husband Lennart's two grand passions, their dogs and drag racing. They had two black Labradors that were allowed to go along when Annika and Lennart drove around Sweden on weekends to wherever there happened to be drag races. Lennart was the one who actually competed, but Annika was always there to cheer him on and provide a bag lunch and a thermos of coffee. Basically, it was always the same people they met at the races, and over the years they had formed a tightly knit group. They all considered each other the closest of friends. At least two weekends each month there were races, and persuading Annika to work on those days was hopeless.

He looked down at his notes.

"Well, I was wondering if you could help me do a little inventory of Alexandra Wijkner's life. Starting with her death and double-checking the chronology backward in all the data we received. How long she was married to Henrik. How long she had lived in Sweden. Check her information about the schools in France and Switzerland, et cetera, et cetera. Do you understand what I'm looking for?"

Annika had taken notes on a pad as he talked and now looked up with an affirmative glance. He felt quite sure that she would find out everything worth knowing. Above all, she would find out if some of the information he had received wasn't worth the paper it was written on. Because there had to be something that didn't add up, he was absolutely sure of that.

"Thanks for the help, Annika. You're a gem."

Patrik began to get up from the chair, but a brusque "Sit!" from Annika made him freeze and sink back onto the chair cushion. He understood at once why her Labradors were so well trained.

She leaned back with a pleased smile and he understood that his first mistake had been to go into her office in person instead of simply leaving her a note. He should have known that she always saw right through him. Besides, her nose for romances was utterly preternatural. He might as well raise the white flag and capitulate, so he leaned back and waited for the barrage of questions that was undoubtedly in the offing. She began softly and insidiously.

"You certainly were exhausted today."

"Mmm . . ."

Not that he wasn't going to make her work a little for the information.

"Was there a party last night?" Annika kept fishing as she probed with Machiavellian guile for cracks in his armor.

"Well, I suppose you could call it a party. It probably depends on one's point of view. How would you define 'party' anyway?" He threw out his arms and opened his eyes wide in innocence.

"Oh, skip the bullshit, Patrik. Just tell me. Who is she?"

He said nothing, tormenting her with his silence. After a few seconds he saw a light go on in Annika's eyes.

"Aha!" Her exclamation resounded triumphantly as Annika waved her finger in the air, certain of victory.

"It's that woman, what's her name, what's her name . . ." She snapped her fingers as she feverishly searched her memory. "Erica! Erica Falck!"

Relieved, she leaned back in her chair again. "So-o-o, Patrik . . . how long has this been going on. . , ?"

He never ceased to be amazed at the unerring precision with which she always hit the target. It was no good denying it, either. He could feel a blush spreading all the way from his head to his toes, and it spoke more clearly than anything he might say. Then he couldn't help the broad smile that spread across his face, and that was the last nail in the coffin as far as Annika was concerned.

After a five-minute interrogation Patrik finally managed to drag himself out of Annika's office. He felt as if he'd been run through the wringer. But it hadn't been unpleasant to talk about Erica, and it was with difficulty that he returned to the task he had given himself to deal with immediately. He put on his coat, told Annika he was off, and headed out into the winter weather, where big snowflakes had begun falling lightly to the ground.

Outside the window Erica saw the snow fluttering down. She was sitting at her computer but had turned it off and was now staring at a black screen. Despite a pounding headache she had forced herself to write ten pages about Selma Lagerlöf. She no longer felt any enthusiasm for the biography, but she was bound by her contract, and in a few months it had to be done. The conversation with Dan had put a damper on her good mood, and she wondered whether he was telling Pernilla everything at this very moment. She decided to make use of her worry about Dan for something creative and rebooted her computer.

The draft of the book about Alex was on the computer desktop, and she opened the file, which now held a good hundred pages. Methodically she read through the pages from beginning to end. It was good. It was even very good. What worried her was how all the people in Alex's circle of friends and family would react if the book were published. Naturally Erica had disguised the story a bit, changing the names of people and places, and allowing herself some flights of imagination. But the core of the book was unmistakably based on Alex's life, as seen through Erica's eyes. The section about Dan in particular was giving Erica a real headache. How could she leave out him and his family? At the same time she felt that she had to write this story. For the first time an idea for a book had really filled her with enthusiasm. There were so many other ideas that hadn't panned out and that she'd rejected over the years; she couldn't afford to lose this one. First she intended to concentrate on finishing the book, then she would deal with the problem of how to handle the feelings of those involved.

Almost an hour of energetic writing had passed when the doorbell rang. At first she was annoyed at being disturbed now that she had finally gotten going, but then she thought maybe it was Patrik and leapt out of her chair. She did a quick check of her appearance in the mirror before she bounded down the stairs to the front door. The smile on her lips faded instantly when she saw who was standing outside. Pernilla looked terrible. She appeared to have aged ten years since Erica saw her last. Her eyes were swollen and red from crying, her hair was uncombed, and she seemed to have forgotten her coat in her haste; she was shivering in a thin cardigan. Erica let her into the warm house. With an impulsive gesture she put her arms around Pernilla and hugged her as she stroked her back the same way she'd stroked Dan's only a couple of hours before. It robbed Pernilla of what little self-control she had left, and she wept with long wrenching sobs on Erica's shoulder. After a while she raised her head. Her mascara had smeared even more, giving her an almost comical, clown-like look.

"I'm sorry." Pernilla looked through her haze of tears at Erica's shoulder, where the white sweater she was wearing had been colored black by the mascara.

"It doesn't matter. Don't worry about it. Come in."

Erica put one arm around Pernilla's shoulders and led her into the living room. She could feel Pernilla shaking all over, and she didn't think it was only because of the cold. For a second, she wondered why Pernilla had chosen her to go to. Erica had always been Dan's friend much more than Pernilla's. She thought it was a little odd that Pernilla hadn't gone to one of her own girlfriends, or her sister. But now she was here, at any rate, and Erica had to do everything she could to help her.

"I've got a pot of coffee on. Would you like a cup? It's been on for about an hour, but it's probably fairly drinkable."

"Yes, thanks."

Pernilla sat down on the sofa and hugged her arms to her chest, as if she were afraid of falling apart and wanted to hold herself together. In a way this was probably true.

Erica came back with two cups of coffee. She placed one on the coffee table in front of Pernilla and the other in front of herself, sitting down in the big wing chair so that she was facing Pernilla on the sofa. She waited for Pernilla to begin.

"Did you know?"

Erica hesitated. "Yes, but not until very recently." She hesitated again. "I urged Dan to tell you."

Pernilla nodded. "What should I do?"

The question was rhetorical, so Erica let it go unanswered.

Pernilla went on. "I knew that from the start I was just a way for Dan to get over you."

Erica began to protest, but Pernilla stopped her with a wave of her hand.

"I knew that was true, but I thought things changed with time and that we really loved each other. We get on well and I trusted him completely."

"Dan loves you, Pernilla. I know he does."

Pernilla didn't seem to be listening to her; she kept talking while she gazed into her coffee cup. Erica saw that she was gripping the cup so hard that her knuckles were white.

"I could live with it if he was having an affair and blame it on an early midlife crisis or something. But I can never forgive him for getting that woman pregnant."

The fury in Pernilla's voice was so strong that Erica had to fight an impulse to move back. When Pernilla raised her head and looked at Erica, the hatred in her eyes was so fierce that Erica felt an icy premonition. She had never before seen such a white-hot, intense fury. For a brief moment she wondered how long Pernilla had actually known about Dan's relationship with Alex. And how far she would be prepared to go to exact revenge. Then she rejected the idea as quickly as it had appeared. This was Pernilla, a housewife with three children, married to Dan for many years, not a raging fury acting as an avenging angel against her husband's lover. But there was still a cold ferocity in Pernilla's eyes that scared Erica.

"What are you going to do now?"

"I don't know. I don't know anything right now. I just had to get out of the house. That was the only thought I had in my head. I couldn't even look at him."

Erica sent a sympathetic thought to Dan. He was surely in his own private hell right now. It would have felt more natural if it were Dan who had come to her for comfort. Then she would have known what to say, which words would reassure him. She didn't know Pernilla well enough to know how to help. Perhaps it was enough just to listen.

"Why do you think he did it? What wasn't he getting from me that he got from her?"

Now Erica understood why Pernilla had to come to her instead of going to one of her many close friends. She believed that Erica possessed answers about Dan. That she would be able to give Pernilla the key to why he'd acted the way he had. Unfortunately, Erica would have to disappoint her. She had always known Dan as honesty incarnate; it had never even occurred to her that he might be unfaithful. She was never as shocked as when she rang the last number called on Alex's telephone and heard Dan's voice on his voicemail. If she were really honest, she would admit to feeling a great disappointment at that moment—the disappointment of discovering that someone she was close to was not the person she had always thought he was. That's why she understood that Pernilla, besides feeling betrayed and deceived, had also begun asking questions about who Dan really was—this man she had lived with all these years.

"I don't know, Pernilla. I was actually terribly shocked. It wasn't like the Dan I know."

Pernilla nodded. It seemed to console her a bit that she wasn't the only one who'd been fooled. She nervously picked at invisible threads on her baggy cardigan. Her long, dark-brown hair with traces of a permanent had been hastily pulled back in a knot, giving her an unkempt look. Erica had always been a bit scornful about the way Pernilla looked; she should have been able to do a lot more with her appearance. She kept getting her hair permed even though permanents went out of fashion at about the same time mid-length men's jackets did. And she always bought her clothes from cheap mail-order department stores, with low prices and a fashion sense to match. But Erica had never seen her look this shabby.

"Pernilla, I know it's incredibly hard just now, but you're a family, you and Dan. You have three wonderful girls and you've had fifteen good years together. You shouldn't do anything hasty. Don't get me wrong, I don't condone anything he's done. Perhaps you can't stay together after this. Maybe it's impossible to forgive him. But wait to make any decisions until it's sunk in a little. Think carefully before you do anything. I know that Dan loves you; he told me that as recently as today. I also know that he deeply regrets what he did. He told me that he wanted to break it off with her and I believe him."

"I don't know what to believe anymore, Erica. Nothing of what I believed before was true, so what should I believe now?"

There was no answer to that, and the silence settled heavily between them.

"What was she like?"

Once again Erica saw a cold fire burning far back in Pernilla's eyes. She didn't have to ask who she meant.

"It was so long ago. I didn't know her anymore."

"She was beautiful. I saw her here in the summertime. She was just like I wanted to be. Beautiful, elegant, sophisticated. She made me feel like a peasant. I would have given anything to be like her. In a way I can understand Dan. Put me and Alex next to each other and it's obvious who would win."

Pernilla tugged in frustration at her practical but unfashionable clothes as if to demonstrate what she meant.

"I've always been envious of you too. The great love of his youth who moved to the big city and left him behind to pine away. The author from Stockholm who really made something of her life and who came back here and boasted to us normal mortals once in a while. Dan always looked forward to your visits for weeks beforehand."

The bitterness in Pernilla's voice dismayed Erica. For the first time she really felt ashamed of her patronizing attitude toward Pernilla. How little she had understood. On closer examination, she had to admit that she'd found a certain satisfaction in noticing the difference between herself and Pernilla. Between her 500-kronor visits to a hair salon on Stureplan and Pernilla's home perms. Between her designer clothes purchased on Biblioteksgatan and Pernilla's off-the-rack blouses and long skirts. But what difference had it made? Why had she in her weaker moments been happy about that difference? She was the one who had left Dan. Was it only to satisfy her own ego, or had she actually been envious that Pernilla and Dan had so much more than she did? Deep inside had she envied them their family life and perhaps even regretted that she hadn't stayed in Fjällbacka? That she wasn't the one who had the family that Pernilla now had? Had she consciously tried to make Pernilla feel small because she was actually jealous of her? The thought was disgusting, but she couldn't push it away. It made her feel ashamed to the bottom of her soul. At the same time she wondered how far she would have gone to protect what Pernilla had. How far had Pernilla been prepared to go? Erica gave her a thoughtful look.

"What are the children going to say?" It looked as though this was the first time it had occurred to Pernilla that she and Dan weren't the only ones who would be affected. "It has to come out, don't you think? That she was pregnant, I mean? What will the girls say?"

The thought seemed to panic Pernilla, and Erica did her best to calm her.

"The police will have to be told that it was Dan who was seeing Alex, but it doesn't mean that everyone will find out. The two of you can choose what you want to tell the girls. You're still in control, Pernilla."

This seemed to reassure Pernilla, and she took a couple of gulps of coffee. It must have been cold by then, but that didn't seem to bother her. For the first time Erica felt truly angry with Dan. It surprised her that she hadn't felt that way earlier, but now she could feel the fury building up inside her. Was he crazy? How could he throw away everything he had, attraction or no attraction? Didn't he realize how good his life was? She clasped her hands in her lap and tried to convey her sympathy to Pernilla, sitting across the table. Whether Pernilla could take it in or not, she had no idea.

"Thanks for listening. I really appreciate it."

Their eyes met. Less than an hour had passed since Pernilla rang the doorbell, but Erica felt that she had learned a lot in that time, especially about herself.

"Can you manage? Do you have anywhere to go?"

"I'm going home." Pernilla's voice was clear and firm. "She's not going to drive me away from my home and my family. I won't give her that satisfaction. I'm going home to my husband, and we're going to work this out. But not without demands. Things will have to be done differently from now on."

Erica couldn't help smiling in the midst of all the misery. Dan was going to have a good deal to wrestle with, that much was clear. But it was nothing he didn't deserve.

They embraced awkwardly at the door. With all her heart Erica wished Pernilla and Dan only the best as she watched Pernilla get into her car and drive down the road. At the same time, she couldn't help feeling a gnawing uneasiness. The image of Pernilla's hate-filled eyes still lingered in her mind. In those eyes there was no mercy.

All the photos lay spread out on the kitchen table in front of her. All Vera had left of Anders now were pictures. Most of them were old and yellowed. It was many years since there had been any reason to take pictures of him. His baby pictures were in black-and-white, and then there were faded color photos when he grew older. He had been a happy child. A little wild, but always happy. Considerate and polite. He had gravely assumed his role as the man of the house. Sometimes a bit too seriously perhaps, but she had let him have his way. Right or wrong. It was so hard to know. Perhaps there was much she should have done differently, perhaps it hadn't mattered? Who could tell?

Vera smiled when she saw one of her favorite photos.

Anders was sitting on his bicycle, proud as a peacock. She had worked a lot of extra evenings and weekends to buy him that bike. It was dark blue and had a seat that was called a banana seat. According to Anders, it was the only thing he would ever want in his whole life. He had longed for that bike more than anything, and she would never forget the expression on his face when he finally got it on his eighth birthday. He spent every free moment riding around on that bike, and in this picture she had managed to catch him in motion. His hair was long and curly, hanging below the collar of his shiny, tight Adidas jacket with the stripes on the sleeves. This was the way she would always remember him. Before everything began to go wrong.

She had been waiting a long time for this day. Every telephone call, every knock on the door had brought the fear. Maybe this particular call, or this knock, would bring the news that she had dreaded for so long. Until now she had hoped that this day would never come. It was unnatural for a child to die before his parent, and that was probably why it was so hard to imagine the possibility. Hope was the last thing to die, and she had continued to believe that things would work out somehow. Even if it took a miracle. But there was no miracle. And there was no hope. The only thing left now was hopelessness, and a pile of old yellowed photographs.

The kitchen clock was ticking in the silence. For the first time, she saw how shabby her home looked. For all these years, she had done nothing to the house, and it was obvious. She had held the dirt at bay, but she couldn't clean away the indifference that clung to the walls and ceiling. Everything was gray and lifeless.

Wasted. That was what depressed her the most. Everything that had been wasted and squandered.

Anders's happy face mocked her from the pictures. It spoke more clearly than anything else of how she had failed. It had been her task to keep him smiling, to give him faith, hope, and above all love to face the future. Instead she had mutely watched as everything was stripped away from him. She had neglected her job as a mother, and she would never be able to rid herself of the shame.

It occurred to her how little evidence there was that Anders had ever lived. The paintings were gone, the few pieces of furniture he'd had in the apartment would soon be discarded if no one wanted them. In her home, none of his things remained. He had either sold them or destroyed them over the years. The only thing that proved that he had really existed was a handful of photos lying on the table in front of her. And her memories. Of course, he would exist in the memories of others as well, but as a drunken wino, not someone to be missed or mourned over. She was the only one who had happy memories of him. Sometimes it had been hard to summon them up, but they were still there. On a day like today they were the only memories of him that surfaced. Nothing else was allowed.

The minutes turned to hours, and Vera sat at her kitchen table with the photographs in front of her. Her joints grew stiff. Her eyes began to have a hard time distinguishing the details of the photos as the winter darkness slowly strangled the light. But it didn't matter. She was now completely, mercilessly alone.

* * *

The doorbell echoed through the house. It took such a long time before he heard anyone inside that he was about to turn around and go back to the car. But after waiting a while he heard someone cautiously coming to the door. The door opened slowly inward and he saw Nelly Lorentz giving him a puzzled look. He was surprised that she answered the door herself. He had envisioned a stiff butler in livery who would graciously invite him in. But maybe nobody had butlers anymore.

"My name is Patrik Hedström, and I'm from the police in Tanumshede. I'm looking for your son, Jan."

He had rung the office first but was told that Jan was working at home today.

The old lady didn't raise an eyebrow but merely stepped aside and let him in.

"I'll call Jan, just a minute."

Slowly but elegantly, Nelly walked in the direction of a door that opened onto a staircase to the floor below. Patrik had heard that Jan had the cellar apartment in the luxurious house.

"Jan, you have a visitor. The police."

Patrik doubted that Nelly's frail old voice could really be heard downstairs, but footsteps on the stairs proved him wrong. A look filled with hidden meanings passed between mother and son when Jan came up the stairs into the front hall. Nelly nodded to Patrik and went into her room, and Jan came toward Patrik with outstretched hand and a smile showing a lot of teeth. Patrik had the sudden image of an alligator in his mind. A smiling alligator.

"Hello. Patrik Hedström, Tanumshede police station."

"Jan Lorentz. Pleased to meet you."

"I'm investigating the murder of Alex Wijkner, and I have a few questions I'd like to ask you, if you don't mind."

"Of course. I don't know how I can help, but that's your job to decide, not mine, isn't it?"

The alligator grin again. Patrik felt his fingers itching; he wanted nothing better than to wipe that smile off his face. There was something about it that drove him crazy.

"We can go down to my apartment, then we won't disturb Mother up here."

"Certainly, that would be fine."

Patrik had to say that the living arrangements seemed a bit strange. First of all, he had a hard time understanding grown men who still lived at home with their mothers. And second, he couldn't comprehend why Jan put up with being banished to a cellar while the old lady lived upstairs in extravagant luxury in a house of at least two thousand square feet. Jan wouldn't be human if the thought hadn't crossed his mind that Nils would certainly not have been banished to the cellar if he were here today.

Patrik followed Jan down the stairs. He had to admit that for a cellar apartment it wasn't half bad. No expense had been spared. The apartment had been furnished by someone who believed in an ostentatious display of prosperity. There was a lot of gold fringe, velvet, and brocade—no doubt furniture of the finest brands, but unfortunately the decor didn't show itself to best advantage without daylight. The effect was instead a bit like a bordello. Patrik knew that Jan had a wife and wondered which of them had insisted on the decor. Based on his own experience, he would guess the wife.

Jan showed him into a small office. Besides a desk and computer there was also a sofa. They sat down at opposite ends and Patrik took a notebook out of his bag. He had decided to wait to mention Anders Nilsson's death; he didn't want to say anything to Jan about it before he had to. Strategy and timing were important if he hoped to get anything useful out of Jan Lorentz.

He scrutinized the man facing him. He looked too perfect. There wasn't a wrinkle in his shirt or suit. His tie was perfectly tied and he was freshly shaven. Not a hair was out of place, and he radiated calm and self-confidence. Too much calm and self-confidence. Patrik's experience told him that everyone who was questioned by the police behaved nervously, more or less, even if they had nothing to hide. A totally calm exterior indicated that the person in question did have something to hide—that was Patrik's very own home-grown theory. It had proven to be right a remarkable number of times.

"Nice place you have here." It never hurt to be polite.

"Yes, it was Lisa, my wife, who did the decorating. I think she did rather a good job."

Patrik looked around the dark little office, which was sumptuously decorated with shiny marble and pillows with gold tassels. An excellent example of what too little taste in combination with too much money could buy.

"Have you come any closer to a solution?"

"We've uncovered a good bit of information and are beginning to get a sense of what might have happened."

Not entirely true, but it was worth a try to shake him up a bit.

"Did you know Alex Wijkner?" Patrik asked. "I heard for instance that your mother went to the funeral reception."

"No, I can't say that I knew her. Naturally I knew who she was, and in Fjällbacka everyone knows everyone, more or less. But her family moved away many years ago. We used to say hello on the street if we met, but never more than that. As far as Mother is concerned, I can't answer for her actions. You'll have to ask her."

"One of the things that has come out during the investigation is that Alex Wijkner had a, what should I call it . . . relationship with Anders Nilsson. You know him, I assume?"

Jan smiled. A crooked, condescending smile.

"Yes, in this town nobody could avoid knowing who Anders is. He's infamous rather than famous, I would say. He and Alex had an affair, you say? You have to excuse me, but I have a hard time imagining that. A rather odd couple, to put it mildly. I can understand what he would see in her, but I find it very difficult to see why she would want to have anything to do with him. Are you sure you haven't got hold of the wrong end of the stick?"

"We're sure that they did have a relationship. What about Anders? Do you know him?"

Once again he saw a superior smile on Jan's lips, but this time it was even broader. He shook his head in amusement.

"You know what? One could safely say that we don't exactly move in the the same circles. I see him down at the square sometimes with the other alkies, but do I know him? No, actually I don't."

His tone clearly revealed how absurd he thought the question was.

"We associate with people of a quite different social class, and winos aren't normally included," he went on.

Jan waved off Patrik's question as if it were a joke, but Patrik thought he saw a flash of uneasiness in his eyes. It vanished as soon as it appeared, but Patrik was sure he'd seen something. Jan was bothered by questions about Anders. Good, then Patrik knew he was on the right track.

He permitted himself to enjoy his next question even before he asked it, pausing for effect and then asking with feigned surprise: "But if that's true, why did Anders recently place a large number of calls to your number?"

To his great satisfaction, Patrik saw the smile vanish from Jan's lips. The question apparently made him lose his train of thought, and for a moment Patrik could see behind the dandy image that Jan so assiduously cultivated. Behind the artifice, he now saw unalloyed terror. As Jan collected himself, he tried to buy time by lighting a cigar with great care while he avoided looking Patrik in the eye.

"Will you pardon me for smoking?" He didn't wait for a reply, nor did Patrik give him one.

"If Anders rang here I certainly don't understand why. I haven't spoken with him, and I don't think my wife has either. No, that's truly odd."

He sucked on his cigar and leaned back against the sofa with his arm nonchalantly stretched out along the sofa pillows.

Patrik said nothing. In his experience, the best way to get people to say more than they intended to was simply to keep quiet. They would feel a need to fill in the silence if it lasted too long. This was a game that Patrik had mastered. He waited.

"Come to think of it, I think I know what happened." Jan leaned forward and waved his cigar.

"Someone called our answering machine and didn't say anything. All we heard was breathing on the tape. And several times when I answered the phone there was nobody on the other end. It must have been Anders who somehow got hold of our number."

"Why would he call you?"

"How should I know?" Jan threw out his arms. "Envy perhaps. We have plenty of money and that grates on some people. People like Anders are always ready to blame their misfortune on others, especially on people who have actually managed to make something of their lives."

Patrik thought that sounded a bit farfetched. It would be difficult to refute what Jan was saying, but he didn't believe him for a minute.

"I assume that you don't still have those calls you mentioned on the answering machine tape."

"Unfortunately, no." Jan frowned in an attempt to look regretful. "Other messages were recorded over them. I'm sorry, I wish I could help you. But if he rings again I'll make sure to save the tape."

"You can rest assured that Anders won't be ringing your home again."

"Oh? And why is that?"

Patrik couldn't tell whether his puzzled expression was genuine or phony.

"Because Anders has been murdered."

A trail of ashes dribbled onto Jan's lap from the cigar. "Anders was murdered?"

"Yes, his body was found this morning."

Patrik studied Jan closely. If only he could hear what was going on in Jan's head right now, it would all be so much easier. Was his surprise genuine, or was he just an excellent actor?

"Is the perpetrator the same person who murdered Alex?"

"It's too early to say." He didn't want to let Jan off the hook just yet. "So you're quite sure that you don't know either Alexandra Wijkner or Anders Nilsson?"

"I'm actually quite aware of the people I associate with and those I don't. I knew them both by sight, but no more than that." Jan was again back to his smiling, calm self.

Patrik decided to try another line of questioning.

"In Alex Wijkner's home we found an article that she had clipped out of *Bohusläningen* about your brother's disappearance. Do you know why she might have been interested in saving that article?"

Once again, Jan threw out his arms and opened his eyes wide as if to say that he had absolutely no idea. "It was the big topic of conversation here in Fjällbacka many years ago. Perhaps she saved the article as a curiosity."

"Perhaps. What's your view about your brother's disappearance? There are a number of different theories."

"Well, I think that Nils is having the time of his life in some nice hot country. Mother, on the other hand, is completely convinced that he met with an accident."

"Were you very close?"

"No, I wouldn't say that. Nils was quite a bit older, and he wasn't entirely enchanted to have a foster brother to share his Mama's attention. But we weren't mortal enemies either. I think we were mostly indifferent to each other."

"It was after Nils disappeared that you were adopted by Nelly, isn't that right?"

"Yes, that's true. About a year later."

"And with it came half the kingdom."

"Yes, one could perhaps say that."

There was only a bit left of the cigar, and it was threatening to burn Jan's fingers. He stubbed it out brusquely in a gaudy ashtray.

"It's not exactly pleasant that it happened at the expense of someone else, but I can honestly say that I've paid my dues over the years. When I took over the management of the cannery it was going downhill. I restructured the whole company from the ground up, and now we export canned fish and seafood all over the world—to the United States, Australia, South America . . ."

"Why do you think that Nils fled abroad?"

"I really shouldn't be talking about this, but a large sum of money disappeared from the factory right after Nils vanished. In addition, some of his clothes, a suitcase, and his passport were all missing."

"Why wasn't the missing money ever reported to the police?"

"Mother refused. She claimed that it had to be a mistake, that Nils would never have done anything like that. You know how mothers are. It's their job to believe only the best about their children."

He lit another cigar. Patrik thought it was starting to get rather smoky in the little room but said nothing.

"Would you like one, by the way? They're Cuban. Handrolled."

"No thanks, I don't smoke."

"That's a shame. You don't know what you're missing." Jan studied his cigar with pleasure.

"I read in our archives about the fire that killed your parents. That must have been terrible. How old were you? Nine, ten?"

"I was ten. And you're right, it was terrible. But I was lucky. Most orphans aren't taken in hand by a family like the Lorentzes."

Patrik thought it a bit tasteless to talk about luck in that context.

"From what I understand, arson was suspected. Was anything else ever discovered?"

"No, you've read the reports. The police never got any further with the case. Personally, I think my father was smoking in bed as usual and fell asleep." For the first time during the conversation he showed his impatience. "May I ask what this has to do with the murders? I've already said that I didn't know either of the victims, and I can't really see how my difficult childhood comes into this."

"We're investigating even the smallest leads just now. The telephone calls from Anders to your home made me want to check it out. But it doesn't seem to lead anywhere. I beg your pardon for taking up your time unnecessarily."

Patrik stood up and held out his hand. Jan also stood and put down the cigar in the ashtray before he shook Patrik's outstretched hand.

"No problem, no problem at all. It was nice to meet you."

Ingratiating as hell, thought Patrik. He followed Jan up the stairs, close on his heels. The contrast was sharp when he reached the extremely tasteful furnishings of the main floor. Too bad that Jan's wife never got the number of Nelly's interior decorator.

He thanked Jan and left the house with a feeling of having strained gnats and swallowed camels. For one thing, he felt as though he'd caught a glimpse of something in Jan that he should have been able to decipher, something that didn't fit in with that lavishly decorated apartment. For another, there was something not quite right about Jan Lorentz. Patrik returned to his previous thoughts. The guy was just too perfect.

It was almost seven o'clock and the snowstorm had gathered force by the time Patrik finally stood on her doorstep. Erica was surprised at how strong her emotion was when she saw him and how natural it was to throw her arms around his neck. He set down two grocery bags from ICA on the floor in the hall and returned her embrace, holding her close for a long time.

"I've missed you."

"Me too."

They kissed tenderly. After a while Patrik's stomach began to growl. They took that as a signal to take the bags into the kitchen. He had bought far too much food, but Erica put the extra things in the fridge. As if by tacit agreement, they didn't talk about what had happened that day while they fixed dinner. Not until they had satisfied their hunger and were sitting facing each other at the table did Patrik begin to tell her what had happened.

"Anders Nilsson is dead. His body was found in his apartment this morning."

"Were you the one who found him?"

"No, but I got there soon afterward."

"How did he die?"

Patrik hesitated. "He'd been hanged."

"Been hanged? You mean he was murdered?" Erica couldn't conceal her agitation. "Was it the same person who killed Alex?"

Patrik wondered how many times today he'd heard that question. But it was undeniably key to the case.

"We think so."

"Do you have any more leads? Did anyone see anything? Did you find any concrete evidence tying the murders together?"

"Hold your horses." Patrik held up his hands. "I can't tell you any more. We could talk about something more pleasant, you know. How was your day, for instance?"

Erica gave him a crooked smile. If only he knew how unpleasant her day had been too. But she couldn't tell him about it. She had to let Dan tell the story himself.

"I slept fairly late and then I wrote most of the day. Considerably less exciting than your day."

Their hands sought each other across the table. Their fingers intertwined. It felt so lovely and safe to sit there together as the darkness enveloped the house. Huge snowflakes kept floating down like tiny falling stars against the black night sky.

"I spent some time thinking about Anna and the

house as well. I really let her have it on the phone the other day, and I've felt bad about my outburst ever since. Maybe I was being selfish. I was only thinking about how it would affect me if the house were sold, about my loss. But things aren't easy for Anna right now either. She's trying to make the best of her situation, and even though I think she's doing the wrong thing, she's not doing it to be mean. Sure, she can be both thoughtless and naïve sometimes, but she's generally a considerate and generous person, and I've been venting my sorrow and disappointment on her lately. Maybe it would be best to sell the house after all. Start over. I could even buy a new, though much smaller house with the money. Maybe I'm being too sentimental. It's time to move on, to stop regretting what could have been and instead take a look at what I actually have."

Patrik understood that she was no longer talking about the house.

"I'm sorry I have to ask this, but how did the accident happen?"

"That's all right." She took a deep breath. "My parents had been in Strömstad visiting my father's sister. It was dark and rainy, and the cold had formed black ice on the roadway. Papa always used to drive carefully, but they think an animal jumped out in front of the car. He turned hard, went into a skid, and the car slammed right into a tree by the side of the road. They probably died instantly. At least that's what Anna and I were told. There's no way to know whether it was true."

A solitary tear trickled down Erica's cheek, and Patrik leaned forward and brushed it away. He took hold of her chin and made her look straight at him.

"They wouldn't say it if it wasn't true. I'm sure they didn't suffer, Erica. Completely sure."

She nodded mutely. She trusted what he said, and it felt as if a huge burden was lifted from her chest. The car had caught fire, and she had spent many sleepless nights, wondering in horror whether her parents might have lived long enough to feel the fire burning them. Patrik's words quelled her anxiety, and for the first time she felt a kind of peace when she thought about the accident that had killed both her parents. The grief was still there, but the anxiety was gone. With his thumb Patrik wiped away some more tears that rolled down her cheek.

"Poor Erica. Poor, poor Erica."

She took his hand and held it against her cheek.

"There's no reason to feel sorry for me, Patrik. I've actually never been as happy as I am right now, at this moment. It's strange, but I feel so unbelievably safe with you. I don't feel any of that uncertainty I usually feel when I've just slept with someone. Why do you think that is?"

"I think it's because we're meant for each other."

Erica blushed at the magnitude of his words. But she couldn't get away from the fact that she felt the same way. It was like finding her way home.

As if on cue, they got up from the table, left the dishes where they were, and went up to the bedroom arm in arm. Outside a full-blown snowstorm was under way.

It felt strange to be staying in her old room again. Especially since her taste had changed over the years, but the room was still the same. A lot of pink and lace was not really her style any longer.

Julia lay on her back on her narrow childhood bed and stared at the ceiling with her hands clasped on her stomach. Everything was about to disintegrate. Her whole life was falling apart all around her and piling up in a drift of shattered fragments. It was as though she had lived her whole life in a fun house, with trick mirrors in which nothing was what it seemed. She had no idea how things would go with her studies. All enthusiasm had been drained out of her with one blow, and now the school term was going on without her. Not that she thought anyone would notice that she was gone. She had never had an easy time making friends.

As far as Julia was concerned, she might just as well lie here in her pink room and stare at the ceiling until she got old and gray. Birgit and Karl-Erik wouldn't dare do anything but let her have her way. She could live off them for the rest of her life if need be. A guilty conscience would keep their wallets open forever.

It felt as if she were moving through water. All her movements were heavy and difficult and all sounds reached her as if through a filter. At first it hadn't been like this. She'd been full of righteous indignation and a hatred so strong that it scared her. She still felt that hatred, but mixed with resignation instead of energy. She was so used to despising herself that on a purely physical level she could feel how the hatred had changed direction. Instead of being directed outward it had now turned inward and was eating huge holes in her chest. Old habits were hard to break. Hating herself was an art form she had learned to practice to perfection.

She turned over on her side. On the desk stood a

photo of her with Alex; she reminded herself to throw it out. As soon as she could get up she would tear it into a thousand pieces and get rid of it. The look of adoration she saw in her eyes in the picture made her wince. Alex was cool and beautiful as usual, while the ugly duckling beside her turned her round face toward her with a worshipful expression. In her eyes, Alex could never have done any wrong; Julia had always harbored a secret hope deep inside that one day she would hatch from her cocoon and climb out looking just as lovely and self-confident as Alex. She scoffed at her own naïveté. What a joke. And the joke had always been at her expense. She wondered whether they were talking about it behind her back. Whether they were laughing at stupid, stupid, ugly Julia.

A discreet knock on the door made Julia curl up in the fetal position. She knew who it was.

"Julia, we're worried about you. Won't you come downstairs for a while?"

She didn't answer Birgit. Instead she studied with the utmost concentration a lock of her own hair.

"Please, Julia, please."

Birgit came in and sat down on the chair by the desk, facing Julia.

"I understand that you're angry and that you also probably hate us, but you must believe me, we had no intention of harming you."

Julia felt a sense of satisfaction that Birgit looked so worn-out and harried. She looked as if she hadn't slept in several nights. Which she probably hadn't. New wrinkles had formed as crow's feet around her eyes, and Julia thought maliciously that the facelift she was planning to give herself next year for her sixty-fifth birthday might have to be done earlier than planned. Birgit moved the chair a little closer and put her hand on Julia's shoulder. She shook it off at once and Birgit recoiled, hurt.

"Darling, we all love you. You know that."

The fuck she did. What good was this whole charade? They were all quite aware of where they stood with each other. Love? Birgit didn't even know what that was. The only one she had ever loved was Alex. Always Alex.

"We have to talk about this, Julia. We have to support each other now."

Birgit's voice was quivering. Julia wondered how many times Birgit wished that it had been her, Julia, who had died instead of Alex. She saw Birgit give up and how her hand shook when she put back the chair. Before she closed the door on her way out, Birgit gave Julia one last entreating glance. Julia made a point of turning over so that she faced the wall instead. The door closed silently behind Birgit.

Mornings weren't usually Patrik's favorite time of the day, and this one was turning out to be particularly miserable. First of all, he'd been forced to get up from Erica's warm bed and leave her there to go to work. Second, he'd had to shovel for half an hour to dig out his car. And third, the bloody car wouldn't start after he'd dug it out. After repeated attempts he had to give up and go back inside to ask Erica if he could borrow her car instead. That was fine, and luckily it started on the first try.

He dashed into the office a half hour late. The shoveling had soaked him to the skin with sweat, and he

tugged at his shirt a few times to try to fan himself.
The coffeemaker was a necessary first stop before he
could start work. Not until he was seated at his desk
with coffee cup in hand did he feel his pulse begin
to slow down. He allowed himself to daydream for
a moment, sinking into the feeling of reckless, sense-
less love. The night before had been just as wonderful
as the first. They had even managed to muster a tiny
bit of good sense and made sure they got a few hours'
sleep. To say that he was rested would have been an
exaggeration, but at least he wasn't in a coma like the
day before.

The first thing he dealt with were the notes from his
meeting with Jan the day before. It hadn't produced
any new details that aroused his interest, yet he didn't
consider the interview wasted time. It was just as
important for the investigation that he get a feeling for
the people who were, or could be, involved. "Homicide
investigations are about people," one of his instructors
at the Police Academy had often said, and those words
of wisdom had stuck in Patrik's mind. Besides, he
thought he was a good judge of people. During interviews with witnesses and suspects he always tried to
disconnect from the cold facts for a while and concentrate on soaking up impressions from the person facing
him. Jan had generated no directly positive feelings in
Patrik. Unreliable, slippery, and hedonistic were words
that popped up in his head when he tried to gather his
impressions of Jan's personality. It was quite obvious
that the man was hiding more than he revealed. Once
again, Patrik picked up the stack of papers dealing
with the Lorentz family. He still could show no concrete link between them and the two homicides, except

for the phone calls from Anders to Jan. But he couldn't prove that Jan's story about wrong numbers coming to his answering machine was not correct. Patrik picked up the folder on the death of Jan's parents. Something in the tone of Jan's voice when he spoke about the incident bothered Patrik. There was something that rang false. He had an idea. Patrik picked up the phone and dialed a number he knew by heart.

"Hi, Vicky, how's it going?"

The person on the other end of the line affirmed that it was going well. After the introductory pleasantries Patrik got down to business.

"Vicky, I wonder if you could do me a favor. I'm checking on a guy who must have entered the rolls at social services in about 1975. Ten years old, called Jan Norin back then. You think you might have anything on the case? Okay, I'll hang on."

He drummed impatiently with his fingers on the desktop as Vicky Lind at the social services office checked her computer records. After a while he heard her come back on the line.

"You have the data there? Fantastic. Can you see who the social worker was on the case? Siv Persson. That's great. Do you have her phone number?"

Patrik quickly wrote down the number on a Post-it note and hung up after promising to take Vicky to lunch one day. He punched in the number she'd given him and instantly heard a brisk voice on the line. It turned out that Siv did remember the case of Jan Norin, and it was fine if he came over right away.

Patrik grabbed his jacket from the coatrack with such eagerness that he managed to tip over the whole rack in the process. Even worse, on its way to the floor the rack had pulled down both a picture from the wall and a vase of flowers from the bookshelf, all of which created a tremendous crash. For the time being Patrik left everything where it landed. When he got to the corridor he saw heads poking out of every doorway. He just waved and ran out the front door as curious pairs of eyes stared after him.

The social service office was no more than a couple of hundred yards from the police station. Patrik trudged through the snow down the main street. At the end of the street he turned left at Tanumshede Inn and continued halfway down the block. The office was in the same building as the community administration, and he took the stairs. He was shown into Siv's office after cheerfully greeting the receptionist, a girl from his class in high school. Siv Persson didn't bother to get up to shake hands when he came in. Their paths had crossed many times during Patrik's years as a cop, and they respected each other's professional expertise even though they didn't always share the same opinion on how best to handle a case. Part of the reason was that Siv was one of the nicest people he knew, but social workers couldn't always get by with seeing only the best in people. At the same time he admired her for being able to retain her basically positive view of human nature despite all examples to the contrary that she had encountered over the years. Patrik felt that he seemed to have gone in the opposite direction.

"Hi, Patrik. So you managed to make it here in spite of all the snow."

Patrik reacted instinctively to the unnatural cheerfulness of her voice.

"Yes, but a snowmobile would have helped."

She raised her eyeglasses dangling on a cord around

her neck and set them on the tip of her nose. Siv loved bright colors, and today her red glasses matched her clothing. She'd had the same hairdo as long as he'd known her. A pageboy style cut straight as an arrow that reached to her jawline, and short bangs cut just above the eyebrows. Her hair was a shiny copper-red, and the bright colors made Patrik feel more lively just by looking at her.

"It was one of my old cases you wanted to look at, you said? Jan Norin?"

Her voice was still sounding strained. She had already fetched the material before he arrived, and a thick folder lay on the desk.

"Well, we have a good deal of material on this individual, as you see," she went on. "Both parents were addicts, and if they hadn't died in an accident we would have had to intervene sooner or later. They let the boy run wild, and he basically had to raise himself. He showed up at school in dirty, ragged clothes and was bullied by his schoolmates because he smelled bad. Apparently, he had to sleep in the old stable and then go to school in the same clothes he slept in."

She looked at Patrik over the top of her glasses.

"I assume you're not coming here to abuse my trust, but to procure the requisite authorization, if only after the fact, so that you can acquire the data on Jan?"

Patrik merely nodded. He knew that it was important to follow regulations, but sometimes investigations required a certain efficiency, and then the wheels of bureaucracy would have to turn after the fact instead. Siv and he had always had a good, pragmatic working relationship, but he knew she had to ask that question.

"Why didn't you step in earlier?" Patrik asked. "How could the situation have been allowed to get so bad? It sounds as if Jan had been neglected since birth, and yet he was ten years old when his parents died."

Siv gave a deep sigh. "Yes, I know what you mean, and believe me, I've had the same thought many times. But times were different when I started working here, no more than a few months before the fire actually. It took extreme circumstances before the state would step in and restrict the right of parents to raise their children as they saw fit. Many people were advocating a liberal form of child rearing as well, and unfortunately it was children like Jan who suffered. There were never any traces of physical abuse found on him. To be crass, perhaps the best thing would have been if he were beaten, so that he could have gone to the hospital. Then at least we would have started to keep an eye on the family situation. But either he was abused so that it was never outwardly visible, or else his parents 'simply' neglected him." Siv wiggled her fingers to indicate quotation marks around the word "simply."

Patrik felt a sudden wave of sympathy for the boy Jan. How the hell could somebody be a normal human being after growing up under such circumstances?

"But you haven't heard the worst of it. We never had any proof, but there were indications that his parents let men abuse Jan in return for money, or narcotics."

Patrik felt his jaw drop. This was much worse than he could ever have imagined.

"As I said, we could never prove anything, but today we can see that Jan followed the standard pattern that we now know is associated with children who have been sexually abused. For one thing, he had big disciplinary problems at school. The other children may have bullied him, but they were also afraid of him."

Siv opened the folder and leafed through the papers until she found what she was looking for.

"Here it is. In the fourth grade he brought a knife to school and used it to threaten one of the worst bullies. He actually cut him in the face, but the school administration hushed the whole thing up. As far as I can see, he wasn't punished. Several such incidents followed when Jan displayed excessive aggression toward his classmates, but the incident with the knife was the most serious. He was also reported to the principal on several occasions because he had acted inappropriately toward the girls in the class. For such a young boy, he showed a knowledge of extremely advanced sexual behavior and allusions. The reports never resulted in any actions either. No one knew quite what to do with a child with such disturbing ways of relating to the people around him. Today, we would definitely react to such blatant signals and take action of some sort, but you must remember that this was in the early seventies. It was a whole different world back then."

Patrik felt nearly faint with sympathy and rage. How could anyone treat a child that way?

"After the fire . . . were there other incidents like this?" he asked.

"No, that's the strange thing. After the fire he was placed immediately with the Lorentz family, and after that we had no reports that Jan ever had a problem again. I drove over to their house a few times to follow up on the situation, and I found a completely different boy. He sat there in his suit with his hair slicked down and stared at me without blinking as he replied politely to all my questions. It was quite horrible, actually. A person doesn't change overnight like that."

Patrik gave a start. It was the first time he'd ever heard Siv hint at anything negative regarding one of her cases. He understood there was something worth digging into further. There was something she wanted to say, but he would have to ask the right question.

"With regard to the fire . . ."

He let the words dangle in the air a moment and saw that Siv sat up straighter in her chair. That meant he was on the right track.

"I heard certain rumors about the fire." He gave Siv a questioning look.

"I can't be responsible for rumors. What was it you heard?"

"That the fire was arson. In our investigation it's even listed as 'probable arson,' but no trace of the perpetrator was ever found. The fire started on the ground floor of the house. The parents were asleep in a room upstairs and never had a chance. Did you ever hear anything about who might have hated the Norins enough to do something like that?"

"Yes." Her reply was monosyllabic and so quiet that he wasn't sure he'd really heard it.

She repeated in a louder voice, "Yes, I know who hated the Norins enough to want to set fire to them."

Patrik sat silently and let her continue at her own pace.

"I accompanied the police out to the house. The fire department was the first on the scene. One of the fire-fighters had gone to examine the site, to check whether any sparks had blown away from the house and might be smoldering somewhere else. The fireman found Jan in the stable. When the boy refused to leave, they contacted us here at social services. I was a new social worker, and in retrospect I have to admit that I thought it was very exciting. Jan was sitting in the stall, all the way at the back, leaning against the wall, under the watchful eye of a fireman, who was extremely relieved to see us arrive. I shooed off the police and went in to try to console Jan, as I thought I should, and then take him out of there. His hands kept moving in the dark where he was sitting, but I couldn't see what he was doing. When I got closer I saw that he was sitting there fidgeting with something in his lap. It was a box of matches. With undisguised glee he was sorting the matches: burned black ones in one half of the box and new red ones in the other half. The expression on his face was sheer joy. He actually seemed to be glowing from within. It was the most horrid thing I've ever seen in my life, Patrik. I can still see that face before me sometimes when I go to bed at night. I went over to him and carefully took the box of matches away. Then he looked up at me and said, 'Are they dead now?' That was all. 'Are they dead now?' Then he giggled and willingly let me lead him out of the old stable. The last thing I saw as we left was a blanket, a flashlight, and a pile of clothes in a corner of the barn. That's when I understood that we were complicit in his parents' death. We should have taken action many, many years earlier."

"Have you ever told anyone about this?"

"No, what would I say? That I thought he murdered his parents because he was playing with matches? No,

I've never said anything until you came and asked me just now. But I've always suspected that he would have a run-in with the police sooner or later. What is he mixed up in?"

"I can't say anything yet, but I promise to tell you as soon as I can. I'm incredibly grateful that you told me all this, and I'll get busy with the paperwork so that you won't have any problems."

He waved and left.

After he was gone Siv stayed at her desk. Her red glasses hung on their cord around her neck, and she rubbed the bridge of her nose between her thumb and forefinger as she closed her eyes.

At the same moment that Patrik stepped out into the snowdrifts on the pavement, his mobile phone rang. His fingers had already grown stiff in the bitter cold, and he had a hard time getting the little lid of his mobile open. He hoped it was Erica but was disappointed when he saw that it was the station's dispatch number blinking on the display.

"Patrik Hedström. Hi, Annika. No, I'm right outside social services. Okay, but give me a minute or two and I'll be back at the station."

He snapped the lid shut. Annika had done it again. She had found something that didn't add up in Alex's CV.

The snow squeaked under his feet as Patrik jogged in the direction of the station. The snowplow had passed by while he was visiting Siv, and the return wasn't the same struggle as before. Few brave souls were venturing out in the cold weather, and the main street was deserted except for an occasional passerby hurrying along with collar turned up and cap pulled down as protection from the cold.

Inside the door of the station Patrik stamped off the snow that had collected on his shoes. He made a note that snow in combination with street shoes made socks unpleasantly wet. He should have been able to figure that out in advance.

He went straight to Annika's office. She was clearly waiting for him, and from the pleased expression on her face he could see that what she'd found was good, really good.

"Are all your clothes in the wash, or what?"

At first Patrik didn't understand the question, but judging from her teasing smile it was a joke at his expense. The penny dropped a second later and he looked down at what he was wearing. Damn, he hadn't changed clothes since the day before yesterday. He wondered if he smelled a bit, or if he smelled a lot.

He muttered something in reply to Annika's comment and tried to glare at her as evilly as he could. She found this even more amusing.

"Yeah, yeah, I get it," Patrik said. "Now get to the point. Speak up, woman!"

He slammed his fist onto her desk in feigned rage. A vase of flowers responded instantly by toppling over and spilling water all over.

"Oh, sorry, I didn't mean to do that. I'm so damn clumsy . . ."

He searched for something to wipe up the water, but Annika was a step ahead of him as usual and produced a roll of paper towels from somewhere behind the desk. She calmly began wiping off her desk as she gave a now-familiar command to Patrik.

"Sit!"

He obeyed at once, thinking it rather unfair that she didn't throw him a sweet as reward for being so clever.

"Shall we begin?" Annika didn't wait for Patrik's answer but began to read from her computer screen.

"Now let's see. I started with the time of her death and worked backward. Everything seems to add up for the time she lived in Göteborg. She started the art gallery with her friend in 1989. Before that she went to university for five years in France, majoring in art history. I received her transcript by fax today, and she took her exams on time and passed them. She attended high school at Hvitfeldtska in Göteborg. I also got her grades from there. She was no brilliant student, but no slouch either. She consistently stayed in the middle."

Annika paused and looked at Patrik, who was leaning over and trying to read ahead on her screen. She turned it away from him a little so he couldn't read her discovery prematurely.

"Before that it was a boarding school in Switzerland. She went to an international school, L'École de Chevalier, which costs a fortune." Annika put great emphasis on the last phrase.

"According to the information I got when I rang them, it costs about a hundred thousand kronor per semester, not counting room, board, clothes, and books. And I checked—the prices were just as high when Alexandra Wijkner attended."

Her words were absorbed thoughtfully by Patrik, who was thinking out loud. "So the question is, how the Carlgren family could afford to send Alex to that school. From what I understood, Birgit has always been a housewife, and it would be impossible for Karl-

Erik to earn enough money to cover such expenses. Did you check—"

Annika interrupted him. "Yes, I asked who was responsible for Alexandra's tuition, but they don't give out that sort of information. The only thing that could make them more forthcoming would be an order from the Swiss police, but with that bureaucracy it would take us at least six months to get it. I began at the other end instead and started checking the Carlgren family's finances over the years. Perhaps they inherited some money, who knows? I'm waiting for a report from the bank, but it will take a couple of days before we have it. But . . ." another rhetorical pause, "that's not even the most interesting thing. According to the Carlgren family's statements, Alex started boarding school during the spring semester of 1977. According to the school's register she didn't start until spring, 1978."

Annika leaned back in her chair triumphantly and crossed her arms.

"Are you sure?" Patrik could hardly control his excitement.

"I checked and double-checked and even triple-checked. The year from spring of '77 to spring of '78 is missing from Alex's life. We have no idea where she was. The family moved away from here in March 1977 and then there's nothing, not a single shred of information until Alex starts at the school in Switzerland. At the same time, her parents show up in Göteborg. They buy a house, and Karl-Erik starts his new job as CEO of a medium-sized company in the wholesale trade."

"So we also don't know where the parents were during this period?"

"No, not yet. But I'm continuing to search. The only thing we know is that there wasn't any data to indicate that they were in Sweden during that year."

Patrik counted on his fingers. "Alex was born in 1967, so she was, let's see, ten years old in 1977."

Annika checked the screen again. "She was born on January third, so that's right, she was ten when they moved."

Patrik nodded thoughtfully. It was valuable information that Annika had managed to dig up, but right now it only gave rise to more questions. Where was the Carlgren family from 1977 to 1978? A whole family couldn't just disappear. They must have left some sort of trail; it was simply a matter of finding it. At the same time there had to be something more. The information that Alex had had a child earlier still baffled him.

"Didn't you find any other gap in her history? For example, couldn't somebody have taken the tests in her name at the university? Or couldn't her partner at the gallery have run it by herself for a period? It's not that I don't trust what you found out, but maybe you should double-check the facts again. And check the hospital records to see if any Alexandra Carlgren or Wijkner gave birth to a child. Start at the Göteborg hospitals, and if you don't find anything there, then work your way out into the countryside. There must be some record of the birth somewhere. A child can't simply go up in smoke."

"Couldn't she have had the baby abroad? During her time at the boarding school, for instance? Or in France?"

"Of course, why didn't I think of that? See if it's

possible to get anything through international channels. And see if you can find any way to trace where the Carlgrens went. Passports, visas, embassies. Somewhere there must be a record of where they went."

Annika was taking notes for dear life.

"By the way, have any of the others found anything worthwhile yet?"

"Ernst has checked Bengt Larsson's alibi, and it holds up, so we can cross him off. Martin talked to Henrik Wijkner by phone but could get nothing else on the connection between Anders and Alex. He intends to keep questioning Anders's wino buddies about whether Anders might have said anything to them about it. And Gösta . . . Gösta's sitting in his office feeling sorry for himself, trying to work up the energy to go to Göteborg and interview the Carlgrens. I'm betting he won't leave until Monday at the earliest."

Patrik sighed. If they were going to solve this case, it would probably be best if he didn't rely on his colleagues. He'd have to do the legwork himself.

"You didn't think about asking the Carlgrens directly?" Annika said. "There might not be anything suspicious about it. Maybe there's some reasonable explanation."

"They're the ones who gave us the information about Alex. For some reason they tried to conceal what they were doing between '77 and '78. I'll talk with them, but first I want to have a little more to go on. I don't want them to have a chance to wriggle out of this."

Annika leaned back and smiled slyly. "So when are we going to hear those wedding bells ringing?"

Patrik saw that she had no intention of dropping this juicy subject anytime soon. He would have to resign himself to being the station's source of entertainment for a while.

"Well, it might be a bit early for that. We should probably be together for at least a week before we book a church."

"So-o-o-o, you're together, are you?"

He realized that he'd fallen right into that trap feet-first with eyes wide open.

"No, er yes, maybe we are . . . I don't know, we get along so far, but it's all awfully new and maybe she's going back to Stockholm soon . . . oh, I don't know. You'll have to be satisfied with that for the time being." Patrik was squirming like a worm in his chair.

"Okay then, but I want to be kept up to date on what's happening, do you hear me?" Annika wagged her finger at him.

He nodded in resignation. "All right, I'll keep you posted. I promise. Satisfied?"

"Well, that will have to do for now, I suppose."

She got up, came around the desk, and before he knew it he was caught in an exuberant bear hug, crushed against Annika's ample bosom.

"I'm so glad for your sake. Don't mess it up, Patrik, promise me." She gave him an extra squeeze that made his ribs protest. Since he didn't have access to any air at the moment he couldn't reply, but she apparently took his silence as acquiescence and released him, but not until she topped it all off with a firm pinch on the cheek.

"Go home and change your clothes now, you hear? You stink!"

And with that comment Patrik found himself sent back out to the corridor, with a sore cheek and ribs. He felt his rib cage cautiously. He liked Annika a lot, but sometimes he wished that she would be a bit more careful with a poor thirty-five-year-old guy whose physique was on a downhill slope.

Badholmen, the bathing island, looked deserted and forsaken. In the summer it was packed full of happy bathers and noisy children, but now the wind howled desolately across the snow that had fallen like a thick blanket overnight. Erica stepped carefully through the snow covering the rocks. She had felt a great need to get a little fresh air, and here from Badholmen she had an uninterrupted view of the islands and the seemingly endless white ice. Cars could be heard in the distance, but otherwise it was mercifully silent; she could almost hear herself think. The diving tower loomed next to her. Not as high as she had thought it was when she was little—then it seemed to reach all the way to heaven—but still high enough that she would never dare jump from the top platform on a warm summer's day.

She could have stood there forever. Wrapped up in furs, she felt the cold trying in vain to penetrate her clothes. Inside herself, she felt the ice thawing. She hadn't realized how lonely she had been until the loneliness was gone. But what would happen with her and Patrik if she had to move back to Stockholm? It was many miles away, and she felt much too old for a long-distance relationship.

If she was forced to go along with selling the house, was there any possibility that she would stay here?

She didn't want to move in with Patrik before their relationship had been properly tested over a period of time. So the only alternative was to find some other place to live in Fjällbacka.

The problem was that nowhere else appealed to her. If they sold the house she would rather cut all ties to Fjällbacka than come here and watch strangers tramping about in her childhood home. Nor could she really imagine renting an apartment here; that would feel very strange. She felt her happiness slipping away as she piled all these negative thoughts on top of each other. Of course, it would be possible to solve this dilemma, but she had to admit that even if she wasn't exactly ancient, so many years of living alone with only herself to think of had taken their toll, and she didn't feel very flexible anymore. After much deliberation she had decided that she was ready to leave her life in Stockholm, but only if she could keep living in the familiar setting of her childhood home. Otherwise, it would simply be too much change in her universe all at once. She wouldn't be able to face it, no matter how much in love she was.

Perhaps her parents' death had also made her less inclined to make big changes. That change was enough for many years to come. Right now, she wanted to sink into a safe, secure, and predictable life. Previously, she had been afraid to commit herself to a relationship. Now she wanted nothing more than to include Patrik in that secure, and predictable life. She wanted to be able to plan for all the usual stages: living together, engagement, marriage, children, and then many ordinary days, one after another, until one day they could look at each other and discover that they had grown old together. That shouldn't be too much to ask.

For the first time Erica felt a pang of sorrow at the thought of Alex. It was as if she only now grasped that Alex's life was irrevocably over. Even though their paths had not crossed for many years, she had still thought of her from time to time. And she had always known that Alex's life was running parallel to her own. Now she was the only one who had a future, who would get to experience all the sorrows and joys that the years ahead would bring. Every time she thought about Alex now, and for the rest of her life, the image that would appear to her would be that of Alex's pale corpse in the bathtub. The blood on the tiles and her hair that looked like a frozen halo. Maybe that was why she had decided to start writing the book about her. It was a way to relive the years when they were so close to each other, and at the same time get to know the woman Alex had become after they parted ways.

What had worried Erica the past few days was that the material felt a little too flat. It was as if she were looking at a three-dimensional model from only one side. The other sides were equally important if she was going to get an idea of how the figure looked, but she hadn't yet been allowed to see them. What she decided was she needed to start looking more at the people around Alex, not only the main actors, but all the bit players who had been part of her life. Then Erica's thoughts had gravitated primarily to what she had sensed and intuited as a child but had never clearly understood.

Something had happened the year before Alex moved away, and nobody had ever bothered to tell Erica what it was. The whispering had always stopped as soon as she came near; she had been shielded from

something that she now desperately needed to understand. The problem was that she didn't know where
to start. The only thing she remembered from her
attempts to eavesdrop on conversations that were conducted in whispers by the adults was that she heard the
word "school" mentioned more than once. It wasn't
much to go on, but it was all she had. Erica knew that
the teacher she and Alex had had in fifth grade was
still living in Fjällbacka. That was probably as good a
place to start as any.

The wind had picked up and despite her thick layers of clothing the cold began to creep in. Erica felt that
it was time to start moving. She glanced one last time
at Fjällbacka nestled in its protected position with the
mountain towering behind. In the summer it was usually bathed in golden light, but now it was gray and
bare; yet Erica thought it was even lovelier like this. In
the summertime the area was more reminiscent of an
anthill with its constant activity. Now a quiet peace had
settled over the little town, and she could almost imagine it hibernating. At the same time she knew that the
peace was illusory. Under the surface there was just as
much evil as anywhere else inhabited by human beings.
Erica had seen a good deal of that in Stockholm, but
she believed that it was even more sinister here. Hatred,
envy, greed, and revenge, all of it concealed underneath
a huge lid that was created by sentiments such as: "what
would people say?" All the evil, pettiness, and malice
was quietly allowed to ferment beneath a surface that
always had to look so neat and clean. Now that Erica
was standing on the rocks of Badholmen and looking
back at the snow-covered little town, she wondered in
silence what secrets it was guarding.

She gave a shiver, stuck her hands deep in her pockets, and headed back toward town.

Life had become more and more threatening with each year that passed. Axel Wennerström was always discovering new dangers. It had started when he became acutely aware of all the billions and trillions of bacilli and bacteria swirling around him. Having to touch anything became a challenge; if he was forced to do so, he saw armies of bacteria rushing over him, threatening to bring along a myriad of known and unknown diseases that would surely cause him a long and painful death. Then his very surroundings became a threat. Big surfaces presented certain dangers, small surfaces presented others. Ending up in a crowd of people made sweat seep from all the pores on his body, and his breathing would get fast and shallow. The only environment Axel could even partially control was his own home. He quickly realized that he could actually live his life without ever having to set foot outside his door again.

The last time Axel went outside was eight years ago. He had so effectively repressed all possible desire to venture out that he no longer knew whether the rest of the world was there or not. He was content with his life and saw no reason to change a thing.

Axel Wennerström spent his days following a routine that was well practiced by now. Each day followed the same schedule, and today was no different. He got up at seven o'clock and ate breakfast. Then he cleaned the whole kitchen with strong cleaning solutions in order to eradicate any possible bacteria that the food he'd eaten for breakfast might have spread after it was taken out of the refrigerator. He spent the next few hours dusting, wiping off, and putting in order the rest of the house. Not until one o'clock could he grant himself a break and sit down with his newspaper on the veranda. According to a special arrangement with Signe, the letter carrier, he got his newspaper in a plastic bag each morning. That allowed him to repress at least partially the image of all the filthy human hands that had handled the paper before it landed in his mailbox.

A knock on the door made his adrenaline skyrocket. Nobody was supposed to come at this time of day. The person who delivered his food normally came early on Friday mornings. That was the only visitor he usually had. Laboriously, Axel made his way inch by inch toward the door. The knocks came again, insistently. He reached out a shaky hand toward the top lock and unfastened it. He wished he had a peephole, the kind usually found in the doors of more modern apartments, but in his old building there wasn't even a window in the door through which he could view the intruder. He also unlocked the bottom bolt and with a pounding heart he opened the door. He had to check a desire to close his eyes to shut out whatever appalling, nameless creature awaited him out there.

"Axel? Axel Wennerström?"

He relaxed. Women were less threatening than men. For safety's sake he kept the security chain on.

"Yes, what is it?"

He tried to sound as discouraging as possible. He just wanted this person, whoever she was, to go away and leave him in peace.

"Hello, Axel. I don't know if you remember me, but I was in your class at school. Erica Falck?"

He searched his memory. That was so many years ago, and there had been so many pupils. Faintly, the image of a little blonde girl began to appear. That was it, Tore's girl.

"I wonder whether I could have a word with you."

She gave him an urgent look through the crack in the door. Axel sighed deeply, unhooked the door chain, and let her in. He tried not to think of how many unknown organisms she was bringing with her into his clean home. He pointed to a shoe rack to indicate that she should take off her shoes. She obeyed politely and also hung up her coat and scarf. To avoid getting her dirt in the rest of the house he showed her to the wicker furniture on the veranda. She sat down on the sofa, and he made a mental note to wash the cushions as soon as she left.

"It's certainly been a long time."

"Yes, it must be twenty-five years since you were in my class, if I'm figuring correctly."

"Yes, that's right. The years go by so fast."

Axel found small talk frustrating, but reluctantly resigned himself to it. He wished that she would get to the point and tell him why she came here. Then she would leave and he could have his home to himself again. For the life of him he couldn't comprehend what she wanted from him. Old pupils had come and gone by the hundreds over the years; until now, he had been spared actually seeing any of them in person. But now Erica Falck was sitting here before him. He felt on pins and needles as he sat on the wicker armchair facing her. He was so eager to get rid of her. His eyes kept looking at the cushion underneath her, and he could literally see all the bacteria she had brought in creeping and crawling and spreading down from the sofa across the floor. It probably wouldn't be enough to wash the cushion; he would have to clean and disinfect the entire house after she left.

"You're probably wondering why I'm here."

He merely nodded in reply.

"You must have heard that Alexandra Wijkner was murdered."

He had heard about it, and it had stirred up things that he had spent a good part of his life trying to repress. Now he wished even more that Erica Falck would get up and walk out the door. But she was still sitting there, and he had to fight a childish impulse to put his hands over his ears and hum loudly to shut out all the words he knew were going to come.

"I have my own reasons for investigating a number of things associated with Alex and her death, and I'd like to ask you a few questions, if you don't mind."

Axel closed his eyes. He had known that this day would come eventually.

"All right. That will be fine."

He didn't want to ask what her reasons were for asking about Alex. She could keep them to herself, if she wanted to; he wasn't interested. She could ask her questions, but there was nothing forcing him to answer them. At the same time he felt to his astonishment a strong urge to tell everything to the blonde woman sitting across from him. To unload onto someone, anyone, everything he had been holding on to for twenty-five years. It had poisoned his life. It had grown like seeds deep inside his conscience and then slowly spread like a poison through his body and his mind. In his more lucid moments, he knew that this was at the root of his mania for cleanliness and his increasing terror of anything that might endanger the control he had over his surroundings. Erica Falck could ask what she liked, but he would do his utmost to check every impulse to answer. He knew that if he started to lose his grip, dams would burst and threaten to eradicate the shield he had so carefully constructed. That must not happen.

"Do you remember Alexandra from school?"

He smiled bitterly to himself. Most of the children he'd had in school had only left behind faint, shadowy memories, but Alexandra was just as distinct to him today as she was twenty-five years ago. Although he could hardly say that out loud.

"Yes, I remember Alexandra. Although as Alexandra Carlgren, not Wijkner, of course."

"Yes, that's obvious. What do you remember of her in school?"

"She was quiet, a little withdrawn, acted much older than her age."

He saw that Erica was frustrated at his curt reply, but he was making a conscious attempt to say as little as possible, as if the words might take over and begin to flow on their own if he let out too many of them.

"Was she good in school?"

"Well, not especially. She wasn't one of the most ambitious pupils I can recall, but she was intelligent in a quiet way. She was probably about in the middle of the class."

Erica hesitated a moment and Axel realized that now they were approaching the questions that she really wanted to ask. The questions up till now had just been warm-ups for her.

"But her family moved away in the middle of the term. Do you recall what reasons Alex's parents gave for moving?"

He pretended to ponder the question, putting his fingertips together and resting his chin on them in a feigned gesture of trying to remember. He saw that Erica moved forward a little on the sofa, showing her eagerness to hear the answer to her question. He was going to have to disappoint her. The only thing he could tell her was the truth.

"Yes, I think her father got a job in another town. To be honest I don't remember exactly, but I vaguely recall it was something like that."

Erica couldn't hide her disappointment. Once again, Axel felt the urge to rip open his chest and reveal what had been hiding there for all these years. To clear his conscience by pouring out the entire naked truth. But he took a deep breath and pushed back what was threatening to spill out.

Erica continued stubbornly. "But the decision came a bit suddenly, from what I understood. Had you heard anything about it earlier, had Alex made any mention that they were going to move?"

"Well, I don't think it was so strange. Of course it did come up rather suddenly, as you say, if I remember correctly. But these things can happen quickly. Perhaps her father received an offer with short notice, how do I know?"

He threw out his arms in a gesture that said Erica's guess was as good as his, and the frown between her eyebrows deepened. This wasn't the answer she wanted. But she would have to make do with it.

"Yes, but later there was something else," Erica

went on. "I recall vaguely from those days that people were talking about something in connection with Alex. I also remember that I heard the grown-ups mention something about the school. Do you know what that might have been? I only have vague memories, as I said, but it was something that was hushed up in front of us children."

Axel felt all the joints in his body turn rigid. He hoped that his consternation was not as obvious as it felt. Of course he knew that there must have been rumors, there always were. It was impossible to keep anything secret, yet he believed that the damage had been limited. He had even helped to limit it; that was part of what was still eating at him from inside. Erica was waiting for a reply.

"No, I can't think of what that might have been. But there's always so much talk, you know how people are. There isn't any substance to most rumors. I wouldn't attach any importance to it if I were you."

Disappointment was written all over her face. She hadn't found out anything of what she had come here for, he understood that much. But he had no choice. It was like a pressure cooker. If he opened the lid just a crack, the whole thing would explode. At the same time, something was still insisting on getting out. He felt as if someone had taken over his body. He felt his mouth open and his tongue start to shape the words, words that should not be spoken. To his relief Erica stood up and the moment passed. She put on her coat and boots and held out her hand. He looked at her hand and swallowed a couple of times before he took it. He had to check an impulse to grimace. Contact with another person's skin disgusted him beyond all description. She finally walked out the door, but turned just as he was about to close it.

"Oh, by the way, did Nils Lorentz have any connection with Alex, or with the school for that matter, that you know of?"

Axel hesitated but then made a decision. She would find out about it sooner or later, if not from him then from someone else.

"Don't you remember? He was a substitute teacher at the grade school for one term."

Then Axel shut the door, locked the double lock, put on the chain, leaned his back against the door and closed his eyes.

He quickly got out the cleaning supplies and wiped away all traces of the unwelcome visitor. Only then did his world feel safe again.

The evening was off to a bad start. Lucas was in a foul mood when he came home, and she kept trying to stay a step ahead so as not to give him any additional reason to be annoyed. Anna knew that in this situation, when he came home in a bad mood, he would search for any excuse to vent his rage.

She took extra care preparing dinner. She made his favorite dish and laid the table so it looked perfect. She had to keep the kids away by putting *The Lion King* on the video in Emma's room and feeding Adrian from the bottle so he'd go to sleep. She put on Lucas's favorite CD, Chet Baker, and finally she dressed up a bit and put more effort into fixing her hair and makeup. But she soon realized that tonight it wouldn't matter what she did. Lucas had clearly had a really bad day at work, and the rage that was building up inside him had to come out. Anna saw the flash in his eye; it was like walking about waiting for a bomb to go off.

The first blow came with no warning. A slap from the right that made her head ring. She held her cheek and looked up at Lucas as if she still hoped that something inside him would relent at the sight of the marks he had left on her. Instead, it aroused a desire in him to do her even more harm. It had taken her the longest time to understand and accept that he actually enjoyed hurting her. For many years she had believed his assurances that hitting her hurt him as much as it did her, but no longer. She had seen the monster in him before; by now it was quite familiar.

She curled up instinctively to protect herself from the blows she knew would come. When they began raining down on her she tried to focus on a point inside herself, a place that Lucas couldn't reach. It was something she had gotten better and better at doing. Even though she was aware of the pain, she could distance herself from it most of the time. It was as if she were floating on the ceiling and looking down on herself as she lay curled up on the floor while Lucas vented his wrath on her.

A sound made her quickly return to reality and slip inside her own body again. Emma was standing in the doorway with her thumb in her mouth and her blanket in her arms. Anna had gotten her to stop sucking her thumb over a year ago, but now she was sucking it hard to comfort herself. Lucas hadn't noticed her yet as he stood with his back to Emma's room, but he turned around when he saw that Anna's eyes were fixed on something behind him.

Swiftly, before Anna could stop him, he went over

to his daughter, roughly lifted her up, and shook her so hard that Anna could hear her teeth rattling against each other. Anna started to get up from the floor, but everything felt as though it were happening in slow motion. She knew that she would always be able to play back this scene in her mind's eye—Lucas shaking Emma who looked with big, uncomprehending eyes at her dear Papa who had suddenly been transformed into a terrifying stranger.

Anna threw herself forward at Lucas to protect Emma. But before she reached him she watched in terror as Lucas slammed the little child's body against the wall. Anna heard a terrible crunching noise and knew that her life had now been irretrievably changed. Lucas's eyes were covered by a shiny film. He seemed almost uncomprehending as he looked at the child in his hands before he carefully and tenderly set her down on the floor. Then he lifted her up in his arms again, like a little baby this time, and looked at Anna with shining, robot-like eyes.

"She has to go to the hospital. She fell down the stairs and hurt herself. We have to explain that to them. She fell down the stairs."

He was talking incoherently and heading for the front door without looking to see if Anna was coming along. She was in a state of shock and vaguely followed after him. She seemed to be moving in a dream, but she could wake up from it at any moment.

Lucas kept repeating, "She fell down the stairs. They have to believe us, as long as we tell the same story, Anna. Because we're going to tell the same story, Anna. She fell down the stairs, didn't she?"

Lucas rambled on, but all Anna could do was nod.

She wanted to tear Emma, who was now crying hysterically in pain and confusion, out of Lucas's arms, but she didn't dare. At the last second, when they were already in the stairwell, she awoke from her haze and remembered that Adrian was still back in the apartment. She hurried inside to get him and rocked him protectively in her arms the whole way to the emergency room, as the knot in her stomach kept growing bigger and bigger.

"Will you come over and have lunch with me?"

"Sure, gladly. When should I come?"

"I can have something ready in an hour or so. Will that work for you?"

"Yes, that'll be perfect. Then I'll have time to clean up a bit. See you in an hour." There was a little pause, and then Patrik said hesitantly, "Kisses, bye."

Erica felt herself blush slightly from happiness at this first little but significant endearment used in their relationship. She replied with the same phrase and they hung up.

As she prepared lunch she was a little ashamed at what she had planned. At the same time she felt that she could do nothing else. When the doorbell rang an hour later she took a deep breath and went to open the door. It was Patrik, and he got a passionate reception, which Erica had to interrupt when the egg timer rang as a signal that the spaghetti was done.

"What's for lunch?" Patrik patted his stomach to show his appetite.

"Spaghetti Bolognese."

"Mmmmm, sounds great. You're every man's dream woman, did you know that?"

Patrik sneaked up behind Erica, put his arms around her and began nuzzling her neck.

"You're sexy, intelligent, fantastic in bed, but above all, most important of all, you're talented in the kitchen. What more could a man want. . . ?"

The doorbell rang. Patrik gave Erica a questioning look. She avoided his eyes and went to open the door, first wiping her hands on the kitchen towel. Outside stood Dan. He looked harried and the worse for wear. His whole body drooped and his eyes looked dead. Erica was shocked when she saw him but pulled herself together and tried not to show it.

When Dan came into the kitchen, Patrik gave Erica an inquisitive look. She cleared her throat and introduced them to each other.

"Patrik Hedström—Dan Karlsson. Dan has something he wants to tell you. But let's sit down first."

She carried the pot of meat sauce into the dining room. They all sat down to eat but the mood was oppressive. Erica felt heavyhearted about the situation but knew it was necessary. She had rung Dan that morning and convinced him that he had to tell the police about his relationship with Alex. And she had proposed that he do it at her house, which might make a tough task a bit easier, she hoped.

She ignored Patrik's puzzled look and started things off.

"Patrik, Dan is here today because he has something to tell you, in your capacity as a policeman."

She nodded to Dan, inviting him to begin. Dan was looking down at his plate, and he hadn't touched his food. After another moment of embarrassed silence, he began to speak.

"I'm the man Alex was seeing. I'm the father of the child she was expecting."

There was a clatter as Patrik dropped his fork onto his plate. Erica put her hand on his arm and explained, "Dan is one of my oldest and dearest friends, Patrik. I found out that Dan was the man Alex had been seeing here in Fjällbacka. I invited both of you to lunch because I thought it would be easier to talk about it in these surroundings rather than at the police station."

She could see that Patrik did not appreciate that she had meddled like this, but she would have to deal with that later. Dan was a good friend, and she intended to do everything she could so that the situation didn't get even worse. When she spoke with him on the phone he had told her that Pernilla had taken the kids and gone to her sister's in Munkedal. She needed time to think, she'd said. She didn't know what was going to happen, and she couldn't promise anything. Dan saw his whole life falling apart around him. In a way it would be a relief to tell the police. The past few weeks had been so difficult. At the same time he'd been forced to grieve for Alex in secret, he had jumped each time the telephone rang or there was a knock on the door, convinced that the police had figured out that he was the man Alex had been meeting. Now that Pernilla knew, Dan was no longer afraid to tell the police. Nothing could be any worse than it already was. He didn't care what happened to him, just so he didn't lose his family.

"Dan has nothing to do with the murder, Patrik. He'll tell you everything you want to know about himself and Alex, but he swears that he never hurt her in any way, and I believe him. I hope that the police can try to keep this confidential. You know how people talk, and Dan's family has already suffered enough. Dan too, for that matter. He made a mistake and believe me, he's paying a very high price for it."

Patrik still didn't look particularly pleased, but nodded as a sign that he was listening to what she had to say.

"I'd like to talk with Dan alone, Erica."

She didn't object but got up politely and went out to the kitchen to wash up. From the kitchen she could hear their voices rising and falling. Dan's dark, deep voice and Patrik's somewhat lighter one. The discussion occasionally sounded heated, but when they came out to the kitchen after almost half an hour, Dan looked relieved. Patrik still looked stern. Before he left, Dan gave Erica a hug and shook Patrik's hand.

"I'll let you know if we have any more questions," said Patrik. "You might have to come in and give a written statement as well."

Dan only nodded mutely and left after a final wave to them both.

The look in Patrik's eyes did not bode well.

"Don't ever, ever do that again, Erica. We're investigating a murder and we have to do everything the proper way."

He scrunched up his forehead when he was angry, and she had to check an impulse to kiss away the wrinkles.

"I know, Patrik. But you had the child's father high up on the list of suspects. I knew that if Dan came into the station you'd put him in an interrogation room and probably start getting tough with him. Dan wouldn't be able to stand that right now. His wife has taken the kids and left him, and he doesn't know if they're

ever coming back. In addition to that, he's lost someone who meant something to him, no matter how you
may look at it. He lost Alex. And he hasn't been able
to show his grief to anyone or talk to anyone about it.
That's why I thought that we could start by talking
here, in a neutral environment and without any other
police involved. I understand that you have to interro-
gate him some more, but now the worst is over. Please
forgive me for deceiving you, Patrik. Do you think you
can ever forgive me?"

She pouted as seductively as she could and snuggled
up to him. She took his arms and put them around
her waist and then stood on tiptoe so she could reach
his lips with hers. She tentatively stuck in the tip of
her tongue, and it didn't take many seconds before she
felt a response from him. He pushed her away after a
moment and looked steadily into her eyes.

"You're forgiven for this time, but don't ever do it
again, do you hear me? Now I think we should heat up
the rest of the lunch in the microwave and take care of
this rumbling stomach of mine."

Erica nodded, and arm in arm they went back to
the dining room where lunch still lay mostly uneaten
on the plates.

When Patrik had to get back to the station and was
on his way out the door, Erica remembered what else
she had wanted to tell him.

"You know, I told you that I had a vague memory that there was talk about something in connection
with Alex just before her family moved away, and that
it had something to do with school. I tried to check
up on it, but didn't find out very much. But I was
reminded that there was another connection between

Alex and Nils, besides the fact that Karl-Erik worked at the cannery. Nils was a substitute teacher at the grade school for one semester. I never had him as a teacher, but I know that he taught Alex's class from time to time. I don't know if this has any significance, but I thought I'd tell you about it anyway."

"So-o-o, Alex had Nils as a teacher." Patrik stopped to think on the front porch.

"As you say, maybe it's of no importance, but right now all connections between Nils Lorentz and Alex are of interest. We don't have too much else to go on." He gave her a serious look. "There was one thing Dan said that really stayed with me. He said that toward the end Alex had talked a lot about having to settle up with her past. That it was important to dare take care of things that were difficult, so she could move on. I wonder whether that could have any connection with what you're saying, Erica."

He fell silent for a moment but then jerked himself back to the present and said, "I can't rule out Dan as a suspect, I hope you understand that."

"Yes, I understand, Patrik. But go easy on him if you can. Are you coming over tonight?"

"Yes, I just have to go home and get a change of clothes and things. But I'll be here around seven."

They kissed good-bye. Patrik went back to his car. Erica stood there on the steps watching him until the car vanished from sight.

Patrik didn't drive straight back to work. Without actually knowing why, he'd brought along the keys to Anders's apartment as he was leaving the station. He decided to stop there and have a look around in peace and quiet. What he needed now was something, anything, that could give him an opening in the case. It felt as though he was running into blind alleys wherever he turned, and as though they would never find the killer, or killers, whoever it was. Alex's secret lover, just as Erica had said, had been at the top of the list of suspects, but now Patrik was no longer so sure. He wasn't prepared to write off Dan completely, but he had to admit that the trail no longer felt as hot.

The mood in Anders's apartment was eerie. In his mind's eye Patrik still could see the image of Anders slowly swaying back and forth from the rope, even though he had already been cut down by the time Patrik saw him. He didn't know what he was searching for, but he put on a pair of gloves so as not to disturb any evidence. He stood right underneath the hook in the ceiling where the noose had been fastened and tried to get an impression of how it was done. How had Anders been hoisted up there? It was simply impossible to figure out. The ceiling was high and the noose had been tied directly below the hook. It must have taken considerable strength to raise Anders's body that high. Of course he had been quite thin, but in view of his height he still must have weighed a good deal. Patrik made a mental note to check Anders's weight when the autopsy report arrived. The only explanation he could find was that several people had lifted him up there together. But how come there weren't any marks on Anders's body? Even if he had been sedated somehow, lifting the body up there should have left some marks. It just didn't add up.

He went further into the apartment and looked closely at everything. Since there wasn't much furniture besides the mattress in the living room and a table with two chairs in the kitchen, there wasn't a lot to examine. Patrik noticed that the only things providing storage space were the kitchen cabinets, and he went through them one by one. They had already been gone through once before, but he still wanted to make sure that nothing had been missed.

In the fourth drawer he checked, he found a notepad, which he took out and placed on the kitchen table for closer inspection. He held up the pad at an angle to the window to see whether there were any impressions on it. He saw quite rightly that what had been written on the top page had made an impression on the paper underneath, and he used an old proven trick to try to make out some of the text. Using a pencil he found in the same drawer, he lightly rubbed the side of the pencil lead across the page. He could only make out parts of the text, but it was enough to tell him what the message was about. Patrik gave a low whistle. That was interesting, very interesting. It set all his gears in motion. He carefully put the pad into one of the plastic bags he'd brought along from the car.

He continued his search of the drawers. Most of the contents were sheer junk, but in the last one he went through he did find something interesting. He looked at the piece of leather he was holding between his fingers. It was exactly like the one he had seen at Alex's house when he and Erica were there. It had lain on her nightstand and he had read precisely the same burned-in inscription that he now read here: "T.T.M. 1976."

When he turned it over he saw that just like the one at Alex's house, there were some blurry spots of blood on the reverse. The fact that there was a link between

Alex and Anders that they didn't yet understand was nothing new. But what did puzzle him was the gnawing feeling he got when he looked at the piece of leather.

Something in his subconscious was demanding attention. Something was trying to tell him that the little patch was significant in some way. Patrik was obviously missing something here; he just couldn't see it. But he did know that the patch told him that the connection between Alex and Anders went far back in time. At least until 1976. The year before Alex and her family moved away from Fjällbacka and vanished without a trace for twelve months. A year before Nils Lorentz disappeared for good. Nils, who according to Erica had been a teacher at the school that both Alex and Anders had attended.

Patrik realized that he needed to talk to Alex's parents. If the suspicions that were beginning to take shape in his mind were correct, they were the ones in possession of the final answers, the answers that could put together the pieces he already thought he could see.

He picked up the notepad and the leather patch in their plastic bags and glanced once more at the living room before he left. Again he saw the image of Anders's pale, skinny, swaying body in his mind's eye. He vowed to get to the bottom of this, to find out why Anders had ended his sad life in a noose. If the glimpses he had seen so far were right, it was a tragedy beyond all comprehension. He sincerely hoped that he was wrong.

Patrik found Gösta's name in the phone book and dialed the number to his extension at the station. He would probably be interrupting him in a game of solitaire.

"Hi, it's Patrik."

"Hi, Patrik." Gösta's voice sounded as weary as always on the other end. Boredom and despondency had given him both an outer and an inner weariness.

"Look, have you scheduled a visit to the Carlgrens in Göteborg yet?"

"No, I haven't gotten around to it yet. I've had a lot of other things to take care of."

Gösta sounded defensive. Patrik's question put him on guard; he was nervous that he would be criticized because he still hadn't carried out his assignment. He simply couldn't bring himself to do it. Picking up the phone and placing a call seemed impossible; getting into the car and driving to Göteborg was insurmountable.

"Would you have any objection if I made the visit in your place?"

Patrik knew that this was simply a rhetorical question. He was well aware that Gösta would be overjoyed to get out of it. As he had thought, Gösta replied with newfound joy in his voice, "No, absolutely not! If you feel that you want to take over, be my guest. I have so much else to get done, that I don't know how I'd be able to fit it in anyway."

They were both aware that they were playing a game, but their roles had been established years ago and they worked well for both of them. Patrik could do what he wanted to do, and Gösta, secure in the knowledge that the job was being done, could go back to his computer game.

"If you could find their number for me, I'll ring them at once."

"Yes, of course, I have it right here. Let's see . . ." Gösta read off the number.

Patrik wrote it down on the pad he always had fastened to the dashboard of his car. He thanked Gösta and hung up so he could call the Carlgrens. He crossed his fingers that they would be at home. He was in luck. Karl-Erik answered after the third ring. When Patrik explained his business he sounded hesitant at first, but then agreed that Patrik could come by and ask a few questions. Karl-Erik tried to find out what sort of questions they were, but Patrik said only that there were a few hazy points that he hoped they could clarify for him.

He backed out of the parking space in front of the apartment building and turned first right and then left at the next intersection toward the highway to Göteborg. The first part was slow, with meandering small roads through the forest, but as soon as he got out onto the highway things went much faster. He passed Dingle, then Munkedal, and when he came to Uddevalla he knew he was halfway there. As always when he was driving, he played music full blast. He thought there was something very relaxing about driving a car. He sat for a moment outside the big light-blue villa in Kålltorp, gathering his faculties. If his hunch was right, he was about to shatter this family idyll inexorably. But sometimes that was his job.

A car drove up the driveway. She didn't see it, but she heard the sound on the gravel. Erica opened the front door and peered out. Her mouth fell open in astonishment when she saw who was getting out of the car. Anna waved wearily to her and then opened the back doors to lift the children out of their car seats. Erica slipped on a pair of clogs and went out to help her.

Anna hadn't said a word about driving over, and Erica wondered what was going on.

Anna looked pale in her black coat. She carefully lifted Emma down to the ground, and Erica loosened the belt of Adrian's car seat and lifted him up in her arms. She got a big toothless smile in thanks and felt a smile spreading over her own face in reply. Then she gave her sister a questioning look, but Anna just shook her head as if to say, "Don't ask." Erica knew her sister well enough to know that Anna would tell her when she was good and ready. Before that it would be impossible to drag anything out of her.

"Imagine what fine visitors I'm going to have today. Imagine that you've all come to see Auntie."

Erica babbled and smiled at the baby in her arms and then looked down to say hello to Emma too. She had always been a big favorite of Emma's, but this time she didn't return her smile. Instead she clutched her mother's coat tightly and stared suspiciously at Erica.

Erica walked ahead into the house with Adrian. Anna followed close behind, holding Emma by one hand and carrying a small bag in the other. Erica saw to her astonishment that the baggage area of the mini-van was packed full, but she made a supreme effort not to ask any questions.

With clumsy, unpracticed hands she took off Adrian's outer clothing while Anna helped Emma out of her coat, although with considerably more skill. Only then did Erica see that one of Emma's arms was in a cast up to the elbow. She gave Anna a shocked look. Again her sister almost imperceptibly shook her head. Emma was still looking at Erica with big, serious eyes and staying close to her mother the whole time. She had stuck her thumb in her mouth; that also told Erica that something serious had happened. Anna had announced a year ago that she had finally weaned Emma from sucking her thumb.

With Adrian's warm baby body solidly anchored in her arms, Erica went into the living room and sat down on the sofa with him on her lap. Adrian looked at her with fascination. Little smiles flitted across his face, as if he couldn't decide whether he wanted to laugh or not. He was so sweet that Erica almost thought she could eat him up.

"Did you have a good trip?"

Erica didn't know exactly what to say, but small talk would have to do until Anna decided to tell her what was going on.

"Yes, it's a fairly long drive. We went through Dalsland. Emma got carsick on the curvy roads through the forest, so we had to stop several times on the way for her to get some fresh air."

"I suppose that wasn't much fun, Emma, was it?"

Erica made an attempt to establish contact with Emma. The girl shook her head but kept peering out from under her bangs and holding on to her mother.

"I thought you could take a nap now, Emma," said Anna. "Do you think that will be all right? You haven't slept a wink the whole trip, so you must be very tired."

Emma nodded in agreement and as if on command she began rubbing her eyes with her good hand.

"Can I put them to bed upstairs, Erica?"

"Yes, of course. Put them in Mama and Papa's bedroom. I'm sleeping there now, so the beds are all made up."

Anna took Adrian from Erica, who to her delight grunted in protest at being lifted out of his nice aunt's arms.

"The blankie, Mama," Emma reminded her when they were already halfway up the stairs, and Anna came back down to fetch the bag she'd left in the hall.

"Would you like some help?"

Erica thought it looked a little difficult for Anna to be balancing Adrian on one arm and carrying the bag in the other, while Emma stubbornly refused to relinquish her hold on her mother.

"No thanks, it's okay. I'm used to it."

Anna gave her a crooked, bitter smile that Erica had a hard time interpreting.

While Anna put the children to bed, Erica busied herself making fresh coffee. She wondered how many pots she had drunk lately. Her stomach was going to start protesting soon. She froze in the middle of holding a scoop of coffee over the filter. Damn. Patrik's clothes were spread over the entire bedroom, and Anna would have to be an idiot not to put two and two together. Her mocking smile when she came down the stairs a minute later was confirmation enough.

"So-o-o, Sister. What is it that you haven't told me? Who's the man who has such a hard time hanging up his clothes properly?"

Erica felt herself blush.

"Well, er, it all happened rather fast, you see."

She could hear herself stammering and Anna was even more amused. The weary lines in her face were briefly smoothed out, and Erica caught glimpses of her sister the way she used to be, before she met Lucas.

"All right, who is it? Stop mumbling and give your

little sister the juicy details. You could start with his name, for instance. Is it somebody I know?"

"Yes, it is actually. I don't know if you remember Patrik Hedström?"

Anna hooted and slapped her knee. "Patrik! Sure I remember Patrik! He used to follow you around like a little puppy with his tongue hanging out. So he finally got the chance . . ."

"Yes, I mean, I knew that he had a slight crush on me when we were younger, but I had no idea how he really felt . . ."

"Good Lord, you must have been blind! He was head over heels in love with you. God, how romantic. Here he's been pining for you all these years, and finally you look deep into his eyes and discover the great love of your life."

Anna clutched her heart dramatically, and Erica couldn't help laughing. This was the sister she knew and loved.

"Well, it wasn't quite like that. He's been married in the meantime, but his wife left him a few years ago and now he's divorced and lives in Tanumshede."

"So what does he do? Don't tell me he's just a carpenter. I'd be sooo jealous. I've always dreamed about hot carpenter sex."

Erica childishly stuck her tongue out at Anna, who stuck hers out in turn.

"No, he's not a carpenter. He's a cop, if you must know."

"A cop, my, my. A man with a truncheon, in other words. Well, that's not so dumb either . . ."

Erica had almost forgotten what a tease her sister could be. She simply shook her head as she poured coffee into two cups. Anna made herself at home. She went to the fridge, took out the milk, and poured a little in her cup and a little in Erica's. The teasing smile disappeared from her face, and Erica understood that she would now find out the reason why Anna and her kids had suddenly appeared in Fjällbacka like this.

"Well, my love story is over. For good. I suppose it really has been for years, but it was only now that I realized it."

Anna fell silent and gazed sadly into her coffee cup.

"I know you never liked Lucas, but I really did love him. Somehow I managed to rationalize why he hit me. He always asked forgiveness and swore that he loved me, at least he used to. Somehow I managed to convince myself that it was all my fault. If only I could be a better wife, a better lover, and a better mother, then he wouldn't have to hit me."

Anna was answering Erica's silent questions.

"Yes, I know how absurd it sounds, but I was incredibly good at fooling myself. Since he was a good father to Emma and Adrian, that excused a lot. I didn't want to take their Papa away from them."

"But something happened?"

Erica was prodding Anna. She could see how hard it was for her to talk about this. Her pride was hurt, and Anna had always been an incredibly proud person who would only reluctantly admit when she was wrong.

"Yes, something happened. Last night he went off on me like he usually does. More and more often lately, actually. But yesterday . . ."

Her voice broke and Anna swallowed a couple of times to stifle her tears.

"Last night he went off on Emma. He was so furious, and in the middle of everything she came into the room and he couldn't stop himself." Anna swallowed again. "We drove to the emergency room, and they confirmed that she had a fracture in her arm."

"I assume you reported Lucas to the police?"

Erica felt rage forming a hard knot in her stomach, a knot that was growing bigger and bigger.

"No." The word came almost inaudibly from Anna and the tears started rolling down her pale cheeks. "No, we said that she fell down the stairs."

"But dear God, did they really believe that?"

Anna gave Erica a crooked smile. "You know how charming Lucas can be. He completely turned the heads of the doctor and the nurses, and they felt almost as sorry for him as they did for Emma."

"But Anna, you have to report him to the police. Surely you can't let him get away with this?"

She looked at her weeping sister. Sympathy was competing with fury. Anna was shrinking before her eyes.

"It will never happen again, I intend to see to that. I pretended that I was listening to his excuses, and then I packed up the car and drove off as soon as he left for work. I never intend to go back to him; Lucas will never have a chance to hurt my children again. If I'd reported him to the police they would have brought in social services, and then maybe they might have taken the children from both of us."

"But Lucas is never going to sit still for you taking the children, Anna. Without a police report and an investigation, how are you going to prove that you should have sole custody of the children?"

"I don't know, I don't know, Erica. I can't think about it now, I just had to get away from him. The rest of it will have to be worked out later. Please don't yell at me!"

Erica set down her cup on the table, got up from her chair, and put her arms around her sister. She stroked her hair and murmured consoling words. She let Anna cry on her shoulder and felt her sweater getting wetter and wetter. At the same time her hatred toward Lucas grew. She really wanted to punch that fucker in the mouth.

Birgit looked out at the street, hidden behind her curtain. Karl-Erik could see from her hunched shoulders how tense she was. She had been pacing anxiously up and down ever since the police rang. For the first time in ages, he felt utterly calm inside. Karl-Erik intended to give the police officer all the answers—if he asked the right questions.

The secrets had been burning inside him for so many years. In a way it had been easier for Birgit. Her manner of handling the situation had been to deny that it ever occurred. She refused to talk about it and fluttered on in life as if nothing had happened. But it did happen. Not a day had passed when he hadn't thought about it, and each time the burden had felt even heavier to bear. He knew that from the outside it looked as if Birgit were the stronger of them. At all social events she glittered like a star while he was the gray, invisible man at her side. She wore her beautiful clothes, her expensive jewelry, and her makeup like a suit of armor.

Whenever they came home after yet another glittering, exhilarating evening, and she took off her armor, she seemed to collapse into nothingness. All that was left was a quivering, insecure child who clung to him for support. During their entire marriage he had been torn between conflicting feelings for his wife. Her beauty and fragility aroused tenderness and a protective instinct that made him feel like a man. But her unwillingness to face life's more difficult aspects sometimes drove him to the brink of madness. What made him most furious was that he knew that she wasn't stupid, but her upbringing had taught her that a woman must at all costs conceal the fact that she had any sort of intelligence. Instead, she should focus all her energy on being beautiful and helpless. And pleasing others. When they were newlyweds he hadn't seen this as anything odd; that was the spirit of the times back then. But times had changed, placing whole different demands on both women and men. He had adapted, but his wife never did. So this day was going to be very hard on her. Karl-Erik believed that deep inside she knew what he was intending to do. That was why she had been pacing back and forth across the room for almost two hours. But he also knew that she didn't intend to let him drag their family secrets out into the open without a fight.

"Why does Henrik have to be here?" Birgit turned toward him, anxiously wringing her hands.

"The police want to talk with the family, and Henrik is part of the family, isn't he?"

"Yes, but I think it's unnecessary to get him mixed up in this. The police will probably just ask some general questions. Do we really have to drag him all the way out here for that? No, I think it seems unnecessary."

Her voice rose and fell with unspoken questions. He knew her so well.

"Here he comes."

Birgit quickly stepped away from the window. It took a moment before the doorbell rang. Karl-Erik took a deep breath and went to open the door, while Birgit retired to the living room where Henrik was already sitting on the sofa, deep in his own thoughts.

"Hello, I'm Patrik Hedström."

"Karl-Erik Carlgren."

They shook hands politely. Karl-Erik estimated that the police officer was about Alex's age. He often did this these days: thought about other people in terms of Alex.

"Come in. I thought we could sit in the living room and talk."

Patrik looked a bit taken aback when he saw Henrik, but recovered quickly and greeted both Birgit and Henrik politely. They all sat down around the coffee table and there was a long moment of oppressive silence. Finally Patrik spoke.

"Well, I realize this was a bit sudden, but I'm grateful you could see me on such short notice."

"We were just wondering if something has happened. Have you found out anything new? We haven't heard from you in a while . . ." The sentence petered out and Birgit looked hopefully at Patrik.

"The investigation is progressing slowly but surely, and that's about all I can say at this point. The murder of Anders Nilsson has also thrown a whole new light on the case."

"Yes, that's obvious, but have you determined whether the person who murdered Anders is the same person who murdered our daughter?"

Birgit's chatter had a frenetic tone to it that made Karl-Erik check an impulse to lean forward and place a soothing hand on hers. Today, he had to steel himself against assuming the protector role in which he was so well practiced.

For a moment he allowed himself to drift away in his mind, away from the present to a past that now seemed so distant to him. He looked around the living room with something that resembled distaste. They had fallen so easily for the temptation, one could almost smell the blood money. The house in Kålltorp was more than they ever dared dream of when the children were small. It was big and airy, with the fine details from the thirties preserved, even as they had indulged all the modern creature comforts. With the salary from his job in Göteborg, they could finally afford all of this.

The room they were sitting in was the largest room in the house. Much too overfurnished for his taste, but Birgit had a penchant for shiny, glittery objects and everything was as good as brand new. About every three years, Birgit would begin to complain that everything looked so worn out. She would tell him how bored she was of everything in their house, and after a few weeks of her entreating looks he usually gave in and pulled out his wallet. It was as though she could keep reinventing herself and her life over and over again, by replacing everything. At present she was into a Laura Ashley period, and the room was so full of rose patterns and flounces that it felt suffocatingly feminine. Karl-Erik knew that he wouldn't have to tolerate it for more than a year, max. If he got lucky on the next redecoration Birgit would be partial to Chesterfield armchairs and the English hunting motif. On the other hand, if he was unlucky it would probably be tiger stripes next time.

Patrik cleared his throat. "I have a number of questions, and I'd appreciate your help in clarifying a few matters."

Nobody said anything so he continued. "Do you know anything about how Alex and Anders Nilsson happened to know each other?"

Henrik looked shocked, and Karl-Erik said he had no idea. It pained him to say that, but it couldn't be helped.

"They were in the same class, but that was so many years ago."

Birgit squirmed nervously as she sat on the sofa next to her son-in-law.

Henrik said, "I recognize the name. Didn't Alex have some of his paintings for sale at the gallery?"

Patrik nodded. Henrik went on, "I don't understand, was there supposed to be some further connection between them? What reason could there be for someone to murder both my wife and one of her artists?"

"That's precisely what I'm trying to work out." Patrik paused before he continued. "Unfortunately we were also able to confirm that they had an intimate relationship."

In the silence that followed, Karl-Erik saw many emotions vying on the faces of the two people sitting across from him, Birgit and Henrik. He himself was only mildly surprised, but it quickly gave way to acceptance. What the police officer had said must be true. It was only natural if one considered the circumstances.

Birgit held her hand over her mouth in an expression of horror, and Henrik's face slowly lost all its color. Karl-Erik saw that Patrik Hedström was not enjoying his role as the harbinger of bad news.

"That can't be right." At a loss, Birgit looked at the others but found no support. "Why would Alex have a relationship with someone like that?" She gave Karl-Erik an urgent look, but he refused to meet her eyes and instead stared down at his hands. Henrik said nothing; he looked as if he had collapsed.

"You don't know whether they continued to stay in contact after you moved away?" asked Patrik.

"No, I can't imagine they would. Alex cut all her ties when we moved away from Fjällbacka." Again it was Birgit who spoke while Henrik and Karl-Erik sat in silence.

"There's another thing I'd like to ask about. You moved to Göteborg in the middle of the term when Alex was in the fifth grade. Why was that? The move seemed very sudden."

"There was nothing strange about it. Karl-Erik got a fantastic job offer that he simply couldn't refuse. He had to decide quickly; they needed someone right away. So that's why it all happened so fast." She wrung her hands incessantly as she talked.

"But you didn't register Alex in any school in Göteborg, did you? Instead she started at a boarding school in Switzerland. What was the reason for that?"

"With Karl-Erik's new job we found ourselves in much improved financial circumstances, and we simply wanted to give Alex the best opportunities we could," said Birgit.

"But weren't there any good schools in Göteborg?"

Patrik implacably hammered away with his questions. Karl-Erik couldn't help admiring his commitment. Once he had also been that young and enthusiastic. Now he was just tired.

Birgit went on, "Of course there were, but just imagine what a social network she could acquire by going to a boarding school like that. There were even a couple of princes at the school. Just think what contacts like that could do for a girl."

"Did you go to Switzerland with Alex?"

"Naturally we went down there to register her at school, if that's what you mean."

"Well, that wasn't quite what I meant." Patrik looked in his notebook to refresh his memory.

"Alexandra left here in the middle of spring semester 1977. She was registered at the boarding school in the spring of 1978, and that was also when Karl-Erik began his job here in Göteborg. My question is therefore, where were you during that year?"

A furrow had formed between Henrik's eyebrows, and he shifted his gaze back and forth between Birgit and Karl-Erik. Both were avoiding his eyes. Karl-Erik felt a grinding pain spreading outward from his heart area and slowly increasing in strength.

"I don't understand what you're getting at with all these questions. What does it matter whether we moved in '77 or '78? Our daughter is dead and you come here asking us questions as if we're the guilty ones. There must have been some mistake somewhere. Someone wrote it down wrong in some register, that's what it must be. We moved here in the spring of '77 and that's when Alexandra began school in Switzerland."

Patrik gave Birgit an apologetic look as she got more and more upset. "I'm sorry, Mrs. Carlgren, to be causing you any discomfort. I know you're going through a difficult time, but I have to ask these questions. And my information is correct. The two of you didn't move here until spring 1978, and for the whole year before that there is nothing to prove that you were even in Sweden. So I have to ask once again: where were you during the year between spring of '77 and spring of '78?"

With desperation in her eyes Birgit turned to Karl-Erik for help, but he knew that he could no longer give her the kind of help she wanted. In the long run, he believed that he was doing this for the good of the family; he also knew that, in the short run, it might crush her. But he had no choice. He gave his wife a sad look and then cleared his throat.

"We were in Switzerland. Alex, my wife, and I."

"Hush, Karl-Erik, don't say any more!"

He ignored her. "We were in Switzerland because our ten-year-old daughter was pregnant."

He wasn't surprised to see Patrik drop his pen in his consternation over what he'd just said. Whatever the police officer had reckoned on, or suspected, it was something else entirely to hear it said out loud. How could anyone have imagined something so awful?

"My daughter was exploited—raped. She was only a child."

He felt his voice break and pressed his fist hard against his lips to try to collect himself. After a while he was able to go on. Birgit refused even to look at him, but now there was no turning back.

"We could tell that something was wrong, but we

didn't know what it was. She had always seemed happy, secure. Sometime in the beginning of the fifth grade she began to change. She turned quiet and uncommunicative. None of her friends came over anymore, and she could be away for hours at a time. We didn't know where she was. We didn't take it that seriously, thinking it was only a phase she was going through. A preliminary stage to her teenage years maybe, I don't know."

He had to clear his throat again. The pain in his chest was increasing. "It wasn't until she was in her fourth month that we discovered she was pregnant. We should have seen the signs earlier, but who could believe . . . We couldn't even imagine . . ."

"Karl-Erik, please." Birgit's face was like a gray mask. Henrik looked numb, as if he couldn't believe what he was hearing, which he probably couldn't. Even to his own ears Karl-Erik could hear how incredible it sounded when he spoke the words aloud. For twenty-five years the words had been gnawing at his guts. Out of consideration for Birgit he had stifled his need to speak out, but now the words came pouring forth and he couldn't stop them.

"We couldn't consider an abortion. Not under those conditions. Nor did we give Alex any opportunity to make a choice, even if she could have done so. We never asked her how she felt or what she wanted to do. Instead, we hushed it all up. We took her out of school, went abroad, and stayed there until she gave birth to the child. No one could know anything about it. Because what would people say?"

He could hear for himself how bitter that last sentence sounded. Nothing had been more important than that. It had taken precedence over their own daughter's happiness and well-being. He couldn't even place the entire blame on Birgit for making that choice. She had never been the one who was most concerned about outward appearances. After years of self-examination, he had been forced to admit to himself that he let her have her way based on his own wish to retain an unblemished appearance. He could feel sour stomach acid creeping up his throat. He swallowed hard and went on.

"After Alex had the baby, we registered her at the boarding school, returned to Göteborg and got on with our lives."

Every word was dripping with bitterness and self-contempt. Birgit's eyes were filled with fury, perhaps hatred as well. She stared at him intensely as if to use sheer willpower to make him stop. But he knew that the process had begun the same moment that Alex was found dead in the bathtub. He knew that the police would root around, turn over every stone, and drag out into the sunlight everything that crawled. It was better that they tell the truth in their own words. Or in his words, as it turned out. Perhaps he should have done it earlier, but he had needed the time to muster the courage. Patrik Hedström's telephone call was the last push he needed.

Karl-Erik knew that he had left out a good deal, but a weariness had settled over him like a blanket, and he let Patrik take up the thread and ask the questions that would fill in the gaps. He leaned back in the armchair and gripped the armrests hard.

Henrik was the first to speak. His voice was noticeably shaky. "Why didn't you tell anyone? Why didn't

Alex say anything? I knew that she was hiding something from me, but not this."

Karl-Erik threw out his hands in a resigned gesture.
There was nothing he could say to Alex's husband.

Patrik had fought hard to retain his professionalism, but it was obvious that he was shaken. He picked
up the pen he had dropped on the floor and tried to
focus on the notebook in front of him.

"Who was it that attacked Alex? Was it someone at
the school?"

Karl-Erik only nodded.

"Was it . . ." Patrik hesitated. "Was it Nils Lorentz?"

"Who's Nils Lorentz?" asked Henrik.

Birgit answered him, with steel in her voice. "He
was a substitute teacher at the school. He's the son of
Nelly Lorentz."

"But where is he now? He must have gone to prison
for what he did to Alex, didn't he?" Henrik looked
like he was wrestling hard to understand what Karl-
Erik had said.

"He disappeared twenty-five years ago," Patrik
explained. "No one has seen him since then. But what
I also want to know is why no police report was ever
filed. I've searched through our archives, and there's
never been any complaint to the police against him."

Karl-Erik closed his eyes. Patrik wasn't asking the
question as an accusation, but that was how it felt.
Each word felt like needles piercing his skin, reminding him of the terrible mistake they had made twenty-
five years ago.

"We never lodged a complaint. When we understood that Alex was pregnant and she told us what
happened, I stormed up to Nelly's house and told her

what her son had done. I had every intention of reporting him to the police, and I told Nelly as much, but——"

"But Nelly came and talked with me and suggested that we could solve it without getting the police involved," said Birgit as she sat on the sofa, her back straight as a poker. "She said that there was no reason to humiliate Alex any further by having all of Fjällbacka whispering about what had happened. We could only agree, and we decided that it would be to her benefit if we could handle the matter within the family. Nelly promised that she would take care of Nils in a suitable manner."

"Nelly also arranged a very well-paid job for me here in Göteborg," said Karl-Erik. "I assume that we were no better than most people, dazzled by the promise of gold." Karl-Erik was being brutally honest about himself. The time for denials was past.

"That had nothing to do with it. How can you say that, Karl-Erik? We were only thinking of what was best for Alex. What good would it have done her if everyone had known? We gave her a chance to move on with her life."

"No, Birgit, we gave ourselves a chance to move on with *our* lives. Alex lost that chance when we decided to hush things up."

They gazed at each other across the coffee table, and Karl-Erik knew that some things could never be repaired. She would never understand.

"And the baby? What happened to the baby? Was it given up for adoption?" asked Patrik.

Silence. Then a voice came from the doorway.

"No, the baby was not given up for adoption. They decided to keep the baby and lie to her about who she was."

"Julia! I thought you were up in your room!"

Karl-Erik turned to see Julia standing in the doorway. She must have tiptoed down the stairs, because no one had heard her coming. He wondered how long she'd been standing there.

She was leaning against the doorjamb with her arms crossed. Her entire shapeless body radiated spite. Even though it was four in the afternoon, she still hadn't changed out of her pajamas. She looked as if she hadn't showered in at least a week. Karl-Erik felt sympathy mix with the pain in his chest. His poor, poor little ugly duckling.

"If it hadn't been for Nelly, or should I say 'grandmother,' you never would have said anything, would you? You never would have gotten around to telling me that my mother is not my mother, but my grandmother, and Papa is not Papa but my grandfather, and above all that my sister is not my sister, but my Mama. Are you following this, or should I go over it one more time? It's a bit complicated."

The sarcastic comment was directed at Patrik. It almost looked as if Julia enjoyed seeing the dismayed expression on his face.

"Perverse, isn't it?" She lowered her voice to a theatrical whisper and put her finger to her lips. "But hush, you mustn't tell anyone. Because what would people say? Imagine if they started gossiping about the well-to-do Carlgren family."

She raised her voice again. "But thank goodness Nelly told me everything last summer when I was working at the cannery. She told me what I had a right to know. Who I really am. My whole life I've felt like an outsider, that I didn't belong in this family. Having a big sister like Alex certainly wasn't easy, but I worshiped her. She was everything I wanted to be, everything I was not. I saw the way you looked at her and the way you looked at me. And Alex never seemed to care much about me, which only made me worship her even more. Now I understand why. She could probably hardly stand to look at me. The bastard child who was born out of rape. And you forced her to be reminded of it every time she looked at me. Do you really not see how cruel that was?"

Karl-Erik flinched at her words as if he'd been slapped. He knew that she was right. It had been horribly cruel to keep Julia, and in that way force Alex to relive over and over the monstrous event that had marked an end to her childhood. Nor had it been fair to Julia. He and Birgit could never forget the way she had been conceived. Apparently Julia had sensed it from the very beginning, because she came into the world shrieking. She had continued to scream and struggle against the world during her whole childhood. Julia had never missed an opportunity to behave badly, and he and Birgit had been too old to handle a young child, especially one as demanding as Julia.

In a way it had been a relief when she came home one day last summer with the rage oozing from every pore and confronted them. It had not surprised them that Nelly on her own authority had told Julia the truth. Nelly was a nasty old woman who only cared about her own interests. If it would benefit her in some way to tell Julia what she knew, then she would do so. That's why they had tried to stop Julia from accepting the offer of the summer job, but Julia had stubbornly stood her ground, as usual.

When Nelly told Julia the true story, a whole new world opened up for her. For the first time there was someone who really wanted her, someone she belonged to. Despite the fact that Nelly had Jan, it was the bond of blood that counted for her. She had told Julia that when the time came she intended to leave her fortune to her. Karl-Erik understood very well how this had affected Julia. She was full of anger toward the people she had thought were her parents, and she worshiped Nelly with the same intensity she had once displayed toward Alex. All this flashed through his mind when he saw her standing in the doorway, outlined by the soft light coming from the kitchen. The sad thing was that—even if it was true that they had looked at Julia many times and were reminded of the horror in the past—she would never realize how much they loved her. But she had been like a stranger in their home, and they had felt awkward and helpless before her. They still felt that way. Now they would probably be forced to accept that they had lost her for good. She was still physically living in their home, but mentally she had already left them behind.

Henrik looked as if he could hardly breathe. He leaned his head forward toward his lap and closed his eyes. For a moment Karl-Erik wondered whether it had been right to ask Henrik to come here and participate. He had invited him because he thought that Henrik deserved to know the truth. He too had loved Alex.

"But Julia . . ." Birgit reached out her arms to Julia in an awkward, entreating gesture. Julia just turned her back to her in contempt, and they heard her stamping up the stairs.

"I'm really sorry," said Patrik, throwing out his

hands in a gesture of resignation. "I knew that something wasn't right, but I never would have imagined this. I don't know what to say."

"We don't know what to say ourselves. Especially to each other." Karl-Erik looked at his wife.

"How long did the abuse go on? Do you know?"

"We're not really sure. Alex didn't want to talk about it. Probably at least a couple of months, maybe up to a year." He hesitated. "And there you have the answer to your earlier question."

"Which one do you mean?" said Patrik.

"The one about the connection between Alex and Anders. Anders was also a victim. The day before we were going to move, we found a note that Alex had written to Anders. It seems that he too had been molested by Nils. Obviously they had understood somehow, or found out, that they were both in the same situation—how I don't know. And they turned to each other for comfort. I took the note over to Vera Nilsson. I told her what had happened to Alex and what had probably happened to Anders. It was one of the hardest things I've ever done. Anders is . . . or was," he corrected himself quickly, "all she had. I suppose I hoped that Vera would be able to do what we weren't brave enough to do—report Nils and hold him responsible for what he had done. But nothing happened, so I assume that Vera felt just as weak as we did."

Unconsciously he had begun to massage his chest with his fist. The pain kept growing in intensity. It had begun to radiate out to his fingers.

"And you have no idea where Nils went?"

"No, no idea. But wherever he is, I hope he's suffering, that devil."

The pain was now like a landslide. His fingers had begun to go numb and he knew that something was wrong. Seriously wrong. The pain made his field of vision contract, and even though he could see the others' mouths moving it was as if all images and all sounds were coming to him in slow motion. At first he felt happy that the anger had gone from Birgit's eyes, but when he saw that it was replaced by worry he understood that something serious was happening. Then the darkness flooded in.

After the panicky ambulance ride to Sahlgrenska Hospital, Patrik sat in his car and tried to catch his breath. He had followed the ambulance in his own car and stayed with Birgit and Henrik until they got word that although Karl-Erik's heart attack was serious, he was past the most critical stage.

This day had been one of the most upsetting in his life. He had seen a lot of misery in his years as a police officer, but he'd never heard such a heartrendingly tragic story as the one Karl-Erik had told that afternoon.

Even though Patrik recognized the truth when he heard it, he still had a hard time accepting what he'd heard. How could anyone go on with their life after going through what Alex had endured? She was not only abused and robbed of her childhood, she had also been forced to live the rest of her life with a constant reminder of it. No matter how Patrik tried he couldn't understand her parents' actions. He couldn't imagine letting the perpetrator get away if his child were abused, nor could he imagine that he would choose to try to hush things up. How could keeping up appearances be more important than his own child's life and health? That was what he had such a terribly hard time understanding.

He sat in the car with his eyes closed, leaning against the headrest. Twilight was falling and he should be starting the drive home, but he felt weak and apathetic. Not even the thought that Erica was waiting for him could induce him to drive home. His ingrained positive attitude to life had been shaken to its core. For the first time, he felt doubtful that the good in human beings was really greater than the evil.

On another level he also felt a bit guilty. The shocking story had touched him deeply, but at the same time he had felt a professional satisfaction when the pieces of the puzzle one by one fell into place. So many questions had been answered this afternoon. Yet he now felt an even greater frustration than before. He had found the explanation to so much, but he was still fumbling in the dark when it came to who had murdered Alex and Anders. Perhaps the motive lay hidden in the past, perhaps it had nothing to do with the past at all, although he found that hard to believe. In spite of everything, this was the only connection he had found between Alex and Anders.

But why would someone want to murder them because of abuse that had taken place more than twenty-five years ago? If that were the reason, why do nothing until now? What had set in motion something that had lain dormant for so many years and then resulted in two murders in the space of a couple of weeks? The most frustrating thing was that Patrik had no idea what direction to take now.

The afternoon had meant a big breakthrough in the

investigation, but at the same time it had led into a blind alley. Patrik went over in his head what he had done and heard that day, and it struck him that he had one very concrete lead with him in the car. Something he had forgotten in the aftershocks of the visit with the Carlgrens and the tumult that followed Karl-Erik's dramatic heart attack. Once again, Patrik felt the same enthusiasm he had experienced that morning. He realized that he had a unique opportunity to follow up this lead more closely. All he needed was a little luck.

He turned on his mobile phone, ignoring the three messages on his voicemail, and rang Information to get the number of Sahlgrenska Hospital. He got the switchboard and asked to be connected.

"Sahlgrenska Hospital."

"Yes, hello, my name is Patrik Hedström. I wonder whether you have a Robert Ek working in the forensic medicine division."

"One moment, I'll check."

Patrik held his breath. Robert was an old classmate from the Police Academy who had gone on to study to be a forensic technician. They had hung out together during the course but then lost contact. Patrik thought he'd heard through the grapevine that Robert was now working at Sahlgrenska, and he crossed his fingers that this was true.

"Let's see. Yes, we do have a Robert Ek working there. Would you like me to connect you?"

Patrik silently cheered. "Yes, please."

There were a couple of rings and then he heard Robert's familiar voice.

"Forensic medicine, Robert Ek."

"Hi, Robban, can you tell who this is?"

There was silence for a couple of seconds. Patrik never thought that Robert would recognize his voice, and was just about to help him out. But then he heard a howl from the phone.

"Patrik Hedström, you old dog! What the hell, it's sure been a long time! How come you're calling? Not exactly an everyday event, I mean."

Robert was teasing him, and Patrik felt a little ashamed. He knew he was terrible at keeping in touch with people. Robert had been a lot better at it but had given up after a while when Patrik never called back. He felt even more ashamed because now that he was finally calling, it was because he needed a favor. But he could hardly back out now.

"No, I know, I'm so damned bad at staying in touch. But right now I'm actually sitting in the parking lot outside Sahlgrenska, and I remembered hearing somewhere that you were working here. I thought I'd check to see if you were in so I could pop in and say hello."

"Sure, damn it. Come on in, no problem."

"How do I find you? Where's your office?"

"We're in the cellar. Go in through the front entrance, take the lift down, turn right and go all the way to the end of the hall. There's a door at the end, and that's where we are. Just ring the bell and I'll let you in. It'll be cool to see you again."

"Same here. So I'll see you in a couple of minutes."

Again Patrik felt ashamed that he was about to exploit an old friend. On the other hand, Robert owed him big-time. At the academy Robert had been his roommate. He was engaged to a girl named Susanne, but at the same time he was carrying on a hot affair with one of their female classmates, Marie, who was also engaged. This had gone on for almost two years, and Patrik couldn't even count the number of times he'd saved Robert's skin. He had provided numerous alibis, demonstrating his rich imagination when Susanne called and asked if he knew where Robert was.

After the fact he didn't think it seemed very honorable behavior, either for him or for Robert. But they were so young and immature back then. To be honest, Patrik had also thought it was rather cool—he had even been a bit envious of Robert, shagging two girls at once. Of course, eventually the bubble burst, and it ended with Robert having neither an apartment nor a girlfriend. But being a born charmer, Robert hadn't needed to sleep on Patrik's sofa for too many weeks before he found a new girl and moved in with her.

At the same time Patrik had learned that Robert was working at Sahlgrenska, he also heard that he was now married with kids, which he had a very hard time imagining. Patrik intended to find out whether that was true or not.

He made his way down the seemingly endless hospital corridors. Even though it had sounded simple when Robert gave him directions, Patrik managed to get lost twice before he finally stood before the correct door. He rang the bell and waited. The door flew open.

"Hey-y-y-y!"

They embraced heartily and then took a step back to see how time had fared for each of them. Patrik saw that the years had been kind to Robert; he hoped that Robert thought the same about him. For safety's sake he sucked in his stomach and puffed out his chest a bit more.

"Come in, come in."

Robert led the way to his office, which was tiny, with barely enough space for one person, let alone two. Patrik studied Robert more closely as he sat down on a chair facing him in front of his desk. His blond hair was just as well-combed as when they were younger, and under the white lab coat his clothes were just as well-ironed. Patrik had always thought that Robert's need for neatness functioned as a counterbalance to the chaos he always tended to create in his personal life. His eyes were drawn to a photograph on a shelf behind the desk.

"Is that your family?" He was not entirely successful in concealing the astonishment in his voice.

Robert smiled proudly and took down the photo from the shelf.

"Yep, this is my wife, Carina, and my two kids, Oscar and Maja."

"How old are they?"

"Oscar is two and Maja is six months."

"That's great. How long have you been married?"

"Three years now. I'll bet you never would have believed that anyone could make a father out of me."

Patrik laughed. "No, I have to admit, you would have had to give me high odds on that one."

"Well, you know, when the devil gets old, he gets religious. What about you? You probably have a whole flock by now."

"No, it didn't really turn out that way. I'm divorced, actually. No kids, which is probably lucky under the circumstances."

"I'm sorry to hear that."

"It's not that bad. I've got something going right now that seems very promising, so we'll see."

"So, how come you're popping up like a jack-in-the-box after all these years?"

Patrik squirmed a little. He was once again reminded of how embarrassed he felt at not being in touch for so long, and then coming here to ask a favor.

"I've come down on police business and heard you were working here in forensics. I have a case I'd like some help with, and I simply don't have time to run it through the usual channels. It would take weeks before I got an answer, and I just don't have the time or the patience."

Robert looked as if his curiosity had been aroused. He put his fingertips together and waited for Patrik to go on.

Patrik leaned down and took from his bag a piece of paper wrapped in plastic. He handed it to Robert, who held it under the bright desk lamp to see more closely what it was.

"I took the paper from a pad at the home of a murder victim. I can see that there are impressions from something that was written on the sheet above it, but they're too faint for me to make out more than fragments. You probably have the equipment here to enhance this sort of impression, don't you?"

"Ye-e-es, we do indeed."

Robert's reply was a bit hesitant as he continued to study the piece of paper under his lamp. "But as you say, there are rather strict rules about how requests should be handled and in what order. We have lots of stuff piled up waiting."

"Sure, I know. But I thought this wouldn't take long and it would be easy to check. I thought that if I asked you as a favor to take a quick look and tell me whether anything can be gotten from it, then maybe . . ."

Robert frowned as he thought over what Patrik had said. Then he gave him a sly smile and got up from his chair.

"All right, I suppose I shouldn't be so bureaucratic. It'll only take a few minutes. Come on."

He led Patrik from the crowded office and through the door opposite his own. The room they entered was big and bright and filled with all sorts of strange-looking equipment. It was squeaky clean and had a clinical look that came from the white walls and all the workbenches and cabinets in gleaming chrome. The apparatus that Robert needed was at the far side of the room. With the greatest of care he removed the paper from the plastic and placed it on a glass plate. He pressed a button and a bluish light came on. The words on the paper immediately stood out in all desired clarity.

"Have a look. Was this what you were hoping for?"

Patrik quickly read through the text. "This is exactly what I was hoping for. Could you leave it there a minute while I write it down?"

Robert smiled. "I can do better than that. With this machine I can take a picture of the text and you can take it with you."

A broad smile spread across Patrik's face. "Excellent! That would be perfect. Thank you!"

Half an hour later Patrik left the hospital with a photocopy of the sheet of paper from Anders's notepad. He had made a solemn promise to get in touch with Robert more often, and he hoped that he'd be able to keep that promise. Unfortunately he knew himself all too well.

He did a lot of thinking on the drive home. He loved driving in the dark. The silence as he was enveloped by the velvet-black night, broken only by the lights of occasional oncoming cars, made him think more clearly. Bit by bit, he added what he already knew to what he had now read on the piece of paper. When he pulled into the driveway of his building in Tanumshede he was quite sure that he had solved at least one of the riddles that were plaguing him.

It felt strange to go to bed without Erica. Odd how quickly one got accustomed to something, as long as it was something pleasant. He found that he now had a hard time sleeping alone. It had surprised him how deeply disappointed he was when Erica rang his mobile on his way home to tell him that her sister had come to visit unexpectedly. She thought it would be better if he slept at his own place. He'd wanted to ask more but heard from Erica's voice that she couldn't explain, so he made do with saying that he'd call her tomorrow and that he missed her.

Now his sleep was filled with images of Erica as well as thoughts about what he would have to do in the morning. For Patrik it was a very long night.

When the kids were asleep for the night they finally had a chance to talk. Erica had quickly thawed out some frozen dinners since Anna looked like she needed to get something in her stomach. Erica had forgotten to eat as well and now her stomach was growling.

Anna mostly poked at her food with her fork. Erica felt a familiar sense of anxiety about her younger sister. Just like when they were little. She wanted to take Anna in her arms, rock her and tell her that everything would be all right, kiss the hurt and make it go away. But they were grown up now, and Anna's problems far exceeded the pain of a skinned knee. Confronted by this problem, Erica felt powerless and helpless. For the first time in her life her little sister seemed like a stranger, and she found herself awkward and unsure of how to talk to her. So she sat in silence, waiting for Anna to point the way. After a long wait she finally did.

"I don't know what to do, Erica. What's going to happen to me and the children? Where are we going to go? How will I support us? I've been a stay-at-home mum for so long that I don't know how to do anything else."

Erica saw Anna's knuckles turn white as she gripped the table, as if in a physical attempt to keep a grip on the situation.

"Shhh, don't think about that now. It's all going to work out. You just need to take one day at a time, and you can stay here with the kids as long as you like. The house is yours too, remember?"

She permitted herself a crooked smile and saw to her joy that Anna responded in kind. Anna wiped her nose with the back of her hand and picked absent-mindedly at the tablecloth.

"I just can't forgive myself for letting it go so far. He hurt Emma. How could I let him hurt Emma?"

The snot began running again, and she used a tissue instead of her hand.

"Why did I let him hurt Emma? Didn't I know deep inside that it was going to happen someday? Did I choose to shut my eyes for the sake of my own comfort?"

"Anna, if there's one thing I'm absolutely sure about, it's that you would never consciously let anyone hurt your kids."

Erica reached across the table and took Anna's hand in hers. It was shockingly thin. Her bones felt like a bird's, as if they would break if she squeezed too hard.

"What I still can't understand is that in spite of what he did, there's still a part of me that loves him. I've loved Lucas for so long that the love has become ingrained in me, it's a part of who I am. No matter what he did, I can't get rid of that part. I wish I could take a knife and physically cut it out of me. I feel disgusting and dirty."

With a shaking hand she touched her chest as if to show where the evil was.

"That's not unusual, Anna. You don't have to be ashamed. The only thing you have to do now is concentrate on feeling well again." She paused. "But you do have to report Lucas to the police."

"No, Erica, no, I can't."

The tears ran down her cheeks and a few drops hung from her chin before they fell and made wet marks on the tablecloth.

"Yes, Anna, you have to. You can't let him get away with this. Don't tell me you can live with yourself if you let him almost break your daughter's arm without having to pay the consequences!"

"No, yes, I don't know, Erica. I can't think straight, it's like my whole head is full of cotton. I can't think about this right now, maybe later."

"No, Anna. Not later. Later it'll be too late. You have to do it now! I'll go down to the police station with you tomorrow, but you have to do it, not only for the children's sake but also for your own."

"I'm just not sure I have the strength for it."

"I know you do. Unlike you and me, Emma and

Adrian have a mother who loves them, a mother who is ready to do anything for them."

She couldn't prevent the bitterness from seeping into her voice.

Anna sighed. "You have to drop that, Erica. I accepted a long time ago that Papa was the only parent we really had. I also stopped worrying about why that was. How do I know? Maybe Mama never wanted to have kids. Maybe we weren't the kids she wanted to have. We'll never find out now, and it doesn't do any good to dwell on it. Although, of the two of us, I was probably the one who was luckier. Because I also had you. Maybe I never told you this, but I know how much you did for me. I know what you meant to me when we were growing up. You had nobody, Erica, nobody to take care of you except Mama. But you mustn't be bitter, promise me that. Don't you think I've seen how you withdraw as soon as you meet somebody and it looks like it might get serious? You withdraw before you risk getting hurt. You have to learn to let go of the past, Erica. It seems like you have something really good going right now. You mustn't retreat this time too. I do want to be an aunt someday."

They both started laughing through their tears, and it was Erica's turn to wipe her nose with a paper napkin. All the emotion in the room made the air feel supersaturated, but at the same time it felt as if they were doing some spring cleaning of the soul. There was so much that had gone unspoken, so much dust in the corners, and they both could feel that it was time to take out the dust mop.

They talked all night, until the winter darkness began to be replaced by a gray morning mist. The children slept longer than usual, and when Adrian finally announced that he was awake with a piercing shriek, Erica offered to take care of the kids and let Anna sleep for a couple of hours.

She felt in lighter spirits than she could ever remember feeling. Naturally she was still furious about what had happened to Emma, but she and Anna had said a lot during the night that should have been said long ago. Some truths had been unpleasant but necessary to hear, and it surprised her how easily her sister could see right through her. Erica had to admit to herself that she had probably underestimated Anna. She may even have been a bit patronizing and only seen her as a big, irresponsible child. She was much more than that, and Erica was glad that she had finally managed to see the real Anna.

They had also talked a lot about Patrik, and with Adrian on her arm Erica now gave him a ring. He didn't answer at home, so she tried his mobile instead. Placing a call turned out to be a bigger challenge than she was used to, since Adrian was overjoyed by the marvelous toy she had in her hand and tried desperately to make it his own. When Patrik answered his mobile after only one ring all the night's weariness vanished as if by magic.

"Hi, darling."

"Mmm, I like it when you call me that," Erica said. "How's it going?"

"Okay, thanks. There's a bit of a family crisis here. I'll tell you all about it when I see you. A lot has happened, and Anna and I stayed up all night talking. Right now I'm watching the kids so she can get some sleep."

He heard her stifle a yawn.

"You sound tired."

"I *am* tired. Hitting the wall. But Anna needs sleep more than I do, so I have to stay awake a couple more hours. The kids aren't old enough to take care of themselves yet."

Adrian babbled in agreement.

Patrik made a snap decision. "There's another solution to the problem."

"Oh yeah, what's that? Should I tie them to the banister for a couple of hours?" She laughed.

"I'll come over and take care of them."

Erica gave an incredulous snort. "You? Take care of the kids?"

He put on his most aggrieved voice. "Are you implying that I might not be man enough for the job? If I can take down two burglars single-handedly, I can certainly handle two extremely short human beings. Or don't you trust me?"

He paused for effect and heard Erica sigh theatrically on the other end.

"All right, you may be able to handle it. But I'm warning you, these are really small wild animals. Are you really sure you can stand the pace, at your age I mean?"

"I'll try. I should probably bring my heart medicine just in case."

"Okay, offer accepted. When can you get here?"

"Right now, actually. I was already on my way to Fjällbacka for something else and I've just passed the minigolf course. So I'll see you in about five minutes."

She was standing in the doorway waiting for him when he stepped out of the car. On her arm she had a boy with round cheeks and flailing arms. Behind her, scarcely visible, stood a little girl with her thumb in her mouth and her other arm in a cast and sling. He still didn't know the reason for Anna's sudden appearance, but from what Erica had told him about her brother-in-law combined with the sight of the little girl's plaster-wrapped arm, a nasty suspicion emerged. He didn't ask. Erica would tell him what happened when she had a chance.

Patrik said hello to all three of them in turn. Erica got a kiss on the mouth, Adrian a pat on the cheek, and then he squatted down to say hello to a solemn Emma. He took her good hand and said, "Hi, my name's Patrik. What's yours?"

The reply came after a long delay. "Emma." Then she stuck her thumb back in her mouth.

"She'll thaw out," said Erica as she handed Adrian to Patrik and turned to Emma.

"Mama and Auntie have to take a nap, so Patrik came over to take care of you for a while. Is that okay? He's a friend of mine and he's very, very nice. And if you're very, very nice Patrik might take an ice cream bar out of the freezer for you."

Emma gave Erica a suspicious look, but the chance for an ice cream bar exerted an irresistible attraction, and she nodded reluctantly.

"So I'll leave them to you and see you in a while. Try to make sure they're in one piece when I wake up, if you would."

Erica vanished up the stairs.

Patrik turned to Emma, who was still giving him a suspicious look.

"So, what do you say? Shall we play a game of

chess? No? How about having a little ice cream for lunch? You think that sounds fine? Okay. Last one to the fridge gets a carrot instead."

Slowly Anna struggled back to consciousness. It felt like she'd been dozing a hundred years, like Sleeping Beauty. When she opened her eyes she had a hard time orienting herself at first. Then she recognized the wallpaper from her childhood room and reality crashed over her like a ton of bricks. She sat up at once. The kids! Then she heard Emma's happy shriek from downstairs and remembered that Erica was watching them while she slept. She lay back down and decided to snooze for a few more minutes in the warm bed. As soon as she got up, she'd have to deal with everything; this way she could buy herself a few more minutes of escape from reality.

Slowly it penetrated her brain that it wasn't Erica's voice she heard from downstairs, mixed in with Emma and Adrian's laughter. In a cold, icy moment she thought that Lucas was here, but then she realized that Erica would rather shoot him on the spot than let him in the front door. She had a hunch who the visitor might be, and in curiosity she crept out to the landing and looked through the bars of the banister. Down in the living room it looked as if a bomb had gone off. The sofa cushions along with four dining room chairs and a blanket had been turned into a fort, and Adrian's blocks were scattered all over the floor. On the coffee table were strewn so many ice cream wrappers that Anna hoped Patrik was a big ice cream eater. With a sigh, she realized that it would probably be extremely difficult to get her daughter to eat either lunch or dinner. The daughter in question was riding on the shoulders of a dark-haired man with a pleasant face and warm brown eyes. She was laughing so hard she was practically choking. Adrian apparently shared her glee as he lay on a blanket on the floor, wearing only a nappy. But the one who seemed to be having the most fun was Patrik, and it was at that moment that he forever won a place in Anna's heart.

She stood up and cleared her throat to draw the attention of the three playmates.

"Mama, look, I got a horsie."

Emma demonstrated her total power over the "horsie" by pulling hard on his hair, but Patrik's protests were much too mild for the little tyrant to care.

"Emma, you have to be nice to the horse. Or else you might not be able to ride him anymore."

This remark prompted a certain caution in the rider. For safety's sake she patted Patrik's mane with her good hand to make sure she wouldn't lose her riding privileges.

"Hey, Anna, long time no see."

"I know. I hope they haven't worn you out too badly."

"No, we've been having a lot of fun." He suddenly looked a bit worried. "I've been very careful with her arm."

"I believe it. She looks like she's getting along fine. Is Erica sleeping?"

"Yes, she sounded so tired when we talked on the phone this morning that I offered to step in."

"And with gusto, obviously."

"Yes, although it's gotten a bit messy. I hope Erica won't get mad when she wakes up and sees the way I've totally sabotaged her living room."

Anna found his concern quite charming. It seemed that Erica had already whipped him into shape.

"I'll help you clean up. But first I need a cup of coffee, I think. Would you like one?"

They drank coffee and talked like old friends. The way to Anna's heart was through her children, and the adoration in Emma's eyes was unmistakable when she climbed all over Patrik, who only waved off Anna's attempts to tell her daughter to leave him in peace for a while. By the time Erica came down with bleary eyes about an hour later, Anna had quizzed Patrik about everything from his shoe size to why he got divorced. When he finally said that he had to go, all the girls protested, and Adrian would have too if he hadn't been taking his afternoon nap.

As soon as they heard his car drive off, Anna turned to Erica with eyes wide.

"God, what a mother-in-law's dream. He doesn't have any younger brothers, does he?"

Erica just laughed happily in reply.

Patrik had been given a few hours' reprieve from the task he knew he had to deal with—something that had made him toss and turn all night. He had seldom dreaded anything as much as he did this, but he knew it was an unavoidable part of the profession he had chosen. He now knew the solution to one of the two murders, but it didn't make him happy.

Patrik drove slowly from Sälvik down toward the center of town. He wanted to postpone this as long as possible, but it wasn't far and he got there sooner than he wanted to. He parked the car in the lot by Eva's Mart and walked the rest of the way. The house stood at the top of one of the streets that sloped steeply down toward the boathouses along the water. It was a fine old house, but it looked as though it had been neglected for many years. Before he knocked on the door he took a deep breath, but as soon as his knuckles touched the wood he was the consummate professional. He couldn't let his personal feelings be involved. He was a cop and as such was bound to do his job, no matter what Patrik the private citizen might feel about the task.

Vera opened the door almost immediately. She gave him a questioning look but stepped aside at once when he asked to come in. She preceded him into the kitchen and they sat down at the kitchen table. Patrik was struck by the fact that she didn't ask him what he wanted, and for a moment he thought it might be because she already knew. Regardless of the reason, he somehow had to present what he wanted to say in as considerate a way as possible.

She calmly rested her eyes on him, but he saw dark circles under them, a sign of her grief after her son's death. On the table lay an old photo album, and he guessed that if he opened it he'd see pictures of Anders from his childhood. It was hard for him to come here, to visit a mother who was grieving for a son who had only been dead a few days. But once again Patrik had to push aside his natural protective instincts and instead concentrate on the job he had come to do. To find out the truth about Anders's death.

"Vera, the last time we met it was under very sad circumstances, and I just want to start by saying that I'm truly sorry about your son's death."

She merely nodded in reply, then waited silently for him to go on.

"But even though I understand how difficult this is for you, it's my job to investigate what happened to Anders. I hope you understand."

Patrik spoke slowly and clearly, as if to a child. Why, he didn't know, but he felt that it was important for him that she really understood what he was saying.

"We've investigated Anders's death as a murder, and we've also searched for a connection with the murder of Alexandra Wijkner, a woman with whom we know he had a relationship. We haven't found any traces of a possible killer, nor have we found evidence as to how the murder itself was committed. This has really put us in a quandary, to be honest. No one has been able to come up with any really good explanation as to how the course of events may have unfolded. But then I found this at Anders's apartment."

Patrik placed the photocopy of the piece of paper on the kitchen table in front of Vera, with the text facing her. An expression of astonishment passed over her face and she looked several times from the paper to Patrik's face and back. She picked up the paper and turned it over. She ran her fingers over the letters and then put the paper down on the table again, still with an expression of shock on her face.

"Where did you find this?" Her voice was hoarse with sorrow.

"At Anders's place. You're surprised because you thought that you took the only copy of this letter, isn't that right?"

She nodded.

Patrik went on, "You did, actually. But I found the notepad that Anders wrote the letter on, and when he pressed the pen into the paper it also left an impression on the sheet underneath. That's how we were able to retrieve the message."

Vera gave him a wry smile. "I didn't even think of that, of course. It was clever of you to work it out."

"I think I know approximately what happened, but I'd really like to hear you tell it in your own words."

She fingered the paper for a moment, feeling the words with her fingertips, as if she were reading Braille. A deep sigh, and then she complied with Patrik's friendly but firm request.

"I went over to Anders's place with a bag of food. The door was unlocked, but it almost always was, so I just called out and then went in. It was calm, completely quiet. I saw him at once. I felt like my heart stopped that instant. That was exactly how it felt. As if my heart stopped beating and there was only stillness in my chest. He was swaying a little. Back and forth. As if there were a wind inside the room, which of course I knew was impossible."

"Why didn't you call the police? Or an ambulance?"

She shrugged her shoulders. "I don't know. My first instinct was to run up and get him down somehow, but when I entered the living room I saw that it was too late. My boy was dead."

For the first time since she started talking he heard a slight quaver in her voice, but then she swallowed hard and forced herself with uncanny calm to go on.

"I found this letter in the kitchen. You've read it, you know what it says. That he couldn't go on living. That life was one long torment for him and now he couldn't fight it anymore. All his reasons to continue were gone. I must have sat there in the kitchen for an hour, maybe two, I don't really know. In an instant I stuffed the letter in my purse, and then I only had to take the chair he used to climb up to the noose and put it back in its place in the kitchen."

"But why, Vera? Why? What purpose did it serve?"

Her gaze was steady but Patrik could see from her trembling hands that her outward calm was a sham. He couldn't even imagine what horror it must have been to see her son hanging from the ceiling, with a thick blue tongue and eyes popping out. It had been hard enough for him to look at Anders, and now his mother would have to live the rest of her life with that image in her mind.

"I wanted to spare him more humiliation. For all these years people have looked at him with contempt. People pointed and laughed. Put their noses in the air when they walked past, feeling superior. What would people say when they heard that Anders had hanged himself? I wanted to spare him that shame, and I did it the only way I could think of."

"But I still don't understand. Why would it be worse if he took his own life than if he was murdered?"

"You're too young to understand. The contempt for suicides still sits deep in people here in the coastal regions. I didn't want people to talk like that about my little boy. They've talked enough rubbish about him over the years."

There was a touch of steel in Vera's voice. For all these years she had devoted herself to protecting and helping her son, and although Patrik still didn't understand her motive, it was perhaps only natural that she continued to protect him even after his death.

Vera reached for the photo album on the table and opened it so that both she and Patrik could see. Judging by the clothing, the pictures must have been from the seventies. Anders's face smiled at him, open and carefree, from all the slightly yellowing photos.

"He was certainly fine, my Anders."

Vera's voice was dreamy and she stroked a finger across the pictures.

"He was always such a nice boy. There was never any problem with him."

Patrik looked with interest at the pictures. It was unbelievable that this was the same person whom he had met only as a wreck. Lucky that the boy in the photos didn't know what fate had awaited him. One of the pictures aroused his interest even more. A thin, blonde girl stood next to Anders, who was sitting on a bicycle with a banana seat and chopper handlebars. She showed just the hint of a smile as she peered out shyly from under her bangs.

"This must be Alex, isn't it?"

"Yes." Vera's tone was curt.

"Did they play much together when they were little?"

"Not often. But sometimes, sure. They were in the same class, after all."

Patrik cautiously entered a sensitive area. He mentally tested the water with his toes before each step he took.

"I understood that they had Nils Lorentz as a teacher for a while?"

Vera gave him a searching look. "Yes, that's possible. It was a long time ago."

"There was some talk about Nils Lorentz, from what I hear. Especially since he later simply disappeared."

"People talk about all sorts of things here in Fjäll-backa. So they probably talked about Nils Lorentz as well."

It was obvious that he was now poking at a fester-ing wound, but he had to keep going and probe even deeper.

"I spoke with Alex's parents, who made certain claims about Nils Lorentz. Claims that also affected Anders."

"I see." She was obviously not going to make it easy for him.

"According to them, Nils Lorentz sexually assaulted Alex, and they claimed that Anders was also abused."

Vera sat ramrod stiff on the edge of the kitchen chair, and she didn't reply to Patrik's statement, which he had intended as a question. He decided to wait her out, and after a moment of internal struggle she slowly closed the photo album and got up from her chair.

"I don't want to talk about ancient history. I want you to go now. If you want to charge me for what I did when I found Anders, then you know where to find me. But I don't intend to help you root about in things that would best be left buried."

"Just one question: did you ever talk to Alexandra about this? From what I understood she had decided to deal with what happened, and it would have been natural for her to speak with you as well."

"Yes, she did. I sat there in her house about a week before she died, listening to her naïve ideas about com-ing to terms with the past, taking all the old skele-tons out of the closet, and so on and so forth. Modern drivel in my opinion. Today, everyone seems obsessed with washing their dirty linen in public, claiming it's so healthy to reveal all their secrets and sins. But some things should remain private. I told her that as well. I don't know whether she listened to me, but I hope so. Otherwise, I only had a stubborn bladder inflammation to show for the trouble of sitting there in her freezing house."

And with that Vera signaled that the discussion was over and walked toward the front door. She opened it for Patrik and said a very guarded farewell.

When he found himself standing out in the cold again with his cap pulled down over his ears and his mittens on, he literally didn't know which foot to stand on. He hopped a few times to warm himself up and then headed briskly for his car.

Vera was a complicated woman, he had gathered that much from their conversation. She belonged to a completely different generation, but in many ways she was in conflict with that generation's values. During her son's childhood she had supported him by her own labor, and even after he reached adulthood and should have taken care of himself, she continued to keep him under her wing. In her way, she was a liberated woman who over all those years had gotten along without a man. At the same time, she was bound by the rules that existed for women, and men for that matter, from her generation. He couldn't help feeling a certain reluctant admiration for her. She was a strong woman. A complex woman, who had endured more than any person should have to endure in a lifetime.

He didn't know what the consequences might be for Vera when it came out that she had interfered to make Anders's suicide look like a murder. He would definitely need to turn in that information to the police station, but he had no idea what would happen after that. If it were his decision, he would choose to look through his fingers, but he couldn't promise that's what would occur. From a purely legal point of view it was possible to charge her with obstructing an investigation, for example, but he sincerely hoped that wouldn't happen. He liked Vera, he couldn't get away from that. She was a fighter, and there weren't many like her.

When he got into his car and flipped open his mobile, he discovered a message waiting for him. It was from Erica. She reported that there were three ladies and a very, very small gentleman who hoped he would have dinner with them this evening. Patrik glanced at the clock. It was already five, so he decided without great internal debate that it was probably already too late to go to the station. And what did he have at home to do? Before he started the car he rang Annika at the station and gave her a brief report on what he'd accomplished, but he left out the details since he wanted to report on the whole situation when he had Mellberg face to face. He wanted at all costs to prevent the situation from being misinterpreted, and to prevent Mellberg from mobilizing some enormous operation simply for his own amusement.

As Patrik drove back to Erica's house, the thoughts of Alex's murder kept returning. It frustrated him that he had run into yet another blind alley. Two murders meant twice the chance that the killer had made a mistake. Now he was back at the beginning once more, and for the first time he thought he might never find the person who had murdered Alex. That made him strangely sad. It felt somehow that he knew Alex better than anyone else did. What he'd found out about her childhood and life after the assaults had moved him deeply. He wanted to find her killer more than he'd ever wanted anything in his whole life.

But he had to accept the situation. He had now reached another blind alley, and he didn't know where he should go from here, or where to look. Patrik forced himself to let it go for the time being. Right now he was going over to see Erica, her sister, and especially the kids, and that was exactly what he needed this evening. All this misery had made him feel frayed inside.

Mellberg drummed impatiently with his fingers on the desktop. Where the hell was that young whippersnapper? Did he think this was some sort of damned day care? That he could come and go as he liked? Of course it was Sunday, but anyone who thought he could take a day off before this was all over was seriously mistaken. Well, he would soon disabuse him of that notion. At his station, it was strict regulations and clear discipline that counted. Good honest leadership. It was the watchword of the times, and if anyone had ever been born with leadership qualities, then he was the one. His mother had always said that he would make something great out of himself. Even if he had to admit that it may have been taking a bit longer than either of them had expected, he had never doubted that his excellent qualifications would pay off sooner or later.

That's why it was so frustrating that they seemed to be stuck in these investigations. Mellberg felt that his big chance was so close that he could taste it. But if his miserable team didn't start delivering results soon, he might as well give up any hope of a promotion and a move back to Göteborg. Slackers, that's what they were, village cops who could hardly find their own ass with both hands and a flashlight. He'd had some hope for young Hedström, but it seemed as if he, too, would disappoint him. Patrik still hadn't reported the results of his trip to Göteborg, so it might turn out to be nothing more than an entry on the expense side of the books. It was ten past nine and he still hadn't seen any trace of him.

"Annika!" He yelled in the direction of the open door and felt his irritation rise even higher when it took a good minute before she deigned to respond to his call.

"Yes, what is it?"

"Have you heard anything from Hedström? Is he still asleep in his warm bed, or what?"

"I should hardly think so. He rang and said that he had a little trouble getting his car started this morning but that he was on the way." She looked at the clock. "He should be here in fifteen minutes or so."

"What the hell, he could walk here if he wanted to."

Annika hesitated and to his astonishment he saw a little smile play over the corners of her mouth.

"Well, I don't think he was at home."

"Where the hell was he then?"

"You'll have to ask Patrik that," said Annika, turning to go back to her room.

The fact that Patrik seemed to have a good excuse for being late annoyed Mellberg even more, for some reason. Couldn't he plan ahead and allow for some extra time in the morning in case he had car trouble?

Fifteen minutes later, Patrik knocked discreetly on

the open door and came in. He looked out of breath and red-cheeked and seemed unabashedly happy and brisk even though he'd made his boss wait for almost half an hour.

"Do you think this is a part-time job here, or what? And where the hell were you yesterday? Wasn't it two days ago that you drove to Göteborg?"

Patrik sat down in the visitor's chair across the desk and calmly answered Mellberg's barrage of questions.

"I apologize for being late. The car wouldn't start this morning, and it took over half an hour to get it going. Yes, it was the day before yesterday that I went to Göteborg, and I thought I'd report on that first, before I tell you what I did yesterday."

Mellberg grunted in reluctant agreement. Patrik told him what he'd found out about Alex's childhood. He included all the disgusting details. At the news that Julia was Alex's daughter, Mellberg felt his jaw drop in the direction of his chest. He'd never heard anything like it before. Patrik continued to tell him about Karl-Erik's emergency trip to the hospital and how he'd had a piece of paper from Anders's apartment analyzed on the spot. He explained that it had turned out to be a suicide note, and then he gave an account of what he'd done yesterday and why. Patrik then summed it all up for an unusually quiet Mellberg.

"So one of our murders has turned out to be a suicide, and as for the other, we still have no idea who did it or why. I have a feeling that it has something to do with what Alexandra's parents told me, but I have absolutely no evidence or actual facts to support that theory. So now you know everything that I know. Do you have any ideas about how to proceed?"

After another moment of silence, Mellberg managed to regain his composure. "Well, that was certainly an amazing story. I would have put my money on that guy she was screwing, rather than a rehash of some old incident from twenty-five years ago. I suggest you talk to Alex's lover boy and tighten the thumbscrews a little extra this time around. I think that would prove to be a considerably better use of our resources."

As soon as Patrik told him who the child's father was, Mellberg had moved Dan up to the top of the list of suspects.

Patrik nodded, a bit too willingly in Mellberg's suspicious mind, and stood up to go.

"Oh, uh, good job, Hedström," Mellberg said reluctantly. "Are you following up on that now?"

"Absolutely, Chief, consider it done."

Did he catch a trace of sarcasm there? But Patrik looked at him with an innocent expression and Mellberg waved off the suspicion. The fellow probably had enough sense between his ears to recognize the voice of experience when he heard it.

The purpose of a yawn was to get more oxygen to the brain. Patrik was very doubtful whether it was doing him any good. The fatigue from the night he'd spent at home tossing and turning had caught up with him, and sleeping with Erica had been vetoed by a majority decision. He looked wearily at the by now familiar piles of paper on his desk and had to quell an impulse to take all the documents and toss them in the wastebasket. He was sincerely sick of this whole investigation by now. It felt as if months had passed, while actually it had been no more than two weeks. So much had happened and yet he hadn't made any progress. Annika went past his office and saw him rubbing his eyes. She came back with a much-needed cup of coffee and set it in front of him.

"Feeling bogged down?"

"Yes, I have to admit that it's a little rough going just now. But all I have to do is start over from the beginning. Somewhere in these stacks of paper is the answer, I know it. All I need is a tiny little lead that I missed before." He tossed his pencil on top of the piles in resignation.

"Anything else?"

"What?"

"I mean, how's life, apart from the job? You know what I mean."

"Yes, Annika, I know exactly what you mean. What do you want to know?"

"Is it still bingo?"

Patrik wasn't sure he really wanted to know, but against his better judgment he asked anyway. "Bingo?"

"Yes, you know. Five in a row . . ." Then she left, shutting the door with a mischievous smile on her lips.

Patrik chuckled to himself. Yes, you could probably call it that.

He forced his thoughts back to the task at hand and scratched his head meditatively with a pencil. There was something that didn't fit. Something that Vera had said just didn't seem right. He took out the notebook he'd been writing in during their conversation and went through his notes methodically, word for word. An idea was slowly forming. It was only a small detail, but it might be important. He pulled out a sheet of paper from one of the piles on his desk. The impression of chaos was deceptive. He knew precisely where everything was.

He read over this item with great meticulousness and circumspection, and then reached for the telephone.

"Yes, hello, this is Patrik Hedström from the police in Tanumshede. I was wondering if you'll be home for a while, I have a few questions. You will be? That's great, then I'll be over there in twenty minutes. Where exactly do you live? Just on the way into Fjällbacka. Take a right just after the steep hill and it's the third house on the left. A red house with white trim? Okay, I should be able to find it. Otherwise I'll call you back. See you soon."

Scarcely twenty minutes later Patrik stood outside the door. He'd had no problem finding the little house, where he guessed that Eilert had lived for many, many years with his family. When he knocked on the door it was opened almost at once by a woman with a pinched-looking face. She introduced herself effusively as Svea Berg, Eilert's wife, and showed him into a small living room. Patrik could see that his call had triggered feverish activity. The good china was on the dining room table, and seven kinds of pastry were piled on a tall three-level cake plate. This case was going to give him a real spare tire by the time it was over, Patrik sighed to himself.

Even though he instinctively took a dislike to Svea Berg, he instantly liked her husband when he encountered a pair of lively, clear-blue eyes above a firm handshake. He could feel the calluses on Eilert's hand and knew that this was a man who had worked hard his whole life.

The sofa cover looked wrinkled when Eilert got up, and with a deep frown Svea was there to smooth it out with a reproachful glance at her husband. The whole house was squeaky clean, without a wrinkle, and it was hard to believe that anyone actually lived in the place. Patrik felt sorry for Eilert. He looked lost in his own home.

The effect turned almost comical when Svea quickly alternated between the ingratiating smile when she was facing Patrik to the reproachful grimace when she turned to her husband. Patrik wondered what it was her husband had done to bring on such disapproval. He suspected that Eilert's mere presence was a source of vexation for Svea.

"Well, Constable, take a seat and have some coffee and cakes."

Patrik sat down obediently on the chair facing the window, and Eilert made a move to sit on the chair across from him.

"Not there, Eilert, you know that. Sit over there."

Svea pointed dictatorially to the chair at the head of the table, and Eilert obeyed politely. Patrik looked around as Svea dashed about like a lost soul, pouring coffee as she simultaneously smoothed out invisible wrinkles in the tablecloth and curtains. The home had apparently been decorated by someone who wanted to give the appearance of a prosperity that did not exist. Everything was a bad copy of the real thing, from the curtains that were supposed to look like silk with plenty of flounces and rosettes in a "progressive" design to the plethora of knickknacks made of silver plate and imitation gold. Eilert looked like a fish out of water in all this simulated pomp.

To Patrik's frustration, it took a while before he could get on to his actual business. Svea babbled incessantly as she slurped loudly from her coffee cup.

"This coffee service, you understand, was sent to me by my sister in America. She married a wealthy man there and she's always sending me such fine presents. It's very expensive, this service."

She raised her elegantly decorated coffee cup with great ostentation. Patrik was rather skeptical of the value of the service, but wisely chose not to comment.

"Yes, I would have gone to America as well, if I weren't always in such delicate health. If it hadn't been for that, I probably would have married a rich man there too, instead of sitting in this hovel for fifty years."

Svea cast an accusatory eye at Eilert, who calmly let the comment pass. It was undoubtedly a tune he'd heard many times before.

"It's gout, the constable should know. My joints are all used up, and I'm in pain from morning till night. It's lucky I'm not the type to complain. With my terrible migraines as well, there would be plenty to complain about, but it's not in my nature to complain, you understand. No, one must bear one's afflictions with equanimity, as they say. I don't know how many times I've heard, 'How strong you are, Svea, going on day in and day out with your infirmities.' But that's the way I am."

She modestly lowered her eyelids as she made a great show of wringing her hands, which in Patrik's layman's eyes looked anything but gout-ridden. What a damned harpy, he thought. Painted and dolled up with far too much cheap jewelry and a thick layer of

makeup. The only positive thing he could say about
her appearance was that at least it matched the decor.
How on earth could such a mismatched couple as
Eilert and Svea have stayed married for fifty years? But
he assumed it was a generational thing. Their generation got divorced only for considerably worse reasons
than mutual differences. But it was a shame. Eilert
couldn't have had much fun in his life.

Patrik cleared his throat to interrupt Svea's torrent
of words. She obediently fell silent, and her eyes hung
on his lips to hear what exciting news he might come
out with. The gossip grapevine was going to start up
as soon as he stepped out the door.

"Well, I have a few questions about the days before
you found Alexandra Wijkner's body. When you were
there looking after the house."

He stopped and looked at Eilert, waiting to hear
what he would say. But Svea began first.

"Yes, I do declare. That something like that would
happen here. And that my Eilert would discover the
body. No one has talked about anything else the past
few weeks."

Her cheeks were glowing with excitement, and
Patrik had to restrain himself from offering a sharp
comment. Instead he gave a sly smile and said, "If
you'll forgive me, I wonder if it would be possible
for me and your husband to speak undisturbed for a
while. It's standard protocol in the police that we only
take testimony when persons not directly concerned
are not present."

A pure lie, but he saw to his satisfaction that Svea,
despite her great annoyance at being excluded from
the center of all the excitement, accepted his author-

ity in the matter and reluctantly got up from the table. Patrik was rewarded at once with an appreciative and amused glance from Eilert, who could hardly conceal his glee at seeing Svea so ignominiously robbed of her gossip tidbits.

When she had reluctantly dragged herself out of the kitchen, Patrik went on, "Now where were we? Yes, you were going to start by telling me about the week before, when you were at Alexandra Wijkner's house."

"Why is that important?"

"I'm not sure just yet. But it could be important. So try to remember as many details as possible."

Eilert thought for a moment, using the time to stuff his pipe carefully from a packet of tobacco marked with three anchors. He didn't speak until he had lit the pipe and puffed a couple of times.

"Now let's see. I found her on a Friday. I always used to go there on Fridays to check on everything before she arrived in the evening. So the last time I was there was the Friday before that. No, actually, we had to go to our youngest son's fortieth birthday party on Friday, so I went there on Thursday evening instead."

"How was the house then? Did you notice anything unusual?" Patrik had a hard time concealing his eagerness.

"Anything unusual?" Eilert puffed slowly on his pipe as he thought. "No, everything was fine. I did a round through the house and the cellar, but everything looked good. I locked the house carefully when I left, as always. She'd given me my own key."

Patrik felt compelled to ask straight out the question that was gnawing inside him. "And the furnace? Was it working? Was there heat in the house?"

"Oh yes, certainly. There was nothing wrong with the furnace then. It must have gone out some time after I was there. I don't understand what importance that has. When the furnace went out?" Eilert temporarily took the pipe out of his mouth.

"To be quite honest, I don't know if it is important. But thank you for your help. It might be important."

"Just out of curiosity, why couldn't you have asked me that on the phone?"

Patrik smiled. "I suppose I'm a bit old-fashioned. I don't think I get as much out of phoning as by talking with someone face to face. Sometimes I wonder if I should have been born a hundred years ago instead, before all these modern inventions."

"Nonsense, boy. Don't believe all that rubbish that it was better in the old days. Being cold, poor, and working from eight o'clock till sunset is nothing to envy. No, I use all the modern conveniences I can. I even have a computer, hooked up to the Internet. I'll bet you wouldn't believe that of an old man like me." He pointed knowingly at Patrik with his pipe.

"I can't say that I'm surprised, actually. Well, now I must be going."

"I hope I was of some use, so you didn't have to drive here for nothing."

"Not at all, I got exactly the information I wanted. And I got to taste your wife's excellent pastries too."

Eilert gave a reluctant snort. "Yes, she certainly can bake, I can say that for her." Then he sank into a silence that seemed to encompass fifty years of hardship.

Svea, who had undoubtedly been standing with her ear to the door, could stand it no longer and came into the room. "So-o-o, did you find out everything you needed?"

"Yes, thank you. Your husband has been quite accommodating. And I'd like to thank you for the coffee and the excellent pastries."

"Think nothing of it. I'm glad you liked them. So Eilert, if you'll start clearing the table I'll show the constable to the door."

Obediently Eilert began collecting the coffee cups and plates as Svea accompanied Patrik to the front door under a constant stream of words.

"Close the door hard after you. I can't stand a draft."

Patrik heaved a sigh of relief when the door closed behind him. What a frightful woman. But he had gotten the confirmation he wanted. Now he was quite sure that he knew who had murdered Alex Wijkner.

At Anders's funeral the weather was not as nice as for Alex's burial. The wind tore at exposed skin and made everyone's cheeks blossom with the cold. Patrik had dressed as warmly as he could, but it wasn't enough against the relentless chill. He shivered as he stood by the open grave when the coffin was slowly lowered down. The ceremony itself had been short and dreary. Only a few people had come to the church, and Patrik had sat discreetly on the pew in the back. Only Vera was sitting up in front.

He had been dubious as to whether he should follow along to the burial site, but decided at the last second that it was the least he could do for Anders. Vera hadn't changed expression the whole time he watched her, but he didn't think her grief was any less for it. She was simply a person who didn't like to show her feelings in public.

Patrik could understand and sympathize with that. In a way he admired her. She was such a strong woman.

After the burial ceremony was over, the few guests in attendance went their separate ways. With her head bowed, Vera walked slowly up the gravel path toward the church. The cold wind was whipping hard, and she had tied her scarf like a kerchief over her head. For a second Patrik hesitated. After an internal struggle that increased as the distance grew between him and Vera, he made up his mind and hurried to catch up with her.

"Lovely ceremony."

She smiled bitterly. "You know as well as I do that Anders's funeral was just as pathetic as most of his life. But thanks anyway. It was nice of you to say so."

Vera's voice bore the mark of many years of fatigue. "I probably should be grateful, really. Not so many years ago he wouldn't have even been allowed to be buried in the public churchyard. He would have been given a spot off to the side, outside church-sanctified ground, a spot specially reserved for suicides. There are still many of the older folks who think that suicides don't go to heaven."

She fell silent for a moment. Patrik waited for her to continue.

"Will there be any legal consequences from what I did to cover up Anders's suicide?"

"No, I can guarantee that there will not. It was regrettable that you did what you did, and certainly there are laws about it, but no, I don't think there will be any consequences."

They passed the parish house and walked slowly in

the direction of Vera's home, which was only a couple of hundred yards from the church. Patrik had worried all night about how he should proceed, and he had reached a cruel but he hoped successful solution.

Nonchalantly, he said, "What I think is most tragic in this whole story with Anders's and Alex's death is that a child also had to die."

Vera turned vehemently toward him. She stopped and grabbed hold of his sleeve.

"What child? What are you talking about?"

Patrik felt thankful that, against all odds, a lid had been kept on that particular piece of information.

"Alexandra's child. She was pregnant when she was murdered. In her third month."

"Her husband . . ."

Vera stammered, but Patrik continued with forced coldness. "Her husband had nothing to do with it. They had clearly not had any relations in several years. No, the father seems to be someone she used to meet here in Fjällbacka."

Vera was holding so hard onto his sleeve that her knuckles turned white.

"Good Lord. Good, good Lord."

"Yes, it's certainly cruel. To kill an unborn child. According to the autopsy report it was apparently a little boy."

He was grimacing inside but forced himself not to say any more. Instead he waited for the reaction he was counting on.

They were standing under the big chestnut tree, fifty yards from Vera's house. When she suddenly exploded in motion he was taken by surprise. She ran surprisingly fast for her age, and it took a couple of seconds for Patrik to recover from the shock and run after her. When he reached her house the front door was wide open and he cautiously stepped inside. Sobbing sounds were heard from the bathroom down the hall, and then he heard her violently throwing up.

It felt wrong to stand there in the hall and wait with cap in hand, listening to her vomiting, so he took off his wet shoes, hung up his coat, and went in to the kitchen. When Vera came out a few minutes later the coffee-maker was bubbling and there were two cups on the kitchen table. She was pale, and for the first time he saw tears. Only a hint, like a glitter in the corner of her eye, but it was enough. Vera sat down stiffly on one of the kitchen chairs.

In a few minutes she had aged many years, and she moved slowly, like a much older woman. Patrik let her have a few more minutes' respite as he poured coffee for them both. But the moment he sat down he let her know with a stern look that the moment of truth had arrived. She knew that he knew, and there was no turning back.

"So I murdered my grandson."

Patrik took it as a rhetorical question and didn't reply. If he did he'd be forced to lie. Once he'd come this far he couldn't back up. In time she would find out the truth. But first it was his turn.

"I knew it was you who murdered Alex when you lied about being there the week before she died. You said that you sat in her cold house freezing, but the furnace didn't break down until the week after that, the week she died."

Vera was staring into space, and it seemed that she didn't even hear what Patrik had said.

"It's strange. It's only now that I actually realize that I took another person's life. Alexandra's death was never very real to me, but Anders's child . . . I can almost see him before me . . ."

"Why did Alex have to die?"

Vera held up her hand. She would tell him everything, but at her own pace.

"There would have been a scandal. Everyone would have pointed at him and talked about him. I did what I thought was right. I didn't know that he would still be the object of everyone's ridicule. That my silence would eat him away inside and strip him of everything of value. It was so simple. Karl-Erik came to me and told me what had happened. He had talked with Nelly before he came to me, and they had reached an agreement. Nothing good would come of having the whole town know about it. It would be our secret, and if I knew what was best for Anders, I would keep my mouth shut. So I shut up. I kept quiet for all those years. But each year robbed Anders of more than the one before. Each year he kept wasting away in his own private hell, and I chose not to see my role in it. I cleaned up after him and supported him as best I could, but the only thing I couldn't do was to make what happened go away. Silence can never be taken back."

She had drunk her coffee in a few greedy gulps and raised her cup to Patrik. He got up and fetched the pot and poured her some more. It seemed as though the habit of drinking coffee was what helped her keep a grip on reality.

"Sometimes I think the silence was worse than the assaults. We never talked about it, not even inside these four walls, and only now do I understand what it must have done to him. Maybe he interpreted my silence as a reproach. That's the only thing I can't stand. That he might have thought I was blaming him for what happened. I never thought that, not even for a second, but I'll never know now whether he knew that."

For a second the façade looked as if it might crack, but then Vera straightened up and forced herself to go on. Patrik could only imagine what an enormous effort it took.

"Over the years we found a sort of equilibrium. Even though life was miserable for both of us, we knew what we had and where we stood with each other. Naturally I knew that he still saw Alex occasionally and that they had some sort of strange attraction for one another, but I still believed that we could go on as we always had. Then Anders told me that Alex wanted to expose what had happened to them. She wanted to clean all the old skeletons out of the closet, I think was what he said. He sounded almost indifferent when he mentioned it, but for me it felt like an electric shock. That would change everything. Nothing would be the same if Alex dragged up old secrets after so many years. What good would it do? And what would people say? Besides, even if Anders tried to pretend that it hadn't affected him, I knew him better than that. I believe that he didn't want her to make it public any more than I did. I know—knew, my son."

"So you went to visit her."

"Yes. I went there that Friday evening hoping to talk some sense into her. Make her understand that she couldn't single-handedly make a decision that would affect us all."

"But she didn't understand."

Vera gave a bitter smile. "No, she didn't."

She had finished her second cup of coffee before Patrik had even finished half of his first one, but now she set the cup aside and folded her hands on the table.

"I tried to appeal to her. I explained to her how difficult it would be for Anders if she made public what had happened, but she looked me straight in the eye and claimed I was only thinking of myself, not Anders. He would be glad if it finally came out, she said. He had never asked us to keep quiet, and she also told me that I, Nelly, Karl-Erik, and Birgit hadn't considered them when we decided to keep the whole thing secret. We were only interested in keeping our own reputations unsullied. Can you imagine such cheek!"

The rage that a moment before had been ignited in Vera's eyes was extinguished just as quickly as it appeared and was replaced by an indifferent, dead look. She continued in a monotone.

"Something burst inside me when I heard her make such an outrageous claim. When I had done everything with Anders's best interests at heart. I could almost hear a click in my head, and I simply acted without thinking. I had my sleeping pills with me in my purse, and when she went into the kitchen I crumbled a few tablets into her cider glass. She had poured a glass of wine for me when I arrived. When she came back from the kitchen I pretended to accept what she'd said and offered to drink a toast as friends before I left. She seemed grateful for that and drank her cider to keep me company. After a while she fell asleep on the sofa. I hadn't really thought out what I should do next. The sleeping pills were an impulse on the spur of the moment, but I got the idea that I would make it look like a suicide. I didn't have enough sleeping pills to force a fatal dose into her. The only thing I could think of was to slit her wrists. I knew that many people did it in the bathtub, so it felt like a feasible idea."

Her voice was toneless. It sounded as if she were relating a completely normal everyday event, not a murder.

"I took off all her clothes. I thought I could probably carry her, since my arms are strong from all those years of cleaning, but it was impossible. Instead I had to drag her into the bathroom and maneuver her into the tub. Then I slit her arteries in both arms with a razor blade I found in the medicine cabinet. After cleaning the house once a week for several years, I was familiar with everything about it. I washed off the glass I drank out of, turned off the lights, locked the door, and put the spare key back in its place."

Patrik was shaken, but forced his voice to remain calm.

"You understand that you'll have to come with me now, don't you? I won't have to call for reinforcements, will I?"

"No, you don't have to do that. May I just gather up a few things to take with me?"

He nodded. "Yes, that will be fine."

She got up. In the doorway she turned around.

"How was I to know she was pregnant? Of course, she didn't drink any wine, I thought of that, but I had no idea that was why. Maybe she only drank in moderation, or had to drive somewhere. How should I know? It was impossible for me to know, don't you think?"

Her voice was pleading, and Patrik could only nod mutely. In time he would tell her that the child wasn't

Anders's, but for the time being he didn't want to disturb the balance of trust they had established. There were several more people she would have to tell her story to before they could close the case on Alexandra Wijkner for good. But something was bothering him. His intuition told him that Vera still hadn't told him everything.

Later, when he got into the car he took out his copy of the letter that Anders had left behind, as his last message to the world. Slowly he read through what Anders had written, and once again Patrik felt how strong the pain was behind those words on the page.

6

The irony of my life has often struck me. How I have the ability to create beauty with my fingers and my eyes, while in everything else I'm only able to create ugliness and destruction. That's why the last thing I'm going to do is destroy my paintings. To obtain some kind of consistency in my life. Better to be consistent and only leave shit behind than to appear to be a more complex person than I deserve.

Actually, I'm very simple. The only thing I ever wanted to do was to erase a few months and events from my life. I don't think that would have been too much to ask. But perhaps I deserved what I got in life. Perhaps I had done something terrible in a previous life that made me have to pay the price in this one. Not that it really makes any difference. But if so it would have been nice to know what I was paying for.

Why am I now choosing this particular moment to leave a life that has been meaningless for so long, you may ask? Yes, go ahead and say it. Why does anyone do something at a certain point in time? Did I love Alex so much that life lost any and all meaning? That's probably one of the explanations you'll be grasping for. I don't actually know if that would be entirely true. Death is a friend that I've lived with for a long time, but only now do I feel that I'm ready. Perhaps it was precisely the fact that Alex died that made my own freedom possible. She was always the unattainable one. It was impossible to make the slightest dent in her shell. The fact that she could die suddenly opened wide the possibility that I might go in the same way. I have long been packed and ready, all that remains is to climb aboard.

   Forgive me, Mama.
   Anders

He had never managed to shake off the habit of getting up early, or in the middle of the night as some might say. It was something that in this case proved to be useful. Svea didn't react when he got up at four a.m., but for safety's sake he sneaked cautiously down the stairs with his clothes in his hand. Eilert dressed silently in the living room and then took out his suitcase which he had carefully hidden in the very back of the pantry. He had planned this for months, and nothing had been left to chance. Today was the first day of the rest of his life.

The car started on the first try despite the cold, and at twenty past four he left behind the house where he had lived for the past fifty years. He drove through a sleeping Fjällbacka and didn't step hard on the gas before he passed the old mill and turned off toward Dingle. It was a good 125 miles to Göteborg and Landvetter Airport, and he could take it easy. The plane to Spain didn't leave until around eight o'clock.

He was finally going to live his life the way he wanted to live it.

He had been planning this for a long time, for many years. The aches and pains got worse with each passing year, and so did the frustration over his life with Svea. Eilert thought he deserved better. On the Internet, he had found a little boardinghouse in a small town on the Costa del Sol. A bit away from the beaches and the tourist area, so the price was reasonable. He had sent e-mails and checked that he could live there year-round if he wanted. In fact, the landlady would give him an even better price if he did. It had taken a long time to save up the money under Svea's vigilant eye that watched everything he did, but finally he had succeeded. He reckoned that he could support himself for about two years on his present savings if he lived frugally, and after that he would simply have to find a way. Right now nothing could restrain his enthusiasm.

For the first time in fifty years he felt free, and he found himself giving the old Volvo a little extra gas out of sheer joy. He would leave the car in the long-term parking lot. Svea would find out where it was soon enough. Not that it mattered. She had never gotten a driver's license but used Eilert as unpaid chauffeur whenever she needed to drive anywhere. The only thing that weighed on his conscience a little was the children. On the other hand, they had always been more Svea's children than his, and to his sorrow they had become just as petty and narrow-minded as she was. He was undoubtedly partly to blame, since he worked long hours and then found all sorts of excuses to stay away from home as much as possible. But he had still decided to send them a postcard from Landvetter to tell them that he had left of his own free will and that they didn't have to worry. He also didn't want them to instigate any big police hunt to find him.

The roads were empty as he drove along in the dark, and he didn't even turn on the radio. He wanted to enjoy the silence instead. Now that his life was beginning.

* * *

"I just have a hard time understanding it. I can't believe that Vera would murder Alex so that she wouldn't talk about assaults against her and Anders that took place over twenty-five years ago."

Erica swirled her wineglass meditatively.

"You should never underestimate the need not to make waves in a small town," said Patrik. "If the old story about the assaults were to come out, people would have a new reason to point their fingers. On the other hand I don't believe Vera when she says that she did it for Anders's sake. Maybe she's right that Anders didn't want everyone to know what happened to them. But I think it's mostly Vera who couldn't stand the thought of what people would be whispering behind her back. Especially if it got out that Anders wasn't merely the victim of sexual assault as a child, but that his mother did nothing about it; in fact, she helped cover everything up. I think it was the shame that she couldn't bear. She killed Alex on the spur of the moment when she realized that Alex wasn't going to budge. Vera got an impulse, which she carried out in a methodical and cold-blooded way."

"How is she taking it now? Now that she's been exposed, I mean?"

"She's surprisingly calm. I think she was immensely relieved when we told her that Anders wasn't the father of the child, and so she hadn't murdered her unborn grandchild after all. Now she doesn't seem to care what happens to her. And why should she? Her son is dead, she has no friends, no life. Everything has been uncovered, and she has nothing more to lose. Only her freedom, and that doesn't mean much to her right now, or so it seems."

They were sitting in Patrik's apartment sharing a

bottle of wine after having dinner together. Erica was enjoying the peace and quiet. She loved having Anna and the kids staying with her, but sometimes it was too much, and today had been one of those days. Patrik was tied up in the interrogation all day, but when he finished he came and collected her along with her little overnight bag. Now they were sitting curled up on the sofa like any hardworking older couple.

Erica closed her eyes. The moment was wonderful and frightening at the same time. Everything was so perfect, and yet she couldn't help thinking that this might mean it would be all downhill from here. She didn't even want to think about what would happen if she moved back to Stockholm. She and Anna had skirted the question of the house for several days; as if by tacit agreement, they had decided not to deal with it yet. And Erica believed that Anna was in no condition to make any big decisions, so she had let it lie.

But tonight she didn't want to think about the future. Better not to think about tomorrow at all and instead try to enjoy the moment as much as she could. She pushed away all the gloomy thoughts.

"I talked to the publishers today," she told Patrik. "I mentioned the book about Alex."

"So, what did they say?" The eager look in Patrik's eyes pleased her.

"They thought the idea sounded brilliant and wanted me to send them the material I have right away. I still have to finish writing the book about Selma Lagerlöf, but they gave me an extra month, so now I've promised to have the biography ready by September. I actually think I can manage to work on both of them at the same time. It's been going fairly well so far."

"What did your publishers say about the legal aspect? Do they think there's a risk of being sued by Alex's family?"

"The law on freedom of the press is quite clear. I have the right to write about her, even without their approval. But of course I hope that they'll be supportive, after I have a chance to explain the project to them and what I envision for the book. I really don't want to write a sensational story with no substance. I want to write about what actually happened and who Alex really was."

"And what about the market? Did they think there would be interest in this sort of book?"

Patrik's eyes were gleaming. Erica was pleased that he was so enthusiastic on her behalf. He knew how much this book meant to her and wanted to share her interest.

"We both think there should be quite a lot of interest. In the States, the demand for true-crime books is enormous. The biggest author in the genre, Ann Rule, sells millions of copies. Here in Sweden, it's quite a new phenomenon. There are a few books along that line, such as the one that was written a couple of years ago about the case of the doctor and the pathologist, but nothing that's purely true crime. Just like Ann Rule, I would want to put a lot of effort into the research. Check facts, interview everyone involved, and then write a book that was as true as possible to what actually happened."

"Do you think that Alex's family will agree to be interviewed?"

"I don't know." Erica twisted a lock of hair around her finger. "I really don't know. But I'm definitely

going to ask them, and if they don't want to participate I'll have to find a way around it somehow. I have
an enormous advantage because I already know a lot
about them. I must say I'm a little hesitant to ask them,
but I'll just have to deal with it. If this book sells well,
I wouldn't have anything against continuing to write
about interesting legal cases, and then I'd have to get
used to being a little pushy with relatives. That's part
of the job description. I also think that people have a
need to speak their piece, to tell their story. Both from
the victim's and the perpetrator's point of view."

"In other words, you're going to try and talk to
Vera as well."

"Yes, absolutely. I have no idea whether she'll agree
to it, but I intend to try at any rate. Maybe she'll talk,
maybe she won't. I can't force her."

She shrugged her shoulders in a gesture of indifference, but clearly it would be a much better book if she
could get Vera to participate. What she'd written so far
was only an outline; now she had to get busy putting
some meat on the bones.

"What about you?" She turned a little on the sofa
and put her legs in Patrik's lap, who took the hint and
obediently began massaging her feet.

"How was your day? Are you the big hero at the
station now?"

The deep sigh from Patrik indicated that this was
not the case.

"No, you don't think Mellberg would give credit
where credit was due, do you? He's been shuttling back
and forth all day between the interrogation room and
various press conferences. His most frequent pronoun
in conversations with reporters has been 'I.' I'd be sur-

prised if he even mentioned my name. But what the heck. Who wants to see their name in print anyway? I arrested a murderer yesterday and that's enough for me."

"You're certainly being noble about it all." Erica punched him playfully on the arm. "Admit that you would have liked standing up there in front of the microphone at a big press conference, puffing out your chest and telling them about how brilliantly you managed to figure out who the murderer was."

"All right, it would have been kind of cool to get at least a little mention in the local paper. But that's not going to happen. Mellberg is going to steal all the glory for himself, and there's not a damn thing I can do about it."

"Do you think he'll get that transfer he wants so much?"

"If only he would. But I suspect the chiefs in Göteborg are quite pleased to have him where he is. I'm afraid we'll probably have to put up with him until he retires. And that day seems very remote right now."

"Poor Patrik." She stroked his hair, and he took this as a signal to jump on her and pin her to the sofa.

The wine had made her limbs heavy, and the heat of his body spread slowly to hers. His breathing changed; he was breathing harder. But Erica still had some questions for him. She struggled up to a sitting position, and with moderate force she shoved him away, back to his own corner.

"But are you satisfied with everything? What about Nils's disappearance, for instance? You didn't find out anything more from Vera?"

"No, she claims not to know anything about it.

Unfortunately, I don't believe her. I think she had an even more serious reason for protecting Anders than that people would find out that Nils had assaulted him. I think she knew precisely what happened to Nils, and that secret had to be preserved at all costs. But I have to admit it bothers me that it's still only speculation on my part. People just don't go up in smoke. He's out there somewhere, and there's somebody who knows where. But I do have a theory."

Patrik then went through the probable course of events step by step and explained the circumstances behind his idea. Erica saw that he was shivering, despite the heat in the room. It sounded unbelievable, and yet strangely plausible. She also understood that Patrik would never be able to prove any of what he was saying. And even if he could, it probably wouldn't do any good. So many years had passed. So many lives had already been destroyed. No good would come of destroying one more.

"I know that this will never lead to anything. And yet I want to know, for my own sake. I've been living with this case for several weeks now, and I want to find some sort of resolution."

"So what are you going to do? What can you do, for that matter?"

Patrik sighed. "I'm simply going to ask for a few answers. Nothing ventured, nothing gained, right?"

Erica gave him a searching glance. "It doesn't seem like such a good idea, but I'm sure you know best."

"I hope so. Could we leave death and sorrow behind for the rest of the evening, and concentrate on each other instead?"

"I think that sounds like a brilliant idea."

He crawled over on top of her again, and this time no one pushed him off.

When he left home Erica was still in bed. He hadn't had the heart to wake her but quietly got up, dressed, and drove off.

He had sensed a certain surprise but also a cautious anticipation when he booked this meeting. The condition had been that they meet discreetly, and Patrik had no problem going along with that. That's why he was now up at seven on a Tuesday morning. As he drove toward Fjällbacka in the dark he passed only a few oncoming cars. He turned off at the sign that said Väddö, and drove a little farther before parking in the lot. His was the only car there. Then he waited. After ten minutes, another car turned into the lot and parked beside his. The driver stepped out, opened the passenger door of Patrik's car and got in. Patrik left his car idling so he could leave the heater on, otherwise they would soon be frozen through.

"It seems rather exciting, meeting in secret like this under the cover of darkness. My only question is why." Jan was completely relaxed, but he had a puzzled look on his face. "I thought the investigation was over. You have Alex's murderer, don't you?"

"Yes, that's true. But there are still a few pieces that don't really fit, and it's bothering me."

"I see. What exactly doesn't fit?"

Jan's face betrayed no emotions. Patrik wondered whether it would turn out that he had got up at this ungodly hour for nothing. But now that he was here, he might as well finish what he'd started.

"As you may have heard, Alexandra and Anders were molested by your stepbrother, Nils."

"Yes, I heard that. Terrible. Especially for Mother's sake."

"Although it wasn't really news to her. She already knew about it."

"Of course she did. She handled the situation in the only way she knew how. With the greatest possible discretion. The family name had to be protected, that's obvious. Everything else was secondary."

"And how do you feel about it? About the fact that your brother was a pedophile and that your mother knew about it and protected him?"

Jan didn't let the question throw him off balance. He brushed off some invisible flecks of dust on his lapel. Then he merely raised one eyebrow when he replied after thinking for a few seconds.

"Naturally, I understand Mother. She acted the only way she could, and the damage was already done, wasn't it?"

"Yes, I suppose one could look at it that way. But the question is, where did Nils go after that? Has anyone in the family ever heard from him?"

"As far as that goes, we naturally informed the police like good citizens." The irony was so expertly blended into his tone of voice that it was hardly noticeable. "But I can understand why he chose to disappear. What was left for him here? Mother had already figured out what sort of person he was, and he couldn't keep working at the school. Mother would have seen to that. So he took off. He's probably living in some nice hot country with easy access to little girls and boys."

"I don't think so."

"Oh no, why not? Have you found the proverbial skeleton in the closet somewhere?"

Patrik ignored his bantering tone of voice. "No, we haven't. But I have a theory, you see . . ."

"How thrilling."

"I don't think Nils molested only Alex and Anders. I think that his primary victim was someone he had within close reach. Someone who was most easily accessible. I think that you were molested as well."

For the first time Patrik thought he saw a crack in Jan's shiny, polished exterior, but the next second he once again had control, or at least so it seemed.

"That's an interesting theory. What do you base it on?"

"Not much, I must admit. But I found a common link between the three of you. In your childhood. I saw a little leather patch in your office when I visited you. I assume it's fairly important to you, isn't it? It symbolizes something. A pact, a solidarity, a blood oath. You've saved it for over twenty-five years. Anders and Alex saved theirs as well. On the back of all of them there's a smudged fingerprint in blood, and that's why I think that you all swore a blood oath in the melodramatic way that children do. Then three letters were burned onto the front of the patch: T.T.M. I haven't managed to decipher that. Perhaps you could help me out on that point?"

Patrik could see how two different forces were almost literally struggling within Jan. On one hand, common sense told him not to say anything at all; on the other hand, the desire to share a secret should not be underestimated, the urge to confide in someone. Patrik was confident in Jan's ego and put his money on the fact that it would be irresistible for him to unburden his heart to someone who would listen with interest. He decided to try to facilitate Jan's decision.

"Everything we say here today will remain between us. I have neither the energy nor the resources to follow up on something that happened twenty-five years ago. And I hardly think I could find any proof if I tried. This is for me personally. I have to know."

The temptation was too great for Jan.

" 'The Three Musketeers,' that's what 'T.T.M.' stands for. Silly and ridiculously romantic, but that was how we saw ourselves. It was us against the world. When we were together we could forget about what had happened to us. We never talked about it with each other, but we didn't need to. We understood without words. We made a pact that we would always be loyal to each other. With a piece of broken glass we each made a cut in one finger and mixed our blood and then stamped the emblems with it.

"I was the strongest of the three of us. I was forced to be the strongest. The others could at least feel safe at home, but I was always looking over my shoulder. At night, I lay with the covers pulled up to my chin and listened for the footsteps I knew were coming, first down the hall and then closer and closer."

It was as if a dam had burst. Jan talked at a furious pace, and Patrik kept quiet so he wouldn't interrupt the flow of words.

Jan lit a cigarette, rolled down the window a crack to let out the smoke, and went on. "The three of us lived in our own world. We met when nobody else was looking and sought comfort and consolation with each other. The strange thing was that although we should actually have served as a reminder of the evil for each other, it was only together that we could escape for a while. I don't even know how we knew.

Or why we first sought out each other's company. But somehow we knew. It was inevitable that we would seek each other out. I was the one who decided that we should solve the problem in our own way. Alex and Anders saw it as a game at first, but I knew it would have to turn serious. There was no other way out.

"One cold, clear winter day we went out on the ice, my foster brother and I. It wasn't hard to entice him to come along. He was overjoyed that I had taken the initiative, and he was looking forward to our little expedition. I had spent many hours on the ice that winter and knew precisely where to take him. Anders and Alex were waiting there. Nils was surprised when he saw them, but he was so arrogant that he never saw us as a threat. We were only kids, after all. The rest was easy. A hole in the ice, a shove, and he was gone.

"At first we were so relieved. The first few days were wonderful. Nelly was beside herself with worry over where Nils had gone, but I lay in my bed at night and smiled. I was listening to the absence of footsteps. Then all hell broke loose. Alex's parents had found out about things—how, I don't know—and they went to Nelly. Alex probably caved under all the pressure and questions and told them everything, both about me and about Anders. Not about what we did to Nils, but about everything that happened before that. If I ever thought that I would meet with sympathy from my foster mother, I learned my lesson back then. Nelly never again looked me in the eye. She never again asked where Nils was. Sometimes I wonder whether she suspected something."

"Vera was also told about the assaults."

"Yes, but Mother was clever. She played on Vera's need to protect Anders and keep up appearances. She didn't even have to pay her off, or bribe her with a good job to make her keep quiet."

"Do you think that Vera found out as well, sooner or later, what happened to Nils?"

"I'm completely convinced of it. I don't think that Anders would have been able to keep something like that from Vera for all those years."

Patrik was thinking out loud. "So presumably Vera murdered Alex not only to keep her quiet about the assaults, but because she was afraid that Anders would be indicted for murder."

Jan's smile was almost gleeful. "Which is almost comical. First of all, the murder falls under the statute of limitations, and second, no one would bother bringing indictments against us now, so long afterward, in view of the circumstances and the fact that we were only children then."

Reluctantly Patrik was forced to agree with him. There wouldn't have been any consequences if Alex had gone to the police and told them everything that happened. But presumably Vera didn't understand that; she believed that there was a real danger that Anders would be convicted of murder.

"Did you stay in contact afterward? You and Alex and Anders?"

"No. Alex moved away almost immediately and Anders retreated into his own little world. Of course, we did see each other occasionally, but we hadn't spoken to each other in twenty-five years until Anders rang me after Alex's death, screaming and yelling that I was the one who had murdered her. Naturally

I denied it. I had nothing to do with her death, but he wouldn't give up."

"Didn't you know that she had thought about going to the police and telling them about Nils's death?"

"Not before she died, no. Anders told me that afterward." Jan nonchalantly blew some smoke rings in the car.

"What would have happened if you had known?"

"I suppose we'll never know, will we?" He turned to Patrik and regarded him with his cold blue eyes. Patrik shuddered. No, they would never know.

"As I said, no one would ever have bothered to send us to prison for what we did. But of course I'll be the first to admit that it has complicated my relationship with my mother a bit."

Then Jan abruptly changed the subject.

"They were apparently screwing, according to what I heard, Anders and Alex. Talk about beauty and the beast. Maybe I should have had a go myself, for old times' sake . . ."

Patrik felt absolutely no sympathy for the man next to him. It's true that he had gone through hell as a child, but there was something more than that in Jan. Something evil and rotten that oozed out of his pores. On pure impulse Patrik said, "Your parents died under tragic circumstances. Do you know anything more about what happened, other than what came out in the investigation?"

A smile played at the corners of Jan's mouth. He rolled down the window another inch or two and flicked his cigarette butt out the window.

"An accident can happen so easily, can't it? A lamp falling over, a curtain fluttering. Tiny incidents that join forces and cause a major event. Then again, it could be said that it's purely God's will that accidents happen to people who deserve them."

"Why did you agree to meet with me? Why are you telling me all this?"

"I was surprised myself, actually. I hadn't intended to come, but curiosity got the best of me, I think. And we all have a need to tell someone about what we've done. Especially when that someone can't do anything about the deeds he's hearing about. Nils's death lies far back in time, it's my word against yours, and no one would believe you, I'm afraid."

Jan climbed out of the car but turned around and leaned inside.

"I believe that crime actually does pay for some people. One day I'm going to inherit a considerable fortune. If Nils had lived I doubt that I'd be in this situation."

He saluted facetiously with two fingers to his brow, closed the door and walked back to his own car. Patrik could feel a malicious grin spreading over his face. Jan obviously didn't know about Julia's relationship with Nelly or the role she would play on the day the will was read. The ways of God were undeniably inscrutable.

The warm breeze caressed his furrowed cheeks as he sat on the little balcony. The sun warmed and healed his aching joints; he was moving more easily with each day that passed. Every day, he went to his job at the fish market where he helped sell the catch that came in early in the morning from the fishing boats.

Here there was no one who tried to take away from

older people their right to make themselves useful. Instead he found himself more respected and appreciated than ever before in his life, and slowly but surely he had begun to make friends in the little town. It's true there was a bit of trouble with the language, but he could tell that he was managing all right with gestures and good intentions, and his vocabulary was also growing steadily. A little drink or two after a good day's work also helped loosen the bonds of shyness; he found to his surprise that he was starting to turn into something of a chatterbox.

As he sat there on the balcony looking out over the lush vegetation that merged into the bluest water he had ever seen, Eilert felt that he would never get any closer to paradise than right here.

An added bit of spice in his life was the daily flirting with the buxom proprietress of the boardinghouse, Rosa. Occasionally, he permitted himself to toy with the thought that over time it might even develop into something more than a playful flirtation. The attraction was there, no question about that, and people were not made to live alone.

For a moment, he happened to think of Svea back home in Sweden. Then he dismissed that unpleasant thought, closed his eyes, and enjoyed a well-earned siesta.

READING GROUP GUIDE FOR
THE ICE PRINCESS BY CAMILLA LÄCKBERG

Description

When the remote, beautiful Alex Wijkner is found dead of an apparent suicide in the sleepy fishing village of Fjällbacka, Sweden, her childhood friend Erica Falck is shaken to the core. Erica and Alex haven't spoken in years, but now Erica, back in her hometown after the deaths of her parents, finds herself haunted by their shared past, their lost friendship, and the suspicion that something isn't quite right about Alex's death.

Joining forces with local detective Patrik Hedström, Erica delves into the mystery of Alex's death, peeling away layers of secrets to reveal the shocking, deeply disturbing past that reaches into the dark heart of Fjällbacka and threatens to tear aside its idyllic façade.

Questions for Discussion

1. Erica's initial involvement in the mystery of Alex's death is purely coincidental, but as time goes on she becomes obsessed with uncovering the truth about her childhood friend's past. What do you think motivates Erica to pursue this case so relentlessly?

2. Both a gifted painter and Fjällbacka's neighborhood drunk, Anders Nilsson lives a contradictory existence. As Läckberg writes, "he was born with an insatiable need for beauty, at the same time that he was condemned to a life of filth and squalor" (page 160). What was your first impression of Anders, and how did it change as the novel progressed?

3. Alex and Anders form a close bond based on the shared trauma of their pasts, a relationship that is truly loving but also profoundly marked by sorrow. Reread Anders's description of Alex on page 217. What do you make of their relationship?

4. Erica continues to write her book about Alex's life despite having many reservations. Läckberg writes, "For the first time an idea for a book had really filled her with enthusiasm. There were so many other ideas that hadn't panned out and that she'd rejected over the years; she couldn't afford to lose this one" (page 300). Do you think the project is exploitative, or even selfish, or will Erica offer a respectful, balanced account that humanizes her subject? Do you think Erica has the right to publish this book?

5. Anna and Erica's strained relationship improves

markedly after Anna leaves her abusive husband. How do both women begin to view each other differently once Lucas is out of the picture? What do you think they will ultimately decide to do with their parents' house?

6. How do Anders's italicized passages contribute to the narrative as a whole? When did you discover the identity of the man in these scenes, and what was it that tipped you off?

7. Karl-Erik and Birgit's decision to raise Julia leaves Alex with a constant reminder of the trauma of her childhood. But as Läckberg writes, "The sad thing was that—even if it was true that they had looked at Julia many times and were reminded of the horror in the past—she would never realize how much they loved her" (page 386). Do you think Karl-Erik and Birgit were well intentioned in their decision, or were they simply trying to sweep the tragedy under the rug?

8. *The Ice Princess* is rife with examples of dysfunctional and adulterous relationships—from Alex and Henrik, to Dan and Pernilla, to Anna and Lucas. Do you think Läckberg intentionally paints a bleak portrait of marriage in general? Will Erica and Patrik fare any better as a couple?

9. Despite the quaint and scenic backdrop that Fjällbacka provides, the town has a dark and disturbing past. Discuss how the setting of this book influences the story. How does the uncovering of Fjällbacka's secrets parallel the demise of some of its most prominent residents?

10. The difficulty of parent/child relationships is a recurring theme in *The Ice Princess,* from Erica's

frustration with her cold and distant mother, to Vera's fierce protectiveness of Anders, to Julia's deep-seated bitterness toward Karl-Erik and Birgit. How are the characters in this book influenced by their relationships with their parents?

11. Vera Nilsson's motive for murder stems from a desperate need to salvage her son's reputation: "'Everyone would have pointed at him and talked about him,'" she says. "'I did what I thought was right'" (page 429). Do you think Vera is at all sympathetic? Why or why not?

Enhance Your Book Club

1. Fjällbacka is the setting for all of Camilla Läckberg's novels as well as her hometown. Do a little online research about Fjällbacka and bring whatever information you find to your next book club meeting. Is the town what you imagined it to be, based on what you read in *The Ice Princess*?

2. According to the author's website, Erica's favorite movie is *Notting Hill* and Patrik's is *The Usual Suspects*. Rent one or both of these movies with your book club and discuss why you think Läckberg chose them as her characters' favorites.

3. For your next book club meeting try your hand at some Swedish cuisine! Check out http://en.wikipedia.org/wiki/Swedish_cuisine for inspiration.

4. Find out more about Camilla Läckberg by visiting her website, http://www.camillalackberg. com, which includes biographical information, a blog, a list of her other titles, interviews, and fun facts about her writing technique, the town of Fjällbacka, and recurring characters. Turn the page to read the first chapter from the next novel in Camilla Läckberg's bestselling series.

In the fishing community of Fjällbacka, life is remote, peaceful—and for some, tragically short.

THE PREACHER

A Novel

CAMILLA LÄCKBERG

Available from Free Press in April 2012

1

The day was off to a promising start. He woke up early, before the rest of the family, put on his clothes as quietly as possible, and managed to sneak out unnoticed. He took along his knight's helmet and wooden sword, which he swung happily as he ran the hundred yards from the house down to the mouth of the King's Cleft. He stopped for a moment and peered in awe into the sheer crevice through the rocky outcrop. The sides of the rock were six or seven feet apart, and it towered up over thirty feet into the sky, into which the summer sun had just begun to climb. Three huge boulders were solidly wedged in the middle of the cleft, and it was an imposing sight. The place held a magical attraction for a six-year-old. The fact that the King's Cleft was forbidden ground made it all the more tempting.

The name had originated from King Oscar II's visit to Fjällbacka in the late nineteenth century, but that was something he neither knew nor cared about as he slowly crept into the shadows, with his sword ready to attack. His father had told him that the scenes from Hell's Gap in the film *Ronja Rövardotter* had been filmed inside the King's Cleft. When he had watched the film himself, he felt a little tickle in his stomach as he saw the robber chieftain Mattis ride through. Sometimes he played highwaymen here, but today he was a knight. A knight of the Round Table, like in the big, fancy-colored book that his grandmother had given him for his birthday.

He crept over the boulders that covered the ground and made ready to attack the great fire-breathing dragon with his courage and his sword. The summer sun did not reach down into the cleft, which made it a cold, dark place. Perfect for dragons. Soon he would make the blood spurt from its throat, and after prolonged death throes it would fall dead at his feet.

Out of the corner of his eye he saw something that caught his attention. He glimpsed a piece of red cloth behind a boulder, and curiosity got the better of him. The dragon could wait; maybe there was treasure hidden there. He jumped up on the rock and looked down the other side. For a moment he almost fell over backward, but after wobbling and flailing his arms about he regained his balance. Later, he would not admit that he was scared, but just then, at that instant, he had never been more terrified in all the six years of his life. A lady was lying in wait for him. She was on her back, staring straight up at him with her eyes wide. His first instinct was to flee before she caught him playing here when he wasn't supposed to be. Maybe she would force him to tell her where he lived and then drag him home to Mama and Papa. They would be so furious, and they were sure to ask: How many times have we told you that you mustn't go to the King's Cleft without a grown-up?

But the odd thing was that the lady didn't move. She didn't have any clothes on either, and for an instant he was embarrassed that he was standing there looking at a naked lady. The red he had seen was not a piece of cloth but something wet right next to her, and he couldn't see her clothes anywhere. Funny, lying there naked. Especially when it was so cold.

Then something impossible occurred to him. What if the lady was dead! He couldn't work out any other explanation for why she was lying so still. The realization made him jump down from the rock, and he slowly backed toward the mouth of the cleft. After putting a few yards between himself and the dead lady, he turned around and ran home as fast as he could. He no longer cared if he was scolded or not.

Sweat made the sheet stick to her body. Erica tossed and turned in bed, but it was impossible to find a comfortable position. The bright summer night didn't make it any easier to sleep, and for the thousandth time she made a mental note to buy some blackout curtains to hang up, or rather persuade Patrik to do it.

It drove her crazy that he could sleep so contentedly next to her. How dare he lie there snoring when she lay awake night after night? She gave him a little poke in the hope that he'd wake up. He didn't budge. She poked a little harder. He grunted, pulled the covers up, and turned his back to her.

With a sigh, she lay on her back with her arms crossed over her breasts and stared at the ceiling. Her belly arched into the air like a big globe, and she tried to imagine her baby swimming inside of her in the dark. Maybe with his thumb in his mouth. Although it was all still too unreal for her to be able to picture it. She was in her eighth month but still couldn't grasp the fact that she had another life inside her. Well, pretty soon it was going to be very real. Erica was torn between longing and dread. It was difficult to see beyond the childbirth. To be honest, right now it was hard to see beyond the problem of no longer being able to sleep on her stomach. She looked at the luminous dial of the alarm clock: 4:42 a.m. Maybe she should turn on the light and read for a while instead.

Three and a half hours and one bad detective novel later, she was about to roll out of bed when the telephone rang shrilly. As usual she handed the receiver to Patrik.

"Hello, this is Patrik." His voice was thick with sleep. "Okay, all right. Oh shit, yeah, I can be there in fifteen minutes. See you there."

He turned to Erica. "We've got an emergency. I've got to run."

"But you're on vacation. Can't one of the others take it?" She could hear that her voice sounded whiny, but lying awake all night hadn't done much for her mood.

"It's a murder. Mellberg wants me to come along. He's going out there himself."

"A murder? Where?"

"Here in Fjällbacka. A little boy found a woman's body in the King's Cleft this morning."

Patrik threw on his clothes, which didn't take long since it was the middle of July and he only needed light summer clothes. Before he rushed out the door he climbed onto the bed and kissed Erica on the belly, somewhere near where she vaguely recalled she once had a navel.

"See you later, baby. Be nice to Mama, and I'll be home soon."

He kissed her quickly on the cheek and hurried off. With a sigh Erica hoisted herself out of bed and put on one of those tentlike dresses that for the time being were the only things that fit her. Against her better judgment she had read lots of baby books, and in her opinion everyone who wrote about the joyful experience of pregnancy ought to be taken out in the public square and horsewhipped. Insomnia, sore joints, stretch marks, hemorrhoids, night sweats, and a general hormonal upheaval—that was closer to the truth. And she sure as hell wasn't glowing with any inner radiance. Erica muttered to herself as she slowly made her way downstairs in pursuit of the day's first cup of coffee. Maybe that would lift the fog a bit.

By the time Patrik arrived, a feverish amount of activity was already under way. The mouth of the King's Cleft had been cordoned off with yellow tape, and he counted three police cars and an ambulance. The techs from Uddevalla were busy with their work and he knew better than to walk right into the crime scene. That was a rookie mistake that didn't prevent his boss, Superintendent Mellberg, from stomping about among them. They looked in dismay at his shoes and clothing, which at that very moment were adding thousands of fibers and particles to their sensitive workplace. When Patrik stopped outside the tape and motioned to his boss, Mellberg climbed back over the cordon, to the great relief of the Forensics.

"Hello, Hedström," said the superintendent.

His voice was hearty, bordering on joyful, and Patrik was taken aback. For a moment he thought that Mellberg was about to give him a hug but, thankfully, this turned out to be wrong. Nevertheless, the man appeared completely changed. It was only a week since Patrik had gone on vacation, but the man before him was really not the same one he'd left sitting sullenly at his desk, muttering that the very concept of vacations ought to be abolished.

Mellberg eagerly pumped Patrik's hand and slapped him on the back.

"So, how's it going with the brooding hen at home? Any sign that you're going to be a father soon?"

"Not for a month and a half, they say."

Patrik still had no idea what had brought on such good humor on Mellberg's part, but he pushed aside his surprise and tried to concentrate on the reason he'd been called to the scene.

"So what have you found?"

Mellberg made an effort to wipe the smile off his face and pointed toward the shadowy interior of the cleft.

"A six-year-old boy sneaked out early this morning while his parents were asleep and came here to play knights among the boulders. Instead he found a dead woman. We got the call at six fifteen."

"How long have Forensics had to examine the crime scene?"

"They arrived an hour ago. The ambulance got here first, and the EMTs were immediately able to confirm that no medical help was needed. Since then they've been able to work freely. They're a bit touchy . . . I just wanted to go in and look around a bit and they were quite rude about it, I must say. Well, I suppose one gets a little anal crawling about looking for fibers with tweezers all day long."

Now Patrik recognized his boss again. This was

more Mellberg's sort of tone. But Patrik knew from experience that it was no use trying to alter his opinions. It was easier just to let his remarks go in one ear and out the other.

"What do we know about her?"

"Nothing yet. We think she's around twenty-five. The only piece of fabric we found, if you could call it that, was a handbag. Otherwise she was stark naked. Pretty nice tits, actually."

Patrik shut his eyes and repeated to himself, like an inner mantra: *It won't be long until he retires. It won't be long until he retires . . .*

Mellberg went on obliviously, "The cause of death hasn't been confirmed, but she was beaten severely. Bruises all over her body and a number of what look to be knife wounds. And then there's the fact that she's lying on a gray blanket. The medical examiner is having a look at her, and we hope to have a preliminary statement very soon."

"Has anyone been reported missing around that age?"

"No, nowhere near it. An old man was reported missing about a week ago, but it turned out that he just got tired of being cooped up with his wife in a trailer and took off with a chick he met at Galären Pub."

Patrik saw that the team around the body was now preparing to lift her carefully into a body bag. Her hands and feet had been bagged according to regulations to preserve any evidence. The team of forensic officers from Uddevalla worked together to get the woman into the body bag in the most efficient way possible. Then the blanket she was lying on also had to be put into a plastic bag for later examination.

The shocked expression on their faces and the way they froze instantly told Patrik that something unexpected had happened.

"What is it?" he called.

"You're not going to believe this," said one of the officers, "but there are bones here. And two skulls. Based on the number of bones, I'd say there are easily enough for two skeletons."